JACQUELINE LICHTENBERG

THOSE
—OF MY—
BLOOD

BENBELLA BOOKS
Dallas, Texas

First BenBella Books Edition October 2003

BenBella Books
6440 North Central Expy, Suite 508
Dallas, TX 75206 (214) 750-3600
www.benbellabooks.com

Printed in the United States of America

10 9 8 7 6 5 4 3 2 1

Library of Congress Cataloging-in-Publication Data

Lichtenberg, Jacqueline.
    Those of my blood / Jacqueline Lichtenberg.
      p. cm.
    ISBN 1-932100-09-1 (alk. paper)
    1. Vampires—Fiction. I. Title.
PS3562.I3T48 2003
813'.54—dc22

                                                                    CIP
                                                          2003015455

Cover illustration copyright © 2002 by Marianne Plumridge
Cover design by Melody Cadungog
Interior designed and composed by John Reinhardt Book Design

Distributed by Independent Publishers Group
To order call (800) 888-4741
www.ipgbook.com

*To Chelsea Quinn Yarbro for the "good vampire" Saint Germain,
who fears his hunger because he might kill,
and reaches out in love for the strength he needs.*

———

*To George R. R. Martin for Fevre Dream,
and Joshua York's struggle to use science
to live with his vampirism without killing humans.*

———

*To Andre Norton who bought my story,
"Through the Moon Gate," for her Witch World anthology,
and thus let me add a vampire to the Witch World—
only on condition that he wasn't "evil."*

- ACKNOWLEDGMENTS -

I want to acknowledge a variety of help with this novel.

Jean Lorrah—professor of English, and sometime co-author of my Sime~Gen books as well as creator of the Savage Empire universe—in her review of my first novel, the Sime~Gen novel *House of Zeor,* called one of my protagonists a *"vampire in muddy boots"*—which is true. The primary archetype behind the Sime~Gen concept is the vampire archetype. After seven Sime~Gen novels, I decided I was ready to try the real thing because it finally struck me that Jean and I both love "Star Trek" for how it uses one minor component of the vampire archetype—dangerous relationships—with love rather than "evil" and "horror."

About the same time I was writing *Those of My Blood,* Jean Lorrah was writing her vampire novel, *Blood Will Tell* which was first published as an e-book and won two awards. Now it is out from BenBella Books (www.benbellabooks.com) and soaring on amazon.com. These two vampire novels appeal to the same readers who love Sime~Gen which is now being published by Meisha Merlin™ Publishing Inc. (www.meishamerlin.com). Watch for new editions of Jean's Savage Empire novels, as well as my own *Dreamspy* from BenBella Books and *Molt Brother* and *City of a Million Legends* easily available on amazon.com.

Diana Stuart, the romance writer who often deals in fantasy elements such as werewolves, gave me vital technical tips as did Jane Toombs, who works in romantic historicals as well as historical romances.

Claire Gabriel, a consummate professional in the general fiction field who has come to sf/f through "Star Trek," returned after a ten-year absence to let a later draft of this manuscript keep her up till 2 A.M.—repeatedly. Since she has a deep aversion to vampire novels but loved this one, and didn't get nightmares, I'm most especially pleased.

Judy Segal, science teacher, literary agent, and dear friend, who does not believe in nor enjoy stories about vampires, read and enjoyed a very early draft of this one.

Anne Pinzow, a professional video producer and sometime slush pile reader for publishers and agents, made time to read and comment on a later draft, as did Roberta Klein-Mendelson whose professionalism lies in stagecraft, but who is also writing a vampire novel. Katie Filipowicz Steinhoff who has been deeply involved in Sime~Gen fanzine production, and has proofed many a manuscript for me, made time to go over this one while running her school library.

Marjorie Robbins, who has served Sime~Gen fandom and www.simegen.com valiantly in many capacities including as head of the Sime~Gen Welcommittee, worked hard to reduce the workload of mail I handled so I'd have time to write this novel. Through the Sime~Gen fanzines she published *Householding Chanel Inquirer* and *First Transfer,* (which are now available online) and she has kept Sime~Gen fans in touch with the progress of *Those of My Blood* and kept me aware of how much they are looking forward to my vampire novel.

Susan M. Garrett, publisher of the *Vampire Quarterly,* has kept fannish interest in vampires alive and well fed.

Victor Schmidt introduced me to Frank Kurt Cylke, the director of the National Library Service for the Blind and Physically Handicapped, the division of the Library of Congress that records books and which has recorded some of my novels. I have gained great respect for these people and their high professional standards, but from my readers, I have also gained a deep appreciation of the hunger among the users of the national service for total access to my writing as well as to other "Star Trek" and sf publications.

As a result of this, Kerry Lindemann-Schaefer, who at the time edited and published one of the Sime~Gen fanzines, *Ambrov Zeor,* Marjorie Robbins, Ellie Miller, and a host of other volunteers energized and organized by Karen MacLeod, editor and publisher of *Companion in Zeor,* (publishing new stories online) have run an auction and book sale to raise money for a pair of the special tape recorders needed, and the Sime~Gen fans started to put all the Sime~Gen fanzines and many other materials on tape before they were made available online. Victor Schmidt, a quality assurance technician for the national recording service, strives mightily to help us achieve the highest possible standards.

As we have struggled with this task, our admiration for Mr. Cylke's achievements at the National Library Service has grown daily. There is no substitute for the quality product his service turns out, and we can only hope that sighted readers will write their Congressmen urging greater appropriations for the recording program. Of the over eight hundred titles in sf/f published in one year, they could only record seventy-two, a colossal achievement but far short of adequate. Online and e-book availability of text the handicapped can use reading-software to access is changing all that.

In another context, I have to thank my chiropractor, Larry Suchoff. Every writer with a bad back knows what I'm thanking him for.

For contact with any of the above-mentioned individuals, with Sime~Gen fandom, or its publications, or for current status and availability on Sime~Gen or any of my other novels, see www.simegen.com/jl/ or email jl@simegen.com or simegen@simegen.com.

If this fails to reach me, I may be contacted through any of my publishers or via Sime~Gen Inc. POB 1244, Murray, KY 42071.

In conclusion, I must thank Russell Galen who deserves an Award of Valor and the Grankite Order of Tactics Class of Excellence for the heroic efforts he put forth on behalf of this book.

Stuart Moore, my editor at St. Martin's Press who had the courage to make a leap of faith, has given me the courage to do what had to be done with this book.

Glenn Yeffeth who recognized the connection between *Those of My Blood*, *Dreamspy* and Sime~Gen and is giving these books their first trade paperback editions.

And now I come to the foundation of all the efforts alluded to above. My husband, Salomon, does what husbands do and it works. Who'd dare to ask for more?

ONE

The tarmac of the Quito spaceport shimmered in the harsh sun. The group of scientists bound for Project Hail on Luna milled about within the red-painted circle under the sign reading, HIGH SECURITY PASSENGER PICKUP.

They all wore Project Hail flight suits. Most had stacked their identical flight bags, each stenciled with the Project logo, at the place where the people-mover would soon pick them up. Two armed guards flanked the pile.

Dr. Titus Shiddehara, clutching his own flight bag, hovered at the edge of the crowd, with them but not of them. He scanned them, searching for the one who would be his adversary, reminding himself not to squint against the sun.

Remember to act human, Connie had admonished him, *and whatever you do, this time keep your objectivity.* Titus intended to do just that. Connie had made it very clear when she'd chosen him for this mission that, this time, his life depended on his objectivity.

Far to his left reporters crowded up against a guarded fence. They formed a churning mass of humanity punctuated by the snouts of video and sound recorders, sat-phones, antennas and other rigs.

One reporter, wearing a fashionable red fedora and reflective sunglasses like Titus', watched—a stillness amidst their motion.

All around, guards in World Sovereignties uniforms patrolled the fence and surrounded the press box. Titus' adversary would be inside the guards' line.

Off to Titus' right were clusters of squat buildings. Out on the field, launch pads held commercial skytrucks. Project Hail's skybus was on the main pad, fuming as workers swarmed over it. They'd be boarding soon. If anything was to happen, it would happen now. Yet all was still.

Behind Titus was the civilian passenger terminal. Squinting despite himself, Titus saw two stragglers emerge and cross the tarmac to join the group. He wished his group had not been told to stand out here, in the brutal mountain sun. He couldn't see any security advantage to

1

loitering so near the fence, and even the layers of sunscreen he'd slathered over his skin didn't protect him from scorching.

He squatted down to search his bag for his gray silk scarf. It could shade the back of his neck.

"Dr. Shiddehara! Something wrong?" called one straggler. Her voice was rich and melodious, the accent French, and the tone that of an administrator who would now take over. Titus rose to meet Dr. Mirelle de Lisle. She was in her mid-thirties, short and compact, with a healthy complexion. Her hair was bound up in a hat with the Project logo on the band, a hat just like Titus wore except that hers bore the sigil of Cognitive Sciences. She had pushed it back rakishly so the brim framed her face. Titus wore his pulled low on his forehead for maximum shade.

Behind her came an older man with receding white hair and a well-controlled paunch. He carried his flight bag, and with his other hand slapped his hat against his thigh as he walked. Neither of them was the adversary Titus expected.

Titus called, "There's nothing wrong that I know of."

Mirelle came right into his personal space as the French were wont to do, negligently dropping her flight bag next to his. Titus stepped back. She retreated, sketching a French shrug, then she changed nationalities right before his eyes by simply shifting her body language. "Nothing wrong? But you were scowling so. The reporters offend you, no?"

Occasionally, a reporter's voice was heard shouting a question or asking someone to turn for the camera. Titus shook his head. "My thoughts were elsewhere."

She readjusted her manner and edged closer. "There are many better things to think about than reporters." She hardly seemed to be the same person who had lectured the group with such austere competency on the use of translators.

And as she advanced this time, Titus found, to his amazement, that he didn't need to step back. Formality melted away, and he felt a warm intimacy toward this woman.

Abruptly on guard, he focused his attention on her. The adversary could be a woman—but no—Mirelle was human. Yet she was controlling his responses as surely as if she were using Influence—the power of his people.

A rich smile of pure admiration crept over his face. Obviously, Communications Anthropology wasn't just psychology or linguistics.

It included applied kinesics developed into a social power to which even his kind were not immune.

She returned his smile, one hand on her hat as she looked up at him. He fought the warmth she roused in him, unsure which of the women she showed the world was the real Mirelle de Lisle. But he wanted to find out.

The man with her touched her elbow with a proprietary gesture. "Dr. Shiddehara," he said. "Didn't I hear you tell the press earlier that you're confident you can identify the alien space ship's home star?"

Now Titus placed the man: Abner Gold, a metallurgist from the Toronto Institute of Orbital Engineering who had trained at Sandia on weapons research, before World Sovereignties banned such companies. *Definitely not my adversary.*

"Dr. Gold," greeted Titus. "Yes, given sufficient data on the ship, its occupants, and its approach trajectory, I can narrow the field to a handful of stars—assuming the ship came from its home star." *But it couldn't have.*

"So your best calculations could turn out to be wrong?"

"Oh, yes, there's always—"

"You see, Mirelle? I told you—the Project is a waste of money Earth can ill afford. There's a good chance we'll pick the wrong star to aim our message at. But even if Dr. Shiddehara guesses right, we've no business wasting money sending a probe out to beam those aliens a message. The ship's most likely from a long dead civilization, and now there's no one out there for us to 'Hail.'"

Titus yanked at his hat brim, turning away to hide the mixed relief and grief that idea aroused. His eye fell on the red hat of the reporter who now stood in the press box, an area inside the gate defined by a rope barricade. He was sighting through his telephoto lens—directly at Titus.

Adjusting the sunglasses he needed in addition to his darkening contacts, Titus turned his back on the reporter and agreed, "Mathematics supports your argument, Dr. Gold. We've all seen the calculations based on the galaxy's size, and the distribution of stars likely to have habitable planets. The odds are against two similar civilizations meeting." *But we have met! Only I'm glad you don't know it. Humans would slaughter those of my blood.*

Gold crowed triumphantly, "What did I tell you, Doctor! Even the Project's chief astronomer agrees with me."

3

Mirelle slanted an open smile at Titus. "Call me Mirelle, both of you. Everyone here answers to Doctor!"

Gold grinned, offering his hand. "Call me Abner."

She shook hands with Gold, then gave Titus her hand. Her touch warmed him in a way that only a human woman could, and he had to remind himself he'd just taken a good meal. "Titus," he offered. Her handshake was firm, brief, and seemed honestly her own. *Is this the real Mirelle?*

Then she turned to Gold, all brisk, polite professional. "Abner. Titus isn't an astronomer. He's an astrophysicist. And—I don't think you let him finish. Did he?"

"No, I hadn't finished," Titus said. *"If* there are people out there, then there's no reason to assume we won't encounter each other— because we are *looking* for each other. And we'll be in a much stronger position if we go to them than if we wait for them to come to us." *Maybe.*

"You see, Abner, he does too believe in the Project! You're the only one who thinks it's a waste."

"The majority is rarely right." Eyeing Titus, Gold made it a challenge. "I wouldn't expect an astrophysicist to believe the Project's hand-waving argument."

"Your problem, Abner Gold," Mirelle declared, "is that you have no faith in people. And if you have no faith in human people, how could you ever make friends with nonhuman people?" Suddenly, as if shocked by her own words, she glanced into Titus' sunglasses, weighing, measuring.

"Friends with an alien?" scoffed Gold, but Mirelle kept staring at Titus.

Titus entertained the paranoid notion that she knew he was exactly such an alien as Project Hail sought to contact. With her skills, she might have seen something unhuman in him. *Was that what all her flirting was about? Testing me?*

He recalled another of Connie's admonitions: *The only live elderly agents are thoroughly paranoid agents.* On the other hand, certain human women were attracted to his kind.

"Why would anyone want to make friends with an alien?" asked Gold. "Trade, maybe, but *friends?"*

Mirelle stared at Gold, and shrugged, "Why not?"

Titus focused on Mirelle as he prepared to break the promise he had made to himself when he'd discovered his power—never to use it against a defenseless human. He'd known, when he took this

4

mission, that he'd have to set aside his scruples—but now that the moment was on him, he shuddered.

He hadn't realized his shudder was visible until Gold grinned. "So you finally see it! If they're *aliens* they can't be friends. The best we can hope for, even *if* our message is received, is some very expensive trading and a nonaggression pact. But friends are best made at home."

"*Au contraire.* I have found some of my best friends—and more than friends—very far from home. Titus only just realized how reluctant he is to break a promise."

She's reading my mind! Titus swallowed his panic. Stage magicians used muscle reading to simulate telepathy and muscle reading was a primitive version of Mirelle's science. He focused his Influence on her, suggesting that he was just an unremarkable human, not worth such close scrutiny.

He expected a facile rationalization as her interest was shunted aside. Instead, she continued speculatively, "I am most curious—break what promise, Titus?"

"Oh, nothing much." He redoubled his effort to Influence her, assuming she was a Resistive, a human difficult to Influence. A puzzled look flitted across her face. For no apparent reason she glanced over her shoulder.

"Titus, look over there. That reporter—the one in the red hat—is photographing us!" She waved sunnily, posing beside Titus, then she dragged him toward the press box, and in that instant, he knew.

She was a susceptible. She'd already been Influenced heavily, but not marked to warn off others of his blood. She was being used—certainly without her knowledge. He could hardly control the disgust that twisted his lips at this abuse. All thought of his own safety was wiped from his mind as he focused all his strength to free her of that control.

She smiled and chattered brightly, grabbing Titus' hand and towing him toward the reporter—who now slipped under the rope barricade, pointing his video pickup at them.

As he came closer, Titus felt the unmistakable throb of Influence and knew the reporter was controlling Mirelle. Older, more powerful than Titus, he was mockingly declaring himself an enemy, a member of the Tourist faction who didn't consider themselves of Earth at all.

Titus focused on one of the W.S. guards, an older man with a ruddy complexion and beefy jowls, and attracted his attention. The man flipped open his cell phone.

Sensing the use of Influence on the guard, the Tourist grinned knowingly at Titus and played his role to the hilt, calling out. "Doctors, do you think it friendly to 'hail' an alien civilization from a false location?"

All of earth had been debating that ever since the Project Hail compromise had been announced—to send an instrument package out of the solar system to a remote point from which it would signal the aliens and wait for a reply in order to establish contact without revealing Earth's location.

"Don't answer him, Mirelle," commanded Titus, with Influence. "Look at the press pass in his hat band. You don't want to be quoted in *that* . . ."

It almost worked. The Tourist chuckled and said, his words so veiled in Influence that to nearby humans they were inaudible, "Titus, you and all of Connie's Residents can't stop us. So you may as well save yourself the ordeal of starving on the moon."

It wasn't the words so much as the friendly tone that got to Titus. The man believed Titus couldn't stop the Tourists' agent from sending their SOS out with the humans' message, an SOS that would reveal Earth's location and ask for rescue. To underscore Titus' helplessness, the Tourist reporter wrenched control of Mirelle from Titus and she replied to the reporter's question, speaking right toward the Tourist's microphone. "It's a terrible duplicity, and when the aliens discover what we've done, they may never trust us."

Infuriated, Titus blasted a shaft of Influence at the guard, summoning the man as if there were a riot brewing.

The guard ran, a hand on his sidearm holster. To Titus' surprise, the Tourist didn't try for control of the guard. The guard barked at the reporter, "The last press conference was this morning! Get back or I'll have your pass lifted!" Then he added courteously to the scientists, "Look there! You're about ready to board now."

Titus, still trying to break through the superior Influence controlling Mirelle, gasped as it cut off. With a grin, the Tourist turned back to the press box and became lost in the crowd, saying to Titus alone, "I don't know about you, but I'm getting in out of this sun before it fries me."

Mirelle yielded to Titus' guiding hand. He plucked up his bag from beside hers and Gold's, still shaking.

A people-mover had pulled up to the scientists and a Project transport officer stood beside it with an electronic clipboard and a bullhorn. "Compartments one through ten, rear cabin, now boarding. When you arrive at the skybus, please step to the inspection station. This will be your last formal inspection, folks, so please be patient with us."

People consulted their boarding cards, while some translated the barely intelligible, amplified words for those who hadn't understood. The flight bags were heaped on the rear deck of the vehicle. Titus gingerly placed his in a side nook, and then sat where he could keep an eye on it.

They rolled smoothly out across the tarmac to where the gantry still surrounded their skybus. The bright light glancing off the brilliant hull nearly blinded him. His skin, even under layers of clothing, felt singed. He yearned for the shade around the skybus.

The bus would lift them to the Luna shuttle. In a few days, they'd be on the moon and working at Project Station, the lab built around the crashed starship. In a few moments, he'd be beyond the reach of his friends, beyond his supply lines. He still hadn't identified his adversary, the Tourist who would try to send that SOS to the home planet of his kind.

As they filed out of the people-mover, Titus edged to the front of the line, stopping only when two others glared at him. *Mustn't be conspicuous.* He took a place just behind Mirelle and braced against more exposure to the sun.

Titus wondered if his adversary was an Influenced human. A suggestion to plant the Tourists' device in the humans' instrument package could lie dormant in a human mind until the right moment. He could not control a shiver of disgust at the idea of using a human to destroy human civilization. When the Residents had called on him, he'd pledged to die rather than allow the Tourists' SOS to be beamcast, but perhaps his life wouldn't be enough. He couldn't get the reporter's pitying certainty out of his mind.

The line filed along a bright red carpet that led through a sensor arch, past a long white counter, then on to the gantry's elevator. A smartly uniformed Sovereignties space Marine guarded the elevator. The official photographer stood by to take pictures as each of them entered the lift.

Titus had no time to savor the moment when the first of his blood would go back into space at last. The final challenge was upon him. He had to concentrate.

Behind the counters two men and two women stood at computer terminals ready to process the scientists. Security was tight because of threats from humans opposing Project Hail. But after what they'd already been through, this final check seemed perfunctory. Titus watched as Mirelle went under the arch and paused on the weighing platform.

One attendant took Mirelle's flight bag and jacket to pass it under the scope, while another inserted her boarding card into the reader. No problem. Titus' card would program the computers to register his special supplies as ground coffee and tobacco—old-fashioned vices common at his social level, and permissible cargo.

Then they checked her fingerprints and retina pattern. The prints were no problem. Titus' had never been altered, but all the computer records from before his "death" had been switched to "Shiddehara," so his new identity was firm. The retina scan was the danger.

He prepared to use Influence on the scanner clerk, so he would not notice the nonhuman anomalies. The computers had already been programmed to identify his retina pattern as Dr. Titus Shiddehara, and he was in fact that person.

Mirelle passed through the check without a bleep and went toward the elevator.

Titus tendered his boarding card, and watched while it was inserted in the reader. Then he handed over his flight bag and jacket, and sauntered through the arch, concentrating on the retina scan technician. He presented his fingers to the plate on the counter while he probed for a contact—and met a blank wall. *An immune?* The bogeyman to all Titus' kind was a human immune to the Influence.

As he was passed to the retina scan technician, he remembered the reporter and knew, *Not immune, Influenced!*

"Ed, come look at this," called the man on the flight bag scanner. "Looks like contraband. Drugs."

The retina technician glanced at the scanner plate. "Would you mind opening the bag for us, Doctor?"

"No, of course not," replied Titus as he edged along the counter to see the plate and fumbled at his keys. "I have the key here." Both men were Influenced, but the reading was genuine—drugs. *So that's what the Tourist meant! While he held my attention, they switched bags! And they had someone reprogram the computer so my card doesn't force the scanner to show coffee.* An image of Gold left guarding the bags while Mirelle pulled Titus away flashed through his mind. There had been uniformed transport officers moving through the crowd carrying things. *Idiot! Amateur!*

Titus probed for the Influencer who had a grip on these men. It wasn't the reporter. He was too far away. Then his eyes flew to the last technician in line, the woman who handed back boarding cards and flight bags. *Another Tourist!* She'd been standing right there all the time, and he'd never even seen her. She was there to keep him from Influencing the technicians to let him through.

With a furious strength born of outrage, Titus struck—and found himself in a pitched battle for control of the two humans hovering over the bag scanner. To any onlooker it must seem as if everyone were considering a minor problem. Titus threw his whole strength into the battle. The Tourist was obviously more experienced at jousting for control of humans, but Titus held and pushed, closing his eyes, ignoring the sweat of fear that coated him, ignoring the constant pain from the light, ignoring the terror of True Hunger that gripped him. But he had never done this before. He had never developed strength and skill for it.

Titus' grip weakened. The Tourist's lips twisted in a smug grin. Mirelle's melodious voice cut across everything. "Titus? Shall I wait for you?" Suddenly, Titus found a new strength. *You won't use them to destroy their own kind!*

The Tourist's grip snapped and Titus had the humans. He could feel their bewilderment as the screen now appeared to register coffee and tobacco, candy, clothing, and reading matter. Eyes locked to the Tourist's, Titus answered, "I'll be right there! It's just a scanner glitch. They've fixed it now." He put Influence behind the words.

"Yeah, it's fixed," agreed the retina technician. "Knew it couldn't be right. Go on through."

Titus reached over and claimed his card from the slot in front of the Tourist. Never taking his eyes from her nor letting up his hold, he retrieved his jacket from the hopper, hooked it over one shoulder and escorted Mirelle back to the elevator. When they were far enough away, he cut his grip on the two human technicians and abandoned the Tourist to her own devices. He'd scored a victory, but perhaps in winning, he had lost. He had to find out what was really in his bag.

In the elevator, Mirelle said, "What happened? I was so worried they might stop you from boarding."

There was no shred of Influence operating on her now. She meant it. "Government computers—obsolete junk. I hope they've equipped Project Station better than that!"

"I don't know about computers except how to use them, but I don't want to spend a year on the moon without you."

If she wanted, of her own free will, to flirt, Titus was willing. He could use a friend, especially a delectable, human one. "Nor would I wish to be on Earth while you were on the moon."

The skybus was compartmentalized in case of pressure failure, with five seats to the compartment. The red and gray plush, gimbaled seats swiveled to face each other around a tiny table, big enough to play cards.

Mirelle and Titus were ushered to the same compartment, where Titus was given the seat near the porthole. Placing his bag between his feet, he began to crank the shutter across the port to cut the horrible light. As it was closing, he glanced out and noticed a runabout pulling up to the check station, where a long line still waited. The Tourist agent was called over and someone else sent to her work station.

Squinting, Titus recognized the replacement as one of Connie's operatives. She had countered the move against Titus ten minutes too late. *I should have gone to the end of the line, and damn the sun.*

The Tourist agent had to retire, leaving Titus' opponent to the same kind of trial Titus had faced. Despite his burning eyes, he wanted to watch his unknown adversary attempt to board. *If he hasn't already.*

"What's so interesting?" Mirelle leaned over him pushing her face to the porthole.

He brushed his lips against her neck, and she shivered, innocently unaware why her response was so strong, and obviously no longer playing her games. Titus, concentration disrupted, closed the shutter and murmured, "Perhaps the year won't be lonely—for either of us."

He reminded himself sternly that he wasn't the least bit hungry. Despite that, their mutual response was intense. Mirelle might be a problem. She was obviously one of those humans who were both susceptible and deeply attracted to his kind. Restraining himself by force, he set about winning her true friendship in the usual, agonizingly slow, fashion.

When Abner Gold was shown to their compartment, Titus excused himself and went to the lavatory, taking his bag with him. When he got the bag open, his heart froze. His packets of powdered blood, his vital supply not just for the trip but for emergencies, had been replaced with plain white packets—half a million in street drugs, no doubt. *Getting me out of jail would have kept Connie too busy to send a replacement.*

10

He flushed it all down the toilet, hoping it wouldn't be noticed when the collector was cleaned. Now he knew what the reporter had meant about starving on the moon. He clamped his teeth over the chattering fear. He would survive on the supply to come in his luggage—if it arrived. He would not let the Tourists know they'd scored.

When he returned to his seat, Mirelle wouldn't let him stare out the window pretending to brood while he watched the check-in line. She coaxed him into the conversation even though Gold preferred to monopolize her.

Gold was just past middle age, while Mirelle might have passed for almost forty. Titus, however, appeared to be in his twenties instead of his actual thirty-eight. Gold was suffering the normal responses of an older man watching a mature woman flirting with a much younger man. He felt compelled to best Titus at something in front of Mirelle, and Titus knew he had to let him or surely make an enemy.

At this point, the fourth passenger in their compartment joined them. White-haired, with a receding hairline and a middle-aged paunch, he moved as if he'd been commuting to orbit for years and could stow his things and strap himself in blindfolded. He dismissed the attendant with a wave and settled down to read as if there was nobody else there.

Titus found a deck of cards inside his chair's arm rest. "Anyone like to play cards?"

Gold shrugged. "Let's see if our fifth plays bridge. We'll have plenty of time before docking at Goddard."

All the passengers had boarded, and still their fifth did not show. An awful suspicion began to creep over him. If this was the only seat left, and someone was late, chances were good it would be his adversary. The Tourists would want their agent to watch Titus, and Connie would want Titus to watch the Tourist. *Not that there's anything either of us could do at the moment.*

He felt and heard the distant clanging shudder and adjustment in air pressure as the hatch was finally closed. *There's no one coming. Connie's blocked them!*

Then he felt a powerful presence nearing, a palpable Influence he was very afraid he recognized.

"Strap in quickly, Doctor," advised the attendant who ushered the tall gentleman in. To Titus she said, "You can take out the cards again when we're in free-fall. They'll adhere to the table, or you may keep them on their holders. You'll find the holders in the chair arms."

Titus barely heard her.

The adversary stood with his back to them, as he doffed hat and jacket. "Sorry to be late." His too familiar voice was cultured, his accent indefinable. "I was detained in traffic in Lima." He appeared middle-aged, but stick-figure thin, as were all of their kind. He turned to face Titus.

Father!

"You seem surprised to see me, Titus," he answered, aware of the humans listening. "I admit, I hadn't expected you'd be here." He added with genuine concern, "Are you sure you can withstand the rigors of this job?"

This was the man who'd dug Titus out of a premature grave and wakened him to his current life by giving of his own blood, the man who had resurrected Titus to the life of a vampire.

Titus swallowed the lump in his throat and chose his words for the humans around them. "I was reliably informed that you had declined the Project's invitation."

"I had—until I heard you'd accepted." He added with peculiar emphasis, "Now, I'm glad I'm here. I will be able to . . . observe . . . your work as no one else of my persuasion."

Titus read him clearly. In his centuries of life, Abbot Nandoha had acquired many specialties. There was no sabotage Titus could do that Abbot couldn't undo.

And Abbot was saying quite plainly that he would stop at nothing—absolutely nothing—to get that SOS out.

TWO

As the attendant left, Titus answered, "I'm flattered . . . Dr. Nandoha." He suppressed a shiver of cold dread and tried to sound implacable. "And I intend to observe your work—as closely as I can." What else could he do? Not only was Abbot much older and stronger than Titus, but he was also his father. Titus was completely in his power. There was no point in his trying to fight Abbot, and Connie knew that.

He suddenly envisioned the quiet battle she had been waging in Quito, trying to delay Abbot, to have him replaced. *No wonder she let them get my bag, and almost let them get me!* She only had eight operatives planted in the Project, and all of them were on Earth. Titus was the only one to make it to the moon.

To break the tension, Gold spoke up. "Well! It does seem you know each other. Titus, introduce us."

Titus gestured to his far right. "Abbot, the gentleman by the door— I mean hatch—is Dr. Abner Gold, metallurgist. The lady here is Dr. Mirelle de Lisle, Cognitive Sciences. And—" The man facing Titus across the porthole had never said a word. He was totally absorbed in a newsletter printed in cyrillic characters. "I didn't catch *your* name, Doctor?"

The man was fiftyish, hawk-nosed, with muscular forearms and painfully short fingernails. "Sir?" prompted Titus. The man finally looked up as if returning from a far distance. He raised both bushy white eyebrows and gazed innocently at Titus, who repeated, "I didn't catch your name."

"Mihelich, Andre Mihelich."

Titus repeated their names and specialties, but Mihelich did not offer anything further until Titus asked, "Which department are you working in?"

"Biomed." With that, he returned to his newsletter. Since he hadn't answered to "Doctor," Titus deduced that Mihelich was one of the nurses or techs in the huge medical department that did both research and healthcare. From the few words he'd spoken, he seemed to be a North American.

Into the resounding silence, Titus said, "Doctors, this is Dr. Abbot Nandoha, electrical engineer, circuit designer, and computer architect. Where will you be working, Abbot?"

From his seat across from Mirelle and Titus, Abbot answered, "Generating plant—supplying power to your computers, Titus, and life-support to the Station."

He could go anywhere without question. Titus shook off despair. Things couldn't get any worse now.

"Well!" said Abner Gold. "Bridge, anyone?"

"Actually," said Mirelle, "poker's more my game. Perhaps if we play poker, Dr. Mihelich will join us?"

Just then, the speakers came on announcing liftoff. Simultaneously, their little table sank into the floor, and their seats swiveled and flattened as the Captain readied for thrust. Soon, the faint murmur singing through the bulkheads became a thick vibration that blotted out all other sound.

13

Then Titus felt his back forced into a proper posture by the gathering g-forces. He relaxed into it. Though the decibel level reached the upper limits of toleration, the sound had the reassuring coherence of finely tuned machinery. It was not threatening. It inspired confidence. Even awe.

For the first time, Titus was able to open himself to the experience of leaving earth. His ancestors had come here in a far more sophisticated craft. But he and his kind had long worked with humans to create this crude vehicle. And now—at last—they were returning to space.

The emotion was as overwhelming as the sound. He caught his father watching him, features distorted by acceleration. There was a fierce joy on Abbot's face that expressed just how Titus was feeling. He did his best to return it, and for a moment the extra sense that guided the use of Influence flared between them, a fierce embrace.

As they shared their private triumph, Titus knew Abbot loved him just as Titus' human father, the man who'd raised him, had loved him. Of his genetic father, Titus knew only that he'd been a vampire, and was probably dead. Abbot had wakened Titus, nurtured him, and now wanted him to share this step in the liberation of The Blood from lonely exile.

The sweet warmth of that embrace stole over Titus, feeding his starved soul. There were so few of them scattered over Earth; they couldn't afford to let factions split them. They understood one another's needs, knew each other's moods, and could rely on each other no matter what the imposition. They were a family. The warmth of belonging was something Titus had rarely felt since his human family had buried him—mistaking him for a dead human.

Until this moment, drowning in the universal roar, helpless in the grip of forces stronger than himself, Titus had not realized how deeply deprived his life had been. There was a hollow ache where there should have been parents, sister, brother, wife, and children of his own.

With a gasp, Titus twisted his head away, breaking the contact with Abbot's eyes. *Wife.* It was like a hot knife in his heart. *Inea. Two more days and we'd have been married.*

He clamped his lips shut. He'd vowed never to say her name again. It was over—done. She was human. And she had seen his body dangling from the overturned car by the seat belt—abdomen pierced by torn metal.

But the emptiness ached and ached, and Abbot knew how to use it. *No, that's not fair.* It wasn't Abbot's fault that Titus had crashed the

14

car, or that Titus had made the change too young. None of Titus' problems were Abbot's doing. He swallowed the emptiness, thrust aside the pain, and looked at Abbot. Summoning a grin to match Abbot's, he refused to be drawn back into the whirl of emotions. Yet, with the most negligent effort, Abbot could sweep him back into the depths, manipulate him into doing or saying anything.

Only this time, he didn't. He let the echoing contact fade, giving mercy that truly felt like love. It *was* genuine love, but still Abbot would kill him, truly and permanently, in order to send that SOS. His loyalty to The Blood—the luren species, on Earth as well as out in the galaxy—was above all personal considerations, and Abbot expected no less of Titus.

As the noise and vibration finally let up and an eerie silence descended, Titus decided he had to fight. Connie, and everyone else—not the least of all, unsuspecting humanity—was depending on him. He had to buy time for Connie to act.

At last, the couches folded back into chairs and a voice instructed them to keep seat belts buckled during free-fall. Attendants would escort anyone who needed to use the facilities. Compliance with this safety rule was a condition of employment on the Project.

Mirelle rummaged in her chair arm. "Ah! A lovely poker deck! Poker, not bridge, no?" The back of the deck showed a glorious view of Goddard Station, with Earth glowing in one corner and stars in the background.

The mysterious Andre Mihelich resumed reading, ignoring Mirelle. Titus asked her, "Poker? You were serious?"

"Of course, Titus. But not to worry—we won't play for money. We will play for each other's palmtops."

"What!" Gold laughed. "What could an anthropologist do with a TI-Alter programmed for metals analysis?" They had each brought their personal favorite combination devices, loading in the calculator and other software they'd need because the lunar facility did not yet have a reliable network up and running. "I had to pull out networking to fit in all I'd need. It's hardly more than a calculator now!"

Mirelle laughed. "That's the point! You see, the winner redistributes the PDAs, deciding who gets whose. To get your own back, you have to work the one you have."

"But I know nothing about metals beyond basic theory," protested Titus, "and less about anthropology or any of the Cognitives."

15

She gazed up at him, close enough that she might discern his contact lenses now that he'd removed his sunglasses. "Titus, how much do you expect I know about astrophysics?"

Titus eyed Abbot but detected no Influence. "I carry a Bell 990. I doubt you'd know how to turn it on." She could have dealt easily with his old Sharp, but he'd had to upgrade for this job, then do some savage reconfiguring just as Gold had. Titus pulled his jacket out from under the seat and produced the 990. No bigger than his palm, it was programmed for all his routine calculations, and had his standard reference tables in ROM with a gig of Project notes. On the moon, it could take him weeks to set up a new 990 or have one reprogrammed from his home files without network access.

Abbot raised an eyebrow in sardonic amusement.

They thought they got my handheld with my bag! Score one!

Titus passed the 990 to Mirelle and watched her turn the smooth case over. "I don't even know how to open it!" From her bag she extracted a stubby looking, thick instrument that she handed to Titus. "Can you make this do anything?"

Titus didn't recognize the manufacturer. He found the activation switch, but every command he tried produced an error message in a different language. Gold chuckled and reached toward Titus. "Here, let me try."

He had no better luck, and handed it to Abbot who said, "Custom-made, isn't it? How many languages does it speak?" Abbot, Titus expected, could use anything that had ever been made, all the way back to the abacus, and was proud of it.

"It was a gift—from an admirer. I designed the commands. It's unique."

Gold fingered his silver-cased Alter and the screen lit up.

"Then how are we supposed to figure out how to use it before we get to the moon?"

Abbot put her instrument on the table and spun the table until she could reach it. Taking it, she said, "Watch." She touched a sequence on the pad and the screen lit up with a picture of the Rosetta stone. "I'll do it again. See? Now each of you show us one easy function." When they had, she added, "All we have to do is remember all three functions until the end of the game, and then whichever PDA we end up with, we can get our own back by making the one we have talk."

"Suppose I get yours but can't make it show a Rosetta stone?" Gold asked Mirelle.

"Then, Abner, whoever has yours may demand a favor. We'll say it can't cost more than the PDA. As soon as the favor is rendered, the instrument is returned. Also—since we all must get to work immediately—it has to be a favor that can be done right away."

Gold eyed Mirelle. "Even a very personal favor?"

"Certainly. This is poker. It gets *very* personal."

Abbot signaled for a cabin attendant and began unstrapping himself. "If you folks will excuse me for a—"

"Don't do that!" warned Gold. "They catch you loose and they'll send you right back to Earth."

Abbot subsided. "Thank you, I had forgotten."

He's in a panic!

Abbot poked at the signal again.

"Not feeling well?" asked Mirelle. "I have some pills."

"Oh, no—I'm fine."

She cranked the free-fall shuffler. "Mind if I deal?"

Clearly, Abbot didn't want to play this game, but could find no graceful way out of it short of using Influence to divert them. Abbot himself had taught Titus the cardinal rule: *Influence is a last resort.* Too much, and people notice their own odd behavior.

Oblivious to all this, Mirelle went on. "We'll secure our PDA's in the middle of the table. There's a small net around here somewhere—"

While she and Gold searched the edge of the table for the compartment and found the net, passing it around to collect instruments, Abbot fidgeted. Titus had never seen his father squirm before.

When Gold passed the net, Abbot made a business of fumbling with the Varian. Suddenly, Titus knew. *There's a piece of the SOS transmitter in there!*

Abbot met Titus' gaze, and his eyes narrowed. Titus said, "This should be interesting. I've never won at poker against you, and I've never seen you stymied by any computer. But there's always a first time for everything."

Abbot relaxed, and with a cool smile passed the net back to Mirelle. Fastening the net as close to the middle of the table as she could reach, Mirelle announced, "I warn you gentlemen, I do intend to win. I hope each of you does too."

Abbot replied, "Rest assured, I do." And to Titus, he added, "And I shall."

I did it! He's going to play!

While Mirelle dealt the cards into four holders and spun the table to distribute them, Titus thought hard. Connie had said that the Tourists' transmitter was being shipped to Project Station in seven components, which would then be assembled to look like a legitimate part of the probe vehicle. In place, it would function as what it resembled, but it would also contain the powerful transmitter that would use the probe's antenna to send a signal hidden under the humans' message. Two of the Tourists' transmitter components would be programmed at Project Station: the targeting computer that would turn the antenna in case the humans sent their signal in the wrong direction, and the component holding the message itself.

Three components were at the station already, two more were being shipped as cargo, and two were being hand carried by their agent. By Abbot. One, at least, in the Varian.

Abbot would surely carry the ones he could least expect to fabricate at the station in case of loss or damage.

As if following his thoughts, Abbot said, "Titus, I am going to win."

"We'll see. If we play simple draw poker with no outside *influences* affecting the *rules*, I just might win."

"That's the spirit!" exclaimed Mirelle. "Simple draw poker it is. No wild cards, no optional hands."

Abbot raised an eyebrow at Titus. "All right, we'll make it a contest of pure poker skill—no other *influences*."

He's either overconfident or I've underestimated him. In the past, Abbot's apparent arrogance had always turned out to be extreme modesty. Titus wiped cold sweat off his palms. In a truly fair game, Titus knew he might even win. But—

The escort attendant poked her head in the door and called pleasantly, "Dr. Nandoha?"

He waved her away. "Never mind. I've become engaged." There was no way Abbot could take the Varian with him without using Influence to make the others overlook his odd behavior.

Mirelle located the package of miniature magnetic poker chips. "Who wants to be banker?"

"You do it, Mirelle," suggested Abner. "You're the only woman here, and we all know what we're playing for—don't we, fellows?" He glanced from Abbot to Titus.

Mirelle shrugged. "I'll divide the chips and if you run out, you're out of the game. No bookkeeping. Whoever ends up with the most chips wins. We play until docking maneuvers and settle up in line at the boarding gate."

"We should be able to settle up here," objected Abbot.

Mirelle spun the table distributing the chips. "Abbot! You doubt your ability to remember computer commands?"

Titus was disturbed by the way Abbot held her gaze. He knew all too well how Abbot used human women, and he despaired as Abbot's lips trembled hungrily.

But the other was no more hungry than Titus at the outset of the mission. Abbot mastered himself easily. "I have not had cause to doubt my abilities in a great while."

They fell to playing in a concentrated silence, each of them focused on the discard pile, calculating odds, measuring each others' expressions for any hint of worry. Abbot, no doubt, wasn't worried. He had nearly total recall.

While Abner Gold pondered his second bet, Titus caught Andre Mihelich peeking at the game over his newsletter.

"Raise ten," announced Abner, sliding a stack of chips out, taking care that they adhered to one another and the bottom one stuck firmly to the table.

"Call," announced Mirelle prettily.

She was yet a different person now. She acted as if each development was the delight of a lifetime. But she didn't chatter. Titus wished she'd just stop playing her anthropological game. Every once in a while, when something got through to her, she revealed flashes of her true self that intrigued him unbearably.

Titus put his cards down. "I'm out." He'd been holding a pair of threes and a pair of twos. He figured Mirelle had at least a flush, and Abbot a full house or above, for he hadn't drawn any cards.

Abbot and Gold called. Mirelle won with a flush just one card higher than Abbot's. Then they each won a round, Titus raking in the highest pot as he bluffed out the two humans when Abbot folded. But two rounds later, Mirelle was ahead and Titus caught Abbot glaring at him. Titus grinned back, knowing his father wouldn't bring Influence to bear after promising not to.

Play became brisk and silent, a battle of nerve in which even Mirelle settled into stony concentration. Mihelich lowered his newsletter and stared. Responding to the tension between Titus and Abbot, the humans also played as if their lives depended on it. In a way, they did. The luren who'd respond to the Tourists' SOS would regard humans as cattle and Earth's civilization as an inconvenience to be wiped away. With all the space stations long ago rendered defenseless by W.S. treaty, it would be no contest.

Then Titus sensed a thrum of Influence gathering about Abbot. He might consider it fair to read the other players' cards or the next cards to be drawn. Looking straight at his father, he roused his own Influence and cast a wave that interfered with the older vampire's nearly tangible power. At will, Abbot could overpower anything Titus could do. Titus said, "I'm glad we're playing straight, uncomplicated draw poker. It reveals the mettle of one's opponents."

"Honor takes many forms," Abbot mused. "Sometimes real honor lies in the sacrifice of honor." Simultaneously, the Influence tension abated. Without even counting his chips, Abbot shoved them all to the center of the table.

Gold stared at the pile. He couldn't match the bet. He folded and mopped his forehead with a handkerchief.

Mirelle matched the bet with one red chip to spare.

Titus' hands shook as he counted chips. He was holding a royal flush, but there were eight hands that could beat his. He was pretty sure Abbot didn't have one of those, or he wouldn't have been worried enough to use Influence. But Mirelle might have that hand. *Not might, does!*

Titus matched the bet, with one white chip left over. Titus stared at her red chip. *She's won.*

"Throw it in, Titus," urged Mirelle. "Raise."

It was a symbolic gesture, nothing more. Mirelle had won, but would be under Abbot's Influence in a flash as soon as the game was over. With a shrug, Titus pushed the remaining white chip out. "Raise one."

Abbot placed his cards face down in their holder. "I'm out." His eyes never flickered, but his Influence gathered. He'd dictate to Mirelle how to distribute the calculators.

Mirelle fingered her red chip and explored Titus' eyes. Then she gazed at Abbot. "I did say the one with the most chips at the end of the game would win, and that's me. But I'd rather match hands with Titus. Winning seems to mean a lot to him. Perhaps if he wins, we'll find out why."

Titus felt Abbot start, a frisson of alarm that shivered through the thick fabric of Influenced space between them. Abbot had always dominated humans. He had never bothered to understand them. Titus smiled. She had chosen him over Abbot, and he marveled at how warm that made him feel.

She snapped her cards down on the table. "Hearts. King. Queen. Jack. Ten. Nine."

Titus, realizing she was in this only for fun, extended the tension much as he would prolong foreplay because a woman liked it. As if about to announce his win, he snapped his cards down. "Spades. Eight. Nine. Ten. Jack. Queen."

She burst out laughing. Twisting in her seat, she could just barely reach Titus' shoulders to embrace him. "Titus, you are wonderful! But even so, I'm glad I won."

Then she reached for the net. "I'll take Abner's TI-Alter, and give my custom job to . . . " Titus felt the Influence build. He tried to block Abbot. She paused and looked as if she'd forgotten what she'd intended to say then started over, "Since it seems to matter to Titus and Abbot more than I'd ever expected, I'm going to award Abbot's Varian to Titus. And my custom to Abbot. Which leaves Titus' Bell to Abner." With a little frown, she said, "Doesn't that make perfect sense?"

"Are you sure that's the way you want it, Mirelle?" asked Abbot.

"Well . . . "

In a hard voice, Titus answered, "She's sure. The game isn't *over* until we settle up!"

She cocked her head to one side, and Titus felt her strive against the Influence aimed at her. If a resistive human had fought Influence half so valiantly, the luren would have little chance in public. But Mirelle was susceptible. She said doubtfully, "I think I'm sure. The object of the game is to make it interesting. And since Abbot seems to want to keep his Varian out of Titus' hands, the best way to make the game interesting is to put it into Titus' hands."

Even though Abbot could have made her change her mind, these people would be confined with them for a year. It was essential not to arouse their suspicions. As he hesitated, the warning chime sounded and Titus collected the Varian, passing the others out as Mirelle had specified while they hurried to stow the cards and chips before docking maneuvers.

No sooner had the ship stopped pulsing and surging than the attendants appeared to escort them through the linked hatches and into Goddard Station—the first stepping stone into space, orbiting high above Earth's surface.

21

The station rotated, providing gravity. The lights were bright, but not too strong for Titus' dark contacts. The air had the blank feel of dustless, processed air marbled with streaks of human odor. Under the hum of machinery, there was the sharp sound of human voices confined in a metal shell.

Abbot had contrived to stay behind Titus all the way from the skybus to an area where the scientists had to pass a brief instrument check to determine their response to the low gravity. Titus walked with one hand in his pocket on Abbot's Varian. Seeing his chance, he squirmed through the press, muttering apologies, and headed for the hatch marked MEN. Glancing behind, he saw Abbot detained by a knot of laughing Turkish engineers teasing a Greek mathematician.

Titus dodged around three women huddled over a glossy flex screen showing a bubble chamber tracing, arguing heatedly. He caught half a sentence and chipped in, "No, if it were, it would go clockwise. Ask that tall, skinny gentleman over there." He pointed at Abbot.

As the women followed his gesture, he ducked through a crack in the wall of people and backed into the men's room. Two men pushed out past him discussing better designs for low-grav urinals. Titus locked himself in a stall and attacked the Varian's case, using his thumbnail as a screwdriver. He heard the door open, and thought he was lost. The screw wouldn't budge. Then, with the steps coming toward him, it turned. Someone went into the adjacent stall, and Titus knew it wasn't Abbot—should have known all along.

Calm down, he admonished himself. At last the case opened. He sorted through modified boards and connectors. *He tricked me! He wanted me to believe there was a transmitter component in here!*

Abbot was capable of such subtlety, and Titus was ashamed for not having considered that before. But then a small bit of circuitry fell out into his hand. It was as long as his palm, and no more than five millimeters thick, but he could see the circuitry etching inside, and the microprocessor. It was an advanced design, glittering like a diffraction jewel, and it wasn't attached to the Varian.

The hatch opened again, and the room was flooded with Influence, silent, overwhelming.

Titus' breath caught in his throat. He clamped his teeth onto his lower lip as he fought to turn his palm over and spill the component to the floor where he could crush it with his heel. His hand trembled, but refused to turn.

He summoned his own power to combat Abbot's Influence. From the adjacent stall came the sound of human retching. Cloaking his words, so the human wouldn't notice, Abbot whispered, "Put it back, boy, and I'll let the human rest."

"If he knew what he was suffering for, he'd surely volunteer," returned Titus and made another supreme effort to drop the jewel-like chip and crush it.

Against the pall of Abbot's Influence, he could not force his hand to turn. With a silent snarl, he focused his power, feeling weak and helpless against the elder's might. He was a twig, and the older vampire an immense oak. He redoubled his effort, but his hand only shook violently.

His fingers, white with strain, uncurled a bit. Not from any conscious direction of Titus' but simply from the strain, his arm spasmed, jerking his hand. The chip slid off his palm and fell lazily in the weak gravity, Coriolis force curving its trajectory. It glanced off the toilet rim and clanked into the polished steel bowl, which contained no water. The chip clattered to rest on the mirror-bright surface, easy to retrieve if not for the searing ultraviolet rays triggered when the solid entered the field.

At the tink of plastic hitting metal, Abbot swarmed up the wall, his concentration wavering when he had to pay attention to how he moved in the light gravity. With a cry of triumph, Titus fell against the flushing bar. Abbot's Influence clamped down again, but the toilet mechanism sucked the component away into the main sewage tank.

Titus looked up at Abbot, who was spread across the top of the stall gazing into the toilet. The power that had enveloped Titus in an iron grip dwindled. The shock frozen onto Abbot's ageless face told Titus he had struck a major blow.

THREE

Abbot's urbanity returned. He even smiled with paternal pleasure. "I honestly didn't think you could defy me so strongly. You've grown, Titus. I'm proud."

Next door, the human stopped retching. Abbot was now using Influence only to blank their conversation and his conspicuous perch. "But we're on the same side of this, you and I. We're both luren."

"Are we?" Residents preferred to think of themselves as vampires—humans living a post-death existence nourished by pre-death humans—but still natives of Earth. The Tourists, however, insisted on the ancestral name for their species—luren—which presumably meant blood-kin, or The Blood, and regarded themselves as temporarily shipwrecked on a primitive planet.

"We are," said Abbot, "and now humans will signal luren space. Even if you misdirect the message, someone will hear it, eventually. Luren will find Earth. It's all over, Titus. There's no reason for you and I opposing one another over an obscure philosophical point."

It sounded so logical, and Abbot wasn't even driving his words with Influence. Doggedly, Titus repeated the Residents' argument. "Without your SOS, it could take centuries for them to find us. By then, humans may be able to defend themselves." He didn't mention the latest human theory that demonstrated there was no such thing as simultaneity across interstellar distances.

"Humans defend themselves? Never effectively," replied Abbot. He glanced at the human who'd been sick. "They've no natural defenses against us. Are their genes going to change in a century or two?"

Titus' faith in humanity, which had sounded so practical in meeting rooms on Earth, seemed a feeble argument now.

"Titus, with your greatest effort, you have not managed to strike a blow against my mission—but only against *our* Blood. I'll fabricate another targeting device, but it won't fit as neatly. Your destruction has increased the chance that the human inspectors will discover my device. And if they do, and if they discover that my message is not in any human language, what will they think?

"If humans discover us before rescue arrives, they'll slaughter us—just as they did in Transylvania." Abbot's genuine anguish echoed off the hard walls. "We're so close to going home, safe, and you have to do this!"

Shame overcame Titus and he could summon no answer.

The paging speaker interrupted, a pleasant woman's voice urging, "Dr. Nandoha, Dr. Abbot Nandoha, please report to medical. Dr. Nandoha, to medical immediately."

Abruptly, Abbot was gone, the outer door closing softly behind him. Titus leaned on the stall door, shaking.

―――――

Two hours later, all the scientists had been processed through medical and assembled in the moonship lounge to await boarding of the orbit-jumper *Barnaby Peter.*

Mirelle had gathered her poker players around one end of the bar. Behind the bar a huge screen, clear as an open window, displayed an exterior view of *Barnaby Peter.*

Titus played with the bulb of Rum Collins he'd ordered for appearance's sake and gazed into the depths of space. Inwardly, he was drained. His best effort would not prevent the Tourists from bringing a ravening horde of luren to Earth, a horde that would devour the only home he'd ever known, and crush him under their heels because he was no more luren than the humans they would feed on.

"Titus, pay attention!" Mirelle nudged up to his side and waved an open hand in front of his eyes. "I said we're settling up now. Are you ready to work the Varian?"

He had been only peripherally aware of them playing with the instruments. He fished the Varian out of his jacket and laid it on the bar. Negligently, he poked keys and it responded with a syncopated "Jingle Bells." Mirelle laughed, delighted, but Titus could summon no response within himself.

He touched her hand, drinking in her warmth and that intangible *life* which was the component of blood that could not be synthesized. He began to thaw inwardly, to recall how precious a human could be, and the real reason he was here, fighting a battle he couldn't win. However small, the chance of winning was worth his life. Humanity was worth it.

"Well, then, here you are," said Abner Gold as he slid the Bell 990 over to Titus. "Took me eight tries to work yours, though. Forgot the quotation marks and kept getting the Southern Cross instead of the Big Dipper." He glanced at Abbot and added jocularly, "The embarrassing part is that I couldn't see the difference!"

Mirelle laughed at the strained joke, her voice ringing through Abbot's glum silence as he nursed a Screwdriver he had no intention of drinking. Looking past Abbot, Titus saw Mihelich watching the bet-settling ceremony with more than passing interest. As their eyes met, Mihelich turned away as if he hadn't been watching them at all.

Mirelle said, "Okay, Abbot. Can you work my custom?"

With a slow smile, he poked at the controls, producing the Rosetta stone closeup she had shown them. Then he tapped another command. The image rotated. "Good enough?"

25

Abbot seemed genuinely amused by the human game. Titus marveled as he returned the Varian, *sans* its most vital component. But as Abbot accepted the gutted instrument, his eyes lingered on Mirelle, then measured Titus.

Self-consciously, Titus moved away from her. "Mirelle, let's see what you can do with Abner's Alter."

"Nothing so fancy," she said and put the instrument on the bar. Abbot moved her custom up next to Gold's Alter.

With great concentration, she plucked out a combination and got a Periodic Table with the metals outlined in purple. "Is that right? I wouldn't know if I got the wrong one."

"There is only one," assured Gold, not bothering to hide his disappointment. "The table is the basis of our message to the aliens, you know."

"That's not my part of the project," she replied.

"No?" asked Abbot, searingly alert. "So why a linguist on this project? Your other communications skills won't be much called for, so are you going to spend all your time translating at meetings?"

"Don't you think that will keep me busy? And then there are all those documents on subjects I know nothing about."

Her bored resignation rang false, and suddenly Titus wondered just why she was on the project. *A medic who isn't a doctor and a linguist who isn't working on the message*—Mihelich had cut himself off from others, and Mirelle had been dissembling so persistently it was hard to say who she really was. Titus glanced about and spotted other loners. Could there be something else going on besides Project Hail?

If the humans were up to something different from what had been announced, it was imperative that the Residents find out about it, and quickly. Mirelle had to be the key.

Just then a man's voice announced, "Attention members of Project Hail. I am honored to present to you, the on-site director of the Project, Dr. Carol Colby."

People turned toward a woman who stood on a chair, a microphone in one hand and an electronic clipboard in the other. She was wearing the same Project Hail uniform as the rest of them, an unprepossessing blue coverall with indigo piping. She had her flight jacket tied around her waist by the arms. Her sandy hair was cut short and flipped back, secured by a headband that held a headset near one ear.

"There isn't much time, so I'll make this short." Her pleasant contralto voice suggested a trained broadcaster or singer. She appeared no more than fifty, and was trim-figured, with pale skin. Titus saw a scattering of people move to a counter by the boarding ramp where translator headsets were plugged in.

"Everything is ready at Project Station, your quarters and labs— even the computers are up and running, and we're expecting the wireless network soon. We've worked hard to reach this point so quickly, and I must now ask something even more special of you.

"As you know, having come directly from Earth today, sabotage has not been rare despite Project security. The controversy is so heated, the project could be canceled.

"You're all volunteers, here because you believe in the Project, so I'm confident you'll respond well when I ask you to work longer hours than you expected and with less network support than you're accustomed to. Our supporters on Earth can give us another eight months at the outside. So we launch the probe in eight months, not fourteen. Can you do it?"

A roar of voices chanted "Yes!" in a dozen languages.

Titus noticed a small knot of men and women moving toward Colby, leading the chanting.

"Abbot?" asked Titus, nervously cloaking his words in Influence. "What are they up to?"

"I see no threat, only suppressed amusement."

Titus wondered if he'd ever develop such powers. He forced his attention back to the director, who was saying, "Since this decision was taken only hours ago, we haven't yet consulted heads of vital departments, so let me put you on the spot here and now. Dr. Nancy Dorenski?"

One of the group of chant leaders presented herself. She was a diminutive brunette.

"Dr. Dorenski, can you complete programming of the message in such a short time?"

"If nothing goes wrong," came a tiny soprano voice, "we can make it."

"Good." Colby made a note on her clipboard with a light pen. "Dr. Shiddehara, Dr. Titus Shiddehara?"

"Here!" answered Titus. "Back by the bar."

"Ah, you speak English!" Her own English had a slight French Canadian tang to it. "Can you locate the point of origin of the aliens in only eight months?"

"There's no way to know, Dr. Colby. But if, as you say, the computers are ready and the crews working on the alien craft complete the

27

analyses I specified, you can count on my department." In truth, he expected that within a month or so he'd have verification of the luren tradition that identified their origin.

On the other hand, as with most legends devoutly believed in, this one might contain only a kernel of truth, embroidered for effect by storytellers impressing children.

Colby continued calling on department heads and all answered as Titus had. He caught Abbot eyeing him narrowly. How long would it take Abbot to make another targeting device? Had he counted on fourteen months? Suddenly the future didn't look quite so bleak. *If only Connie managed to get a decent quantity of blood through to the Station . . .*

Titus' brooding was interrupted when a member of the small group of chanters, a young woman who couldn't be more than twenty-five, dragged a chair up to Colby's and climbed up. "May I borrow your microphone for a moment, Doctor?"

Puzzled, the Director handed the headset over, while the woman held out a packet wrapped in white tissue. "This is from the six technicians of the Air Scrubbing Plant—to help you maintain discipline."

The Director unwrapped the package, unrolling a green cloth and holding it up. It was a T-shirt with the words BIG CHEESE on the front and a moon-shaped slice of cheese balanced on a photograph of the moon. In silence the Director stared at it blankly, then she burst out laughing. She took off the jacket tied around her waist and pulled the huge T-shirt over her head. It went almost to her knees.

Colby took the headset back, and said, "I'll be the Big Cheese on the Moon if you folks remember that this Colby doesn't crumble!" With that, she stepped down, leaving everyone cheering. The boarding announcement cut across the noise, and people lined up to board for the trip to the moon.

Abbot, Titus, and Mirelle rated private cabins far forward of the drive and so were funneled into the same line. Titus wanted nothing so much as to get away from Abbot, but he turned when Mirelle called, "Titus, wait!"

She caught up with him and this time shyly waited for him to take her arm. He hesitated. He had made a pact with himself not to touch human sources of blood. He was used to synthetics, supplemented with ectoplasm only from volunteers. But his blood supplies had been stolen.

And Mirelle had chosen him over Abbot. If he rejected her, she'd turn to his father. Titus could not abide the way Abbot treated his stringers.

He slid his arm around her waist, feeling the layer of hard muscle under feminine contours, and guided her to the line moving up the boarding ramp. She cuddled closer. "Maybe I can get my cabin changed to one next to you?"

"Mirelle, I don't know what to make of you. You're never the same woman twice. What game are you playing?"

She looked up with wounded dignity turning to innocence. Just then Abbot inserted himself into the line beside them, exerting Influence to keep others from objecting to the cut.

"Mirelle," he said, displaying his boarding card. "I've switched to the cabin next to yours." Enhancing his words with Influence, he put his arm around her and murmured in her ear, "This'll be an interesting voyage. We're far enough away from that stuffy physicist"—he indicated Titus— "to have some real fun." Over her head, Abbot met Titus' gaze and hardened his Influence around Mirelle.

Abbot was only exercising the elder's right of choice in taking Mirelle. But the way he did it rankled.

Yet it was the Law of Blood. Titus relinquished his hold on the human. He could barely breathe against the outrage flooding through him. His lips curled in a snarl. *Tourist!* But he dared not spit an obscenity in his father's face. Cloaking his words, he said, "Humans aren't orl. They have the right of choice." Orl were just animals evolved for luren to feed on, but Tourists often used the word for humans.

Abbot whispered to Mirelle, poisoning her subconscious against Titus. "I won't let that *physicist* pry anything out of you. You can always depend on me to protect you."

Offended, Titus choked, "What do you think I am?"

Abbot raised an eyebrow. "Luren, of course." He turned Mirelle toward him and moved his left forefinger toward the point between her brows. His Influence focused to a barely discernible blue-white light emanating from the tip of his finger. If that finger should once touch her, Mirelle would be Marked with the complex pattern of Abbot's personal sigil.

Until Abbot cared to remove the mark, no other luren would touch her. She would become Abbot's puppet, his eyes and ears, his hands, doing his will.

Titus grabbed Abbot's wrist and—surprised that he'd caught the older vampire off guard—yanked him off balance. Startled, Abbot forgot the light gravity and stumbled, drifting to the deck, Influence disrupted.

Security guards converged, moving with that sliding gait that marked experienced spacemen. Mirelle came out of her induced stupor. "Abbot! What were you doing?"

Appalled at himself, Titus spread his Influence, projecting boredom. It was just a clumsy grounder stumbling around. He waved the guards away and bent to help Abbot up.

The older vampire bemusedly added his power to Titus' efforts to distract the guards, then soothed Mirelle. As the line shuffled forward, he grunted, "Titus, that was unprincipled. Undisciplined. UnLawful. And foolish. Didn't I go to considerable pains to teach you the penalties for violating Blood Law?"

"Your people stole my supplies. Who violated Law first?"

"*Supplies!*" he scoffed. "Powdered ichor, cloned, freeze dried—*lifeless!* That stuff isn't covered by Law. Mirelle is. There're other passengers. I deny you nothing in exercising my priority. Defy me again on penalty of death!"

Surrounding Mirelle in a bubble of Influence, Abbot touched her forehead and set his stamp into her aura. She darted a hurt glance at Titus, then succumbed. Her eyes were dull as she gazed adoringly up at Abbot. With a triumphal swagger, he escorted her onto the ship.

Calm enough to think again, Titus realized Abbot hadn't taken Mirelle just because Titus had won her over. He sensed, as Titus did, that she was involved in something clandestine within Project Hail. Abbot took her as Titus had taken the transmitter component, as part of his job.

And there was nothing Titus could do about it. Abbot, as his father, had both right and responsibility to destroy him if he turned unLawful and thus became a danger to luren security on Earth. Abbot never shirked a responsibility.

Once onboard the orbit-jumper, Titus went directly to his cabin and locked himself in. He spent the trip pacing the cubicle, on the floor when there was gravity, in the air when there wasn't. Through his growing hunger, he told himself that Connie would see he was supplied. She was wily enough to get his supplies past the humans and Tourists. But until he got to Project Station and found his baggage empty of blood crystals, he wouldn't think of taking a human. He just would not.

30

By the time they arrived at Luna Station, he was determined that within a month, two at the outside, he'd be on his way back to Earth, his part of the project completed. Meanwhile, he'd have to send a message to Connie demanding she get somebody else to deal with Abbot.

At Luna Station, they were loaded onto Toyota moonbuses for the twelve-hour trip out to the crash site around which Project Station had been built. Titus was in the lead bus, Abbot and Mirelle five cars behind that. With a heavy escort, they caravanned across the lunar landscape, following a well-worn track.

The scientists were all beyond misery and into dim-witted exhaustion by the time they first saw Project Station.

It was inside the new crater formed by the alien ship's impact. Dust from that impact still orbited, interfering with the observatories' work. The station consisted of a circle of interlocked domes clustered about the wreck. Trails worn by vehicle treads crisscrossed among the domes, some marked out by large boulders or cairns, leading off the station out over the jagged horizon.

Titus knew these were made by maintenance crews going out to work on the far-flung solar collector installations that powered, via landlines, both Project Station and Luna Station. But some of them also led to the eight Arrays, the huge assemblies of antennas that would be tied into his own observatory computers, Arrays through which he'd map the sky.

The outer circle of Project Station's domes housed power and environment plants, and, off to one side, Titus identified a motor pool park and maintenance shed. A tall, ridiculously slender antenna mast lofted high over the complex, and held reflectors and dishes for Earth or local communications.

Far off on the rim of the crater, Titus could see a field of solar collectors, most tilted toward the sun. For part of the month, the station had its own power. At "night" they were powered by landlines from the distant solar collectors, by battery, and by experimental generators.

Through the driver's forward screen, they could all see the probe's launch pad. The probe itself was still under cover in the huge hangar at the edge of the station, its gaping maw floodlit, dozens of suited figures around it. The probe was being designed and constructed here using every bit of knowledge that had been wrung out of the alien craft. It would be launched toward a point of Titus' choosing, and programmed to beam a message where Titus designated.

31

The domes housed the labs and offices from which the scientists would continue to study the alien craft. Beneath those labs were the residences, connected by airtight underground corridors. Theoretically, only those working on the alien craft, the probe, or Maintenance had to go out into vacuum. But they had all been trained for it—just in case.

"It feels like a safe place to live," remarked a man at the back of Titus' transport.

"Safe, I don't know," responded a woman up front, "but live, yes. It's bigger than any campus I've worked on, and I've lived happily without going off campus for months and months at a time. They say there's even a shopping mall."

The driver contributed a laugh. "Yes, but everything's so overpriced you'll only buy what you can't live without." She steered into the motor pool parking lot where a dozen suited spacemen swarmed over their bus.

In turn, each of the carriers was attached to a dome's lock to discharge passengers. Titus suffered stoically through the brief ceremony of welcome. He was hungry. He told himself it was more a psychological than a real physical crisis. Since he'd first rebelled against Abbot, he'd never doubted the source of his next meal. But his patience was dangerously thin by the time they were escorted in groups of six—an airlock full or an elevator full—to their assigned quarters where, presumably, their luggage would be waiting.

The trip took an unconscionable length of time, as they were given maps and their guide encouraged them to trace out their route. At each intersection, he stopped and lectured on emergency procedures. Eventually, one of the women with Titus' group chanced to object, "We've learned all this in training. I'm tired and I want to get to my room!"

"And that, Doctor, is why I must repeat it. You learned it, so you think you know it. You think that being tired is a reason to make haste and take shortcuts. That's the attitude that gets people killed out here."

From then on, the guide was more meticulous, making each of them work the controls on every emergency device they passed. The fourth time Titus was required to heft down a fire extinguisher and blow foam on the floor, he said, "You know, don't you, that we're so tired we're not listening well."

"Yes, of course," agreed the guide. "That's the point. You've *learned* this stuff, but now it's going in on the deepest, unconscious level so you'll *react* rather than think." He grinned. "It's the principle behind an M.D.'s grueling internship. Take it from me, it works."

"You're an M.D.?" asked Titus with interest. He had not forgotten Mihelich, the outsider like Mirelle.

The young man nodded. "We all do extra duty, especially when new groups arrive. Yours is the biggest so *everyone* has to work overtime getting folks settled. Yesterday, three astronomers and five engineers hauled your luggage around. The moon doesn't know from class." He waggled a finger at Titus. "You may find yourself assigned to cook next week!"

Titus chuckled. "I doubt that. At least not twice!" The others laughed, and agreed that none of them could cook either. As they entered their residence corridor, Titus moved up beside the young physician. "What's your name?"

"Philips. Morrisey Philips. Yours?"

Tucking the name firmly into his memory, Titus gave his current alias. He'd been Shiddehara since his wakening, with only short times under other names to build identities he might need. "How big is the medical department?"

"Big enough. Why? Feeling bad? You'll have another round of checks soon to adjust your gravity medication."

"I'm fine," said Titus. "But perhaps I'll drop over to check out the place tomorrow. Will you be on duty?"

"Most likely. Always am. Here you are, number forty-three." He presented Titus a key. "This way, folks."

Eagerly, Titus opened the door and went in. Instantly, he was relieved to see his luggage piled in the middle of the floor, looking untouched. Locking the door behind him, he turned on the overhead light and squinted against the intrusive brilliance. He attacked the cases, dumping the contents in a frantic search for the packets of dark powder.

"Ah!" Untouched.

The relief made him sag onto the bed clutching two bags to his chest. Then he was acutely embarrassed at the mess he'd made. He forced himself to unpack meticulously and stow his belongings properly. He collected the little bags, boxes and bottles of precious nutrients, and the vials of tablet supplements with all their different, false, labels on the counter that served as a kitchen.

He noted that he would have to refill his prescription for blood pressure medication, and dumped today's tablet down the disposer.

The drug rendered humans sensitive to ultraviolet, and the false prescription was his excuse not to use the solarium.

There was a sink, wet bar-sized Frigidaire, and a Sears microwave. Over this was a cabinet with dishes, cooking implements, and basic supplies including the ubiquitous Nescafé, Earl Grey tea, and a package of Osem crackers with Fortnum & Mason marmalade which bore, on an attached card, the compliments of the King of England. Titus found a quart pitcher and managed to fill it with water. Then he warmed the water in the microwave and dissolved his powder.

His hand shook as he poured some of the solution into a disposable cup. He made himself carry the pitcher and cup to the small table and sit down before even tasting the divine liquid.

Only then did he give himself up to the shivering ecstasy of it. He'd drunk three cups before he came to awareness of the room he must call home for the duration.

It was cheerfully decorated in yellow and brown with a short pile carpet and heavy drapes across the wall beside the door. Peeking, Titus discovered he had a round window, a porthole actually, with a view of the corridor.

The room was large. With the bed folded up into the wall, there was enough space to throw a party. One closet held an extra Samsonite table and several ultra-light chairs. Another door led to a bathroom which was plastered with bright signs prescribing dire penalties for wasting water.

An alcove harbored a desk and computer terminal. There was a lounge and some easy chairs. On one wall, a viewscreen displayed a moonscape at Earthrise, but Titus saw the bank of controls below it and realized this was his vidcom as well as his outside window. Playing with it, he discovered the Project Station cable channels and found the news and two entertainment selections. Then he read the instructions.

There was a slot for media of all kinds, even tapes. Surely recordings would be traded briskly at the shopping mall.

He found the channels that showed angles from cameras set all around Project Station, and even one of the alien craft. *If they can do all this already, how come the wireless network for the PDA's isn't . . .*

Arrested in mid-thought, he feasted on the sight. He had no more idea what he was looking at than any human on Earth. Except he was certain now—certain down deep in his bones—that it was a luren ship.

It was a space vehicle, only vaguely streamlined. Tiny suited figures moving about the area attested to its size. It had housed and fed fifty luren. By the humans' count, there had been two hundred orl aboard. The one-to-four ratio was standard in space, or so legend held.

This had been a cargo carrier, and its holds were filled with intriguing artifacts. The investigation had been going on now for two years, and a cloak of governmental secrecy still shrouded every detail. Some of it was classified above even Titus' rating. "Weapons," they whispered, but Titus doubted that. Weapons would be shipped on an armed vessel. This seemed like nothing but a trader.

I'll have to go out there—get a look at the corpses.

He laughed at himself, amazed at what a meal could do for his ambition. Finishing the artificial blood, he told himself the station was so big he might complete his job here and still avoid Abbot, avoid defying him again. Things might not turn out too badly at all.

He was washing up when the vidcom chimed and an unfamiliar face appeared in one corner of the huge screen. "Dr. Shiddehara? This is Shimon Ben Zvi. I'm sorry to wake you after your trip, but something very odd is happening to your computer, and we think you ought to know about it. Dr. Shiddehara?" Clearly the man, who spoke with a distinct Israeli accent, couldn't see or hear Titus.

Abbot! Abbot's done something! With quick, grim strokes, Titus opened the connection and answered, "This is Dr. Shiddehara. What's this about my computer?"

"Oh, Doctor! I'm Shimon—in charge of operations for you. Carol, uh, Dr. Colby told us you were counting on the computer being up and ready to meet the new deadline. And it was but about an hour ago it began throwing strange error messages—ones that aren't even in this unit! I *know* they aren't in this unit—"

"I trust you," Titus assured him. "Your degree is from the Technion, right? They told me you were the best."

"I am, but Doctor, I think you should come look at this. I don't think it's salvageable with less than three weeks of work. And Carol said—"

"Three weeks! All right, I'll be right there." He started to switch off. "Wait! Shimon. Where is there? I mean, how do I get there from here?"

"They should have given you a map." Shimon gave him a room number in another dome, on an upper floor. "Shouldn't take more than ten minutes to get here from almost anywhere else."

"I'll be there in twenty."

Fifteen minutes and five wrong turns later, Titus swung through the door to Lab 290, paused at the top of the three shallow steps that led down to the floor, and stared into chaos. Ten or fifteen people in white overalls were shouting and gesticulating as if working to patch an air leak. A large one.

Some of them had access panels off the walls exposing circuit boards. One wheeled an instrument cart over to a pair who were gutting one of the many consoles. Another pair argued in Japanese. Someone swore in Russian and was answered luridly in a thick, incomprehensible Aussie dialect.

Far in the back of the room, glass walls set off the observatory area. It was tied to the antenna mast he had seen on the way in, and to the antenna arrays, thus to all the observatories in orbit around Earth and around the sun. His observatory could direct or debrief most of the instruments in the solar system, even some of the farthest probes, and cross-correlate any new data with all archived data from the last several decades. A slender, somewhat feminine figure shrouded in white bent intensely over a screen in that glassed-in area, ignoring everything going on outside.

Titus drew a deep breath, and bellowed, "Silence!"

In the ensuing breathless quiet, something crackled and suddenly sparks jumped and smoke rose from several different locations. Agonized comments popped along with the sparks. "Oh, shit!" "Ditto." "*Randall!*"

The Aussie muttered, "Told you those fuses weren't enough."

A fire extinguisher whooshed.

"That's done it. Somebody turn up the air circulators."

This last was Shimon Ben Zvi, rising from the cloud of vapor, coughing. Out of that same cloud, appearing like an apparition from a horror movie, came Abbot Nandoha, his white coveralls accentuating the pallor of his face.

"I knew it," groaned Titus.

Innocently, Abbot raised one eyebrow. Cloaking his words in Influence, the older vampire explained, "All I did was insert a little glitch in the operating system. Their frantic chasing of it did all the rest. Oh well, I did play some tricks with the voltage too of course." He smiled. "That should give me time to build a new targeting device."

Through gritted teeth, not cloaking his words, Titus said "This is my lab. Get out and don't come back."

36

Still cloaking his words, Abbot said, "I see your meal wasn't very satisfying. Mind your temper, Titus. I've always said your temper was your worst flaw." He sidled around Titus and sauntered out the door.

Clean air began to dissipate the fog. People gathered in small groups staring at the mess. Even the person from the glass-enclosed observatory emerged to join them.

Shimon looked up from the ruin. "At *least* four weeks, Dr. Shiddehara." At this, everyone turned toward Titus. The woman from the back squeezed through the group and squinted up at him through the haze. A frown gathered on her face as she mouthed his name, *Shiddehara.*

But even through the frown, Titus recognized her. Her hair was cut differently, and she was nearly twenty years older. The planes of her face, honed down to emphasize the nose and cheekbones of the British aristocracy, were oddly coupled to the sensuous mouth and dimpled chin he had loved to kiss. His heart paused then skittered into a panic rhythm, spurred by joy and terror. *Inea!*

A puzzled wonder replaced her frown as she moved up to him, staring fixedly at his face. To her, he was dead, mangled in a car crash and buried. Yet certainty grew in her as she approached, a certainty born of shock and not yet tempered by embarrassment at the mistaken identity.

If he spoke, she'd recognize his voice. She'd blurt out his identity. No matter what he did, somebody would check. Project Security was vicious. All the luren on Earth could be in danger from this one human. Titus knew he ought to use Influence to blur her perception of him until she got used to it and decided it was just a haunting similarity.

But he could not.

He had always hated Influencing humans. They were defenseless against such treatment. For this mission, he'd resigned himself to the necessity, but he couldn't use it on Inea. She was sacred in his memory and in his heart.

———— FOUR ————

They stood frozen, the others watching Inea as her shock turned to love and then to disbelief overlaid with unshakable conviction. At last she whispered, under the rush of the air conditioning. "Darrell?"

He couldn't deny his born name.

"Darrell Raaj," she asserted so softly only he could hear. Her eyes burned with awe and fear.

The fear finally broke through his paralysis. Unable to summon Influence to mask his words, he answered in the same almost inaudible tone, "Inea, don't betray me. Please. I beg you. Don't. By everything we've ever meant to each other, don't."

She blanched, barely mouthing, "It *is* you!"

For a moment, he thought she'd faint, and he could catch her and sweep her away to get some fresh air. But no, she was made of sterner stuff. He should have known that.

Recovering, she glanced about at everyone then buried her face in her hands as if embarrassed, saying aloud, "I'm so sorry, Dr. Shiddehara. You remind me of someone I knew a long time ago. Perhaps he was a relative of yours?"

It was Titus' turn to fight off a swoop of lowered blood pressure. Even in this gravity, his knees sagged. Until this moment, he had not realized how very much he loved Inea Cellura. He found his voice at last. "Later, we can discuss the resemblance in detail. But right now"— his voice broke, and he coughed to cover his emotion— "right now, I think we'd better get to cleaning this up. Shimon, I'll want to see you in my office. Uh" —he glanced around in a feeble attempt at humor— "I do have one, don't I?"

Everyone laughed, and it broke the tension.

"This way, Titus," said Shimon, leading him to a corner where partitions made of two sheets of flexcite with levelors sandwiched between them created an office around an executive desk and two chairs. The levelors were open, making the partitions transparent. There were empty shelves and files in dreary government-issue tan, and a Cobra desk terminal.

Titus collapsed into his chair, which had a back higher than his head. He concealed his shaking hands from Shimon and glanced out through the partition. Inea leaned heavily against a desk, watching him with big, round eyes. Then she shook her head and turned away to help clean up.

Titus gestured, "Close the levelors, would you Shimon?"

The Israeli stroked the control and the walls opaqued.

"Shimon, I have to report to Carol, so I have to know exactly what's happened and how it affects our goals." He rummaged in the drawers but found no paper, and turned on the Cobra link. "Does this thing have a word processor?"

38

"Inea shook you up, didn't she?"

"Inea . . . " Still dazed, he answered automatically, as if reciting a lesson. "Is that her name?" Since his death, such dissembling had become an ingrained habit.

"Inea Cellura. Her degree's in astronomy. Worked at Arecibo. She's supposed to be your assistant, but she's been running the observatory station all by herself for weeks now. I wonder who she mistook you for?"

"Would you expect me to know?" She'd always scorned his passion for astronomy because his fascination with the possibility of other life forms in the galaxy disturbed her. Obviously, she'd changed. A knot of apprehension which he hadn't even known was there unraveled and he wiped a sheen of cold sweat from his upper lip and pulled the Cobra toward him.

"If I were you," mused Shimon, "I'd like to be the one she mistook you for. She's maybe not so pretty, but with the pretty ones who get you physically, it fades fast. With her kind, it gets better each time."

Not pretty? How could anyone say she wasn't pretty? "You've slept with her?" *I've no right to be jealous!*

"Not yet. But if you want her don't worry about me. She's not Jewish and maybe not even available." He glanced at the shut blinds. "Except maybe to you."

Shimon will be a good source of contacts if it ever comes to that. As revolting as the idea was, the thought gratified Titus, for it signaled that he was still able to think defensively. He couldn't afford a careless move now.

Titus' fingering produced the Cobra's standard word processing prompt under a Quill trademark which faded to the seal of Brink's Security and the request, "Please enter your security clearance, personal code, and passwords."

Irked, Titus hit ESCAPE but the thing bleeped at him.

"Yeah," commiserated Shimon, "you must secure everything—even grocery lists."

Titus complied and began taking notes. "The first thing I need to know—my memory, the one I shipped up here that contains my special star catalogue—is it intact?"

"The catalogue and our copy were erased while we were backing it up. I must order a new board before I can reprogram from your backup—*after* I discover why it did that."

Titus sagged. The backup had been in his flight bag. "I don't have a backup with me. Make a list of the hardware we need. I'll obtain a copy of my catalogue. As you've guessed, it's customized for just such a hunt as we're about to stage. Now, give me a rundown on what happened."

Titus listened, mentally tracing the damage, for there was one question he couldn't ask. Built into the system, there had been a black box Shimon had been instructed under Influence not to tamper with. It was Titus' link to Connie on Earth. He had no idea if it could be replaced.

It had been designed for this project, and could send and receive messages hidden in the checksums that ensured the accuracy of all telecommunications. The two computers repeated sequences back and forth and filtered out the data from the noise. Titus' black box simply preempted several of the repetitions to send Titus' message, which the computer on the other end discarded as noise but the black box on Earth captured and decoded for Connie's operatives.

Now it appeared that Abbot's sabotage had destroyed the device. How could he tell Connie what had happened? How could he get her to re-supply him with blood? How could he get her to send someone else to deal with Abbot?

He spent some time berating himself for not predicting Abbot's swift move. Abbot had, after all, spent the voyage resting and refreshing himself with his new human. He had not arrived hungry and exhausted, but—

Titus' mind leaped. Abbot had learned something from Mirelle— something about the clandestine project within Project Hail. *That* had made it necessary for him to gain some time. Rebuilding the device Titus had destroyed was only an excuse. He'd never have taken such a risk for that. *But then why did he do it?*

Titus had no time to pursue that question. The rest of the day went into assessing the damage and scouring the station for hardware. His computer system was a complex of interlinked units designed to accept, store, and digest the input from all Earth's observatories, to create and continually update detailed, multi-dimensional maps of space.

Their one small lab room contained more computing power than had existed on all of Earth a decade before. It was designed to become the astrogation and command center of Earth's interstellar exploration fleet—or battle fleet.

Within four hours, Titus realized they were racing Abbot from storeroom to storeroom, gleaning the dregs he left them. Grimly, Titus began to anticipate Abbot's moves, and garnered two or three hauls that would chisel days off the repairs. He listed the items he suspected Abbot had swiped out from under them by deleting them from inventory or by misfiling them on the shelves. Later, he'd find them himself.

By the time he left the lab, Titus had requisitioned everything that had to be ordered from Luna Station or Earth. He had a thorough report entered into his Bell 990. And he had an appointment with Carol Colby.

He had spent hours framing his report in such a way that he would not appear, to the humans, to be blaming Abbot for what had occurred but that would signal to any Resident who saw it that he couldn't handle Abbot.

With Colby, he used all his persuasion augmented only by a touch of Influence. She assigned him a priority level that would override Abbot's. Whatever equipment his father had not used or altered, Titus just might get back. And to do that, he was prepared to break into storerooms and scour the shelves in person.

As he left the Director's office, Titus was convinced that this Colby, as she'd boasted, didn't crumble. She'd set a deadline of two weeks to get Titus' system up, and she'd put in a direct call to Earth for his supplies. Titus couldn't begin to estimate the monetary cost of saving two weeks downtime, but an idle crew also ate money like crazy, so the expense of the call was, no doubt, justified.

Turning toward the nearest elevators, Titus knew he had to go out to the alien craft, investigate the medical dome and discover what Abbot had learned from Mirelle. But he was tired, his coordination off so much that his newly learned walking technique deserted him every few steps.

He hadn't slept since the night before departure. Yet if he did not move swiftly, Abbot would again have the jump on him. On the other hand, like any human, he could make ghastly mistakes from fatigue. He hated to admit it, but Abbot was right. Powdered blood was not as good a restorative as freshly cloned blood, and neither could compete with a human. As he pondered the elevator doors, one pair opened and Inea strode out.

She stopped short, and stared up at his face, weighing, assessing, and finally admitting again, "Darrell."

"Titus," he corrected gently. His eyes feasted on her. All the love was still there, but with something stronger added. He'd never felt like this for a human before.

The lengthy silence was finally broken by the arrival of another elevator, full of office workers arriving for the next shift. Titus had no idea what time of day it was supposed to be. He didn't even know what shift he was supposed to work.

"Titus, then," she granted. "We've got to talk."

He blinked hard. "I'm not ready for this."

"Me neither. I've been up for twenty-four hours, and though my feet don't hurt, I'm exhausted. But I won't be able to sleep until I get an explanation. You owe me that—don't you think?"

He wanted to scoop her into his arms and never let her go. "I owe you everything. Where can we talk?"

"My place isn't far."

"Invite me in," he warned, "and you'll never keep me out." *It's that way with those of my blood.*

"Is that a threat, Da—uh, Titus?"

"In a way. You might change your mind about me." The terror of that thought choked him. Then he told himself he was not the first of his blood to face this kind of ordeal. There were rules for handling this particular interview.

She searched his face again, gnawing her lower lip. In a very quiet voice, she said, "Just tell me one thing. Did you murder that boy they buried in your place?"

His heart shuttered and he checked the corridor for surveillance equipment. In fact, he wasn't even certain personal quarters were exempt from surveillance. Brink's was known for thoroughness, and the laws here were ambiguous to say the least. But if the situation was that bad, he was lost already.

"Inea, I swear to you, I did not."

"Then I won't change my mind. Come on."

She led the way to another bank of elevators, then down into a residence complex. The doors here were closer together than the ones in Titus' hall, and when she threw open her door, he saw how luxurious his quarters were.

Here, the floor was bare save for two scatter rugs, and the hall window was masked only by blinds. There was no kitchenette. The small desk took up most of the room, even with the bed folded away. One comfortable chair faced a tiny vidcom screen. A media case labeled *Guggenheim Tour* lay beside the recorder slot. But there were a few intensely personal touches. On one shelf, there was an arrangement of moon rocks around a small, artificial bonsai. At the bedside, a macramé hanging made from discarded packing was used to hold the vidcom remote control, a red-handled hairbrush, and an array of framed snapshots.

Noticing his expression, she explained, "I don't spend very much time here. The required exercise in the gym soaks up hours, and I eat at the refectory around the corner. Just down the hall, there's a solarium with really comfortable reading chairs. The rest of the time, I'm at work."

"Actually, you've got a lovely place. Invite me in?" The psychic potential that filled the boundaries of the room was at once enticing and an absolute barrier to Titus.

She tilted her head. "What's the matter with you?"

Abbot would have thought nothing of Influencing the invitation from her. "Invite me in and I'll explain."

Exasperated, she burst out, "Will you get your butt in here, before I—"

Titus stepped smoothly across the threshold and closed the door, palming the lock. "Thank you," he said, sincerely. The atmosphere sent ripples of pleasure through him.

Hands on hips, she shook her head at him in wonderment. "All right, you're in. Now explain."

He thrust aside the delight of just being here, and dropped into the desk chair. "Let me think how to say this." But the first thing the guidelines required was to bring her under Influence so she'd never repeat any of it. *I can't!*

"If you didn't kill anyone, what are you afraid of telling me?"

"Inea, please believe me; you have to believe. I wouldn't kill a human being. Ever. Can you accept that?"

"Why would I disbelieve it?" She perched on the edge of the easy chair. "Whoever was in your coffin—"

"Inea," he interrupted. "*I* was in my coffin. I crashed the car. I was sitting right next to you. And I died."

Clearly, she thought him insane. "Look, I don't recall a thing from that night until I woke up in the hospital and they told me I had a concussion but could go home for your funeral. But now you're alive. And you're no Jesus Christ! Obviously, it wasn't you in the car with—"

"I *was* in the car. I died. I'm a vampire."

There was sympathy under her dismay now, the kind of sympathy reserved for the hopelessly deluded.

43

"Do you want me to prove it? Or would you prefer to nurse your doubt until the evidence mounts and you can't deny it anymore?"

"How could you possibly prove you're a vampire? Turn into a bat and flutter about the room?"

He laughed. He hadn't expected such a challenge, yet he should have. He had thought of himself as a vampire so long, that he had forgotten the myths surrounding his kind.

"What's so funny?"

"The conservation laws! Basic biology! Shape change is impossible. And I mass nearly ninety kilos. Have you ever seen a bat that big? Inea, idiot-love, it couldn't fly!"

"Idiot-love?!"

It was his oldest endearment for her. But she was a scientist now. "Inea, I didn't mean—I'm sorry . . . "

"No—it *was* kind of a stupid thing to say. You really believe you're a vampire? There's a disease—"

"But victims of it don't get it by rising from the dead. And that's what happened to me."

"So you walk at night and suck young maidens' blood?"

Facetiously, he corrected her. "They don't have to be so young, and maidenhood isn't a requisite."

She shifted tactics. "Listen, if it's kinky sex you want, you'd better find yourself another—"

"Oh, shut up!" he snapped.

She folded into herself, shocked.

Contrite, he offered, "I'm sorry. I shouldn't have—I mean, I guess I'm just sensitive because—how I live—" Miserably, he finished, "Maybe I just haven't made my own peace with it yet. They say it takes more than a century."

"Century! God! You really believe it. But you look normal—a little pale, a bit underweight maybe, but normal."

"I am normal. For me."

"And you expect me to believe you're a vampire? I can see you reflected in the vidcom screen."

"Of course I reflect. I'm solid flesh and blood." It would be easier just to Influence her to believe. But he couldn't. He had to convince her completely and honestly, and get her free will promise of silence.

"The legends are wrong, but you're a vampire? Darrell, what kind of a game is this? Are you into espionage?"

44

"My name is Titus Shiddehara. I had to change it because Darrell Raaj died—legally, anyway. So please call me Titus. It could be dangerous for me if you don't."

"But you really are the famous astrophysicist? You're not substituting for him?"

"Yes, I'm really Titus Shiddehara. After I . . . awakened . . . and was on my feet again, I went on to college just like I'd planned. Only my name and . . . lifestyle . . . has changed."

"All the proof I have is your assertion. Vampires are supposed to wither at the sight of crucifixes. Maybe I could find a Catholic and—"

"I don't wither before crucifixes or any religious object. I'm not evil. I told you, I don't kill humans, virgins or otherwise. And I wasn't created by the devil."

"Then why do you call yourself a vampire?"

"Because my body can regenerate after injuries that would kill a man. Because I can't live on food, but have to have blood. And . . . I have other powers."

"Powers? What powers?"

He considered carefully. If there ever could be anything real between them again, he had to be honest now. "I can make you think I can turn into a bat, or smoke, or anything. I can control animals, even wolves." He searched her eyes, watching for rejection. "I can control you."

"Now we're getting somewhere!" She leaped to her feet and opened the bathroom door to reveal a full-length mirror. "Remember how I could never let myself be hypnotized? W.S. had a tough time with my security clearance because of it. You go ahead and make me think you've turned into a bat that doesn't reflect in this mirror, and I'll believe you."

It's not the same as using Influence to make her believe me. Still, he felt wrong about it.

"I'm waiting."

She had to believe or her promise of silence would be only a joke to her, not a solemn vow. Or worse yet, she'd consider it her duty to him to have him committed. "Okay."

He exerted Influence, testing her resistance. She was strong, but not remarkably so. In a puff of smoke, he became for her a medium-sized bat that fluttered at her head, squeaking, but not reflecting in the mirror.

She flung up her arms and ducked, then peeked up at the mirror. Stunned, she gaped at the empty desk chair.

Getting into the drama of it, Titus went to the middle of the room, summoned a memory of an old *Dracula* film, then had the bat fly over to his new location, whirl into smoke, and coalesce into a black-caped figure in evening dress. Swirling the cape magnificently to show off its ruby lining, he gave her a courtly bow.

When he rose, she slumped into a faint, floating downwards in the meager gravity.

He dropped the illusion, and knelt beside her, taking her head in his lap. He straightened her body, wanting to chafe her hands and pat her cheeks to wake her up, but knowing that he only wanted to alleviate his own anxiety. She'd come out of it when her blood pressure normalized. The longer it took, the more time her mind would have had to adjust, the better it would be for her. So he cradled her in his arms with a terrible tenderness, surrendering to curious shudders of pleasure.

He didn't notice when her eyes fluttered open, but then she sighed deeply and murmured, "Darrell . . . " Her memory surged back, and she shrank from him, starting to twist free of his grasp.

"Inea, it was just an illusion! Think! How could I have turned into a bat! That's silly! It can't be done."

"I saw what I saw." Influence always carried a sharp conviction that the senses gave absolute truth. Many humans, when finally convinced otherwise, went completely insane.

"Yes, you saw it. I'm not sure how this power works, but I do know that for you, it really happened." Titus flinched away from the inherent contradictions between his physicist's knowledge of how things worked, and the pragmatic facts of what he could do to people's nervous systems.

"Do it again," she challenged, face hardened.

Astonished, he replied, "No. You're not a toy, or even a laboratory animal, that I can play with your perceptions at my own whim or for my convenience. I'm never going to use that power on you again. I want you to *know* beyond any doubt that whatever you see, know, or feel is *real.*"

He was lying by omission. No human on Project Station could trust any physical sense while Abbot was around. And Abbot would declare Titus unLawful if he ever discovered what Titus had done here or what he had yet to do. Titus would have to keep Abbot ignorant of Inea. He couldn't let Inea be stolen from him and marked like Mirelle and then used as a hostage. That's what Abbot would do if he ever realized what Inea meant to Titus.

At length, she announced, "You must be using some power to make me believe that promise."

"The power of love. The power of honesty. Nothing any human couldn't use."

She studied him again. "Human. You're not, are you?"

"Never was. Though my mother was human, my father—not my mother's husband, but the man who begot me—wasn't. And I'm not. I didn't know that until I awakened. It was a terrible shock."

"I can imagine." She sat up, folding her legs into a full lotus and holding her head. "Why do I believe you?"

"I'm glad you do."

"Because you need someone to believe you?"

"No, because I need to convince you so you won't ever mention this to anyone—not here, and not on Earth. Not anywhere, not ever. As I offer my promise, I need yours."

Her eyes opened wide. "Or you'll throw a whammy on me so I can't tell?"

Her reason almost obliterated by shock, she was still capable of that insight. His heart threatened to spill over with love. "That's what I'm supposed to do," he choked out. "You can imagine why. If—humans—discovered us . . . "

"How many of you are there?"

He shrugged. "A couple thousand, no more."

"How many humans do they kill each year?"

"I don't know. Not many. Since about 1850, killing humans has been a crime. It leads to pogroms against us. So the law is vigorously enforced."

This too was a half truth. Deaths of human stringers were investigated by the Death Committee, composed of both Tourists and Residents, but the Tourists usually claimed their stringers died naturally simply from being fed upon. Even if the stringers had been mildly abused, the Tourists usually got away with it if they didn't leave a mess to attract human attention. Marked stringers were possessions. "Inea, now we live mostly on manufactured blood. Our numbers are not increasing. We're not a burden on humanity, and we're not a threat. Your silence would not harm humanity."

"Why do I always believe you? I'm not a credulous person."

"No, but you've always known truth when you hear it. Look, pledge me your silence just until you discover that what I've told you is flatly untrue." *What will I do when she discovers what I haven't told her?*

"You'll take my naked word?"

"If you'll take mine. Have I ever betrayed you?"

"You were alive. But you didn't come back to marry me. You let me think you were dead. You let me go on as if you'd died. But you were alive! How could you—"

"They wouldn't let me! It's against our laws. I'd given my word to uphold that law. I had to. I needed the help of others of my . . . kind."

She melted. "It must have been awful for you."

"There were some bad moments." He got to his feet. "You haven't promised."

"What will you do if I don't?"

"I'll walk out of here and never speak to you again in any personal way. I'll be nothing but Titus Shiddehara to you. And I'll probably have to do my best to have you cashiered off the Project, just because I couldn't stand being so near you and unable to touch you. I love you."

"And you'd use your power to make me forget who you really are?"

Slowly, deliberately, he shook his head. "I couldn't. I just couldn't bring myself to do that."

He knew it was true, and he also knew what stakes he was putting on the table. Earth's whole luren community could be wiped out within a few years because of his scruples.

"What would keep me from blowing the whistle on you? Supposing, of course, that I could find proof?"

"Oh, I suppose you could find proof. You're awfully clever. But what sense is there in releasing a bloody frenzy of fear and terror, a witch hunt that would burn thousands of humans along with most of us, when we aren't a real threat, and there is a *real* problem demanding all our attention, the problem from out there?"

"What do you know about the aliens?"

"Not as much as I want to know. What do you know about them?"

"You're evading my question."

"I've given my pledge; I'm waiting for your promise."

"If you feel so sure my own common sense would keep me quiet, why do you insist I give you a promise?"

"To salve my conscience. I told you, I'm not supposed to let you walk around knowing what you now know and not, uh, gagged by a whammy." He avoided using luren terms because any accidental reference could betray her to Abbot. "Besides, knowing how hard it is to get promises to roll off your tongue, I think I trust your word more than my whammy." He had only exacted one other promise from her: marriage. And then he'd died two days before the actual ceremony.

She smiled nostalgically. "I haven't forgotten all the times you proposed."

"I haven't forgotten the one time you accepted."

"Are you going to hold me to it?"

Her expression became so neutral that if he hadn't been listening with all his other senses, he wouldn't have known she was throbbing with hope as well as dread.

"Inea, I think we have to renegotiate the contract. After all, even the wedding vows are only until death do us part—and it did. Surely that breaks an engagement, too. But we can start all over again."

"And this gag promise is only until I discover you've lied and your people are indeed a threat?"

"That's all I'm asking."

Grimly, she replied, "That's all you're getting. But that much you do have. Agreed?"

"Agreed."

"Now what about the question you evaded? The aliens?"

"I'm going to continue to evade."

"Why?"

"Basically, to protect you."

"From?"

"I've already told you. I've broken a law for you. You're walking around with a head full of knowledge you shouldn't have, and no gag-whammy to keep you silent. One slip and we're both in an awful lot of trouble."

"How much trouble?"

"Life or death for me. Being gagged for you."

"They wouldn't kill me? For knowing?"

"For knowing? No." *Not legally, anyway. But just let Abbot Mark her, and* . . . He couldn't finish the thought.

"But they'd kill you?"

"Might. It's a pretty terrible crime—endangering all of us. They wouldn't understand—about you and me." He helped her to her feet and resisted the natural embrace, holding her shoulders at arm's length. He wanted to take her to bed as he'd never wanted anything else in his life. But he wasn't going to spoil this with haste.

Rationally, he knew the most they could have together would be a few short decades. She'd die of old age while he still seemed young and had to change identities every few years. But right now, those decades were worth his life, and more. It was something he had to have, no matter the price. And if that meant going to bed alone tonight, then so be it.

She broke away and turned to the door. "You'd better go. I'll get through the night alone. I've done it before."

He gathered himself. "But this time, I'll be there in the morning. And tomorrow night, too, if you like."

"We'll see. I have to think." She opened the door for him. "I'll see you in the morning, Dr. Shiddehara."

"Titus," he corrected.

"Titus."

He was left alone in the busy, well-lighted corridor. But where before his mind had been a deep, black silence of fatigue and despair, it was now filled with plans. Where the station had seemed cold, distant, alien, and unreal, it was now home. There was nothing he couldn't do. It wasn't elation that buoyed him all the way to the elevators. It was strength.

He felt as refreshed as if he'd slept the day through. The renewal showed in his body. The last of the solar irritation was gone from his skin. A vague headache that had plagued him had disappeared. He felt wonderful.

He sent the elevator up to the surface, and set out to visit the alien craft. No doubt Abbot had been there ahead of him, but he would catch up now, and he would win.

—————— FIVE ——————

Titus knew that besting Abbot was a fantasy, but he nursed it like a potent drink as he made his way toward the locks leading out to the alien ship. Abbot had been playing this game for too long. But on the other hand, there was something to be said for youth, flexibility, and desperation. *Not Inea. He's not going to get Inea.*

He had to think. In the day he'd been at the station, Titus had spent no more than four hours in his room. In six hours, he had to be back at the lab, and then they'd be after him for his physical and to log time in the gym. For all he knew, that might be as necessary for his kind as for humans, in order to return to Earth with any bone left.

If he went to the alien craft now, someone might notice that he never rested. They wouldn't make anything of it immediately. Everyone here was an eager volunteer. But dedication was one thing, superhuman performance something else. So he didn't dare approach the alien craft openly.

He loitered at an intersection until the corridor was clear, then cloaked himself with Influence. He'd found that surveillance cameras were located only where emergency crowd control was needed. He evaded them and found the locker room, where there was a locker with his name on it containing a customized spacesuit. He waited until the room was empty, then suited up in haste, using Influence to repel anyone from the door. *Abbot could suit up in plain sight of half a dozen people and keep them from noticing!* thought Titus, ruing his own lack of practice.

Thought of Abbot's mastery of Influence reminded him that he'd have to find some way of keeping the Tourist out of the lab and away from Inea. Just throwing him out of the lab in a fury as he'd done earlier wouldn't be enough. He'd have to work on Colby somehow, get it made an order.

Dressed, Titus tagged along with a group going on shift. There were three engineers, two electricians, a physicist, a chemist, and a metallurgist. Their chatter was strewn with references to the alien craft's design. But one thing was clear: not a tenth of what they had been doing and thinking had yet been reported on Earth, even at top security levels.

Furthermore, nobody yet understood the craft's engines or power source. Speculation was running wild, however. Titus followed the group into the docking bay where the surface truck would pick them up, listening attentively.

"I tell you, that thing has to be FTL. It works on some principle we've never imagined. There's no power source!"

"Look, maybe it lost its sails. Maybe it's not supposed to come this close to a star. Maybe they left their engines out beyond Neptune. That could be why we can't analyze the propulsion—because this module doesn't have any!"

"Maybe this is only a lifeboat detached from a larger ship that suffered a disaster." The third engineer was the youngest. She was also the smallest of the group, dark-haired and comely, with a musical voice. "We can't rule anything out, even though *we* wouldn't build a lifeboat with such a huge cargo bay."

"If it's a lifeboat," argued the first engineer, "it would have propulsion and power for life-support and communications. Maybe it's just a cargo 'crane'?"

One of the others spoke up. "You know, I think you've got something there—a power module left way out in solar orbit. Makes sense. The ship didn't explode on impact. It could be they came in on battery power. We ought to get one of the observatories searching far orbits tangent to the ship's line of approach. Might find their sails."

"It can't be a new idea," said someone else. "I'll bet they're doing a search already."

"And what if they aren't? I'm going to write it into my daily report, and we'll see what happens. That's what they want us to do, you know—think independently so if we all come to the same conclusions, they'll figure we got it."

Titus didn't know if a module of this ship was missing, but according to Abbot, the ship their ancestors had come to Earth in had been faster than light, and it hadn't exploded on impact, either. Titus had always accepted that some mishap had forced that ship down on Earth, but he'd often wondered where they had been going and why. Had they been explorers, colonists, traders, or even tourists? Was this new ship of the same sort, or different?

"There's our ride," called one of the men.

The docking bay's pressure doors stood open, and now a truck churned silently up onto the glazed flooring of the bay. It was an open framework built over two tracks, and it maneuvered quite nimbly though soundlessly in the vacuum.

Titus felt the vibration as the truck scraped the dock. He followed the others, climbing onto the struts and grabbing a cargo strap. The driver was seated on a bench before an array of levers which she manipulated with finesse. "All set?" Without turning to look, she added, "Here we go!"

The truck lurched away from the dock and lumbered out the door into the starry night, kicking up a cloud of dust. The sun was not visible at the moment, for which Titus was thankful. Even though his suit would protect him as nothing he could wear on Earth, he still didn't wholly trust it. It had been designed by humans with human tolerances in mind.

But his anxieties melted away as they rounded the corner of the bay doors and came into full view of the wreck.

Pieces of it that had scattered during the crash had been dragged up beside the main fragment before the station was built around it. The main section was mangled, torn, and half-buried. Floodlights cast sharply defined cones of illumination, stripping away any glamour or drama. The ship looked like heaps of trash in a wrecking yard. But he could see something now that he hadn't seen in the photos taken with instruments tuned to human vision.

Suddenly mindful of the cameras perpetually aimed at the wreck, he moved to shield his suit identification as he squinted against the floodlights. He could just make out markings on the ship's hull; dark rust against darker rust color. Had the humans missed the markings because their eyes didn't register the distinction? It was faint to him, but his eyes were not luren eyes. They were human eyes affected by luren genes.

Perhaps to luren eyes, the markings stood out brightly. He made a mental note to Influence someone to do a spectral analysis of the whole hull. It might hold a clue to the luren eye, and thus to the luren sun.

Part of the inscription was torn away and part was buried in the moon dust. But Titus could read the script. Imagining the missing parts of letters, he transliterated it to English, trying to sound the word, for he didn't know what it meant. *Kylyd.* "Kailaid?"

Possibly this was a word in a different language from that preserved among Earth's luren. Or it might simply be a name, a word that had lost meaning eons ago.

As they approached the rent in the side of the main section being used for an entryway, Titus felt a prickly surge of excitement. Suddenly, the wreck wasn't just a heap of twisted metal anymore. It was a starship. It had an identity, a history, a proud name, and a loyal crew.

Titus skinned through the security check in the shadow of one of the engineers, and found himself free inside the wreck. Nothing had prepared him for this.

Twisted and distorted though it was, the shape of the space the aliens had carved struck a deep nerve in Titus, a human nerve. This place was subtly *wrong*. It was alien.

Titus had traveled all over the world, and had felt the vague unease in foreign buildings, a negligible component of culture-stress syndrome. But this was different. This fairly shouted *wrong!*

He shuddered and ducked aside through an airlock that had been wrenched and buckled at impact. Here floodlights had been strung up since they hadn't yet conquered the ship's systems. The ship's lighting, when they found it, ought to provide Titus with a vital clue to the home star.

Crossbreeds such as Titus usually had an infrared sensitivity peak as well as a much greater ultraviolet peak along with the usual three human peaks of sensitivity. But what of purebred luren?

Not far beyond the twisted hatch, he came upon two work stations set in wide places at either side of the corridor. There were dark stains on the light buff furnishings. Blood.

He examined a chair set low and pitched so the occupant would be half reclining, looking at an overhead panel. Now the panel was just a dark red oval patch on the ceiling, but the darkness had depth, as if he were looking into a tank. He tried to imagine what the display would be like, but he had no idea what was done at this station.

The controls were on the arms of the chair, which were broad and dotted with bits of the same deep dark substance that formed the screen above. Perhaps, with the power on, the display on the chair arms would identify each control's function. That would be necessary if the functions of the controls could be changed.

He was thinking like a human, and he knew it. He wasn't sure anyone on the Project had the imagination to understand luren controls. He regarded the work station with some awe. It was unexpectedly humbling, for he'd always subconsciously assumed he would understand luren artifacts on sight.

Casting about with all his senses, he determined that he was alone. Sitting down, he put his hands on the controls and gazed up into the monitor—if that's what it was. Opening himself, he tried to feel what this place was.

But it only baffled him. *There's a lesson. Raised human, schooled by humans, I am human.* He wished everyone who subscribed to the Tourist philosophy could sit here and feel this. It would end their callous treatment of humans.

Suddenly, the last of the unacknowledged doubts that had depressed him since his skirmish with Abbot in the men's room on Goddard Station vanished. It might be futile to delay the moment the luren found Earth, but it had to be done. With time to study this, humans just might be able to hold their own.

Something whispered at the edge of perception.

Influence! Abbot!

He sprang out of the chair and crouched, muffling his own Influence as much as he dared. Back the way he'd come, through the twisted hatch, Titus saw Abbot stop, hunker down, and open an access panel. He worked within, concentrating, Influence keeping him invisible to the humans who passed.

Titus backed along the hall away from Abbot, searching for a place to hide. Nearby, he found an undamaged door. Eyes focused on Abbot, he put one hand behind him, groping with gloved fingers for the control. His grip fell naturally onto a panel, and before he knew it he was inside the room.

It was a chamber about seven feet by eight feet. As he sensed Abbot move toward him, he worked frantically to shut the door. It slid closed just as Abbot eased through the twisted hatch. Before utter blackness enclosed him, Titus glimpsed Abbot's hand gripping a recording device.

Dispelling his own Influence, Titus leaned against the door, eyes closed, concentrating on Abbot's moves. He couldn't discern the faint vibration that Abbot's feet must be making—the whole ship pulsed with human movement. But that keener sense that accompanied Influence tracked Abbot to the work stations Titus had examined.

Abbot stopped there and Titus sensed the older vampire's intense concentration cloaked under precisely disciplined Influence. Titus didn't dare move. He hardly breathed. He just waited, observing Abbot working.

At last, Abbot moved on past the room where Titus hid, and was gone. When the last whiff of his Influence had faded, Titus heaved a tremendous sigh. Then it hit him. He had spied on Abbot, and had not been noticed. Titus grinned ferociously. He wasn't helpless before an all-powerful master. It was a real contest now.

Titus heaved himself away from the wall, and saw absolute, total darkness.

Activating his suit light, he peered about in the shaft of illumination and found a Westinghouse cable feeding overhead lights. He found the switch and turned them on.

In the center of the bare room, a transparent cylinder about six-feet long lay atop a dark rectangular block.

And inside—inside lay a man.

No! A luren!

The supine figure was unclothed. The skin had the white pigmentation that had turned Titus from the dusky skin color of

55

Southern India to that of a deeply tanned Caucasian in the grave. The abdomen was concave, indicating the shrunken abdominal organs and sparse body fat of the typical Earth-bred luren. His face was long and gaunt.

The only differences were those of degree. This individual was whiter than anyone Titus knew. He was more emaciated. His hair was not gray or white but metallic silver. Titus supposed his eyes would be pale, too.

He seemed "alien" because there was no Oriental, Hispanic, Caucasian, Indian, or Black cast to his features. It was nothing specific. His nose wasn't too prominent, his eyes weren't too odd, his lips not especially different, and his cheekbones seemed normal. His ears were reasonably shaped and placed. Even his haircut wasn't so exotic. It was in the summation of these things that the difference lay.

The body showed no sign of explosive decompression. One side of the chest was depressed. A blow had broken ribs and ruptured organs—minor damage but enough to induce dormancy in a luren or to kill a human. The skull seemed intact.

The protective cylinder had gauges for air pressure, temperature, and radiation. The gauges were attached to a remote-monitored telemetry device.

Inferences leaped through Titus' mind. There had been no hint on Earth that they'd found anything but cell-damaged corpses. This intact specimen was being preserved—probably in pure sterile nitrogen—*for cloning!* It had to be for cloning!

It hadn't been done yet for lack of budget, but they'd do it eventually. All they needed was one perfect germ cell.

What the humans didn't know was that this "corpse" was not dead. His spine and brain were intact. Given a benign environment, he'd revive. But the humans didn't suspect that. Despite, or perhaps because of, all the horror movies ever made, they'd never suspect that.

Suddenly, he realized what he'd done. Turning on the lights had signaled security. They had to be on their way.

He flicked the lights off and fumbled at the door. It resisted. *Calm down. It has to be unlocked or how'd I get in?* It gave, spilling him into the hall, and he took off in the direction Abbot had gone. Behind him, a security officer squeezed through the twisted hatch and headed for the room where the sleeper lay.

Titus rounded a bend, chose a branching corridor, and stopped, lost. He knew he was facing what they had labeled the stern. It was connected to the medical research dome by a pressurized, high-security tunnel. Very likely Abbot had gone that way, for the only other way back into the station was via the surface, past the security checkpoint.

Heart pounding, Titus set off astern, cloaked heavily in Influence. Visualizing the consequences of being caught and connected to the security breach, he sidled through groups of workers. The Project openly sponsored some fifteen hundred investigations underway, both on the alien vessel and in the station's labs. But Titus' mind was on the sleeper. Could he allow the humans to vivisect a helpless luren? If they knew, would they do it anyway? They could have their cloning specimen without destroying the man. But knowing what he did of biologists, Titus was sure they'd do a total autopsy, which would include removing the brain—fatal even for a luren. If they knew he was alive, would they let him wake?

Was it even up to Titus to decide what they should allow the humans to do to the sleeper? *Maybe* Abbot didn't know about the sleeper yet. Titus had to get word to Connie.

That meant rebuilding his computer, hoping the parts shipment from Earth would include a new black box. Had Abbot destroyed the black box on purpose? Did he even know about it? More to the point, could Titus slip a replacement communicator box into the rebuilt computer without Abbot knowing? Was Abbot in direct touch with his Tourists?

Had Connie received and understood Titus' cryptic message buried in the requisition that Carol Colby had sent to Earth? And could Connie's agents smuggle him a communicator? Unlike Abbot, Titus didn't have the skill to build one.

Titus came to an unguarded airlock fitted into a docking port of the luren craft by profligate use of flexible gasket material. The portal was plastered with a frightening array of Day-Glo quarantine signs, but the green light above it was on. He leaned against the bulkhead beside it, trying to concentrate on what was on the other side.

At length, he held his breath and eased into the airlock. Casting a pall of Influence to divert the attention of the guards, he hoped no one would notice what appeared to be an empty lock cycling. After a nerve-wracking interval, he emerged in the Biomed research section where the alien bodies were being studied. It was one area Titus' clearance didn't authorize him to enter.

He would need their results, but he had been banned from their lab. Why? Because they planned a cloning? It seemed so reasonable, and then he remembered Mihelich. If he was connected with cloning . . .

The airlock opened into a corridor where everyone was dressed in bio-isolation suits, the labs opening off it doubly sealed. Through the next airlock, precautions eased and there was one open lab where glass vessels climbed poles up to the ceiling next to one lined with incubator ovens filled with specimen dishes. Two other rooms down the hall held the main biocomputer.

Further on, he found a power and life-support substation capable of maintaining this dome independently of the central systems of the station. Of course Abbot would oversee the operation of that unit, and thus be cleared for this area.

Titus was sorely tempted to linger, to listen and try to find out if cloning capability was being installed here. But it was too dangerous. He had already inadvertently tripped one of security's traps. No more today.

He headed back to his room.

———

Titus spent the next couple of days organizing the repairs. Shimon proved to be a genius, and Inea became invaluable. Though she was no computer hardware expert, she was a wizard at troubleshooting and better with her hands than others.

At his first department heads meeting, Titus Influenced one of the engineers to do a refractory study of the ship's hull. He led the man to believe it would be useful if the military had to detect hostile ships.

When not attending obligatory meetings, sitting on committees, or reading reports of meetings he wasn't supposed to attend, Titus prowled the storerooms. He found eight vital components that had disappeared from inventory—Abbot's work, no doubt. Each time he returned with one of these treasures, Inea would study him thoughtfully.

During working hours, she treated him in a professional manner. There were only a few moments when she would pause to weigh something he said or did, and he would feel he was being judged— no, that all luren were being judged.

He hadn't visited her again, not because he spent most of his off hours trying to crack security seals to get at background on the biomed staff, but because, each evening when they parted, she would say goodnight in a final tone.

At first he thought it was an act designed to tell everyone there was nothing between them, protecting his cover. But when he caught up with her in the elevator, she brushed him off. He was alarmed at how much it hurt to watch her retreating form. But he didn't dare push her.

On the fourth day, Carol Colby called. Titus took it in his office. "Titus, I have good news and bad news. Which do you want first?"

"I'll take the bad first."

"We've got an appropriations fight on our hands. We may not get all the parts you ordered. And we may not get them by special shipment. They're telling me the budget won't cover it. When I told them they had to ship the parts, or at least squirt us a copy of your star catalogue, they laughed at me. It would cost too much to squirt it, they tell me."

"It would," agreed Titus. "It would take hours, and there'd be errors. Sunspot activity is making hash of all data from the far orbital instruments. We're on repeaters."

At least part of his operation had been functioning well. He *was* getting *some* raw data from the far observatories searching the Taurus region along the vessel's approach path. The others hadn't found anything as useful as a jettisoned power module, but he was monitoring a particle-counting array deployed on the surface of Demos. If the luren drive had left a particle trail, they might find it. But not until the computer was up again.

Titus hoped Colby's good news was that they had regained contact with the probe that had tracked the alien in, then ceased talking before dumping its data. Unmanned probes often righted themselves. There were a dozen good people working on the problem, but Titus needed the data soon, for the probe had seen the approach from a different angle.

"Well then," he said heartily, "your good news is that *Wild Goose* has finally reported in?"

"No, my good news isn't that good. Abbot Nandoha has agreed— after considerable persuasion on my part—to help with your repairs. He's technically hired to run our power plant, but his dossier shows he's also a computer architect. I hope he can redesign your system and put you back on line with the parts we have and will be getting soon."

Oh, shit. "I'll bet that took some persuasion."

"Now, Titus, I am aware of the, uh, friction you've generated with Nandoha. I don't expect such behavior from my department heads. You'll make an effort. Am I understood?"

"Yes." She couldn't fire him because nobody else had spent the last ten years identifying stars with planets. A few decades ago, the search had been the main occupation of astronomers. But the grant money had dried up. Now, Titus had the only complete catalogue of such stars, and heaps of unpublished papers. The lack of public interest had forced Titus to make his living teaching. "I will make the effort, Dr. Colby. And in the future, I will take care not to allow fatigue to erode my temper. Please accept my apology."

"Now don't take it too hard, Titus. We're all human. We make mistakes. If I hear nothing more of it, it won't go on your record, your pay won't be docked, and I won't need to bring in a lesser manager for your department."

"Thank you, Dr. Colby."

"Carol—remember?"

Titus forced himself to relax visibly. But this was a message from Abbot. At will, his father could remove him from the project just by creating "friction."

"Look, Carol, I'm not sure it's necessary to take such a vitally needed man off maintaining our life-support. Shimon is a genius in his own right, and has been diligent—"

"Don't argue with me, Titus. I'm giving you Nandoha for a week. In four days, I'll want your list of what still must be brought from Earth. Don't despair, I'll get it for you somehow. But only what Abbot can't do without. Good day."

Titus sat back and stared at the blank screen. *Maybe the anti-Project humans are blocking appropriations because somebody knows about the sleeper.* If they knew, Connie might know by now, too. But he couldn't assume that. He *had* to get a message out to Connie. He needed blood concentrate. He needed someone who could stand up to Abbot. And he had to know what to do about the sleeper.

Before he could report, he had to verify his suspicions about cloning. Mihelich was no orderly. His file was locked behind highest security. Even queries for his published papers were blocked. And while Titus had been wasting time on Mihelich's files, Abbot had outflanked him, Influencing Colby. *He'll control the whole Project before I figure out what's really happening.*

"Titus?"

Inea peeked around the office door.

With an incredible effort, Titus rearranged his face into a welcoming smile. "Come in. What can I do for you?"

She ventured into the room. "What's wrong?"

What could he say? That another vampire was coming to joust with him for possession of her? "Nothing new."

"Titus," she warned.

"Carol says we're not getting our scheduled parts shipment. No appropriation."

"Bad. But it's more than that."

"Shimon's going to blow his Israeli stack when he discovers what Carol has done."

She almost bit at that one, but instead of asking what Carol had done, she shook her head. "More."

Titus wondered how he could be so transparent to a human. "All right," he confessed, as if surrendering. "I'm worried. I can't figure out how to tell you . . . something."

"Just tell."

"You may never speak to me again. I couldn't stand that. It's been bad enough the last few days, with you stalking off every night without a word."

She frowned at him, studying him in that way that made him so nervous. "I'm not ready to talk yet," she said. "Later. I promise."

"Okay. Look, meanwhile could you do me a favor?"

"Like?"

He thought fast. "You've turned out to be very talented with circuitry. When the few components we can get finally do arrive, we won't have time to fool with them. I'm going to send you over to Ernie Natches in Electronics for some quick training. That way you'll be more help when we really need you."

"What precisely do I have to learn?" she challenged.

"Let Ernie decide. He's got benches full of our components he's trying to repair. You can help."

She studied him again, weighing. "You're making this up as you go along."

Diabolical woman. He recalled thinking that in a monotonous undertone during the years he'd been going with her. "Inea, I've got a *lot* of problems. I have to create solutions on the spot."

"What problem is getting rid of me a solution to?"

"Trying to get my computer repaired and keep my ass out of the fire. The worst part is that I spend all my time filling out forms, writing reports, and going to meetings rather than doing physics. I'm becoming a frustrated administrator."

"You're evading again."

"Consider it a favor. I'll owe you. Report to Ernie in the morning, okay?"

"It's not okay, but I'll do it. What do I tell him, that I'm still on your payroll?"

"Of course. He's doing me a favor. Training you."

She went to the door. "What you owe me in return is a *complete* explanation."

"Okay. As soon as we get back to Earth."

"Titus!"

He shrugged.

"You have the best woebegone look of anyone I know. All right, but I get my explanation on the Quito landing pad."

"No deal. The 'port restaurant." He'd never forget that scorching sun.

"Don't quibble!" She left.

Watching her, he noted that it was hard to flounce on the moon. It definitely crimped her style.

The moment she was out the door, he got Ernie on the vidcom. He had only met the man on his odyssey through the stockrooms, but he had been extraordinarily helpful. He owed Ernie several favors and here he was asking for another.

Worse yet, as soon as he finished with Ernie, he had to convince Shimon to rotate to the night shift. With Abbot being brought in as if Shimon couldn't handle his job, there was no way the two would get along.

And still worse, Titus had to face Abbot after publicly expelling him from the lab.

─────── SIX ───────

The next morning, when his father showed up, Titus met him at the lab door, making sure he had an audience. "Thank you, Dr. Nandoha, for agreeing to help us. I hope you've forgiven my temperamental outburst on our first day here."

"Think nothing of it, lad. I'm eager to help."

The civilities over with, Titus retired to his office, leaving his adversary free run of his lab. Abbot would certainly place bugs to monitor not only all of Titus' Project work, but also his Residents' communications. Resolutely Titus bent his efforts to studying the schematics for his computer complex.

It wasn't that the architecture had ever been beyond him, but that it tended to bore him to distraction. Now, however, he had a purpose that drove him. Each evening when Abbot left, Titus went over every unit the man had touched, tracing each component, striving to comprehend the purpose of every modification and looking for Abbot's bugs.

Each day, he found hand-fabricated boards spliced to anonymous button connectors. Some he tested himself, but others, which set up parallel processing with his cosmic cube array, he took to Ernie's shop for testing. Yet he never found anything amiss.

Inea, when he saw her there, was distant and efficient. He couldn't believe how much that hurt him. But when she asked, he replied, "I need you here more than in the lab."

"You want my trust? You shouldn't strain my credulity."

"You'll get your explanation."

"In Quito! You'll need the time to concoct such a prize tale!"

Yet she learned the customized circuitry of the system Abbot was building out of the shreds of the original. She became a parts connoisseur, preferring some fabricated at Luna Station over those made on Earth, and never mind they didn't fit the couplings. Once, Titus heard her cursing at a high-grade chip made at the L-5 factories.

But his vampire senses told him her vehemence originated in her frustrations, not the chip's quality. And the texture of that frustration was definitely sexual.

Taking his life in his hands, he went to her where she bent over the parts-strewn workbench and whispered, "I love you, Inea, and I *want* you."

She kept her head bent over her work, but her bright brimming eyes moved to look up at him. Her hands shook as his hunger aroused her. Now that their physical need was finally winning, he suddenly wasn't sure that was what he desired. Then she said, "I have to think this through."

"It's difficult to think when the physical tension is so great." He cupped his hand over her shoulder, almost daring to touch, his hunger sharpened by her desire, her tears aching behind his own eyes. *I can't stand her suffering.* "The way to solve a difficult and complex problem is to factor it and solve one term at a time."

63

She tilted her head back to keep her tears from dripping on the electrical contacts. "Can't you see that's what I'm trying to do? Don't— don't offer me the easy way out, or I'll give in and then I'll hate myself forever."

He forced his hand back to his side.

She turned to look squarely at him. "I can't think when you're this close because all I know is your suffering."

Positive feedback. Shit. After that, he avoided her shift, spending that time out on the craft.

He couldn't get past the new security on the corridor where he'd found the sleeper, but he did ascertain two things: from the configuration of furniture and hatchways, the *Kylyd* had a dependable internal gravity. If even full luren needed gravity for health, then he and Abbot were at more risk living on the moon than they'd figured. They couldn't use the drugs the humans used to slow bone loss.

Secondly, he found that there were more anthropologists studying the puzzle of the orl than was publicly admitted. As with the engineers, independent groups were amassing their own data and developing divergent interpretations.

He witnessed dissections where luren and orl nerves were stimulated by electrical current, and he read the chemists' reports of tracers used to map the DNA. He listened raptly to physical anthropologists spinning theories about two intelligent species exploring the stars in friendship. "Tell me, Doctors," prompted Titus, "do their visual sensitivity ranges match? And what about optical properties of their organic constituents? Could they be from the same planet?"

"Two intelligent species on the same planet? Unlikely."

"How dare we rule it out?" argued another. "In fact, are you absolutely certain both species are intelligent?"

"They both have hands."

It was too much for Titus. "All apes have hands. Just get me the optical data—if you can."

He made it a blatant challenge, and they redoubled their efforts to determine the capabilities of the optic nerves. But his questions started a new investigation. Could the two species interbreed? Were they two races, not two species?

Titus could not recall any mention of the subject. And so began a new niggling doubt. Suppose orl were intelligent? Suppose his ancestors had been brainwashed by their culture to believe orl were animals? In a twisted way, that was an encouraging thought, for it would mean luren *had* consciences and that modern luren in the galaxy *might* have, under the compulsion of conscience, shifted from being callous victimizers to neighbors who might not enslave Earth for food. After all, it had been centuries since Titus' ancestors crashed on Earth and only about three years since this craft had hit the moon. Things could have changed drastically out there just as they had here, even if there couldn't be a way to determine simultaneity.

From then on, he monitored the anthropology reports that crossed his desk, though his low security rating screened out details. If orl had been aboard *Kylyd* as crew, things had truly changed among luren. Abbot might be right to make contact now, but Abbot would be in for a rude shock when luren rejected the Tourists' archaic callous attitudes.

Could any of the cargo containers aboard *Kylyd* hold a blood substitute? If so, and if it was present in quantities indicating they'd actually lived on it rather than on orl, then luren had indeed changed. Titus spent some of his time trying to find out.

Meanwhile, it became easier to keep away from Inea, for every time he saw Abbot he envisioned what he'd do to Inea if he suspected how Titus felt. His mind froze whenever Abbot was in the lab. He didn't dare consider the fact that should he give in to Abbot, Inea would be safe. If he did dwell on that thought, he knew he'd soon be willing to believe any anthropologist who declared the orl were definitely crew members of equal status. Then he'd help Abbot send his SOS.

The sight of Abbot so distracted him from the lab's business that once Shimon brought him some coffee and asked if he was feeling well. Alarmed, Titus pulled himself together and tried to act normally for the rest of the day.

That evening, he found himself pacing outside Inea's apartment. His whole body could feel the dazzling pull of her apartment's charged atmosphere. He stood staring at her door, yearning for the revitalization he'd once found there.

Dear God! I'm starving.

But he knew it wasn't just the severely short rations he was living on. If this were merely physical hunger, anybody would do. Though he had felt surges of appetite with others, especially if they bled, only here was he overwhelmed with it.

He almost went in. With patience, he could seduce her. She'd never hate herself for giving in to him as she feared she would. When she finally got it all thought through, she'd know he was no threat to humanity or to her integrity. She was right about him. She'd always been right about him, even though she knew barely half the story and still had at least one more shock coming. But, he told himself, one hand spread on the door, she's now an astronomer. Obviously, she's resolved her xenophobia or she wouldn't be on this project. The mere fact that he was not entirely human wouldn't matter after she was sure of his mettle.

But if Abbot finds out how much I care—

He would have to divert Abbot's attention. He couldn't resist much longer, and then he might not have the patience to seduce her. He prayed she'd come to him soon. He would loathe himself if he treated her as Abbot had taught him to treat humans—as he might have to treat some again soon.

He tore himself from her door and fled to the gym to work out in the centrifuge chamber, which helped a little. He got tired enough to sleep.

He had never failed to log the requisite hours in the gym, and made a point of visiting a Skychef refectory, using his meal card and cloaking the fact that he didn't eat. He never quibbled about this use of Influence.

The day after his abortive approach to Inea's door, he lunched in the refectory near his lab and was pitching his tray, considering how he might distract Abbot, when he turned to find Inea sitting with a group near the door. She had perceived his projection of the remains of a hearty meal on his tray and maybe even his illusion that he'd been eating.

Their eyes locked and Titus saw injured betrayal in Inea's. He had told her he fed only on blood. *She thinks I lied.* He took three steps toward her, but she wrenched her gaze aside.

Such rejection emanated from her that he believed she'd accuse him publicly if he approached. He was unprepared for the chilling weakness that seized him as he left her.

He had never encountered anything like that aching chill before. How long could he stand it, and what would he do if he broke—run back in there, grab her by the shoulders and Influence her to accept him? *No! No, I won't.*

He was standing at an intersection, still shaking, when Shimon accosted him with a new problem.

Abbot had created a grotesque array of mismatched parts, claiming it would replace one of the microcomponents they couldn't get from

Earth. Irritated by Abbot's high-handed manner, Shimon still took every opportunity to challenge him. This only enhanced Abbot's entrenched contempt for humans. Abbot had lived through the years when the contents of a simple palmtop filled an entire room.

It took all of Titus' skill to persuade Shimon to give it a try. But in the process, he realized that Abbot must be spending so many hours fabricating items that he couldn't be keeping Titus under surveillance. The idea was both a relief and a torment. There had to be moments when Titus could approach Inea safely—but he had no way of knowing when.

He redoubled his own efforts on all fronts, hoping once more that he could outwit and outflank his father. With luck, he might even locate another transmitter component. *That* would surely keep Abbot busy.

Titus could get along on very little sleep during the moon's night, but as the sun rose over the horizon outside, even with all the protective dome and moon rock over his head, he felt a perpetual drag on his energies, yet couldn't rest. For the first time, he unlimbered the magnetic field generator for his bed. It took some recalibration, but he finally found the setting that brought him peace.

Gratefully, he lay down, chuckling as he always did at the way legends are born. The superstitious, noting the restlessness of the vampire unable to return to the place where he'd awakened to second life, assumed it was the dirt of that grave that was needed. But, in fact, it was the exact magnetic condition of the place of wakening that was vital.

Abbot had once remarked that luren had a mobile life stage before First Death, and a localization thereafter, in the adult stage—much like some primitive sea life on Earth.

The anthropologists studying the sleeping quarters aboard *Kylyd* were going crazy without knowing that a few wires and a battery were all the "bed" a luren needed.

In daytime, Titus allowed himself four hours sleep in each twenty-four, but the shortened sleep period sharpened his appetite. And his supplies were running low.

He normally used a packet a day, but had cut it to a third so the six packets he had left gave him eighteen days. Surely Connie would get a shipment to him by then. But if not, he'd have to use Influence to create a string. He hadn't done that in ten years, since the luren researchers had improved the humans' own process for synthesizing blood. He'd lived on synthetics, with occasional deep contact with humans he truly cared for and who cared for him. He flinched from the thought of forced intimacy with strangers.

But Abbot left him no time to brood. One night, when Titus was showing Shimon and the night shift what Abbot had accomplished that day, Abbot returned to the lab on the pretext of having forgotten his Varian. Titus rose from his crouched position beside Shimon, telling the Israeli, "Go ahead and check that one out. I'll be right back."

Abbot turned from his desk with the Varian held in his right hand. "Putting in overtime, I see. Checking my work?"

"Should I have to?"

Pacing a bit aside, Abbot cloaked his words. With an air of embarrassment, he confessed, "I'm not playing games with you. I really want your computer fixed so you can verify our legends. I didn't mean to do so *much* damage, and I didn't know you lost your spare catalogue at Quito. I'm just trying to make up for a small blunder. We're both really on the same side, you know."

"Are we?" *If* Abbot was telling the truth, then Abbot had made an error, and so had the Tourists. As formidable as they were, they were not invincible. He had to cling to that. Cloaking his own words, he asked, "I suppose you're ready to give up on implanting your transmitter then?"

"Of course not. And all your various secretive activities are only making my job more dangerous. Neither of us want the humans to discover us before the luren arrive. It would be better if you'd stop skulking about so clumsily."

Titus could not take offense. He was clumsy. But how much did Abbot really know? "Skulking about where?"

"Well, the ship, for one place. Don't you realize what a mess you made of the business of the dormant luren?"

Abbot reacted to the dismay that disrupted Titus' heavy cloaking by wrapping his Influence around Titus, shielding his shock from human notice. "You didn't know . . . ?"

Titus had cherished the knowledge that Abbot had not known he was hiding in the sleeper's chamber, observing.

Abbot moved a bit closer. "Listen. We can't afford another botched up job like that one. Thanks to you, they've moved the dormant one into the biomed dome and redoubled the security. What if he wakens where we can't get to him?"

Titus gulped. He knew what happened when an Earth luren wakened without luren help. He had hunted down such feral

68

monstrosities. They were the source of the worst of the vampire superstitions.

"They'll probably vivisect him soon," Abbot went on grimly. "I can't imagine how we can rescue him now. If I were you, I'd feel like a murderer."

"He's not dead yet—"

"And don't assume you're in the clear. They're combing all records looking for whoever might have broken into that chamber. We were both on *Kylyd,* though I was there before you. They can't prove I was there, but I can't prove I was elsewhere. Can you? Don't you see what you've done?"

"How can you be so sure it was me?" His voice shook. When he'd returned to his apartment that day, he'd found a message from Inea on his vidcom. She had triggered the emergency alarm trying to wake him, so she knew he hadn't been home.

Worse yet was the idea of the sleeper coming to on the operating table with a dozen human medics leaning over him. In the ravening hunger of reawakening, he would surely kill most of them before he was subdued.

"Who else could have figured out the door latch? The only others who can work it are two anthropologists and two Brink's men. *They* had clearance. *They* knew the alarm system. They trusted the alien lock to hold against any human. They never figured on another luren who could work the latch."

He didn't know I was watching him! The relief that flooded through Titus almost undid him. "I've learned to avoid the security alarms now. Don't worry. I won't set them off again." *But I didn't figure out the lock.* His hands had worked the alien mechanism by accident. *Quick, change the subject.* "You say it's called Kaileed?"

"I think it's a type of bird. A scavenger. When I was young, it was used as an insult. There's so much you didn't give me time to teach you. If you had, you'd understand and help me with this transmitter."

"What is there to understand except that humans have no defense against luren, and luren have no reason to regard humans as equals? Inviting luren here would just be handing over our human families to slavery—or worse."

"You don't know that. We're here. The very fact that we're luren, too, will protect Earth. If we call in the authorities, we'll have proprietary rights over Earth. If we just sit and wait, we won't get any rights."

"We don't know that Law still holds, or that human-luren hybrids would be legally luren—able to own property." The implications of human-luren cross-breeding had not escaped Titus. They had to be genetically linked, to be races of the same species. But would that make a difference to luren? "Laws can change, you know."

"The Law of Blood is ancient beyond human reckoning. There's no reason to suppose it's changed in principle. Our time sense has changed with our shortened lives, you know. We haven't been exiled so awfully long."

"We don't know how long the ship that brought our ancestors was out of touch with luren civilization before it arrived here. We don't know the parameters of the space drive they used—the time dilation. For that matter, we don't know what sort of drive *Kylyd* has! Neither ship is a generation ship or a sleeper ship, but they can't be instantaneous whatever that might mean."

"There are a lot of old tales I only half remember. Titus, there *could* be virtually instantaneous travel by now, and there *may* be more than just luren in the galaxy. There could be a galactic civilization with inter-species politics. The Blood may need us—and Earth—as much as we need them."

"And you want rescue to come in your lifetime. I can understand that. But give the humans time to study *Kylyd* and they'll meet luren as equals. Without your signal, it could take a couple of centuries for them to get here. By then—"

"—you'll still be young, and you'll have to watch the extinction of Earth's luren. Think what you're saying!" Abbot's intensity was born of true conviction. "We're already losing our heritage. Little things, like the fact that kylyd is the name of a scavenger bird, get lost each generation, and big things do too. You Residents call yourselves vampires, not luren. You think of humans as your families, not a convenient link in the food chain. In a few centuries, there won't be any recognizable luren on Earth to be rescued."

"Are you so sure we'd be recognized now? I saw the dormant one. Would he think he looked anything like us?"

"Have you seen the way humans look at him? Do you doubt that if they knew us, they'd turn on us? Son, don't you know how difficult it was to get you and me into this Project? With today's computer records and photographs, life on Earth isn't what it was when I was your age. It's becoming harder to forge new identities to cover our failure to age. Manipulation of popular or even government opinion is nearly impossible. Soon we'll be rediscovered and humans will erupt in madness to devour us all. Even Residents who consider themselves humans and live on that synthetic syrup you call blood, won't be safe.

"Titus, it wouldn't take much to wipe us out. Humans know our vulnerabilities. We need the help of The Blood."

He might be right. He just might be. While Titus groped for a reply, someone called, "Dr. Shiddehara! I have a tracing now! Come look at this!"

"I'll be right there!" called Titus.

He buried himself in the work, frightened by Abbot's ability to undermine his convictions. He preferred to deal with particle storms in space, gravity lenses, galactic fields, or something really simple, like the origin of time and gravity. Espionage wasn't his game.

Late that night, he woke with a new resolve. To counter Abbot, he'd have to use Influence, and he knew just where it would be most effective.

Dressing in a black Glynnis gym suit and his Suchoff moon shoes, he threw a towel about his neck and went to the gym. He had been unable to crack the project's security codes and get into the files. But he had discovered the duty rosters for the Brink's personnel, and there was one charming young woman, Suzy Langton, who would be in the gym now. It shouldn't be difficult to get the codes from her.

The gym was the largest open area on the station. World Sovereignties had spent lavishly to make it attractive so that people would spend time there. Real plants adorned the dividers separating working areas. Clever engineering controlled noise. Anthropologists had designed a space that many nationalities would find conducive to socializing. Titus surveyed the largest area, where a dozen women were working out on rowing machines while watching a popular adventure show. One of them, who worked in his lab, waved to him.

He waved back, contrasting the cozy feeling the gym created with the crawling discomfort he'd felt at first on *Kylyd*. Here the walls were a neutral light shade, difficult to name. The floors were of a shock-absorbing composition. The ceiling was high, and artwork concealed gym riggings when they were pulled up and stored.

In one place, trellises supported arching vines. In another, rough-cut wooden beams crisscrossed beneath the lights. Beyond that, there was a ceiling that made you think you were looking up into the ocean from a dome on a sunken coral reef. Farther away, there was frescoed vaulting. With dividing hedges and trellises, hanging plants and some trees, there was a sense of privacy without the enclosed feeling of the tiny efficiency apartments.

Off the main room, a glass wall enclosed the swimming pool. Water behaved so differently under lunar gravity that one needed special training to be allowed to swim. Titus had not taken the training. Water altered magnetic currents in disconcerting ways. So he hoped his quarry wasn't a swimmer.

He checked the log of the centrifuge for Langton but finally discovered her working out in the martial arts studio—a huge area divided by colored mats and padded walls. Six different styles were being practiced or taught, modified for lunar gravity. But in a far corner, a green mat was occupied by two Brink's women, one of them Suzy Langton. They were sparring free-style, shifting from one stance to another, from one style to another with smooth efficiency.

Titus threaded his way between the mats, protected only by elastic ropes from which vanquished contestants rebounded gently—or in the case of one young man, not so gently. That youth bounced, grabbed futilely at his instructor, then soared into the padded wall. On the rebound, he caught the ropes and held on, oscillating ludicrously.

Uproarious laughter met this performance, and Titus, seeing the youngster was hamming it up, laughed too. The instructor let his group break ranks and engage in random horseplay. Titus decided this was not just a class in martial disciplines but in mental health and social integration.

If he had time, it might be a good thing for him to participate in. It could keep suspicions at bay—if he could hide his strength.

Suzy Langton, on the other hand, was engaged in a more serious match. She was short, with the shoulders of a circus aerialist and the calves of a ballet dancer, and moved like a world-class gymnast. Her opponent was large and heavier, but they both wore black belts with lunar-gravity knots. Titus swayed, wanting to coach Langton. *Kick!* But Langton spun, squatted, thrust out one foot and swept the other off her feet. Behind Titus, someone applauded. Turning, he found a group of women in brown belts, coated with aromatic sweat from their own class. Among them stood Mirelle.

Abbot's Mark fairly glowed over her forehead, though Titus was the only one aware of it. She didn't see him at first, but surged forward, yelling, "Suzy, watch out!"

Turning, Titus saw that Suzy's opponent had used the light gravity to twist so she landed on her hands and used her legs to grab Langton's neck, forcing her to the mat.

With a grunt, Suzy arched, lunged, and brought her opponent down, where they both grappled for wrestling holds.

Several men had now quit their own mats to join the audience. One called encouragement, "Get her, Kitten!"

Another answered, "That's no kitten. That there's one full-grown panther!"

Titus was inclined to agree. If it came down to it, he wouldn't care to fight either of these women fair. He'd have to use Influence. Normally he'd Influence a violent human to prevent them pitting their strength against his and getting hurt. With trained fighters like these, however, he'd have to combat skill with Influence or get creamed.

"Titus!" At last Mirelle recognized him.

He tore his eyes from the spectacle. "Mirelle. It's good to see you again. Is Abbot around?"

"Should he be?"

"You two seemed to hit it off fairly well."

"Jealous?"

"I was." It occurred to him that if he hadn't found Inea, he would be hurting for Mirelle still.

"Such flattery!" She raked him up and down with her eyes. "I could almost wish Abbot did not want me."

Titus felt his polite smile slip. Given her susceptibility and Abbot's methods, she shouldn't have been able to think such a thing, let alone say it to him. Her feelings must have been much stronger than Abbot had suspected.

"Now *that's* flattering," he responded. But he narrowed his attention, searching for what had been done to her.

She moved closer. "I could wish to see more of you."

"Our work keeps us in separate worlds."

"I don't work all the time."

"What exactly are you doing?" He felt Abbot's Influence surface, but it was a bare whisper of what it might be.

Titus realized, as she fabricated a generality, that Abbot had kept his interference to a minimum so as not to impair her professional acuity or limit her curiosity. He hadn't needed to inhibit her from talking to Titus because Titus lacked the top security clearance and she knew it.

By leaving her able to come on to him, Abbot had found a subtle way to torment both Titus and Mirelle. The Mark on her forehead put her beyond Titus' reach no matter what.

He stepped back, locking his hands behind him. "Do me a favor, Mirelle. Tell Abbot I play by the rules."

She cocked her head to one side. "What do you mean?"

"He'll know what I mean." She'd report every nuance of his behavior to Abbot the moment she saw him again. She was an open channel through which Abbot spied on anything and everything she encountered.

It suddenly struck Titus that Abbot's uncanny ability to know everything must be due to his having Marked and opened a number of humans. It was a standard survival technique which Abbot had taught Titus, but which Titus had forgotten. *Even if he's busy, it might not be safe to go to Inea.*

Her expression changed. "Well, *mon cheri,* you don't have to look at me as if I were half a worm you found in an apple you just bit into." She brushed a finger over his lips and kissed it wistfully. He couldn't help himself. He caught the fingers and kissed them formally, as she continued, "I will deliver your cryptic message, but do not think I would be faithful to Abbot if you gave me a choice." She turned toward the women's locker room.

If Abbot had been there at that moment, Titus would have cheerfully killed his father. He forced his attention back to the match, relieved that Mirelle had left, for he couldn't approach Langton with Mirelle watching and reporting to Abbot.

In a flurry of kicks and punches, Langton downed her opponent again, but this time blood sprang from a cut over Langton's right eye. Negligently, she dashed it aside, sending droplets flying onto the mat at Titus' feet.

He clamped his lips together, but his indrawn breath carried the scent to him above the aroma of human sweat. His eyes fastened hungrily on the haze of ectoplasm dissipating from the tiny drops. He couldn't afford to react in public. He closed his eyes and turned away from the ring, abandoning his quarry until her cut had been closed.

He was about to plunge to the back of the crowd, when his eyes locked with Inea's. She wore a terry robe over a wet bathing suit of azure and pink, her hair plastered to her skull, slick and shiny. Her feet were bare.

His nerves rang with the shock of her beauty. Her eyes leaped out of her face, burning through him in accusation. *She saw Mirelle flirting!* He started toward her. Since blood had been drawn, the level of noise among the spectators had redoubled. They surged in, making it nearly impossible for Titus to move.

Inea watched him struggle toward her, and he thought he saw a trace of sympathy on her face. Then she shook her head at him, turned and fled into the women's locker room.

A moment later, with a yell and a resounding smack of open arms hitting the mat, the contest was over. Two women, also Brink's officers, escorted Langton toward the women's locker room. People surged forward to congratulate her and compliment her on her moves. As she worked her way past Titus, he shook himself out of his daze and stepped forward, catching her elbow. Exerting Influence, he said, "Meet me here when you're dressed. We have something personal to discuss. Besides, I give great back rubs."

Exhausted from the match, she took the impression readily. She aimed a dazzling smile at him and replied as if he were an old friend, "I won't be long."

It was that simple. He could have her tonight, all night, if he wanted. A part of him was tempted. The cut over her eye had bled profusely, and he came away with her blood on his fingers. He couldn't resist raising it to his mouth and sucking until his own skin threatened to break.

There were several ways out of the women's locker room, and he was fairly sure Inea would not use this exit. Yet if she came out first, he'd follow her—make her listen—and never mind Suzy Langton and the Brink's security codes. It occurred to him that he'd lost the cold objectivity Connie had insisted was his only protection during this mission.

Langton emerged first, her cut sealed, and a fresh red wraparound highlighting her trim figure. Her black hair was confined by a white band, and her soft-soled Suchoffs were also white. Summoning himself to the business at hand, Titus stepped forward. "Remember me?"

As he escorted her through a hedgerow into a deserted area where comfortable lounges surrounded a dance floor, he shamelessly Influenced her into a dream world. Nobody would bother them here until the next dance class. He gathered her down onto a lounge in such a way that anyone blundering into the area would assume they wanted privacy.

His lips close to her ear, his Influence clouding her mind so she knew nothing of what she said, only what she felt, he coaxed the information he needed out of her. Brink's conditioning was fierce. He needed all his skill to create an exquisite pitch of arousal, sufficient to mask his purpose.

To do all this and shield them from interruptions was almost more than he could handle, for half his energy went into fighting his own self-disgust.

Once, his lips strayed to the sealed cut, the odor of blood sending him into delirium, and he wanted to make her illusionary experience real. It would be so much better for both of them if he participated in her ecstasy.

At the very last moment, as his teeth were nibbling at the bandage, he turned his face aside. *Even starvation doesn't give me the right to take what I want.*

When he had all the codes, even those she didn't consciously remember, he gave her supreme release and the peaceful oblivion of sleep, a tender gift, an offering to he knew not what god. How could anything make up for what he'd done?

Gently, he wiped all trace of his identity from her memory. He left no Mark to ward off Abbot, hoping that if his father took her, he would believe Titus had only fed and would look no deeper. He, himself, could hardly believe he could have bestowed such an experience on a human woman and still feel as hungry and as achingly unfinished as he did. Yet the thought of the ration awaiting him at home filled him with revulsion.

Refusing to look at Langton again, he rearranged his clothing, schooled his features, and crossed the dance floor to an opening in the hedge. *Never again. I'm never going to do this again.*

As he approached the opening, senses raw, he felt Inea. She crouched behind the hedge, watching him cross the floor. Then she broke and ran, the hedge tossing in her wake.

What she thought she'd seen—what he'd been projecting for anyone passing by to see—was a man and woman hastily coupling with embarrassing intensity.

He broke into a shambling lunar run. "Inea, wait!"

SEVEN

Inea ran from him as if he were truly evil.

It would be so easy to stop her with Influence. Titus skidded to a halt in the midst of a weight lifting class and summoned the revulsion he'd felt as he'd forced each of the codes out of Suzy Langton. *I won't be addicted to Influence.*

"Hey, Mister, anything wrong?" called the instructor, a muscular young woman who had oiled her black skin until she looked like an ebony statue. Abner Gold stood behind her.

Titus noticed an odd intensity in her gaze, but brushed it aside. "Oh . . . just forgot something." He pushed on.

As he emerged from an arch in the vine that shielded the weight lifting area, he found Inea poised on the balls of her feet eyeing him. They were near the entrance to the gym. The rowing team he'd seen working out was gone, and their area was dimmed. Titus cast about for any trace of Abbot. He found nothing, but one of his string could be watching.

Titus moved into the rowing area, and called, "Inea, you didn't see what you thought you saw. Not here and not in the cafeteria. We *really* need to talk. Come sit?"

He settled cross-legged on the floor beside one of the rowing machines, leaning against its side, waiting. He had almost given up hope, when she drifted through the gate.

As she entered the area, he erected a shield around them to divert the interest of passersby. "Let me explain my—apparent—behavior. Please, Inea, please listen."

"I can't imagine what you could say after what I saw."

"Remember the bat?"

She glanced sharply at him. "So?"

"I can make people see anything. In the refectory, you thought I'd eaten a meal. Here you thought I'd taken a woman. I did neither."

"How do I know? You could say anything."

This was why he'd promised himself never to Influence her. "Think," he pleaded. "People must believe I eat, so I must create that impression even if it means using the defensive gift of my kind."

Titus watched as she digested that, and recoiled. "You lied to me. You drank blood from that woman. Is she dead?"

He sprang to his feet. "God, no!"

But she was out and around the divider, racing back to the dance floor. He caught up to her at the dance floor's hedge, grabbed her by the shoulders and held her. "Listen to me!" he whispered fiercely. "I haven't lied to you. I will never lie to you. The cut on Suzy's face nearly drove me out of my mind, but I didn't take anything from her—except the information I need to do my job. She'll never remember me. You've no cause to be horrified—or even jealous."

She relaxed. "All right, then let me go look."

"She'll be waking up soon."

"I'll be quiet."

He let her go. She crept through the hedge. Titus thought he could feel Suzy stirring. Perhaps she had, for a moment later, Inea reappeared. "Well, she's not dead anyway. I guess I shouldn't leap to conclusions."

He put his arm around her shoulders and led her back to the rowing area, this time guiding her all the way in and sitting her down beside him. "Do you still doubt me?"

"I don't know. When I saw you eating in the cafeteria I thought you'd tricked me, but I couldn't imagine why unless you really had killed someone and had him buried in your place."

"Why didn't you go to the authorities right then?"

"I—I wasn't sure. Then I saw your expression when Suzy's blood spattered all over the mat."

He groaned. "Did I really give myself away that badly?"

"No, everyone was lusting after the sight of blood. I don't suppose they're all vampires."

"No. Humans have their own ideas of amusement."

"You didn't find it amusing. It made you hungry."

"Yes."

"Then why didn't you just drink Suzy's blood?"

"You believe I *could* but didn't?"

"I don't know what to believe. If you could do such a thing—if you have to do such things—why didn't you?"

"Because I didn't have her permission."

"Permission? Is that supposed to be funny? You took information from her, you said—I presume with this power of yours. I assume she didn't give permission for that."

"What I took from her was not for myself, but for the benefit of humanity. What I refused was for myself alone."

"You never used to be so selfless—or concerned about honor."

"That's true. The young have so little power, they don't have to agonize over its proper use."

Slowly, she said, "I believe you. It adds up. I've been trying to watch you, but I can't keep up with you. Nobody can go as long without sleep as you do. But why steal information from Brink's? To sell it? Professors don't make much. It takes lots of untraceable money to create false identities."

"But anyone in the market for Brink's secrets couldn't be trusted to use them for the benefit of humankind."

"Why would that stop you?"

He caught her hands and hissed, "I don't use any power, human or otherwise, in such ways! I simply do not!"

Stunned, she let her hands lie between his.

Against his will, his head lowered and his lips sought hers. Barely making contact, he hesitated, feeling her flesh tremble as his body pressed against hers, revealing his state more clearly than words ever could. But he held back.

When she was sure he wasn't going to force her, she relaxed, and he felt the divine power of her. He didn't know which need was more urgent, the growing heat in his groin or the thirst that burned in every cell.

He felt the waves of arousal that beat through her, surging between them, possessing them both, and he knew he had another power over her. Now she wouldn't say no.

He scooped her into his arms and buried his face in her damp hair. "Before I died, when we were engaged," he said, "I never felt like this. It was easy then to wait until our wedding night." He had never felt true arousal until after his wakening, when it became tangled up with the thirst. Luren didn't reach sexual maturity until after First Death.

"When you died . . . I cried myself to sleep each night because we'd waited. I'd rather have been alone and pregnant than alone and a virgin. The next time I didn't wait."

"Did you ever marry? You aren't married now, are you?"

"Divorced. The one I did trap into marrying me—well, I hated myself more than he ended up hating me. If you've learned not to use your power, then I've learned recreational sex doesn't do much for me. This time, Titus, I have to be sure! Especially with what you say, I have to be sure!"

He started to move back, but she clung to him. "It feels so good, Titus. How could it be wrong?"

79

"Yes." He schooled himself to patience, wanting her to have what she needed from him.

But she felt his tension. "Is it that you want to . . . bite my neck?"

He thrust back from her, holding her shoulders at arm's length, embarrassed enough by that truth to laugh it off as another myth. But he owed her more. He shrugged. "Any vein will do. But I no longer drink from humans. I told you."

"Your canine teeth aren't very long."

He laughed. "No, but incisors do break skin, only not too neatly. We use surgical tools so the wound heals fast." He took a deep breath, struggling to quell his urgency. "But all I'm asking now is what any man would want. I'm human, too, remember? I'm asking you to go to bed with me. Nothing . . . kinky. Just what we've always wanted with each other." *Just that. Maybe it will be enough—for now.*

"Is it especially good with . . . vampires? Or is that a myth, too?"

"I'll make it like nothing you've ever known."

"Like you did with Suzy?"

"No! That was illusion. I won't need any illusion with you." But he knew that his hunger sharpened the experience for his bedmates, even when he used no Influence. "I promise, everything between us will be real."

"I keep believing you—and I keep going back to my room wondering if I've gone mad. I haven't got a shred of real evidence to prove what you've made me believe."

"Tell me what evidence you want—it'll be yours."

She put her hands on his cheeks, fingering the roughness of his beard. He waited, but when she didn't name her proof, he pleaded shamelessly, "But in the meantime . . . ?" He pressed his lips to her palm and let them describe his offer.

She listened to his silent message, eyes closed, but when he worked up to the inside of her wrist, she sensed his hunger rising. She jerked free, staring at her hand. "What if you're really a vampire? And what if you're as evil as legend says and if I let you—then I— I'll become—"

"Is that what you've been brooding about?"

"If you really were such a horror, you'd compel me to believe you, so the more I believe you, the more I doubt."

"Actually, that's wise—"*—with Abbot around.*

"Are you telling me you are evil?" She wrenched away, wrapping her arms over her chest. "How melodramatic."

80

"No, not evil. But you've got to prove it yourself." Even Abbot wasn't evil, just scared of the power of his cattle.

"Will you tell me what you took from the Brink's woman?"

"No. It's bad enough that one non-Brink's person has it. No one else will ever get it from me."

"That's not proof. That's not evidence."

"I know. Nothing I can do or say is evidence. You must define for yourself the proof that you would accept. It might be best if you can get it without my knowing."

She scrambled to her feet, stared down at him, then yanked herself around and made for the opening in the divider. Over her shoulder, she warned, "Don't follow me this time."

He felt that if he did, she would surrender. But he also knew what he hadn't understood that time he'd paced outside her door and had almost gone in to seduce her. The next day her doubts would return and spoil everything forever.

He dragged himself back to his room and to a very miserable night. Nothing helped. Unable to sleep, he carefully recorded the codes he'd memorized then tried three times to use them, but he kept keying mistakes.

In the morning, he pulled himself together and went to the lab hoping work would banish his mental conversations with Inea. When he had assigned everyone to a task for the shift, he barricaded himself in his office and, wondering if they'd ever get the wireless network running, patched his handheld into his desk terminal, invoking one of Abbot's handy programs. It caused Security programs to forget that certain files had been accessed. He hadn't dared to use it before because it had been known to fail on other Brink's systems used by banks. But this time he had Brink's own codes, so he went after the records of those heading clandestine departments.

He sweated through every pause, afraid the old program, which had allowed his kind to create identities, was finally obsolete. The Project's systems had to be superior to banking systems, for banks had to show a profit while the government didn't. So government could spend absurdly on security. If Langton's codes had been changed, or if he'd gotten one wrong and he couldn't answer a challenge on the first try . . . he refused to think about that.

At last he found a compilation of hobbies and prior professions of those working in Biomed and Cognitive Sciences. Someone had gone to great lengths to assemble scientists who seemed ideal to perform one sort of task, but were in fact better suited for something else entirely. The two key figures turned out to be Mirelle and Mihelich, with Gold a close third because of his Sandia connections and his work on low-grav bio-cybernetic laboratory instruments.

Mihelich was not just an M.D., but a geneticist, a research cytologist, and a pioneer in cloning techniques with several patents on work done under the auspices of various corporations, so that few people knew of his contributions.

Titus dug out some of the man's more esoteric papers and waded through the alien language of biomed. Clearly, Mihelich was one of ten researchers who understood human cloning well enough to produce a viable luren or orl fetus. And he had gathered all the help and equipment he'd need.

When Titus uncovered the profiles of Dr. Mirelle de Lisle and her co-workers, the scope—the sheer audacity—of the clandestine half of the Project came home to him.

It would be useless to clone an alien without knowing *what* he was. The Cognitive Sciences, which included anthropology, ethnography, ethnology, linguistics, and psychology, yearned to dub themselves Xenology. But there had been no strangers to study until *Kylyd* arrived. Now, the leaders of that movement were on the moon to create an environment suitable for raising alien children.

But the biggest discovery, Titus made by accident. One of Mirelle's reports—which read like a textbook in applied kinesics, a branch of anthropology dealing with communication encoded in subconsciously controlled movement—contained an illegible document that seemed like gibberish until he recognized the phonetic alphabet and looked up the symbols.

An hour later, he stared at a screen full of squiggles he could read as plainly as English. But it wasn't English. It was luren. Distorted pronunciations, strange words, and odd syntax aside, it was the language Abbot had taught him, and the document seemed to be a transcription of a kind of verbal log recording off *Kylyd.*

They've tapped the ship's electronics! And not a hint of that had ever appeared in any official report from Project Station. He backed out of the file stealthily, his mind leaping from the sketchiest hints to rock-hard conclusions.

The first time he'd seen Abbot in *Kylyd,* squeezing through the twisted portal, he'd been carrying something that could have been a recorder. Abbot was an electronics wizard. Abbot had Marked Mirelle, who was on the clandestine side of the Project. Abbot knew what she knew.

Knowing that it had been done by the humans, never mind that official reports said they couldn't even ignite the lighting system, Abbot could have jiggered a recorder to mesh with *Kylyd's* own system. And if so, he could have been pulling data out of the control console he bent over with such absorption while Titus hid in the sleeper's chamber.

Abbot had this transcription as well as others the humans knew nothing about, and Abbot was learning to read *Kylyd's* records. The humans, of course, had no idea what Mirelle's gibberish meant; there was no Rosetta stone.

Why would Abbot spend so much time on language? Just to send the SOS in the right dialect? Hardly. He intended to wake the sleeper. But what did Abbot plan to do with a wakened luren—a pure-blood?— a pure-blood who would become his son—wholly in his power?

Titus shied away from that idea, telling himself it was just wild conjecture, but he was unable to get the thought of the orl out of his mind. What if they had been aboard as crew, not food? What if the galactic luren of today would not regard Earth's humans merely as a food supply? And what if Abbot was right? What if this really was the last chance for Earth's luren to survive intact as luren? *What should I do?*

The question haunted him through the rest of the day, despite distractions, and when the evening crew left, he stayed, coveting time alone during the one shift when the lab was empty. He had to think through, in the most absolutely rigorous fashion, what he must do. He had to build a mental model of the situation and run some trial solutions to his problems to see what the major effects would be.

Knowing life wouldn't be as simple as physics, he was nevertheless methodical as he listed his goals and options in his handheld's private note file. Pondering the result, he suddenly added, "I could waken the luren and father him."

Staring at that absurdity, he heard the lab's hall door open. Inea peeked around the cowling of the airlock.

The lab's lights were on full, but Titus had dimmed the light in his office; the levelors were shut, the door ajar. She found the lab empty, and crossed to the observatory. She grabbed her lab coat off the rack and donned it, covering her lilac and pink gym suit as if she did this every night.

Curious, Titus shut his note file and watched from his door. She bent over a reader, calling up files, reading. He tiptoed to his desk and slaved his unit to hers. She was checking the daily worksheet on the computer repair.

The screen went blank again, and he saw her move to the observatory instruments. Most were receivers tied to the major solar orbit observatories, but some were tuned to the few dozen extra-system probes that were still alive. His observatory recorded everything that came in, but the data was useless until the main server came back on line.

There were three installations on Earth and one in Earth orbit that could synthesize portions of the data, but the Project had the only system able to interpret all the data according to any of the prevailing theories of the universe, and run a continuous comparison of the results against all new data. They had not only capacity, but unique programming on unique hardware.

Inea, a skilled interpreter, could tell by inspection if the raw data was unusual. She pored over the readouts intently.

All his adult life, Titus had postulated the position of the dim, distant star that had to be the origin of the flight that had deposited his ancestors on Earth. It was hidden behind the brighter bodies in the Taurus region, but legend gave him an approximate line and distance. Data captured by the extra-solar observatories that saw *Kylyd's* approach would pinpoint the home star—as soon as *Wild Goose* answered.

Inea raised her head, frowning in frustration at the dissected computers out in the main room, and then back at the screen she was reading. *Has she found something?*

He crossed the lab to the glass partitions of the observatory. At the door, he hesitated. His foot hit a screwdriver abandoned on the floor. Inea whirled, stifling a squeak. "Darr—Titus! Do you have to sneak up like that?"

"I'm sorry. I'm curious about what you're doing here."

"Well, this is my job, you know. And I'm not putting in for the overtime. I won't screw up your bookkeeping."

"Do you come in every day?" *Has Abbot seen her?*

"Y-yes," she confessed. "Is that so terrible?"

"I just didn't expect it."

"I'm an astronomer, not an electrician. On my own time I'll do astronomy." She tilted her head to one side. "Is there some reason I shouldn't be here?"

"No, of course not. Knowing you, I should have realized you'd come." He entered the observatory, and scanned the recorders. "Did you see what came in this afternoon?"

"Yes. I wish I'd been here."

"It could be our big break." The tracings indicated an object where no one had seen one before.

"Yes, if it's a star and its spectrum checks against the data from the alien ship, we won't need your star catalogue."

"I wouldn't go that far, but this afternoon, I asked for the data to be processed on Earth and the results relayed to us. Only by then our server may be up—our shipment from Luna Station is due in two days. Will you be ready?"

"I've been ready for a week. When should I report?"

They discussed the state of the repairs, Titus insisting she report the day after Abbot was due to finish his job on the computers. He didn't explain the timing.

As he dodged her questions, she became more insistent and curious. Then, without warning, she desisted.

As if capitulating, she walked toward the observatory door, hands in her gym suit pockets. Titus followed and was arm's length from her when she turned, and thrust a large silver crucifix in his face.

He backed away, trying to focus his eyes. She took it for aversion and shoved the object up against his nose.

Reflexively, his hands clasped the crucifix. Bright beauty sizzled through his every nerve, stiffening his body as high voltage current would. Forgetting everything, he drank it in as thirstily as if it were blood. A strange ecstasy stole over him. Transfixed, he heard music so sweet he needed to cry. He was filled by an indescribable scent and laughter bubbled through his veins.

In one instant, he was totally consumed and reborn.

The current spent, he drooped, leaning on a desk, propping himself on stiff arms. His head lolled onto his chest as he gulped air. Every vampire sense was alive in him. Inea was a redolent human warmth, the cavernous lab echoed empty, and he felt the distant throb of humanity throughout the dome.

"So you did lie." Inea's voice was ripe with grief.

Dizzy, he yearned for time to assimilate the precious gift that had flowed into him, the strength he so desperately needed. "Inea, I didn't lie," he insisted wearily. "Give me the cross." He groped vaguely in her direction.

She approached, holding it before her like a shield, waiting for him to wither in its light. But it had spent itself. He took it from her taut grip and held it to his lips, feeling her warmth still in the pure silver.

Turning, he sat on the desk corner. He cradled the cross in his hands and smiled up at her. "Thank you. But I can't imagine where you found this."

"There's a Catholic chaplain over in the other dome. He loaned it to me." She added in a small voice, "It almost killed you. Why are you sitting there holding it as if it was your greatest treasure?"

At that, he laughed, a pure spontaneous celebration. "Because it is! Or was." For the first time in days, his hunger had stopped gnawing at him, and he felt he could face down Abbot himself, if necessary. "Listen. I told you I'm not *afraid* of religious objects of any sort, and that's the truth. But a charge such as this one held is rare. It takes a priest of great purity and power to consecrate anything like that— and it's silver . . . " He was dabbling at the edges of metaphysics. There was no rational reason why silver would hold such a charge while other materials didn't.

Perhaps this one had been charged recently?

"Silver bullets are supposed to kill your kind."

"Sure. Any kind of bullets will if they hit a vital spot. Myths. The power stored in this cross discharged into me, in the most exquisite—"

"You mean it was good? A pleasure?"

"A pleasure I could crave endlessly."

"How could a legend get so twisted?"

"Easy. You saw how it disabled me. Even you thought you'd killed me. If you'd run in terror, you'd have been convinced you'd vanquished me—wouldn't you?"

"And that you were too evil to abide a symbol of good."

He nodded, watching her work it through. Then he said, curiously, "But you're not Catholic. Surely there must be chaplains of other faiths here? Why did you choose—"

"But Catholics are the ones who train exorcists and"—her eyes went to the crucifix he fondled— "I guess you passed that test. On the other hand, I have only your word for it that you'd welcome another Catholic whammy."

Catholic whammy? "How about Jewish? See if you can find a kosher mezuzah somewhere and throw that at me."

"You serious? Or are you just doing Brer Rabbit begging not to be thrown into the briar patch?"

He rose, his legs able to hold him now. Brusquely, he told her, "It was your test. You ought to be satisfied. But next time, please give me a couple of seconds warning." He handed over the crucifix. "Take this back to the chaplain and tell him it ought to be reconsecrated. If he was the one who charged it in the first place, it'll work again."

She held it by the long shaft. "That wouldn't prove anything. It didn't prove anything this time."

"Is that my fault? I'm very tired of this game."

"So am I. I thought this would settle it. I honestly didn't expect you to react at all. You did tell me you didn't fear religious objects!"

"And I don't!" he snapped, then realized it was his sexual frustration driving him. "I'm sorry. Everything I've told you is true. But I haven't told you everything there is to tell. I never said I had."

"I've yet to uncover one piece of concrete evidence to substantiate your story."

"I doubt you ever will. Whatever you observe, Inea, you'll be able to find another explanation."

"Years ago, you taught me about Occam's Razor—that the least complex explanation usually turns out to be true. Why assume you're a vampire when human tricks can account for everything you do?"

"Why would I insist on this wild tale when I could let you believe me human and take you to bed right away?"

Reaching, she suggested, "Because you're crazy?"

"Your hypothesis is getting complex. Think about that. Then go find the holographic equipment I snuck in and installed in your room during the few hours I was on Luna before you invited me there. You saw the bat form. You believed it. You're not that easy to trick."

"True." She sighed. "I'll devise something definitive, and I promise it won't be silver bullets. I don't want to hurt you." She sidled past him, planting a shy kiss on his cheek that left him as limp as the crucifix's charge had. And the joy that came in the wake of her kiss was almost as potent.

That night, he slept cherishing the memory of that single, voluntary kiss. He hardly dared imagine what it would be like when she finally took him to her bed.

———

On Abbot's last day of work in the lab, the shipment from Luna Station arrived, escorted from the docks by three rough-cut Brink's guards commanded by Suzy Langton. There was one huge crate and two smaller ones, which were waist high on Titus.

When they broke the seals under the watchful gaze of security, they discovered the larger one contained all the parts they'd expected. The other two crates carried a variety of items shipped from Earth just after Titus' group had left.

While the others were picking over the bounty in the large crate, Titus took the crowbar to the other two, and discovered to his great relief that nestled among bottles of B&J High Purity Solvent which Titus hadn't ordered were a few dozen small packets of dark crystalline powder labeled B&J Additives. Connie had shipped him blood to replace what had been stolen. *She must have acted instantly.*

As he leaned over, his upper body jackknifed into the crate, Titus felt Abbot approach. Before he could hide the evidence, his father peered down into the crate.

But it was a Brink's man who bent over Abbot's shoulder and asked in a deceptively soft Southern accent, "What have you got there? Powdered solvent? I didn't know there was such a thing, but it surely doesn't belong here. Hey, Suzy!"

Everyone followed Suzy over to the smaller crate.

Titus realized he should have cloaked his actions when he opened the crate. He could have removed the packets to his office without anyone noticing. Now it was too late.

Shimon plucked up one of the bags and tossed it from hand to hand. "Odd stuff. Whose do you suppose it is?"

Titus' eyes met Abbot's, hardly daring to plead.

Abbot inspected Titus with a sardonic smile. Then he shrugged and finessed the packet out of Shimon's hands. "I'll find out who it belongs to and take care of it." He spoke to the Israeli, but his attention swept the crowd as he insisted with powerful Influence, "It can't be important."

Titus added his Influence, summoning all his power and trying to emulate his father's tightly leashed control. "It's trivial. Abbot and I will take care of it. You can all safely forget it."

At that moment, Inea swung through the door carrying a toolbox and wearing a lab coat and white gloves. She had her hair bound back in a clean-room cap. "I heard the shipment was here and I came to . . . What's the matter?"

Abbot reached out with his Influence, focusing real power to subdue her curiosity as he insisted, "Not a thing. We have more imp—"

Without thinking, Titus reacted, the whole force of his raised Influence behind the command. "Abbot, *no!*"

———— EIGHT ————

To Titus' surprise, his father recoiled. "Titus, what in the—" Cloaking his words, he swore. "Child, you don't know your own strength! What do you think you're doing?"

Titus' greatest efforts had never before produced such an effect in Abbot. "I—I. . . ."

Perplexed, Abbot inspected Inea, adding, "You're that involved and you haven't Marked her?"

Around them, everyone was staring disinterestedly into the packing case. Titus pulled himself together. "She's not mine," he answered nonchalantly, cloaking as well. He raised his voice and ordered in clear, "Inea, check the observatory first and I'll be right with you. Okay?"

She shrugged and shoved her toolbox into a corner. "Sure," she answered, but he saw her glance over her shoulder at Abbot as she went toward the glass enclosure.

"See?" Titus pointed out. "As you taught me, when you don't need Influence, don't use it."

Abbot shook his head, and Titus was almost sure he'd covered his slip. Inea now seemed to be no one special, just useful.

"Titus, do you want my help with the others or not?"

"I'd consider it a favor." Abbot didn't seem to think he needed help. Titus wondered if he'd gained power from the Catholic talisman, for he had felt wonderful ever since.

Abbot raised his voice with Influence. "If we're going to be up and running this month, we'd better get to work."

Titus added his Influence, singling out individuals and assigning jobs, diverting attention from the crate.

Suzy Langton hefted the top of the crate. "I'll just seal up this stray case and take it back . . ."

"Oh, that won't be necessary," Titus interrupted hastily, and Abbot joined with, "Absolutely not necessary."

She stopped, the awkward top held across her chest. "Well . . . no, it's not necessary. But I ought to do it anyway."

Abbot glanced at Titus, who was keenly aware that Inea might be watching, then took the top from Langton. "I know who it belongs to. I'll take care of it. You wouldn't waste government time going out of your way, would you?"

The Brink's guards shook their heads like kindergarteners agreeing with their teacher. Abbot had them totally under control. But he was working gingerly. They dared not create an illusion that was blatantly incongruous, for with time, these people would remember bits and snatches, worry at them, and compare notes. More than once in their long history on Earth luren had been caught by just such human tenacity.

Titus pointed out, "There's no reason for you folks to wait here. Get on back to your more important work."

Perplexed, Langton hesitantly agreed. Abbot made a show of resealing the crate, grinning confidently at her over his shoulder. At last she led her crew out, seeming satisfied.

"Thanks," said Titus, as he removed the lid again, still unsure why Abbot had helped except that it would be awkward for all luren if a human analyzed the "B&J Additives."

"Don't mention it." Abbot eyed the observatory where Inea worked. "Though since you have *her*—and don't tell me you don't!—I can't see why you want this garbage."

"I don't take blood from humans anymore."

"Then let me have her."

"*Let* you?"

"Well, I took Mirelle. I shouldn't cut in on you every time. Still, I helped you. Since you're not using her—"

"That's a bit of a steep price for such trivial, if timely, assistance. Here, take a couple of packets instead." He held his breath, hoping Abbot would refuse as usual. He needed all of it himself, and Abbot's only reason for accepting would be to cripple Titus' efforts to oppose him.

"Oh, Titus, where did I go wrong with you? You were so promising! But you're young, maybe it's just a phase." He shrugged. "Keep your packets. When you're tired of them, let me know. I've a couple of choice items I'd be willing to share. In a small community, it minimizes the risks."

"No thank you, Father. I can handle my own *if* I must."

90

Abbot scrutinized him again. "Yes, surprisingly enough, I think you can now. Here, let me help you get these packets into your office. You know, they must have been shipped within hours of our switching your bag in Quito? Connie must have known the minute we did it. She's pretty sharp, that one. Not that you're turning out to be so dull, either."

What is he up to? thought Titus as he gathered an armload. The sooner the packets disappeared, the less likely anyone would be to remember them. When they'd finished stuffing the packets into drawers in Titus' office, he watched Abbot reseal the crate and haul it out the door.

Then he spent the rest of the shift pondering Abbot's behavior. He was acting as if Titus were no longer a threat to his mission. Hoping that wasn't so, Titus resolved to destroy another transmitter component as soon as possible.

It wouldn't be easy. Titus had been tracking his father all over the station when he could. Sometimes Abbot noticed him, sometimes he didn't—or pretended not to. For all his efforts, Titus still didn't know where Abbot had hidden the six pieces of his transmitter, or the rebuilt piece. *Surely he's already rebuilt it.*

By now, Abbot, under cover of repairing Titus' system, could have assembled the transmitter. He might even have planted it within the shell of the probe. That would account for his confidence, for Titus didn't have clearance to go out to the probe hangar, and so far he hadn't gone out by using Influence.

However, placing the transmitter so long before launch would increase the chance of a human finding it, so Titus doubted he'd done it yet. His confidence was probably just a ploy to keep Titus off balance, to keep him asking irrelevant questions and wasting energy seeking answers, diverting his attention. But from what? The sleeping luren? The cloning project? The language project? What exactly had Abbot recovered from *Kylyd's* recorders?

Why did Abbot want the computer fixed so fast? To pirate time on it for himself? Titus made a mental note to set some traps in his system. If he were clever, Titus might be able to bleed off Abbot's data while Abbot thought he was getting away with pirating. But that was a longshot. Nobody beat Abbot in a computer duel. Still, Titus would try. He'd beaten his father in other ways he'd never expected to.

But the nagging question was why did Abbot want Titus supplied with blood? To keep him from prospecting among the humans?

Titus straightened up from examining a technician's work. Oblivious to the technician's apprehensive expression, he watched Abbot checking connections. Even way across the lab, the power of him throbbed through Titus. Abbot wasn't starving. And suddenly, it hit him. Abbot didn't want him to find out *who* was on his string.

A shock washed through Titus as his mind leaped into high gear, leaving logic behind. Abbot *knew* he had broken into Mirelle's file. Abbot *assumed* Titus wanted to know what Abbot had learned from her. His feigned confidence was to focus Titus' attention away from Mirelle and Abbot's other stringers, to make him wonder why Abbot felt he'd already beaten Titus.

It made sense, but didn't quite fit Abbot's devious nature. *And he knows me! He's always manipulated me.* All at once, he recalled Abbot staring at Inea then scrutinizing Titus. It came to him with crystal clarity. *It's his unMarked that count!* He had to find them and check their files.

That might be more important than the transmitter. After all, the probe would not go for months yet; the sleeper could be wakened anytime.

Absently, Titus praised the apprehensive technician's work while his plans jelled. He'd mount an all-out, obvious effort to find another transmitter part, and, in the process, he'd sift the station's population for Abbot's humans.

Later, as Abbot finally took his official departure from the lab he warned Titus, cloaking his words, "Look to that girl of yours. You may have to silence her whether you want to or not. I don't like the way she's been watching us."

Titus glanced at where Inea was sitting tailor fashion before an access hatch jigsawing three boards into a space barely big enough for two. "I'll tend to it, don't worry."

"I do worry. Listen, Titus, Mark her. There are two of us here. If you want her, Mark her." He sounded friendly.

It seemed, for an instant, like reasonable advice. Then he met Inea's eyes. *Never! She's not a possession, not an object.* He didn't want a stringer, he wanted a wife, and that was something Abbot would never understand. "I'll keep her quiet."

The moment the door closed behind Abbot, Inea dropped her task and came to Titus, demanding, "What in the world—well, the moon—has been going on here all day?"

"What do you think?"

"Espionage. For some reason, you're afraid of that man. I think he knows you've been spying."

Titus chuckled. "Spying?" *Diabolical woman!*

"The Project's a bone of contention among the Sovereignties." She cocked her head. "What did you smuggle in right under the Brink's guards' noses? Plastic explosive?"

He threw his head back and laughed. Everyone looked at him. He waved them off. "She has a great sense of humor!"

To Inea, he said, "Come into my office." He led the way, blurring their exit in everyone else's minds.

Even before she'd closed the door, Titus whirled and hissed indignantly, "Don't you think I have better sense than to fool with explosives with all that vacuum out there?"

"You could plant it on the probe—set to blow it up out in space. According to the news, there are idiots who'd do it if they could, and rob all mankind of this chance. How do I know you aren't one of those? People change."

Hurt more than he could believe, he turned away, clenching his fists. "I'll show you, if you'll promise just to believe your eyes. Believe in me just that much, and I'll show you what I smuggled in." *Abbot will kill me.*

"I guess I owe you that much."

He dug into his bottom desk drawer, found a packet, and tossed it to her, proud of his mastery of the gravity as it arced directly into her hands. She kneaded the packet and read the label. "I don't understand."

"False label. That's the blood substitute I live on."

She tallied her observations of him. "You've been starving yourself, waiting for this shipment!"

He shook his head. "Just short rations. I was worried, though. Another week—" He shrugged.

"Who sent it to you?"

"A friend."

"Your kind have infiltrated the whole Project!"

"One shipping clerk does not a spy ring make."

"Shipping clerk?"

"You going to start a witch hunt for my friend?"

She thought about that. Her answer, when it came, was low voiced but certain. "No."

"Good. Then I'll introduce you when we get back."

She hefted the packet of cloned blood. "I hope your friend shares your dietary inclinations."

"Yes."

There was a knock on the door. Titus beckoned and Inea tossed the packet back to him. Stuffing it into the drawer, he called, "Come in!"

It was Shimon, carrying a small black box with cables on both ends. "Titus, I was checking the empty crate before trashing it, and I found this in the bottom packing—oh, Inea, I'm sorry to interrupt—" He flushed, and Titus realized that the delay in responding to the knock implied he'd interrupted an intimate moment.

Inea said, "That's all right. What have you found?"

"Wish I knew." He slid it across the desk to Titus. "No manufacturer's mark, no label. Looks like one of Abbot's fabrications. But he labels his stuff."

Not Abbot's fabrication, Connie's! A replacement for the communicator Abbot ruined. Somehow, Abbot missed it. And Abbot thought Connie was swift in getting the blood here! She must have sent this before Abbot wrecked mine.

Titus glanced at Inea. He didn't want to manipulate Shimon in front of her. Without Influence, he said, "It's probably not important. I'll query Luna Station and take care of it."

"Well, you're so busy. And I'm curious. Why don't I handle it for you?" He reached across the desk.

Titus snatched up the box. "Oh, it's *my* job to hassle with stuff like this. You've more urgent things to do."

"It's no hassle. My job is winding down. We'll finish installing and testing tomorrow and be ready for a run by the next day. But your job is just beginning—"

There was no choice. Backing his words with Influence, narrowed and aimed only at Shimon, Titus said, "Since we got all the parts we expected, this is probably just a piece of trash somebody threw into the crate by accident. You did right to bring it to me. I'll take care of it. You've more important work." *Connie would be ashamed of me. I've made a complete hash of fielding both her shipments!*

Very slowly, Shimon recited, "I—have more important work. Yes." To himself, he added, *"Ken. Yesh li avodah."*

"You've been doing excellent work," said Titus with Influence. "You'll get a citation, and I'll put you up for a raise because you never give me any arguments, just results."

Shimon withdrew his hand. "No arguments."

Titus smiled. "Thank you, Shimon."

"Yes, sir." Turning, he nodded to Inea and left.

As the door closed, she breathed, "My God."

"I didn't want to do that to him, but—"

"You didn't have *his* consent."

"No."

"What is that thing?"

He told her a half-truth. "Part of my communications link. So I can signal when I need more . . . blood. I didn't know it was in that crate. Shimon shouldn't have found it." She stared at him as if he were a new sort of bug. "I didn't harm him. He feels very proud of himself. And I will put him in for a citation and a raise. He's earned it." As she considered that, he groped for a diversion. "If I let you taste my concoction, will that prove it all to you?"

Her eyes shifted to the closed door, then back to Titus. "After what you did to that stubborn Israeli, yeah, I think so. If that stuff is really blood—"

"It's pretty close." He thought of the packets hidden about the office. Abbot might expect him to leave most of it here because there was too much to carry in one trip. He might plan to return and abscond with the rest, putting the lie to Titus' theories. He weighed the matter, and decided he'd rather have the blood than proof of Abbot's intentions. Besides, he didn't want to risk Maintenance finding it.

He offered, "Help me carry these home, and I'll show you how it makes up into a very good imitation of real blood."

He found four large net bags and lined them with spare clothing, then stuffed them with packets, putting the black box, which was useless until the computer was up, in one bag. They'd seem to be carrying laundry, which would reinforce Shimon's impression that they were lovers. The rumor would be all over the station within three days. And coming right after he'd demonstrated to Abbot his control of Inea, it would reinforce the impression he wanted Abbot to have, that he was only using Inea, casually establishing his "cover" as a human, just as Abbot had taught him.

Knowing Titus the way he did, Abbot would never believe he'd expose a human he cared for by establishing any public connection between them. And ordinarily, Titus wouldn't. But he had to play out the charade he'd started. Later, he could appear to "drop" Inea, thus blending in with the social tides of the humans around them. He just had to be sure not to give Abbot any more reason to suspect.

"Real blood," muttered Inea as they packed. "There's a difference between this stuff and real blood?"

"Yes, but it can be supplemented. I'll show you."

By the time they reached his apartment, he was almost faint with a hunger made acute by the promise of a complete meal. He had to conceal his hand as he opened the door, for his fingers were shaking with his need for haste.

But when the door opened, they were bombarded with sound. "Oh, I left the vidcom on! Turn it off, will you, please?"

As he went to the sink, Inea drifted to the vidcom and studied the controls uncertainly. Hers was different. "The silver stud on the far right!" he called, drawing water into his pitcher and putting it into the microwave to heat.

"Wait a minute!" she said. "Come look at this."

He was in absolutely no mood for the news, but he went. The screen showed a milling throng—a riot in progress. As Titus came into the zone where the sound focused, he made out the words. " . . . anti-Hail terrorists in Africa today. In London, the Humanists claim credit for the catastrophic breakdown of Project Hail's astrogational computer. Titus Shiddehara, the department head in charge of that unique computer, could not be reached, but Dr. Colby, Hail's on-site director, claims the breakdown was due to a defect in the innovative hardware, not sabotage.

"Elsewhere: United Europe. World Sovereignties Police have caught an alleged assassin headed for Project Hail. The man, a native of Kenya, had obtained a plumber's job on the Project with a false identity. Director Carol Colby was identified as his target.

"Moscow. Chief Astronomer Arkady Abramovitch has testified that he alone is responsible for the attempted sabotage of all eight broadcast antenna arrays on the moon. According to Abramovitch, there is no international conspiracy to stop Project Hail. His objective, he claims, was to demonstrate how lax security left the solar system's entire communications network vulnerable in the face of the potential alien invasion Project Hail is inviting. Abramovitch claims he never intended the bombs to go off.

"This just in from Lesser Houston."

The scene shifted to dusty buildings scintillating in the Texas sun and cut to a woman at a mahogany desk. A sign appeared. "Project Hail Chair, Dr. Irene Nagel."

"Dr. Nagel, what would happen to Project Hail if the assassination attempt aimed at Colby had succeeded?"

"Not much. Dr. Colby's ability as an administrator is nowhere more evident than in the fact that she is very replaceable. Her work is organized so that any of several qualified people could step into her shoes instantly."

"Assassinating the director would not stop the project?"

"No, indeed—"

The reporter cut her off. "Thank you, Dr. Nagel. Now back to Paris for the weather."

Inea punched the off stud. "What do you make of that?"

"Fanatics will stop at nothing."

"Think! If the terrorists now believe Carol isn't a good target, where'll they strike next? At an irreplaceable scientist—" Her expression shifted to wild surmise. "You're not an *assassin,* are you? That isn't why you went after that Brink's woman—"

The microwave bleeped. Testily, he snapped, "*You* think! If I wanted to stop this project, I could just quit. I'm more likely to be the next target! How many others do you know who can do my job here?"

She answered the rhetorical question quite seriously, "The only other who had anything like your expertise in finding stars with planets—stars which might have spawned life on their planets—was Emil Tuttenheim, and he died nearly a decade ago."

He nodded, "Poverty stricken and depressed because his work attracted no funding. Emil was my teacher—and my idol. Look, I'm sorry I yelled at you."

"That's all right. I know you're no assassin, whatever else you may or may not be. I don't know why I said that."

He nodded his acceptance and turned to the microwave. "Look over here." He extracted the pitcher and thrust it into her hands. "Just over body temperature." Setting it on the counter, he opened a packet, dumped the crystals into the water, and stirred.

The odor almost broke his imposed calm. He fumbled down two glasses and filled one. Raising it, he said, "Just to prove it's not poisoned." He gulped it all down, trying not to let his ecstasy seem too apparent. Then he half filled the other glass and handed it to her, hoping she wouldn't drink any. He wanted to lick up every drop.

She held it close to her chest, wrapping both hands around it as if it were brandy, sniffed, wrinkled her nose, then tipped a bit into her mouth. With a strangled noise, she said, "It's awful. But I guess it tastes like blood."

When she handed the glass back to him, a thrill danced up his arm. The blood had absorbed a hint of her ectoplasm. It was the best known medium for the nonmaterial substance luren called ectoplasm. As a scientist, he was loath to use the term. It shouldn't exist—but it did. And he needed it as much as he needed blood. The dead, freeze-dried blood would sponge up ectoplasm from any human it touched. He savored every drop, forgetting to control himself, for, charged even faintly, it was more satisfying than any elixir of the gods.

When it was gone, he noticed her watching, and wondered if he dared. His hunger finally overwhelmed his judgment. He refilled his glass and handed it to her. "Hold it to you. Taste it again if you want."

"Why? It tastes like blood."

"There are differences. This doesn't come from a human. It isn't alive. I need that life as you need vitamins as well as calories. Please. It will cost you nothing."

Self-consciously, she cradled the glass, sniffing at it, then examined him over the rim.

Very gradually, her whole being became suffused with a glow that sent tremors of fear-laced pleasure through him. No human had ever looked at him like this before. But it was instantly addictive. He couldn't live without it now.

"Oh, dear God, Titus, what I've put you through! I'm so sorry! I didn't know."

She believes! He dared to move closer, drawn like a moth to a flame. Dreading yet another rejection, he watched in dismay as his hands rose to cup her cheeks. But she didn't shrink from him.

Hardly aware, he lowered his lips to the glass and drank from between her two hands. It wasn't the same as taking human blood. Yet it was enough.

He raised his head, not hiding what she had done to him. He couldn't speak. He had only his hands to convey to her the depth of his reverence and surrender.

But she seemed to understand. For one long held breath, he thought she was going to kiss him. He was already aroused beyond bearing remembering that one voluntary kiss she had bestowed upon him. Then she shuddered and drew back.

"If you'll brush your teeth, I'll kiss you."

He lifted the glass from her fingers. "And more than kiss? Promise me more."

"More. Everything. Hurry."

When he returned, she was in his bed, wearing nothing but a curl of sheet shading her breasts. Absently, he shed his clothes on the way. Scooping her to him, he sank into the ecstasy of it and discovered his own driving urgency. She matched him move for move, as if she, too, hungered. He'd never had such a human, and it brought him to himself. *Inea!*

He sought control. *No. She has given me what no other has ever freely offered—not just ectoplasm but love. This is for her.*

"What's wrong? Don't I please you?"

She's never been with a man who cared for her pleasure! The realization was like a cold shock. *Oh, Inea!* Humans could use humans more cruelly than luren ever did. He rolled her over onto her stomach and whispered in her ear. "Remember you asked me if it could be better with me than with . . . a human? And I said I'd make it special for you. Well, I will."

He went to work, using the skills garnered over twenty years of more casual encounters, less fully informed consent. He'd used Influence to cast a glamour for his women, but he always made sure that what he took and what he gave balanced out, and in the process he'd learned the intricacies of the female response. Regarding Inea as a strange kind of virgin who didn't know the power of her own body, he used his vampire senses to track her responses, but never focused Influence. What was between them would be real.

When he eased her onto her back, she was flushed and beautiful, hypnotized by her inward sensations. But she touched his arousal, feeling his moist tremors as he fought his body. "Why are you doing this to yourself?"

That she would be so mystified nearly tore his heart in half. "Because you've earned the glory due a woman."

She pulled him down. "But I'm ready."

"No you're not. Not by half. I don't enjoy taking a woman before she's ready." Never mind that his human body wanted it and no more nonsense.

She kissed a line up his abdomen, threatening to drive him over the edge. Her whispered words tickled his flesh. "Let's just see how ready I am."

She moved and his sensitive organ was almost enveloped before he realized he couldn't endure much of that and still bring her to a higher pitch. He pushed her away with a gasp.

"Titus, what is the matter with you!"

Her sharp frustration bit into him, and nothing but whole truth would do. "I want this to be perfect for you. Everything between us is real—and I'll never lie to you. Never. I said what you gave me would cost you nothing—and so it shall be. If you let me do this for you properly, all I took when you let me drink will be restored and more. Otherwise, if you give to me repeatedly, you'll grow weak and depressed, and I'll hate myself. Even with just this once, you'd feel a drain on your vitality."

Her features, wiped clean of the years by her rapture, froze as a new reality intruded. "You really *are* a vampire."

He kissed the base of her neck and traced a line up to her lips. "Yes. I live in your love and wither without it. Let me show you the gift I have for you, if only you'll be patient enough to receive it. Please. Let me."

"If you don't hurry, you'll have to start over."

He let his kiss tell her how much further they could go together. He took his time, following the body currents, stimulating each and every bit of skin and deep muscle until the currents of orgasm would move unobstructed by tension. As he worked his last devotions, he felt the intense surge of ectoplasm, as if energy had come into her from nowhere and she had made it living substance for him to feed on.

It was magic. He dared think no further than that. "Now, you're ready!"

In that deep penetration and matching of even deeper rhythms, his body soaked up the excess substance she poured forth, and the liberating joy of it drove him over the top and into the headlong plunge of release.

It was the greatest perfection he had ever achieved.

NINE

"Titus?"

"Hmm?"

"I think it's morning."

"What?" He sat up, disoriented. The clock said he'd slept ten hours without even rigging his wires around the bed. His clothes were strewn across the floor. On the sink, the glasses and pitcher sat, dry and crusted.

Inea had one arm flung carelessly over her face, her eyes buried in the crook of her elbow. The ends of her fingers brushed his shoulder. They were shaking. He kissed her palm but his touch didn't trigger the expected response. It wasn't just his sated condition, either. "What's wrong?"

"Nothing. Just a nightmare. I hate watching the news before bedtime. Damn Abramovitch, anyway."

Abramovitch? It was an incredible effort to dredge up the association, but then he had it: the Russian who wanted to prove Earth was vulnerable to attack from outer space aliens. *Her xenophobia!* Cold sweat broke out all over him. Had he misjudged her? If she hadn't changed her attitude, though, why was she on the Project at all?

Inea turned to sprawl over the edge of the bed examining the apartment's master controls on the bedstand.

"Do I use the shower first?" she asked. "And how do I charge the water bill to my apartment?"

Alarm lanced through him. Abbot could trace her to him through bills. All Abbot knew for sure right now was that Titus would like to feed on Inea. He had no idea how very much Inea meant to Titus, and so if casual checking turned up no other connection, Abbot would have no reason to look closer at Inea, no reason to consider using her as a weapon against Titus, and thus no reason to discover that Titus had broken the Law of Blood by not silencing her with Influence.

Striving to seem casual, he palmed sleep out of his eyes. "Never mind, my water allotment is generous. Go ahead and shower. The boss can be late."

She rolled off the bed gathering her neatly piled clothing. "Actually, the boss is too zonked to move."

"The boss is replete for the first time since leaving Earth. Maybe for the first time ever." He lay back and flung his elbow over his eyes as she dialed the lights up. "Just let me enjoy it another five minutes."

She passed the mess on the sink without a glance. Squinting under his elbow, he watched her, fascinated by the effect lunar gravity had on her buttocks and breasts, lazily toying with the idea of writing the equations to describe that tantalizing motion: a *Song of Songs* written in physics, celebrating the similarity between the surging foment of stellar plasma and the incendiary effect of semifluid flesh.

He drifted into the abstracted state in which he did physics, letting the delicious relaxation steal over him.

It seemed only moments later when Inea emerged, dressed, combing her sleek wet hair and carrying something in one hand. "I borrowed your comb. I'll bring my things up here tonight—" She saw the mess on the sink. "And when I move in, we'll have to do something about this sort of thing."

Abbot. How can I warn her about Abbot? If Abbot ever did investigate her mind, he'd find that Titus had endangered not just himself, but his own father and all luren, by letting her go unsilenced. Worse yet, if he so much as hinted that Abbot was any sort of danger to him or to her, she'd immediately take steps to investigate Abbot and so attract his attention. But if Titus threw enough of a scare into her to keep her from deviling Abbot, then she'd betray herself through sheer nervousness. No, he didn't dare say anything to her if he valued her life—and his own.

When he didn't answer, she turned, her expression mirroring Titus' consternation. With wild alarm edging her voice, she said, "I can't believe this is just another one-night stand!"

Before he knew it, he was off the bed and hugging her. "No! This is forever. Permanent. Exclusive. I'll marry you—any vows you want—as soon as we get back to Earth."

She stiffened. "Why wait? Or at least, why not live together if we're sleeping together?"

Searching frantically for a way to say it, he led her to the table and sat her down. "Wherever I am, there's always danger. *Always.* If people notice I'm—odd—I might not know until it's gone too far. It happens to those of my blood, and most often in small communities. If it happens to me here, I don't want you hurt."

Absently, she put a small brown vial down on the table, his blood pressure medication. "What makes you think I wouldn't stand up for you now that I know the truth?"

"I wouldn't want you to. When things get that bad, anyone who defends one of us gets burned too. I don't want to risk you."

"*You* don't want to risk *me?* If you think I'm going to wait until Earth to do this again, you're very—"

"Just until tonight. Your place. Okay? Nobody will know I'm there except you. And you'll know. I promise."

He kissed her, but as he got involved, she pulled back, studying him. "I'll be late for work. What'll my boss say?"

"He won't say a thing," he teased. "But your boss's boss may scream at us all."

"Carol? She never screams." She extricated herself and moved to the door. "But Shimon will yell at us if we don't finish tomorrow. Besides, what would Abbot say if we blew it now? He'll go down in history as a genius for reconstructing this system in record time."

"Of course. Records are important." He moved to kiss her temple, but she withdrew slightly. *What's the matter with her?*

She cocked her head to one side, studying him in that way that made him nervous. Then she tossed her wet hair back and added archly, "Besides, you had me train to do this job for Shimon, and I'm going to do it! Just remember *that* the next time you come up with a brilliant idea to send me away. *I* don't waste training, even training I don't need."

With that, she spun out the door. A moment later she popped back in and added, "Eight-hundred Greenwich, on the nose. B.Y.O.B. *I'm* getting pizza and beer." And she was gone.

B.Y.O.B. could mean Bring Your Own Blood. Her quip made him smile despite his sudden uncertainty about her. At least Abbot didn't know what she meant to him, and she didn't know what to make of Abbot. But how long could he keep it that way? Scheduling time with Inea without making her suspicious about his absences, as he chased around looking for Abbot's unMarked stringers, would be a colossal challenge.

When he arrived at the lab, the reassembly of the system was well begun. Shimon had set a pace that both allowed step-by-step testing and kept up the progress rate, spurring everyone on. The man definitely had earned a raise, as had his whole staff. Knowing the thought would get lost in the affairs facing him, Titus called Colby immediately.

"Oh, Dr. Shiddehara!" answered an assistant. He was a lanky, lantern-jawed Black with a vaguely Oriental cast to his features. Titus had heard he'd given up a high post with Consumer's Union to take this job. "I've been trying to reach you. Dr. Colby wants to speak with you."

Uh-oh. "That's good. Put her on."

After a long wait, she came on screen flushed and breathless. She might well have been screaming at somebody. "There you are, Titus. It's about time."

"Yes, indeed. I—"

"Don't talk, just listen. You've been following the press coverage on that assassin? Well, that wasn't the first infiltrator *we* caught. But the publicity has impressed the highest government circles with the size of the anti-Project movement. We're going to lose our appropriation, and our scientific reputations, unless we convince the public we're spending their money wisely. So Nagel was forced to accept terms—I've fought, but I've had to capitulate, too.

"Twenty reporters will be here day after tomorrow to tour the station and report directly to the people. If we handle it right, this nonsense will die down, and the terrorists will be criminals, not heroes. But if we look wasteful or deceitful, that's the end of the Project.

"Now, I need your help, Titus. You're right at the focus of all this because of your computer's cost overrun. It must be up and running day after tomorrow—and it's got to do something spectacular they can take pictures of."

Titus digested that. Abbot must have had wind of this days ago— and that was why he was so eager to help. Abbot, whose mission was to send an SOS., had nearly scuttled the entire Project with his retaliation at Titus that first day.

Abbot the invincible. Ha!

"What are you so happy about?" asked Colby.

Think quick! "Carol, let me get Shimon on the line."

He buzzed Shimon's desk without response, then resorted to the oldest method of office communication. He stuck his head out the door and called, "Shimon! Pick up on Two!"

When he got back to the vidcom, the screen was split, showing Carol briefing Shimon. In the end, Shimon studied Titus' image deadpan. The silence stretched until Titus said, "Shimon, I know we won't need Nandoha's help on this one." His eyes met Shimon's. Shimon knew Titus had fought Abbot's presence as much as he could.

Titus could almost see the wheels turning in the man's mind. He had swallowed his resentment of Abbot's arrogance with professional stoicism, and he even respected Abbot's ability. But he disliked the man intensely. He had, however, grasped early on that Colby's primary measure of an employee's value was the employee's loyalty to the immediate supervisor as well as to the Project. Nodding at last, Shimon declared, "No problem, Dr. Colby. We finish tonight, even we go into overtime. We test tomorrow and set up something visual for the press."

Colby beamed. "I see why Titus has such faith in you. You give me a good show day after tomorrow, Shimon, and you'll get a big raise, retroactive."

"You got it."

Colby signed off, and a moment later Shimon stormed into the office. "*Mochrotayim!* She's got to be kidding!" He paced a furious circle, one hand on his head.

"Thanks for backing me, Shimon. I know it's going to be hard. Just tell me what you need and you'll have it."

He paused, hands on hips. "Titus, if you didn't sent Inea to be trained for this, we'd never make it. Can I tell the crew they'll get double-time for overtime tonight if they'll stay until we've finished?"

"Yes, that's a good idea."

"It could be all night. Just one defective part—"

"I know. Meanwhile, I'll get a demo program written."

Shimon pursed his fingers at the ceiling in the typical Israeli gesture. "*Rega, rega!* Inea's project! It would be perfect! For fun, she wrote this program for a holographic projection of the Taurus region—complete with an animated, stomping thoroughbred bull. The thing rotates so you can view our sun from the other side of the constellation. Then you get an animated closeup of each of the stars—she said it's just a toy because she used ancient data on the starspots. I don't pretend to understand it all. Ask her."

He nodded. "Great, but do we have a projector for it?"

"No, but before the chemists arrived we were using their tank. Maybe we can borrow it again?"

The chemists used a three-dimensional viewing tank to manipulate complex organic molecules. "Is it in color?"

"Yes, and so was Inea's program. She added that last."

It would make an impressive if irrelevant demonstration. "Okay, we'll make a couple dozen copies of a broadcast quality video and be sure Inea's copyright is on it."

It took Titus three hours to organize everything, but at last he took Connie's black box out to the lab. Inea and half the crew were in the observatory, arguing over the schematics, steaming coffee mugs abandoned behind them.

Working fast, cloaked by a minimum of Influence, Titus spliced the communicator into its circuit and replaced the boards that surrounded it, hiding it from view. If it didn't malfunction in the first test, he'd get his message out the first time they contacted Earth. He had already reinforced the entire crew's blindness to the black box. Only Inea could see it, and she wouldn't say anything.

He returned to his office and coded his message to Connie into his desk unit. The moment this system linked to the Project's system in Houston, Sydney, or Beer Sheva, the black box would call out the text from his desk unit and send it to a similar black box on the other end. He only hoped that one of Connie's people, not a Tourist, would pick it up.

In his report, he apprised Connie of his blood situation, and tersely reminded her that, despite his successes to date, he couldn't handle Abbot alone. He also warned her of the clandestine Project, and sketched his plans.

He wished it were all as simple as it sounded.

Idly watching Inea, all he wanted to do was write poetry in physics and make love. But he shook himself out of it, and breezed out of the lab, telling everyone he was going to the ship. Then he went in search of Abbot's stringers.

He'd already checked everyone who ever had access to his own lab and had found no trace of Abbot's meddling. He hadn't expected to. Now he strolled the halls, examining every passerby. He searched refectories and snack bars, and detoured through the gym. His most valuable quarry would be someone Abbot had Influenced but left unMarked, and that was hard to spot. So he moved slowly, and triggered belligerent reactions by staring. *Mirelle could do this without upsetting people!*

With nothing to show for the hour, he headed for *Kylyd*.

From early in his post-doctoral years, he had learned the only way to keep up on the branches of a complex project was with frequent personal appearances. The other department heads did the same, so he was not at all conspicuous.

Having legitimate business on the ship, he donned his suit openly and accompanied a group of workers on the ride out. While the sun had been up, he had dreaded his open trips, but now they were in shadow again.

He wandered about the ship, unsure if he'd recognize Abbot's Mark on a suited human. The life-presence was blocked by the suit, but he had Influenced suited humans. *Something* wasn't blocked by the insulation. *Fractured particles dancing in the moonlight, speeding to oblivion.*

Poetry stirred in his soul, poetry and magic, magic and Inea. *There's no such thing as magic. There's a rational explanation for everything.* Sure. He clomped up a slanted floor through a mangled airlock with an arch cut in it.

He squatted to peer at it. The last time he'd been here, they'd despaired of cutting that metal. Progress.

"Something wrong, Dr. Shiddehara?"

The suit beside him bore a familiar technician's name. He rose and asked about the cutting while he studied the man.

"Oh, Dr. Gold did that yesterday with the magnetic scissors he made in the Biomed lab. You apply a shear planar magnetic field and the stuff falls apart. I guess it's not exactly a metal—well, that's not my field."

He bore no trace of Abbot's touch, but Titus' neck prickled. Biomed. That was one place he couldn't wander freely, but Abbot could. "Magnetic scissors. Fascinating." *Next thing you know, they'll make a sonic screwdriver!*

"I saw Dr. Gold going that way," the technician said, pointing. "He loves to explain it, but I don't think he's found anyone who understands what he's talking about yet."

Titus followed the man's directions and climbed into a wide place where bulkheads had been wrenched open on impact. Two technicians were wrestling a device that looked like a scissors large enough to snip down a maple tree. When they had it positioned, the scissors sliced through the twisted bulkhead. and they cautiously removed the large panel.

Through the new opening, Titus saw Abner Gold's and Carol Colby's suits, and a smaller suit with a Biomed blazon.

Gold gesticulated so emphatically his feet left the deck, and he stumbled. Titus picked his way toward them, mindful that sharp edges could damage his suit, and searched the communications channels until he found Abner's voice.

". . . Sisi, that's not what you told me! Colby, she's lying, but I know what I know. You owe me *answers*. There are certain things I won't be a party to!"

"Calm down, Dr. Gold," admonished the Director. "We are all under a lot of pressure, and it's going to get worse, if we're forced to work in a spotlight. In a few days—"

"Few days! *Now* or I quit! Think about that, Colby! Can you afford to have me quit after what I've accomplished?"

107

"Abner, no one is indispensable. And your attitude displays a certain lack of loyalty which—"

"Loyalty to what? Or doesn't that matter to you? You just do what you get paid to do and never think about—"

"Dr. Gold, you are hereby terminated, your security clearances revoked. Your final pay and—"

"Terminated? You can't fire me. I just quit." He whirled and stalked away, coming toward Titus.

Titus stopped him. He was burning with curiosity about what had ticked Gold off, but he only asked, "Abner, are you sure you want to do this? Think! I didn't hear what it's about, but this Project is history in the making."

Gold took a deep breath and straightened, looking at Titus with a strained smile. "Thank you, Titus, but I stayed up all night considering it all."

"Well, *I* want a copy of your paper on the magnetic scissors. Brilliant work."

Gold beamed. "I'll see you get one."

"After the reporters get through with my lab, I'll come see you off. I assume you'll be leaving with them." *Maybe then he'll tell me what's so terrible he can't countenance it.*

His face fell. "I suppose." Abstracted, he pulled loose. "Good luck, Titus. You're a good man."

The offhand compliment made Titus feel inexplicably good as he turned toward the group watching them. Interestingly, he could perceive the misting pattern of Abbot's Influence around Colby, despite her lack of a Mark. The same signature appeared in the aura around the Biomed tech.

He went up to them. "I'm sorry, Carol, I didn't mean to eavesdrop."

"That isn't the first time I've fired someone, but—damn, I wish I hadn't had to do that!" Deeply disturbed, she grasped at formalities. "Oh, I'm sorry, Titus, have you met Sisi Mintraub? She runs the Biomed maintenance shop. Sisi, this is the famous Dr. Shiddehara."

"Honored," she offered in a sweet soprano.

"Likewise," replied Titus. "Medical hardware, huh? Would you happen to know where the chemists' tank is now?"

"It's not my jurisdiction, but I saw it yesterday. Why?"

He told Carol about the demonstration idea, and she nodded. "Sounds good. Sisi, tell whoever has the tank that if they're not using it, astrophysics needs it for the demo."

"I'll tell them." She flashed a dazzling smile at Titus. "But chemists are a possessive lot."

Colby added, "If necessary, tell them to call me."

When Mintraub had gone, Colby prompted, "Fill me in on this brilliant idea. I think it's the best any department's come up with so far."

"It's from Inea and Shimon, really," he protested, and elaborated on Inea's visuals. "What worries me is that it's not relevant to our work."

"It does *look* relevant, though. On the other hand, you're right, some of the reporters know some science. Could you come up with something *they'd* appreciate?"

"Well, that's what I came out here for. To see if there's anything new on the lighting system. With the system up, I could use a standard star catalogue to pick out some stars with the correct spectrum, at least show them how it's going to be done when I have all the data."

"There was nothing new as of yesterday. But it's worth checking. Lindholm, Rubens, and that Dutch woman whose name I can never remember were down by what we think is the drive chamber. They found a light panel they suspect is still operative, but they won't admit to knowing anything."

"Can't fault them for being cautious. Nothing about this ship follows expectations. Magnetic scissors! Where did Abner ever get that idea?"

"Titus, forgive me, but I don't want to talk about Abner now. And I'm late for an engineers' meeting. If they can solve just one of the power-supply mysteries, we can energize that light panel and discover its output spectrum. Our power just burns them out."

As she walked off, Titus went to chase down the intact light panel and see what could be learned from it.

Hours later, Titus returned to the lab, with very little to show for his afternoon but the appearance of the chemists' tank. Shimon had ordered pizza brought in. People ate while monitoring screens as the test programs ran.

Inea waved Titus over. "I got my pizza. But I've *no* idea when we'll be finished. There're a million glitches."

"Well, look, I'm glad you volunteered to stick with this tonight. Afterwards, well, we'll reschedule afterwards."

"I hope so," she replied firmly.

He was already hungry, but he had to keep his mind off it. "Carol is pleased with your demo." He related his encounter with the Director.

"I didn't get any new spectral data, but I'm going to go work up something using 'best guess' data based on the work done decades ago on the first orbital telescopes and some of the guesses based on clues found in the ship. I can run a simulation for the reporters using that, and just show how we'll plug in the actual data when we get it." He had most of it set up on his PDA.

"Sounds good. Want some help?" She started to rise.

"You're more valuable where you are." Cloaking the words, he let his voice drop to a caress. "What I *want* has little to do with it. Later, Inea, I'll fulfill my promise."

With icy calm, she asked, "What am I to you, a decorative possession or a person?"

"That's unfair. Have I ever given you cause to—"

"Yes." She kept her voice low, but ferocious. "This morning you wanted to protect me, and expected I'd stand by and let you get ripped apart by a mob rather than speaking up for you. And your only reason was *you* didn't want to risk *me,* as if I were an object you own. Now you order me to a technician's job when I could be better employed doing astronomy. Okay, I have to sub here because of the reporters. But you didn't know they'd be coming when you sent me off to learn this stuff. Whyever you did that to me, it wasn't to advance my career. It wasn't from professional respect. So I rubbed your nose in it a little this morning, flouncing off like that, but I didn't really mean it and it *was* in private. Now, right in the middle of the lab, you start telling me what you *really* want me for. And it isn't to write astronomy programs. A *person* writes astronomy programs."

Stunned, Titus shook his head.

"Person or object," she reiterated. "That's the rock on which all my other relationships foundered. I want it straight from the beginning. What am I to you?"

"I don't want to make love to a decorative possession. I've never understood men who did. You don't know how it turned me on to discover your toy program may save this Project's funding. You don't know how I've searched for a *person* like you, but you're one of a kind. I should have known that. I should have gone back to you years ago."

Her lips trembled and her eyes sparkled. "I hope you mean that. I hope you know what it means to say that."

"You'll teach me. And I promise—as soon as this job is done, you'll be back in the observatory. I never wanted to send you away. It was an administrative decision, and you did admit you needed some space to think it all through."

"Titus, I'm not going to kiss you here. No matter what. Understand? It wouldn't be professional."

"I suppose that's best. I'll see you late tonight."

After that, he couldn't concentrate on his model calculation. It was as boring as concocting exams for undergrad courses. It simply wasn't real. But Inea's presence out in the lab was so real, he couldn't keep his mind off it. He wondered if she'd consider that treating her like an object—*like an orl*. It was the most disturbing thought he'd ever had.

When he'd finished his program, he used the Brink's code key to check on Sisi Mintraub. He found nothing of great interest except that she was in charge of the equipment that kept the dormant luren in an isolated and chill environment.

He could see why Abbot cultivated her with as light a touch as he used on Colby. It would be dangerous if she became suspicious, but even worse was the way Security monitored her. They'd notice any inconsistent behavior.

He looked up Sisi's apartment number. It was in the same dome as the shopping mall. She was the only one of Abbot's spies he'd yet found, and since she wasn't Marked, it was no crime for him to use Influence on her.

From his desk, he gazed out his door at Inea working beside Shimon. If he Influenced Sisi, would Abbot retaliate on Inea? But Inea bore no trace of Titus' Influence. Abbot couldn't conceive of any luren feeding on a human without Influence. *That might be all that will save her if Abbot discovers I've been at one of his humans.*

Still—if he Marked Inea, Abbot couldn't touch her. *No. I won't Mark her without her consent.* For that, he'd have to tell her the whole story so she'd know why she had to be Marked. But he was scared of losing her. It was worse since he'd tasted what they might have. But which was the greater risk, Abbot taking her, or him alienating her by being too hasty? Either way, he'd lose her. To protect her, he'd try to approach Mintraub without arousing Abbot's suspicions. *At least that's not treating Inea like a possession!*

Decisively, he went to Mintraub's apartment, but she was out. Deciding he'd rather go hungry until Inea was free than go home and drink dead blood, he went to the shopping mall.

The lift doors opened on a curving mezzanine with an arch of sky blue overhead. Large, lush green bushes were set along the promenade.

A sparkling fountain splashed over moon rock at the far end. Leaning over the railing, he saw a Skychef doughnut shop with tables set on a transparent floor, lit from beneath. He didn't believe his eyes when he saw the first fish. Then a school of large ones flashed by, and he realized he was looking into the breeding tank where Skychef bred all the fresh fish served on the station.

He went down the broad steps, aware that the architects of the Station had designed the public areas to be lavish and the private rooms spartan so people would socialize.

He browsed through some shops. He had heard about the prices, but he was surprised at the small selection, and how the stock was crammed into the tiny shops. In one store, robes hung from shoe boxes stacked up to the ceiling. In another, tables were crammed with swimsuits and underwear. Under the table, shirts were stacked by color and size. The clerks wore Skychef uniforms, and minded the shops as second jobs. They all looked very tired.

Titus remembered how, on arrival, he'd been threatened with a kitchen assignment. He'd escaped that only because now there was staff for the extra duties.

Titus scanned the crowd for any sign of Abbot's Mark or Influence, and noticed many familiar faces. There, strolling with Suzy Langton, was one of the cooks from the Gourmet Lounge near his apartment. The ebony statue who was the weight-lifting instructor was leaving with Abner Gold.

In the back of the fifth store, Titus found an array of cooking utensils for microwaves, and some picnic equipment.

He bought a dark gold Thermos and mug set, with a case. It was rated for microwave use, but apparently the people who had no kitchenette used them for take-out food. He wouldn't be conspicuous carrying his blood from his microwave to Inea's place. Somebody else bought a plug-in warmer, saying that a group of techs were chipping in for it so they could all eat hot pizza while watching videos.

In a lingerie shop, he found a filmy thing so nearly massless it hardly cost more than it would on Earth. He thought of Inea walking into the bathroom this morning. Though he'd enjoyed the view, he thought she'd appreciate a robe. He chose one in her favorite shade of pink—he hoped it was still her favorite—and a toiletries set. "Wrap it and deliver it tomorrow morning," he told the clerk.

He was examining a rack of Glynnis brand sportswear when he spotted someone who looked like Mintraub just leaving the doughnut shop, munching on a long twist. He'd only seen her in her helmet, and then later in official photographs. But it looked like her. He worked his way closer. She was wearing a green gym suit, and had her hair bound up in a pink band. She strode along as if following the shortest path to a goal.

But he lost her when she squeezed into a full elevator. He took the next one and got off at her apartment, but she wasn't there. Back in the elevator, he tried the most popular stop, the connecting corridor to the other domes. She'd been dressed for the gym, so he headed that way.

Signing in, he circulated through the busiest areas, and checked the swimming pool from the observation lounge. He was turning away when he noticed Abbot's Mark. Other than Mirelle, it was the first he'd found.

The woman in question was a slender, statuesque blonde wearing a white bathing suit designed like a plain tank suit. She climbed the highest diving platform and sailed off it, taking advantage of the gravity to execute a marvelous series of maneuvers before slicing cleanly into the water.

"Do you know who that is?" asked Titus of the man beside him, who was wearing a space suit liner, not gym clothes.

"They call her the Diving Belle. I don't know her name, but she's here every night putting on a show. They say she's really one of those stuffy doctors of something or other."

"Oh. Thank you." Titus asked others, but got only the nickname, that she spoke with a Georgian accent, and that she was a physical anthropologist. It was enough to enable him to find her file, but he didn't have to. Abbot had collected another one with clearance to study the alien "corpse."

Since she was Marked, he didn't dare touch the Diving Belle, so he moved on around the gym. Gold was in the weight-lifting class with the ebony statue, working as if taking out a rage. *He has a right. Have to talk to him.*

As Titus passed, the class broke up, but Gold didn't register Titus' presence. He headed blindly for the locker room. There was no trace of Abbot's Influence on him. After that, Titus noticed the ebony statue twice more as he circled. But there was no sign of Sisi Mintraub. He was about to leave when he remembered he owed time in the centrifuge. If he just signed out of the gym, Medical would be after him immediately.

113

But when he logged into the centrifuge, there was Sisi's name on the waiting list right above his. The attendant handed him a suit, saying, "Number three will be ready to roll in five minutes. And don't forget the telemetry."

The five separate centrifuge units started on a regular schedule, but with staggered times so there was no wait.

He changed quickly, determined to get into the same unit Sisi entered. The pale green suit made his complexion more conspicuous, but he set a low grade of Influence around himself so people would perceive his dusky pallor as normal. His human ancestry had blessed him with dark skin, so he didn't seem as stark white as some luren.

When he emerged, he again noticed the ebony statue lingering nearby, but thought nothing of it. Inside the cylindrical chamber, he found his quarry, strapped in with the elastic safety bands, ready to walk the treadmill. She was the only other one on this ride, though the chamber could accommodate eight on treadmills and six more seated.

Titus took the treadmill beside hers and secured his towel to a bar. Attaching the straps, he called, "Don't I know you? We met out at the starship today, didn't we?"

She peered at him. She was quite pretty, and no doubt used to every line in the book.

"I'm Titus Shiddehara," he added.

"Oh! Yes, Dr. Colby introduced us. Did you get the chemists' display tank?"

"Yes. Thank you."

"Amazing you'd recognize me. I didn't know you." The warning chime sounded, and she gripped the handles of the treadmill. "Here we go."

Elegantly muted sound heterodyned up to a pleasant, multivoiced hum as the tank began to rotate, and the platforms swung up onto the sides of the drum. They flexed their knees and blinked away the slight disorientation from the Coriolis force, and then they were both walking in place.

Titus had attached his telemetry monitors to a device that would feed it good human data, so he didn't have to worry about the duty tech noticing anything odd about him. He could concentrate on Mintraub.

─── TEN ───

Titus made small talk, probing for subject areas where Abbot had Influenced her. He'd learned the trick from Abbot but rarely used it. Luren who acted as agents were trained to create and erase identities, tying human records into knots. Occasionally, they hunted luren gone feral, thus honing their skills. But Titus, except for a few episodes, had been a scholar depending on agents to protect him.

He was bemused at his own audacity. To expect to outmaneuver Abbot at this game was more naïve than expecting to best him in computers. Yet even Abbot wasn't invulnerable.

Delicately, he advanced into a sensitized area. "Did you say cryogenics? Haven't there been some marvelous advances in that machinery in the last five years?"

"Yes, but don't you use the new superconductors in physics these days? All our hardware does."

"My new computers had them in the core that was destroyed." He took a deep breath and pitched his voice carefully. "Abbot Nandoha has had to fabricate replacement components based on the older technology."

"He is a genius, isn't he?" she agreed starry-eyed.

Oh, Abbot, that's unfair, implanting hero worship in a human!
"Thorough," Titus allowed.

She rallied to Abbot's defense, and gradually, a picture formed. She knew little of the objectives of either Biomed or Cognitive Sciences, though both drew on her equipment pool. But Abbot had convinced her that she couldn't handle the alien "corpse's" preservation chamber alone. Since she would be involved when they did anything to the "corpse," Abbot would also be called in. Very neat.

Preparing to withdraw, Titus began to reinforce in her a reluctance to mention this casual conversation to Abbot, as if she'd shared trivial confidences with another woman.

Out of the blue she volunteered, "You know, Abbot's a strange one. I often wonder if he *has* an apartment! He turns up at all hours, even keeps a shaver in my desk. And I think he's stashed his toiletries in the cryogenic room and uses the sterilizing shower as if it were his own. How do you account for someone like that? I mean it couldn't take more than fifteen minutes to get to his apartment!"

"People are strange." He hadn't Influenced that out of her. She was jogging along at a good clip, and had augmented his hypnotic effect by going into natural alpha state.

What's really in the sleeper's room? A transmitter component? The whole transmitter? Getting in to find out would be a project itself. Before he even tried, he'd rifle the Brink's files for the cryogenic chamber's alarm system, *and* find out more about Diving Belle. As a physical anthropologist, she'd be in the Cognitive Sciences group, next door to the chamber. But he couldn't ask Sisi about her. Abbot would notice such an inquiry immediately.

Titus came out of his thoughts to find Sisi slowing down, puffing hard. He felt as if he were jogging uphill.

The pleasant hum of the rotators climbed in pitch, and as it did, Titus' knees began to sag. He jabbed at the stop button, at the emergency override, at the attendant call signal—nothing. The panel stayed dark. "Malfunction!" he said. "Dismount and try to make it to one of the chairs!"

"Impossible," she stated with the adamant conviction of an expert mechanic. She kept poking control buttons in varying combinations while Titus tried to dismount.

He estimated they were at two g's now, but his reflexes, if they weren't off too much from low grav, should be up to it. He ripped the telemetry wires free then unhitched his safety belt. The treadmill was forcing him to run faster and faster. If the telemetry had not crashed with the g-control, he'd be in a lot of trouble. His idiot program would have kept sending dead-level healthy signals for one-g stress.

Calculating mentally, he stepped off the treadmill and curled into a forward roll, matching his momentum relative to the floor. It would make a wonderful exam question for his freshmen. He landed hard, the black traction strips on the floor ripping his suit and scraping his skin raw. He sat up, bleeding from his forehead and nose.

Mintraub still clutched the handlebars of the treadmill, her feet trailing out behind her, her body sagging alarmingly under the increasing gravity. He lunged to his feet and staggered to her, shouting, "Let go. I'll catch you."

"No!" she yelled back. "I'm too heavy now." Her knuckles were white, her hands slipping gradually.

He planted his feet to either side of hers. She might weigh two hundred pounds now, which Titus could manage. But he had to get her free before her weight climbed to three hundred and neither of them could move. "Let go!" he commanded with Influence and yanked her loose, pulling them both over backwards. "Got to get to the chairs," he gasped, struggling to his knees. "They're contoured for four g's."

"You're bleeding!" she said.

"So are you." At least his blood was an acceptable color for human blood. It was now all over her gym suit.

She wiped her nose and stared at her bloody hand.

"Don't tilt your head back," Titus advised. "Better to lose a bit of blood than ruin your neck from gravity. Crawl." They had no more than five strides to go, but it took an eternity. The few weeks he'd been on the moon had undermined his strength.

At last they climbed into seats. Titus hit the controls in the armrest. "Dead. It's going to be a long ride."

"Can't be. Safeties kick in at four g's, or the motors burn out. Designed that way. Awful lot of momentum in this baby." Panting, she added through clenched teeth, "If I survive this, I'm going to get the sonuvabitch responsible!"

And if she dies, how do I explain surviving four g's for an hour? His record showed he had high blood pressure and mild claustrophobia. The anxiety would be sending a human's blood pressure reading off the scale.

He'd acquired the phobia by being killed in a car crash and then buried alive. He was thankful it was a mild phobia, but now that he had nothing to do but endure, he worried about how to explain not having a heart attack or stroke.

For the lift-off, he'd been issued special medication—which he hadn't taken, of course. Maybe he could "confess" that and say he'd had it with him now? But why carry it in his gym suit? Irrational fear of the centrifuge? That would get him sent back to Earth, but he couldn't quit until he'd pinpointed the probe's target and Connie replaced him.

And the odor of human blood was making him ravenous.

Then the lights went off.

"Oh, shit. Titus, I hate the dark. Hold my hand."

It was really dark. Other than the dim glow of her body and the warm machinery, it was like a buried coffin.

"Hey, Titus—you all right?"

"Yeah." He took her hand.

"Is it my imagination, or is it getting stuffy in here?"

"Let's not dwell on it." He did a quick calculation. "There's plenty of air for the time we'll be in here. Just relax. Four g's isn't really all that much."

She squeezed his hand. "This helps."

She was right. His universe narrowed to the few square centimeters of skin against his. Somehow, she communicated more to him by that simple touch than words ever could. Hot tears stung his eyes and a bit of moisture leaked out the corners and down his temples. And he didn't know why.

He concentrated on enduring and keeping her confident. "It *is* getting stuffy in here," Mintraub panted.

"Won't be long now." But he was panting, too. *Could somebody be pumping CO_2 in?*

The darkness became reddish, sparkling. It brought back the awful time in his coffin. He had wakened and started using oxygen. There hadn't been much. His raging hunger triggered panic, using more oxygen. He hadn't realized he'd been mentally screaming for help powered by Influence. When Abbot's hand, glowing with vitality, had broken through the coffin lid, flooding cool air, mud, and rain down upon him, he had gone for Abbot's throat like a ravening animal.

Now, with all his adult strength, he struggled to keep his plight from radiating to Abbot. He didn't need any more debts to his father. He wasn't going to let Abbot see him in that feral panic again. He just wasn't going to let that happen.

He clung to that until, like a hand relaxing in death, his mind let go of its thoughts and surrendered to dormancy.

———

" . . . normal enough for someone revived by CPR an hour ago. But I wish we had had telemetry during the centrifuge ride. His eyes show some hemorrhage, but the pupils are the same size . . . . Chuck, look at this. He's wearing contacts—"

Titus grabbed for consciousness, as fingers peeled back his eyelids. He jerked his head away, gasping at the pain.

"Hey, he's conscious."

All at once, Titus realized he was in the infirmary. He must have passed out before the centrifuge stopped. *No! They said CPR. I must have gone dormant.* Feeling clumsy, he summoned Influence and shrouded himself in normality.

Chuck bent over Titus with a pen light.

The light was too bright, and Titus flinched, commanding silently, *You saw what you expected to see as normal.*

"What am I supposed to look at, Dave?"

Dave bent down. Titus widened the command to include him. *No need to look again.*

Dave responded, "Guess I was mistaken. Been studying those corpses too much. Humans aren't that weird."

The two withdrew, and Titus assessed his surroundings. It was a booth formed by drapes around the gurney on which he lay. Equipment carts, a wastebasket, a sink, and a vidcom on the one solid wall completed the examination room.

He tried to sit up but found he'd been strapped down. Chuck pushed him back. "Now just be still a while, Titus. You're going to be fine. But we have to make sure—"

"I *am* fine," argued Titus. "Unstrap me. Where's the woman who was with me?"

Chuck's hands moved of their own accord, but the doctor was better trained than that. He pulled his hands back and asserted, "You must lie still. You've had a cardiac arrest, but I just ran a quick comparison through the computer and there's no damage, no change. Sometimes miracles do happen. But you'll stay with us a couple of days, just in case."

Oh, no I won't. "Where's the woman who was with me?" He was really afraid now. If he'd gone dormant, what of her?

"Don't you worry about a thing. Ms. Mintraub is fine. We've sent her home. She didn't arrest or take a nasty bump on the head like you did."

Behind the curtains, an outer door burst open and a babble of voices filled the room. Titus discerned Abbot's rumble, Carol Colby's clear, commanding tones, and above them all Inea—with an edge of panic, saying, "I insist. I must see him immediately!"

"Inea!" said Abbot, his Influence filling the room. "The doctors have their procedures."

"Inea," called Titus, "I'm right here." He was surprised at the ragged edge to his voice and the raw fear in the pit of his stomach. Thinking fast, he added, "You don't have to worry about the chemists' tank— I've taken care of it all. We'll be ready to test your program in the morning!"

Smugly, he listened to Colby reply. Just maybe it would divert Abbot from the obvious conclusion about him and Inea.

119

By the time Colby had finished admonishing him about his health being more important than the press demonstration she had worked her way through the medtechs and doctors to his cubicle, trailed by the others.

Titus shot a glance at Abbot, and put all his strength into Influence as he told Colby, "I'm fine. Just get me out of here. I've got work to do." *And, dear God, I'm hungry!* Nervous sweat beaded his upper lip. *What if they don't let me go?* His eyes met Inea's, and he faked confidence. But she had seen his fear, and she eyed the medics uncertainly.

Yet it was Abbot who acted. He added the Influence needed to convince everyone that the bandages painted on Titus' forehead, palms, and knees meant nothing. They argued about the cardiac arrest, and Abbot challenged, "Since your instruments show no such evidence, perhaps he was only unconscious. He certainly doesn't seem like a heart patient to me." Abbot set them to convince each other as he wandered about poking at their computers and recorders. Occasionally, he'd flash Titus a magnanimous grin and erase something.

Abbot knew how weak Titus was. After being mashed in the centrifuge, suffocated, then pounded on by some amateur at CPR as the oxygen began to revive him from brief dormancy, how could he feel? But he grinned back at Abbot, determined not to let it show. Not before him, and not before Inea.

The medical discussion raged. Colby was reluctant to order Titus released on her authority, while the doctors refused to take responsibility for bypassing procedures. Titus knew the best way to break the deadlock was to stand up and sign himself out on his own recognizance. But of course there was no way he could reach the fastenings on the straps.

Meanwhile, Inea edged closer to Titus, one ear cocked to the medical discussion. As she began to believe Titus was all right, anger replaced her anxiety. "I forced my way in here because I thought you were in danger from those doctors! I wanted to help you, you cretin! How could you even *think*—let alone *say* right in front of everybody—that I'm more concerned about my damn program than about you?"

Long as she's mad at me, she won't give herself away to Abbot. "Well naturally, I just came to and I thought—" The lie stuck in his throat.

"You thought? You're not capable of thinking! All you know how to do is force people to believe you!"

120

Stung, he hissed, "Idiot-love, *you're* not thinking! And if you don't get me out of these straps right now, all the disasters you expected may come to pass. Or worse."

"Turn to mist and ooze out of them!" She whirled and stalked back to the group's heated discussion, where the humans were now comparing Titus to Abbot.

"I can't quite put my finger on it," Chuck was saying. "It's just a feeling."

"Very scientific," said Colby.

Dave announced, "I'll pull the records and we'll see."

"It's nothing in the records," confessed Chuck. "I've checked. It's just a sense of having missed something—do you know what I mean, Dave? Like doing rounds with a prof who doesn't say a word until you're out in the hall. You feel you've zeroed in on the diagnosis by the book—yet you *know* you've missed something and you're gonna get clobbered."

Titus cloaked his voice and called, "Abbot!"

His father poked his head under the curtain, and Titus glanced at the discussion group through the crack. "We've blown it."

Chuck continued to Colby, "That's why I don't want to let him walk out of here until we know there's no hematoma in the brain from that blow, and absolutely no chance of any damage to the heart. I wouldn't *dare* risk it."

"Very commendable," agreed Colby.

"But—" interrupted Abbot, turning to them. Titus felt his Influence gearing down to a fine, subtle touch. "—a good scientist learns when to take risks. If you're still timidly laboring under the specter of some professor's wrath, you don't have the strength to hold up your end of a team effort. Isn't that true, Dr. Colby?"

"Very true."

Abbot turned to Inea. "I expect Titus feels at a disadvantage, all tied down. Why don't you release him, while Dr. Colby explains everything to these fine doctors."

Abbot's Influence was hardly discernible, but Inea turned to comply as if it were her own will.

"I'm sorry I lost my temper, Titus. I was taught better than to hit a man when he's down."

"Forget it," he replied. "I *wasn't* thinking clearly."

"Chuck," said Colby, "I'm not impugning your *medical* judgment. Abbot's right. There are other factors to consider. The centrifuge was sabotaged and we have reason to believe it was an assassination attempt on Dr. Shiddehara."

Titus bolted upright. "Assassination!"

The two medics tried to push him down again, but Titus swung his feet to the floor. "I'm fine, really I'm fine. Did you catch the bastard?"

"Not yet," replied Colby. "So I don't want you stuck in sick bay, a high profile target. I'd rather have you moving around and working, not sleeping in your own apartment. I'm putting a decoy guard on your door, and another pair to follow you around, but that might not help."

Abbot turned to Titus. "The two centrifuge attendants were knocked out. Expertly. The damage was done very crudely. The assassin doesn't know computers or machinery."

"But he was strong," added Colby. "Very, very strong. Ripped out fail-safe boards by force. And clever. Not a clue to his identity. We'll not underestimate him again."

Titus ignored the searing ache in his body. "I flatly refuse to be put under guard." *Oh, shit. Wrong approach.*

"I'm afraid you have no choice—at least until we catch this 'bastard,' as you so aptly put it."

Titus went to Colby, summoning all his patience, trying not to think about hunger. "Carol, look, I don't want to resign over a matter of principle that has nothing to do with my work here. I'll accept a guard on my door. But don't put a tail on me. One of the guards could be the hitman."

"Brink's? Not likely, but I'm rechecking everyone. Titus, if I let you get murdered—especially after this warning—it may as well be me in the coffin. Listen, we have professionals in these matters here and on Earth. You don't have to worry. Your guards will be screened. You're going to be safer than anyone else on the station."

Inea said, "I've an idea. Give Titus another apartment for tonight— Abbot's or yours, Dr. Colby, or any vacant one. He'll drop out of sight until the reporters leave, then we can trap the assassin using a ringer for Titus."

Colby ran a hand over her face. "The timing of this attack was no accident. The terrorists wanted to divert those reporters from anything good we have to show them. And without Titus, the Project would really be crippled. They'd argue it's hopeless to send the probe out at all. If that's their game, they'll attack again while the press is here."

"Good," said Inea. "Then we only have to live with this for a few hours. You can have extra plainclothes guards around during the demonstration in Titus' lab. But leave him alone in the meantime, and he can get lost. This is not a small place, and there's probably only one assassin on the station. I mean, how could security have slipped up twice?"

"Well, if there was a vacant apartment . . . But we're moving people out and tripling up in order to squeeze the reporters in for a night . . . ."

"Titus can have my place for the duration," offered Abbot. "I'll take his. Nobody would mistake me for him."

Oh, no you don't! He'd never find all the bugs Abbot would leave behind. *How am I going to get out of this?*

Inea was looking at him strangely. Suddenly, she said, "For that matter, who'd confuse *me* with Titus? And it's less remarkable for a woman to invade a man's bedroom—than for another man to just . . . well, move in. I mean, neither of them has that sort of reputation. Here, switch with me." She dug her key out of a hip pocket and shoved it at Titus. "After all, I owe you something for putting my copyright on my program."

Colby agreed to the plan, but the medics insisted on a battery of tests before letting him go. Colby's parting remark proved she accepted Titus' claim to health. "I'll expect a full report on my desk in four days—everything you noticed before and during the incident."

Abbot turned at the door and, cloaking his words, asked, "You're sure you can handle the humans now?"

"Of course," he replied cheerfully. "They got the jump on me when I was unconscious. Thanks for the rescue. I'm in your debt."

"No." He shrugged. "Merely a parent's duty." He left.

Glumly Titus turned from the closing door. Abbot had only been obeying luren law, keeping humans from discovering too much. There was no affection in him.

Titus couldn't brood over his feelings about Abbot. He had to gather all his strength for the ensuing challenge. The medics weighed and measured him, scrutinized his private parts, poked and prodded and attached electrodes, and made him lie on cold tables while slow scanners floated around him.

All of this had been done countless times before, and if Connie's agents' work on the computer records still stood, the results would be the same this time. But Titus had to stay alert, misdirecting, twisting and averting suspicion. These doctors were no ordinary clinicians. They had worked on luren and orl corpses. The trained medical mind never forgot anything and continually integrated new data.

By now, both doctors were haunted by a nightmarish déjà vu when they considered Titus, Abbot, or the aliens. When the Influenced memories finally surfaced, they might well raise a hue and cry. *But before then, Abbot will kill them.* It was universal luren policy—Tourist and Resident alike. They had to protect their secret or be exterminated. But Residents tried to recruit the suspicious, not kill them—a risk the Tourists found unconscionable.

So Titus labored to convince the doctors they'd found nothing unusual. Contusions and abrasions aside, he was very lucky. And that's all it was—luck.

But their disturbed subconsciouses had to fasten on something, so when they suggested he see the Nutritionist about his blood pressure and diet, he capitulated, letting them believe they'd done their medical duty. Then they handed him his package with the gold Thermos which he'd left in a gym locker, and escorted him to the Nutritionist.

He regretted it the moment he stepped into the woman's domain. She was a portly, middle-aged expert with a dictatorial stance, and a face like a bull dog. "I'm Dr. Dorchester, and I've studied your data with great care. I think we can get you off medication in two months if you'll follow my regimen—*and* stop missing meals."

She punched her orders into the kitchen computers so his meal card wouldn't bring him any forbidden substances. "And you've got to increase your calcium intake to one and a half times normal. Do you understand that, Titus?"

"Yes, of course. I will."

"You're too young for such problems. There's no excuse for it. You're certainly not overweight. So you must eat properly, and get more exercise. Then, as soon as you're off medication, I want you to get out in the solarium, not tanning, just a little sun. But you'll have to be careful despite your complexion. You *can* get skin cancer."

"I know." He listened to her lecture on campus living being too sedentary while campus politics produced too much anxiety. Then he accepted her advice eagerly. When he finally escaped, he was exhausted. He wondered if even Carol Colby could stand up to Dorchester.

Free at last, he made his way to his apartment on rubbery legs. He nodded to the guard who wore the Brink's uniform with the Project

Hail patch. Then, hiding the shaking of his fingers, he tucked the Thermos package under one arm and triggered the door signal. *Come on, Inea.*

The guard said, "Pardon, Doctor, but I was told—"

"I know. But the object of the game is to be where I'm not expected to be, no?" He rapped on the door, harder than he'd intended. *Inea!*

"But Brink's doesn't make mistakes—"

"Yes, of course." His teeth were clenched together, but Titus strove to sound pleasant. "The lady is home, isn't she?" Her aura was so strong he could taste it.

"Perhaps she's sleeping?" suggested the guard.

Inea opened the door. In her left hand she held the vial of his blood pressure medication which he'd left on the table. In her other hand were several tablets. "Rip the door off the hinges, why don't you."

He squeezed past her. "It's a hatch, not a door." She shut it and followed him to the kitchenette. "Why do you always do that? Just when I'm all consumed with sympathy for your plight, you make me crazy mad!"

He splashed water into his pitcher and shoved it into the microwave, then unwrapped the Thermos. "I'm sorry. I'm a little crazy myself right now."

As he turned toward her, she stifled an exclamation, then discarded the pills on the table and pulled out the chair. "Sit down! You're not as well as you were pretending to be, are you? Why did they let you go then?"

He just looked at her.

"Oh," she said, eyes round. "Your whammy."

"I had to get out of there."

"Well, so I'd figured when I heard what had happened. That's why I bullied my way in . . . to *help* you—you—"

"Go ahead, call me names if it will help." He rummaged in a cabinet for a packet of crystals, fighting off the idea that Abbot was right about the artificial blood. Luren biology demanded more.

She picked up the vial again and toyed with the pills. "No. I outgrew name-calling years ago. I've had a while to think about this—this mass of contradictions you've handed me. Maybe you haven't lied to me, but you haven't told me the whole truth, have you? You're scared witless, aren't you?"

She's fishing. She doesn't know about Abbot. "Witless? That's not name-calling?"

125

Wearily, she answered, "You trying to pick a fight? Because if you keep it up, you're going to succeed. I'm only asking you to level with me. Are you afraid—so afraid of something that you'd rather offend me than face it?"

The microwave bleeped, and he fetched the Thermos and dumped in crystals and water. With his back to her, he answered, "Isn't there any way to get through to you?"

He turned, aware that his face and stance revealed too much. "I'm not dealing with just ordinary hunger here. I went dormant—as if I'd died. But only for a very little while. Still—I'm starving."

Suddenly, there were tears in her eyes. "I'm such a sucker! You always do this to me. I've never met a man who could do this to me like you do. But as soon as my guard is down, you're going to hit me where it hurts most—aren't you? What will it be this time?"

"What do you mean?"

"You're going to sleep with me, even marry me next year sometime, but you won't live with me. You're going to give my career a big boost by using my program on a media event—but you assign me to a hardware tech's duties instead of writing programs with you. You're unconscious, and I come running to save your precious secret identity—and you call me the worst kind of materialist right in public. Now you plead dire starvation and I can't stand the sight of you suffering, and I'll do anything you ask—and what are you going to do to me next?"

She's right. I'm as cruel as Abbot.

He poured some of the dead blood into the gold mug. His raging hunger refused to focus on the thick liquid. He carried it toward her, gathering her hands to it. "All right," he told her, "what I'm going to do to you next is tell you most of the whole truth."

Her precious ectoplasm was not flowing gloriously into the blood medium. She was barriered against him.

"You're going to tell me what you're so afraid of?"

He shut his eyes. He felt her ectoplasmic envelope reaching out toward him, but then it recoiled. Savagery boiled up in him, and he knew real fear—fear that he'd disgrace himself utterly. *I should have gone to Abbot. A luren has to have luren blood on wakening from dormancy.* But he had been able to hide his condition from Abbot—or Abbot would be here now. And Abbot had known he'd been dormant—he had to have known. But from such a short dormancy, surely he wasn't in any danger of going feral?

Suppose Abbot suspects I'll go to Inea, and he wants that because he wants a feral edge on me? It would be typical of Abbot. *Perhaps he intends to show up when I've admitted neither the blood nor Inea will help this hunger?*

But he wouldn't take Abbot's blood. He simply, flatly refused to give the Tourist any further power over him.

He opened his eyes, his mind suddenly feverishly clear. "This life forces me to contend with fears I'd never dreamed of before. I have the power to make you offer me what I need. And to make you enjoy it. I've sworn not to . . . but I'm tempted. And I'm afraid of that temptation. Worse, I'm afraid I'll use ordinary words to get you to help me. And worse yet, I'm terrified if I don't do either, you won't help me. I believe you will but I'm afraid you won't. Does that make sense?"

She raised the mug. "Here, drink." But there was no tendril of ectoplasm, no energy infusing the chemical.

——— ELEVEN ———

He cradled her hands in his. "No, that won't help. I need your love, *and* your trust. I didn't know how cruel I was. You're right, I haven't been regarding you as a person. I've been making decisions for you with information I kept from you. Trust me now, and I'll give you that information."

"You're shaking."

He closed his eyes, the bright light in the apartment making him see blood red. "Waiting for you is very hard." *God! What happens if I break? What happens if I go for her throat? Oh, please, no!* Petrified by that vision, he hardly noticed when her hardness dissolved and tendrils of ectoplasm grew toward the blood between her hands.

"Waiting for you is very hard, too, Darrell, Titus, and whoever else you may become. Drink before it gets cold."

She pressed the mug against his lips and he felt the warmth that was more than temperature. Stooping, he accepted the gift leashing back the clumsy greed that drove him.

Draining the mug, he enfolded her in his arms and kissed her. She didn't even complain about the blood on his lips.

At last, dizzy with the enticing promise of repletion, but still hungering as never before, he drew back, aware to his very bone marrow how precious she was to him. "We can't stay here. Come to your apartment with me."

She glanced at the Thermos still more than half full. "If you were all that hungry, you must need more."

"I do. I got the Thermos to take it to your place. We have time now. God knows what's going to happen tomorrow."

She pulled a tissue out of the wall dispenser and scrubbed her lips, looking at the discarded tablets on the table. "Go brush your teeth."

She herded him toward the bathroom, but he saw the package he'd ordered delivered sitting on the table beside the refill of his prescription. Inea had opened the refill, not the old empty bottle. He took his package. "Got you something." With ritual protests, she accepted the lingerie and toiletries as the apology he meant it to be. Handing her the toothbrush, he said, "Here, join me."

"All right. But—oh—Carol left you a message."

Over the sink, he mumbled, "Message?"

She garbled back, "Listen. Just before I got Carol's message, I saw that those pills of yours are labeled wrong. I know. My dad used to take those."

Spitting, Titus charged back into the other room and picked up the bottle. She called around the door frame, "See? They don't have the little lines quartering them. If you've been taking them, you could be very sick."

"I don't *take* them! The prescription is just to get me exempted from the solarium. I can't stand sun, remember?" But if someone was trying to poison him, they'd be wondering why he wasn't dead. *And if they found out why* . . . Inea came out asking how he'd fooled the medics, and he answered, "I told you, we have some people who are clever with computer records."

She jiggled a handful of tablets. "Well, your first refill wasn't right, either. Carol said they'd checked the pharmacy and found your pills were still there, and an equal amount of something innocuous was missing. So they and the assassin think you'd been off your medication for weeks before going into that centrifuge. They wonder why you're not dead. They're rushing your medication to my room."

He threw the bottle down. "We'd better get going." He grabbed another kiss as he closed the Thermos.

She pulled him up short. "Carol told me both attendants died, but they said the assassin was very slender and dressed in a ninja costume. If there's a real ninja out there . . ."

It gave him pause. He had minimal training in the use of his luren abilities in combat with humans. "Costumes are cheap. If the attendants interrupted a real ninja, they wouldn't have survived five seconds. Besides, a real ninja wouldn't have been discovered. In fact, I doubt if a real ninja would have plotted to poison me and then stage an 'accident.' That's gangland stuff, not serious martial art."

"I hope you're right."

He handed her the Thermos. "Here, it'll help if you carry this." The gold plastic and foam insulation of the Thermos was as permeable to ectoplasm as its plastic mug.

Watching all around them, Titus led her into a lift and directed it to the level where they could cross to her dome.

Alone with him in the lift, Inea asked, "It's that Abbot Nandoha, isn't it? He's the one you're so scared of. Every time he's around, you do something peculiar. He's certainly thin. Could he have been the ninja?"

In his shock, he laughed out loud.

"I thought you said you'd level with me."

Titus sucked in his laughter, realizing it had more than a tinge of hysteria to it. But the image of Abbot dressed up as a ninja was just too much. "Abbot's part of what I have to fill you in on," he confessed. "But not here."

His legs were still weak he noticed as the lift pulled to a halt. She led the way into an adjacent car bound for her level. It was full, so they couldn't talk.

At her door, she had to remind him, "You have the key."

He fumbled it out of his pocket, and triggered the mechanism. The strong feel of her permeated the space like a song. On her bed was a pharmacy package. As she closed the door, a sudden thought forced him to ask, "Did you ever invite Abbot here?"

"No, of course not—why . . . ?" She stopped in her tracks. "He's a vampire? That's why you're so afraid of him? That doesn't make sense."

"Think hard—have you ever said anything he might construe as an invitation?"

"No. He's a genius in his field, but I loathe the man."

He shut his eyes over the draining relief.

"Here—sit down." She shoved the pharmacy package onto the floor. "You should be in the infirmary." He sat on the end of the bed, and she settled beside him, unscrewed the mug from the Thermos and filled it. Putting the Thermos on the floor, she held the mug and breathed on it. "So tell me about Abbot."

He ran a finger around the cup, outlining her hands, enjoying the feel of her. He could still detect a tremor though, an inward flinching. He had all but conditioned her to expect a verbal blow every time she let her defenses down to him. "I'm so sorry for how I've treated you."

"You're evading again. Abbot. Tell me."

He hovered over the mug. "Blackmail? Ransom for my dinner? Yes, he's . . . a vampire, though he wouldn't put it that way. It's complicated."

"Not now then. Here. Take it."

Instead, he kissed her delicately on the eyelids, the nose, then the lips. He worked down to the mug, his lips on her fingers bespeaking his love. "Abbot, then. After dinner. The whole story." He drank from between her hands.

"I don't know what it is when you do that," she whispered, "but I feel it, all over my body."

"Me, too." He drank steadily, pausing only to refill the mug and grab a moistened towelette from the dispenser near the head of the bed. He wiped his lips each time he drank, and then resumed experimenting with his lips on her skin. As he finished the blood, the scintillating arousal dancing between them intensified. "What do you feel?"

"Wonderful. Do that some more."

He set the mug on the floor and laid her back on the bed. "Like this?" He trailed kisses around her neck.

"Vampire."

And he knew what the difference was. She believed him at last—completely—and trusted him not to hurt her again. There was a wholeness in her gift to him that he could never have evoked with Influence. Even humans he took by consent never knew enough to truly consent, as she had.

He began undressing her. Slowly, hardly disturbing the rhythm, he discarded their clothing and moved them up to lie full length on the bed. Using all his senses, he strove to gift her with as much of value as she had given him.

He made it last a very long time. Together, they finally surrendered to the inevitable.

Titus found tears leaking down his temples as he lay on his back beside her. That pure, clean surge of ectoplasm had touched something too deep for words.

Given this, how could anybody want anything else? Then he understood. Abbot had never had this. He couldn't. Most luren, even

Residents, couldn't. It demanded total commitment, both from the luren and from the human, to create this. But it was more precious than anything, for it had the power to dispel the feral rage. Titus knew that it was not only gone, but that it would never return.

"What are you thinking?" asked Inea.

"I'm glad we came to your room. I don't think it would have been as powerful in my room. And I needed all of it."

"Me too." She wiped away some tears of her own.

"Promise me something."

"Hmm?"

"Never invite Abbot in here."

She propped herself up. "All right. I won't invite him in. Now, *please* explain why real vampires, not the magical kind, *care* about an invitation? That's supposed to be superstition, like crosses and mirrors; evil can't endure good, the sight of itself, or enter uninvited. You like crosses, mirrors reflect you, and yet . . . this!"

"I can't explain it, certainly not in terms of any physics we know. I don't want to look at it too closely, for fear I'll discover that physics as we know it is garbage."

"Can't be that bad. Physics works."

"True. But so does whatever it is we have. One theory is that it has something to do with gravity and magnetic fields. Location is important. You know—the bit about how a vampire has to sleep in his own coffin? We get around it by generating the magnetic field we need to rest in. Simple electronics, but it gives us freedom."

"You mean you don't cart around your native earth?"

"I'm not a potted plant!"

"But what's that got to do with needing an invitation?"

"Some people create a sort of bubble or sphere around their home, almost a kind of personal magnetic field. This is *your* place. I think Abbot could break in, if he wanted to, but more likely he'd just—how did you say it?—put a whammy on you to make you want to invite him in."

"He could do that?"

"He can do everything I can do—only better—and more besides. You have to understand about Abbot. He's not evil. He's rigorously ethical, courageous—even heroic—charitable, and dedicated to his cause. He'd give his life and more for the lives and honor of all of Earth's vampires."

"So you don't think he could have been the ninja? But if he's so wonderful, why do you fear him?"

He looked up at her. *What if she never offers me that gift again?* He wanted to wipe all this from her memory.

"Titus, what's the matter?"

There was nothing for it but to spit it out. "Abbot doesn't share my . . . diet . . . or my goals. He's opposed to everything I stand for— and he's my father."

She sat up. "What!"

He sat up and pulled the cover around them. Trying to be clinical, he launched into the story of how it had been Abbot who had resurrected him from the grave because his own genetic father had disappeared. "By giving me blood after that long dormancy, he became my father—the one whose power I can't successfully oppose. Ever. For any reason." Up to now, Titus knew, Abbot had been toying with him. Even his one success in the men's room at Goddard Station had been more accident than success. When he'd tried to block Abbot from Influencing Inea in the lab, he'd come as close to pitting his power against Abbot's as a son ever could. Abbot had been so astonished, he'd desisted. But Titus knew what would have happened had Abbot chosen to use his power.

"So, knowing he's safe, Abbot uses his power against you? Why?"

"Abbot's a typical Tourist, so I left him to join the Residents as soon as I discovered them." He explained that much of luren politics.

"So the Residents ship you powdered blood, and the Tourists feed on humans like cattle?"

He hadn't used that image to her. "That's exactly how they think of it. So you see, Abbot's a very real danger to you because I can't protect you from him."

"Why would he want to hurt me?"

"He wouldn't. He's no sadist. He wouldn't perceive your pain at all. He would take you simply to get at me."

"Why would he want to do that?"

"I told you he's dedicated to goals and ideals far beyond himself. To protect all vampires, he'd kill me—he'd mourn, he'd suffer—but he'd do it. And in telling you all this, without 'gagging' you, I've broken a law Abbot lives by. I've jeopardized us all. The penalty is death. We're alive because so far, he doesn't know how much you know."

"Oh God. I didn't understand what you meant that first night— death for you, and being gagged for me. Abbot would kill you and take me, wouldn't he?"

"Yes."

She was silent a long time. Then, in a very small voice, she said, "Titus, I want you to put that gag-whammy on me. I don't care, because I won't ever want to tell anyone."

He kissed her.

She grabbed him by the ears and pushed him back. "You do it, you hear me—because—because—"

"Not yet. Listen. There's more."

She shook him. "No. I don't want to hear it until I can't get you into trouble for it. I *believe* you, Titus. I've seen it in that man's eyes. He'd kill without a qualm. I'll bet he was the ninja. He moves like a trained fighter."

"He is. But he wasn't the ninja. If Abbot had wanted to gimmick the centrifuge, he'd have persuaded the computer to do it for him. But he doesn't yet have a reason to kill me. When he does, he'll use a method likely to work. He knows I don't have high blood pressure—he's using the same dodge with a different medication. And he knows four g's won't kill me, while suffocation would only produce dormancy." *But suppose he wanted dormancy, and a feral edge to my appetite? No. He'd have found a more elegant way.*

"I guess it was an absurd idea. If Abbot wanted you dead, you'd be dead."

"Not really. But just remember, if Abbot ever has to kill me, he'll make sure there's no body left for autopsy. That's another law among us—to protect us from discovery."

"Is that why there are two of you on the moon? In case one of you is killed, the other has to dispose of the body?"

"No. That's not the reason, but it is a service I'd perform if I had to . . . even at risk of my own life."

"Tourists and Residents both live by the same basic laws, you said. Would you kill Abbot if he violated a law?"

"No." His quick answer startled him. "I mean, aside from the fact that I literally couldn't because he's my father, I've never actually killed anyone. Not exactly, on purpose, anyway. And our law wouldn't require it of me where Abbot was concerned."

"But you do have laws that require murder?"

"No. Extermination." And he tried to explain what a feral luren was like. "I've helped hunt them," he confessed. "We captured one, once, tried to rehabilitate him. I heard later that they had to kill him. Usually, though, they don't let themselves be taken, so they get killed in the chase."

"So there are evil vampires."

"Yes. If you can call humans who've gone violently insane evil, then yes, there are evil vampires too."

"How can you trust me? Even me? You just told me you'd gone dormant, and that's why you were so hungry. Now you're saying you should have had blood from one of your own kind instead of the synthetic. Are you likely to go feral?"

"No, I'm satisfied now. And I haven't killed anyone."

"Far from it." She squirmed. "I don't see how we can just sit here and discuss killing. It's unreal."

"Well, then let's just go to sleep." He pulled her down, massaging her back.

She let him work the knots out for a while, then popped her head up. "Are you putting that gag-whammy on me now?"

"No!"

She sat up. "Titus, I absolutely, flatly insist."

"No!"

"Will it hurt?"

"No!"

"Will it stop me thinking?"

"No."

"Then why not?"

"Because—" He realized all his reasons were selfish ones. "Because I promised not to use my power on you."

"But I'm telling you to do it. That's different."

"Well . . ."

"Titus!"

"Maybe—" He swallowed dryly. "Maybe after you hear the rest, you'll want to tell the authorities. Then how will you feel about me?"

"Then," she answered reasonably, "I'll just ask you to lift the whammy. It *is* liftable, isn't it?"

"Yes."

"So what's the problem? It's only to protect you from Abbot."

And that's the problem. I don't want her to protect me. She'd objected to him protecting her, and now he knew why. He squirmed, then hit on how to discourage her. "All right, then. I will. On one condition."

"Condition?"

"Next time I want to protect you, you let me."

She blinked. "It's a deal. Go to it."

Diabolical woman. But he had to keep his word.

An hour ago, he'd have been too weak. Now, when he exerted Influence, the power shimmered around him. "You won't speak of my private affairs involving my feeding or living habits or those of the vampires, Tourists, or Residents of any origin, nor will you reveal any detail that would lead anyone to suspect we exist, unless you're assured of privacy and alone with me."

"Okay," she agreed. "Go ahead and cast the whammy."

"It's done. You can't test it until morning, though, because right now you're very busy."

"I am?"

He smothered that with a kiss, then made love to her, slowly and passionately, driven by the fear that he'd lose all of this when she learned the rest.

When they woke, she was ravenous. "We should live in your room with that lovely microwave. Now I've got to get dressed to go eat."

"Wait a minute." He pulled her back. He had promised not to keep information from her anymore, and now she couldn't betray the luren plans. "Abbot mustn't suspect how much you mean to me, so you've got to be careful."

"But you put the whammy on me. Abbot's no threat."

He lay back with an explosive sigh. "Abbot's an incredible threat. Listen." And he explained just what Abbot's original mission was, and how Titus himself had been chosen to stop the Tourists from implanting that transmitter. He tried to talk around his nonhuman origin, to cushion the shock, to delay the ultimate moment. He tried to tell himself she'd accepted him completely and the simple matter of ancestry wasn't that important. But his throat was dry and constricted as he forced out the words he had to speak.

She was white and shaking when he'd finished. "You're part nonhuman—an alien from outer space? But that's not possible. If your mother was human . . . it's not possible."

"Our legends tell us our ancestors crashed on Earth. I don't know where luren evolved or how." It was a relief to be able to use his own terminology with her. "I don't know how or why it's true, but I know that ship out there on the lunar surface was crewed by relatives of my species."

She clutched her pillow. "Titus, don't kid me."

"I'm not. I promised not to keep anything back."

"I just slept with an alien from outer space? That's—that's—*Titus!*"

135

"I was born on Earth," he protested. "Look, when Abbot dug me out of that grave, and explained why I—behaved the way I did—I felt about like you do now. Then he pointed out I'd *always* been . . . nonhuman, and knowing it didn't make me a different person." She hugged herself, rocking. Her lips were still too white. "Well," he added, "it didn't help me much either, at first."

He got off the bed and in a slow agony of apprehension, he dressed, noting his bruises had healed, so he'd have to keep the areas covered. Humans didn't heal that fast. When he glanced at Inea, she was still rocking back and forth, her eyes screwed shut. Finally, he knelt beside her and pried one of her fingers loose to kiss it. "I'm sorry I laid that on you like that. I'd never have done it if you hadn't insisted on the— we call it being silenced under Influence. You took all that about Abbot so well, I hoped—well, I did promise to tell you everything. Inea, I'm sorry."

She pulled her finger back and hunched away from him.

I should ask if she wants me to remove the gag. But demanding such a decision right now would be cruel. "I'll remove the silencing any time you ask." She didn't respond. "You need some time to get over this one. I'll leave now. I don't want to but . . . ."

She didn't move. She was barely breathing.

"But I guess I ought to." Slowly, he rose and went to the door. Turning for one last look, hoping desperately, he wanted to curl up around the searing grief in his own body. Something finally became clear to him. She'd been doing to him exactly what she'd accused him of doing to her. Every time he let his guard down, feeling accepted, she cut him off. He hadn't known he was doing it to her, and he was sure she didn't know what she was doing to him. *How human!*

He put his hand on the door, and spoke to it. "From now on, Inea, I'll try for all I'm worth to stop hurting you."

The airtight seal popped softly as the door opened, but he paused, praying she'd reach out and stop him. "Inea, just remember, the only important thing I've told you is about Abbot. He's the danger. Don't let him suspect we care about each other. Earth is my home, and I'm going to stop him from sending his message."

When she didn't reply, he had to step out and close the door. There were still two things she didn't know: what it would mean if he Marked her as his stringer—that under luren law his Mark would protect her somewhat from Abbot but make her his property—and that *Kylyd* had a survivor whom Abbot intended to revive.

He stood with his back to her door, noticing the subtly different air of the corridor and trying to think. He had about twelve hours until the scheduled demonstration to the reporters. They were, no doubt, here already, and Carol Colby was busy with them. He couldn't help with that. He'd been given his assignment—stay out of the assassin's way.

With a mighty effort, he ripped himself away from Inea's door, forcing down all fear that she'd never touch him again. There were three things he had to accomplish before the demonstration. He had to check the sleeper's new chamber for Abbot's transmitter before Abbot discovered what Sisi had divulged; he had to reconstruct Abbot's moves while Titus had been with Inea; and he needed to know who the ninja was.

As he wandered by a refectory, he remembered he had to "eat" and used his reprogrammed meal card, Influencing the crowd automatically. Gradually, he steadied down, concentration returning, and he thought to scan the crowds for traces of Abbot's work. He was astonished when his mechanical effort brought him to staring at a short Oriental woman with a cap of straight black hair.

She was bussing her tray at the conveyer belt. Her face showed her to be in her forties, with strong character lines and a purposeful expression. She wore the Project uniform pants and jacket with a crisp perfection. But she also wore, no doubt without her knowledge, sign of Abbot's tampering.

He had not, however, Marked her.

When she reached the door, Titus decided to follow her. Out in the corridor, he crowded into the same lift she took, and lost her as she switched to another. But he knew where she was going. All those she had greeted were from Biomed.

Titus joined the stream of workers reporting for their shift, and cloaked himself in a blur of familiarity. He passed through the security checkpoint as a ghost of one of the legitimate workers—a burst of random static on the instruments. Nothing worthy of the guards' attention.

He followed the Oriental woman to the Cognitive Sciences section, and toward the Artificial Intelligence division. Moving through as if on an errand, a blur at the edges of vision, he overheard her called Dr. Kuo.

With just a cursory glimpse of the section's work, he hardly had to look her up. She had to be involved in tapping *Kylyd's* computers, no doubt providing the clues Abbot had needed to take data from *Kylyd's* systems.

But Titus couldn't dawdle about without making people nervous. He'd have to delve into Dr. Kuo's work later. He faded back into the corridor, coming out near the sleeper's new chamber. There were three men and a woman stationed at the end of the short hall that led to the locked door.

One of the men was seated at a desk, apparently unarmed. Before him was a handprint verifier, and a monitor to check current status of clearances. The four guards had surely memorized the few faces cleared to pass that point.

At the end of the approach hall, the door was festooned with security instruments.

Titus ducked into a nearby men's room and holed up in one of the stalls. Until he shut himself in, he hadn't realized how frightened he'd been. He had promised Abbot he wouldn't trigger alarms the next time he visited their relative in there. But did he have the nerve?

Of course, he had studied the alarms, and he had his PDA with him. He opened the back and plucked out the nearly invisible adhesive dot that would bypass the palmreader. Placing it into its slot, he programmed it to tell the reader he was Nandoha, then palmed it.

It took him fifteen minutes to talk himself into it, and even when he stepped back out into the corridor, projecting the semblance of Abbot Nandoha about him, all he could think was, *What if Abbot passes by while I'm in there?*

But that probability was small enough. Even Abbot had to sleep sometime, and it was a big station. Titus had not come here to live his life without risks. He marched himself up to the check station, being Abbot right down to the slight swagger and benign smile. Palm on the plate, he flashed his own I.D. under the other guard's nose. "Nandoha."

"Good morning, Doctor," replied the guard cordially.

Titus nodded and was passed through. He had to go through a sterilizing shower that tortured his skin, then dress in a disposable suit, but then he was inside the chamber. It was a very large bare room—originally built as a chemistry lab. It had dully gleaming pale gray walls, while the lights made him wish for his sunglasses.

Beyond the transparent shrouds of the double-walled bio-isolation airlock surrounding the opaque showering chamber — the whole installation set across the entry — it was also cold. The air inside the room was dry, preventing condensation on the cryogenic chamber itself. And that was the same as it had been. The sleeper's chest was just as torn, the whole body unmoved—dead looking.

But that wasn't what he'd come to see. Titus searched storage bins and working counters littered with instruments. There were half a dozen computer taps, and one stand-alone with a tremendous memory. Obviously, there were a number of investigations in the first stages of being set up. Labels on some unopened crates told the story.

Heaped on one side, Titus found almost everything needed to set up a cloning lab, complete with a Ships-Freuden artificial womb—one that could have its every parameter adjusted by microscopic increments. A powerful research tool, and just what would be ordered to clone an alien.

He wondered if the ultra-pure B&J chemicals that had come to him "accidentally" had actually been for this lab.

He searched every nook and cranny that could be a hiding place, touching nothing with his bare hands, fanatically careful not to disturb anything. But either Abbot had already removed his property, or it had never been here.

As he was about to exit through the shower, he turned back to survey the place, and realized it was packed with electronic equipment. Abbot could have hidden anything inside anything. And since he was now the recognized expert in fabricating components, nobody would question him.

Could that be why he helped rebuild the computer? Could he have destroyed it just to get this credential? But Titus couldn't attribute such infallible foresight to Abbot. His father had erred, and was trying to make the best of it. No doubt he'd had a lot of practice at that in his long life.

Titus left with all the care he'd entered with. Back in the area where he was authorized to be, Titus acknowledged that it was unlikely Abbot had hidden the transmitter or its components too carefully. After all, that would imply that Abbot considered his half-trained son a viable threat.

Possibly, Abbot had planted that false information in Sisi for Titus to find. The computer record of a visit to the sleeper that Abbot had not made would tip him off that Titus had debriefed Sisi as expected. And Abbot would have the last laugh.

Maybe. Titus set off to the gym to try to pick up the trail of the ninja. Then he'd check out Dr. Kuo. If Abbot were planting false trails, it implied there was a true one to be found.

His efforts for the remainder of the time all proved just as fruitless as his visit to the sleeper. The area of the gym housing the centrifuges had been walled off for repairs. But he discovered from one of the dance instructors that parts of the ninja costume had been identified in the waste from the locker rooms.

He spotted Abner Gold and the ebony statue of a weight-lifting instructor, cozily head to head over drinks at one of the bars near the swimming pool. Then he had to dodge a gaggle of reporters on the grand tour. He had no luck discovering what Abbot had been up to while he dallied with Inea and, checking with his own lab, he was told he was not needed. Inea did not answer at her apartment—or his. *She's at work. She wouldn't let the project down.*

Inexorably, his feet carried him to his lab. He had to admit, as he straight-armed the door, that he needed to see her, needed to know she wasn't still sitting on her bed, white-faced and nearly catatonic.

"What are you doing here?" called Shimon across the lab.

A dozen or so faces turned up to Titus.

He descended among the rows of machines. They'd made enormous progress. The floors were clear of litter, and most of the work stations were buttoned up. "Coat of paint and this place would look almost like new," Titus commented with his best smile. "You're all to be congratulated."

"It works like new," offered Shimon. "Want to see?"

"I saw some of the reporters over in the gym. They'll be here soon. You go on with what you're doing." But he found no sign of Inea— not even in the observatory. As casually as he could, he asked, "Anyone see Inea?"

Shimon wiped his hands on a towel. "She finished her work, and left with Abbot. He said he'd buy her lunch to celebrate—what's the matter?"

——— TWELVE ———

"Uh," said Titus.

Discarding the towel, Shimon took Titus' elbow, steering him to his office. "They said you signed yourself out of the infirmary. Maybe you shouldn't have. Here, sit—"

Titus repossessed his elbow. "I'm all right. Do you have any idea where they went?"

Shimon cocked his head in an Israeli mannerism which others in the lab had picked up. "Abbot wasn't after your girl—"

"Don't get the idea she's my girl," commanded Titus with enough Influence to drive it home. "I need to talk to both of them before the press demonstration. Where did they go?"

Mechanically, Shimon said, "Abbot mentioned Segal's Castle, but I don't know . . . ."

Titus realized he'd hit Shimon too hard. "Forget I mentioned it." Titus changed the subject. "Thank you, Shimon. You deserve all the credit for this miracle." He gestured at the reassembled computers visible through the levelors.

"Oh no. No, no, no. Abbot — "

"Abbot only does what's easy for him. You've surpassed yourself. That won't go unnoticed."

———

He found Inea dawdling over coffee at a little table. Crumbs littered the white cloth. There was a red rose in a crystal holder, and a red candle at the center. White china and gleaming silver scattered about showed two had dined.

It took all his nerve to walk across the thick red carpet and sit in the red velvet chair opposite her.

Slowly, as if in a faraway dream, she raised her eyes to meet his. Her eyes were vacant, her expression slack.

She'd been debriefed under strong Influence, but Abbot had not Marked her. He released his breath. If he hadn't silenced her, he would now be the target of two assassins.

There was no sign of Abbot's minions in the restaurant. Titus waved the waiter away, and passed his hand before Inea's eyes. She didn't blink. *Damn that man!* The icy lump he'd been carrying in his midsection since she'd rejected him grew much larger. Titus hadn't done anything like this to Sisi.

Despite his promise, Titus had to use his power on her. She couldn't handle the press like this. In a few hours, she'd revive spontaneously. But they didn't have hours.

Abbot must have left traps for him, traps to make him injure her if he tried to bring her out of it. *He knew I'd find her, or he wouldn't have left her here like this. But why would he want her to miss the demonstration?* He sat back and dismissed awareness of all distractions.

141

"Talk to me," he commanded, interrogating her and watching her aura respond. Finally, it became clear that Abbot had used extreme force because Inea had fought hard. *Maybe I interrupted him, so he just left her for me to deal with.*

It was a good hypothesis. He found no hidden traps—no reason not to wake her. Shrouding himself in the semblance of Abbot, he donned Abbot's voice and set his hand in the focal plane of her eyes. Moving his hand, he trapped her gaze then snapped his fingers and withdrew his hand to the plane of his own face, saying, "Remember!" in Abbot's voice.

Her eyes focused and she recoiled with a stifled squeal.

He cast aside the Abbot illusion, saying, "You may speak freely now. This is a private conversation."

She shrank away. "Who are you! For God's sake, stay the right person!"

"Inea, it's me. Titus. I've broken my promise—"

"It was you all along—but—why—"

"No! That *was* Abbot. He had you in thrall. I used my power to break your trance and restore your memory of what he did. I thought that's what you'd want."

She started to breathe normally, but her hands clutched her nearly empty cup. "I see now why you refused to use those illusions on me again, after that first time. Not knowing what's *real* . . . . Are you really you?"

"Abbot never knew—I had a dog named Tippy, mostly black spaniel. He got fat cadging snacks off your mother."

A smile played around her lips. "I guess you're you."

"Inea—I didn't think Abbot would do that to you. I'd have protected you, come what may, if I'd suspected he'd—"

Expressionlessly, she said, "You *said* he was ethical."

"He warned me—I didn't know what he meant, but he did warn me." He put his hand palm up on the table, not daring to reach out to touch her, but knowing they both needed it.

She ignored his hand. "You couldn't have stopped him. You said so yourself last night."

"I could have Marked you. He wouldn't have touched you then. But all I did was Silence you." And he explained what Marking meant under luren law. "I didn't want to Mark you last night because it would have been a blatant signal that you were important to me. Now it's too late to hide that. But if you want, I'll place the Mark."

"If you'd told me about the Mark—before you told me what you people are—I'd have demanded it. I belonged to you—"

He noted the past tense. The world froze.

When she didn't say anything, he felt compelled to add, "I wanted to tell you all of it, let it be your choice—"

"It's too late. He's already done his worst."

"No, he hasn't. He hasn't Marked you for himself. He hasn't taken you. He left no permanent commands buried in your mind. He only questioned you—brutally. He found out things I didn't want him to know, and made sure I'd find out he knows. But he did nothing to you compared to what he could have done. He did it as a warning to me."

He hadn't told Inea what he was doing against Abbot. His father had learned nothing important—except how precious Inea was to him. "I don't think he'll molest you again because you've come to hate me so." He made his next suggestion with much trepidation. "If you like, I can remove the memory of his interrogation."

"No!" She recoiled. Then she scrubbed at her face with both hands, and when she looked up again, it was the old Inea staring back at him. "You could do it, couldn't you? You could do everything he did!"

Stricken, he nodded. Tarred with the same brush.

Only she added, in a hard, positive voice, "But you wouldn't. You were willing to starve, to face any nightmare, to take any humiliation, rather than do *that!*"

"I might have lost that resolve. I'm only a flesh and blood creature. Don't think I'm—"

"But you're human. That—*individual*—isn't!"

"He prides himself on cultivating what he thinks are luren attributes. But he's as human as I am."

"How can you defend him!"

"I can't. I oppose him as absolutely as I love you."

"Oh, Titus—I—" She fell silent, mouth working as if she wanted to proclaim her love. At last, she put her hand on the table barely touching his. "Give me time. Please."

"I don't have it to give. Abbot is running this game. Let me Mark you as my own. I'll take it away, if you tell me to. But in the meantime, you'll be safe from him."

"You said the Mark itself won't stop him."

"No. It's just a law. But he'd die rather than violate our laws." He had to be brutally honest though. "But as my father, he *could* force

143

me to remove my Mark, then take you. He *wouldn't,* though, unless I push him too far. I've misjudged him a couple of times, but I'm really very positive about how he regards the Mark. He taught me himself. It would take a threat to The Blood to make him violate a Mark, and he'd expect to be executed for it. Before he'd force me to remove my Mark, he'd have to be willing to kill me. He's not. He didn't find out how long you ran around unsilenced. Forgive me, but I checked before I brought you out of it."

She doodled on the tablecloth. "Think. He'll be at the demonstration. If I walk in there Marked, he'll know he's forced you to a move you didn't want to make."

He shook his head. "I don't care what he thinks—" *Neither does she. She doesn't want to wear a brand.*

She balled up her fist and hit the table. "No! You have to care what he thinks! You said you were here to win for all of Earth. If those are the stakes, then *I* am as expendable as any soldier. For once, you listen to me. We're going to walk in there pretending nothing at all has happened. From now on, we're going to seize the initiative, we're going to force him into a corner, and then we're going to whip him good. Have you got that, Dr. Shiddehara?"

A slow warmth thawed the icy lump in his belly. *An ally. Not a Marked stringer. An ally!* "Got it."

He moved to take her hand, but she froze again. Her voice trembled as she whispered, "I'll fight him with you. But that's all I can do now."

I'll win her back. I will.

Titus walked back to the lab beside Inea, restlessly scanning the crowds for Abbot's spies. It was close to the end of the day shift. Gossip raged around them, people talking about the reporters, the assassin, and the threat to close the Project down, sabotage.

The tension in the humans made Titus edgy. Abbot was certainly not about to leap out of some potted shrubbery and devour Inea. He would be in the lab. Colby had arranged for him to take his bows in front of his handiwork.

At the lift, Inea stepped close and asked, "Tell me. Why fight Abbot while working so hard for the Project? If the Probe doesn't go—"

"The majority of Earth's people want the probe to go, and they have the right to decide how to run their world."

The lift they squeezed into was full, so she couldn't answer until they reached the corridor on the lab's level. "Don't the Tourists have an equal right to go home?"

"Certainly. But not at such a price." He repeated his argument that, with time, humans would be able to defend themselves. "And the Residents will help." *If we still exist.* "This is our world. Home. Does that make sense?"

"Yes. But I'm sure not all Residents are like you."

"True. No two alike. Just like humans." He wanted to wrap her in his arms and kiss her forever. But he kept his hands to himself. They rounded the last corner, and found a squad of Brink's security guards outside the lab doors. Their dress uniform trim gleamed, and they stood to attention at full military brace. *Pretending to be an honor guard?*

It took the guards five minutes to validate their identities and pass them through. Inside, his entire crew was lined up, wearing fresh lab coats and solemn expressions. Among them, Titus counted ten new faces—the plainclothes guards.

W.S. emblems had been stenciled on the consoles. Colby was giving an interview in front of his office, between a W.S. flag and a Project Hail banner that hadn't been there before.

A young man with a clipboard rushed up to them. "You'd be Dr. Shiddehara—and you are?"

"Inea Cellura, staff astronomer."

"Fine. Then would you please just step over there with the staff?" He checked off something on his board. "Dr. Shiddehara, would you come with me, please?"

He wanted to pull Inea over with him, but she rolled her eyes, then meekly joined Shimon and the others.

"We'll want a shot of you at the observatory console that controls the Eighth Antenna Array—that is the one nearest this station?" At Titus' nod, the young man continued, "A shot of you aiming the Eighth at Taurus sending a signal to *Wild Goose* will be splendid." He ignored Titus' protest that the Eighth couldn't see Taurus today, and that *Wild Goose* wasn't anywhere near Taurus. "Have you seen Dr. Nandoha?"

"No. I haven't seen him."

"Titus!" exclaimed Colby. "Ladies and gentlemen, I'd like you to meet the man responsible, Dr. Titus Shiddehara."

People tucked notepads under their elbows to patter their hands in polite applause. Titus nodded graciously, and let himself be posed for pictures and rapid-fire interviews. Although every reporter represented more than one publication, the crowd still overtaxed the lab's air system.

When, inevitably, the topic turned to the recent attack on Titus' life, Colby reached behind her to bring an older woman to the fore. She was nearly Titus' own height, and had the splendid black skin of deepest Africa and a Haitian accent.

"This is Rebecca Whithers, the lawyer representing the Project in this matter," said Colby, listing her titles.

Titus couldn't take his eyes off Whithers. The Project uniform clung to her revealing not a "well-preserved" figure, but contours that bespoke vast strength. *Like "Ebony!"*

Associations clicked into a pattern. He had seen Ebony outside the centrifuge as he went in. She was the right size to wear the ninja costume, and certainly had the strength. She'd be unlikely to have real computer wizardry. Caught in the act, she'd have forgotten any precise instructions on how to gimmick the controls.

Meanwhile, the lawyer eloquently fielded questions fired at her in three languages. Then someone shifted back to the technical, and she laughed. "Dr. Shiddehara will have to answer *that!*"

Titus launched into his explanation of how the orbital and extra-solar observatories and probes had tracked the stranger craft into the solar system, how one key probe, *Wild Goose,* had gone dark—but might yet return, giving vital data on the trajectory.

Then he explained how the craft's approach line wasn't sufficient data. Biomed and Engineering would soon provide spectral data. He went on to introduce their demonstrations.

"With all this data, we can choose a logical target for our probe's message. As you've probably heard, we already have a broad region of space identified, the Taurus region."

Everyone laughed. Speculation had been running wild about every known star in that area ever since *Kylyd* had been spotted approaching.

Titus cited probabilities to show it was unlikely any visible star was the aliens' home. Modern instruments—great-grandchildren of the original Hubble orbital telescope used in the nineties— had revealed a few possibilities, but all the data wasn't in yet.

A man Titus thought he recognized stepped forward. "If I might interrupt for a moment, I have something I believe it would be appropriate to present now."

As he approached Titus, the ten guards in the lab tensed. Titus could feel the atmosphere crackle as the man proffered a small black case. "Here, Dr. Shiddehara, is a copy of your famous private star catalogue."

"What!" exclaimed Colby.

"Don't touch that!" yelled a Brink's guard.

Titus' hand froze. The guard who'd yelled ran up and whipped the black box from the reporters' hands, apologizing to the man by name. Titus realized this reporter was famous for the integrity of his investigative reporting.

Titus caught his eye and shrugged ruefully. "Security. After that attack on me—you understand . . . ."

"I see. Well, it is your own catalogue, a gift from sources I can't name, made before the Project's official copy—the one taken from your own home—was tampered with."

"Tampered . . . !" Colby choked, then whirled and shot to the back of the room issuing rapid-fire orders to a Brink's guard. He left, and Colby returned, all cameras on her.

"May I ask that you hold off reporting this until we have verified it. We have, at this time, no reason to believe the Project's copy which arrived on your shuttle has been altered in any way. Most likely, this pirated copy is the one at fault, and I believe only Dr. Shiddehara will be able to discern the truth of the matter."

One man objected. "The press always tries to cooperate, Dr. Colby, but in this case it might be unwise to—"

She interrupted. "By morning we'll have an official statement for you. Arrangements will be made for those of you who wish to file copy tomorrow at noon. In the meantime, we do have a most interesting demonstration here. Doctor?"

Titus introduced Inea and she ran the demonstration.

Still Abbot had not showed up. As the reporters peered into the chemists' tank, Colby fretted, "What could have happened to Abbot? Should I start a search?"

"No," whispered Titus in answer while all eyes watched the marvelous prize brahma bull stamp and snort among the stars of Taurus—the stars of the constellation connected by flashing lines to show the constellation's mythical outline changing with the centuries. "He might be coping with some embarrassing malfunction of station life-support. The reporters would love it."

"Good point. But I'm worried. He said he'd be here."

"He might be camera shy," suggested Titus. Older luren avoided publicity so it would be easier to change identities. He hadn't thought that would be Abbot's main concern right now.

He still hadn't shown up when Titus' own program was ready to run. Titus had to stand amid the computers with Shimon and explain how this was a simplified version of the program they would run on the real data; how he'd inserted plausible guesses for missing facts for the sake of demonstration.

Shimon traced the route of the data through the complex system, through error checking and backup, and went into lurid technical detail for the science reporters, explaining how the system was almost as fast as it had been. Titus interrupted when the others began to stifle yawns. "All right, let's run it and see what it says."

His operator punched in the command, smiling for the cameras. Lights flickered all over the lab as the various systems talked to each other. Over the hum, Titus answered questions about how his catalogue would figure in this process when it was read into the system. He mentioned the method he'd developed to determine if a distant system with a gas giant actually had an Earthlike planet.

He'd never rehearsed this, so he was astonished that his speech ended exactly as the printer began to spill out pages.

"With my assumptions, the program has narrowed it down to fifteen stars, all widely separated. We can't signal so many locations. We can bracket two, perhaps three closely grouped stars and still listen for answers. Remember, this probe will be unmanned. The less it must do on its own, the more likely it will succeed before it malfunctions."

Colby stepped up beside Titus and took his elbow. Behind a broad grin she whispered, "Abbot never showed!" Aloud, she announced, "So you see, Dr. Shiddehara's department is ready. Now if you'll follow my most able assistants, you'll tour the probe. We've made miraculous progress there, and we expect to bring it in under budget.

"I'll see you all in the big conference hall tomorrow morning. Now, please excuse me. It's been a very long day." The group broke up, and Colby added, to Titus, "I've been on my feet for almost twenty hours, and I can't remember the last time I had more than a nap. I've got to get some sleep. If you see Abbot, don't let him talk to the reporters alone. They'll cream him. He's so innocent. But your main job is to tell us which of those catalogues is the real thing."

"That may be impossible. I haven't memorized the data." *Innocent? Abbot? Shit.* "But I'll do my best."

As they watched the guides lining the reporters up for the excursion into vacuum, she added, swaying on her feet, "I'll want you at that meeting tomorrow if you can authenticate one of those catalogues. If not, stay away."

At that point, the doors opened, and everyone turned. Titus expected it would be Abbot, but the figure who stood there was shorter, older, and very human. *Abner Gold!*

He threw up both his arms and shouted for silence. "I have something to tell you. Don't let them stop me!"

The Brink's people surreptitiously closing in on him from all sides froze, looking at Colby. She stood, mouth agape.

Gold announced, "There's a secret project here! They've got a perfectly preserved alien corpse and they're planning to clone it and raise an alien child! Has any W.S. nation ratified such a plan? Or have these mad scientists taken the moral decisions of our race into their own hands?"

Good God!

A roar of questions and demands for proof filled the room. Gold told them which room in Biomed held the corpse. He tossed a memory cartridge to the reporter who had tried to deliver Titus' catalogue. The man caught it, and Gold said, "In there is the whole story—the bills of lading for the cloning equipment, the names of those here insane enough to try such a thing, and," he added with a triumphant glance at Colby, "the total amounts spent on this unauthorized scheme."

Where could he have gotten all of that? Then the image came to him of Gold head to head with Ebony. Had she put him up to this? Or had Gold told her about it?

But if she knew Gold would blow the lid on the cloning project, and if her terrorist group knew his star catalogue was altered, then why would she have tried to assassinate Titus?

Of course! There was more than one group of terrorists. And they each wanted credit for scuttling the Project.

Surely, Ebony had found out about the cloning project from Gold only after she sabotaged the centrifuge. Having failed, she needed another line of attack, and Gold fell right into her lap. Gold wouldn't have spoken to anyone until after Colby fired him. Not knowing Ebony was a terrorist, he wouldn't have gone running to his weight-lifting instructor. But when he saw her next, she'd have pumped him until he spilled the whole story.

Colby climbed the steps by the door and held everyone's attention as three Brink's guards escorted Gold out. One of the reporters called,

"Dr. Colby, the tour of the probe can wait. We must see Biomed and Cognitive Sciences. Now."

"And what would you expect to *see?*" she challenged.

"Proof," retorted a woman reporter.

"Nonsense," said Colby. "You'd see what Dr. Gold described—a perfectly preserved alien corpse, in a cryogenic chamber, in a small lab rigged for *full* sterility procedures, absolutely *full*. None of you will get into that room."

There was an uproar. "We're hiding nothing!" she lied. "We reported we have well-preserved tissue. Dr. Shiddehara mentioned how study of the alien eyes will yield clues to the spectrum of the alien's sun. Skin tissue likewise. Chemical analysis of the flesh may reveal their sun's composition for the planet on which they evolved probably formed from the same matter that condensed into their sun. Calculations are possible. But not if the tissue is contaminated. I repeat, for your safety and the potential reliability of our data, not one of you will enter the chamber." She was sweating.

When the protests subsided, she relented. "You may, however, view the chamber through our monitors. Biomed personnel will answer your questions. You'll find that we do have the capability to attempt a cloning. We couldn't do our primary job without it because those who are expert in the necessary fields are also prominent in the field of clone research. No such project is, however, under way. No such facility has been set up. No such authorization has been given us. No such budget exists. You may check all that."

"Then you deny the charge?"

"That we're mad scientists? Certainly. Are you mad journalists? Do you deny that charge?"

"We're angry journalists!" said a woman representing three science magazines. "We toured Biomed and you never showed us this corpse."

"You saw every phase of the investigations *currently* under way. We've given you a coherent picture of the thrust of our research. I'd think experienced journalists would appreciate that. I would not expect anyone but sensation mongers to be diverted by the hysterical allegations of one deeply disturbed individual. Why don't you continue your tour—which we've arranged to be least disruptive to our work— and later, check the facts behind this so-called evidence you've been given? Then I'll answer your questions.

"But I will not tolerate an ever-escalating melee. This is a research facility, ladies and gentlemen, not a commodity trading pit. Those who wish to tour the probe are welcome to step into the corridor where cars await you. Others may catch the shuttle leaving for Luna Station in half an hour. It has room for the few who've completed the tour here. I will instruct the Brink's guards to see you to the dock."

She turned her back and went out. Someone met her in the doorway, and she waved them on into the lab.

Titus expected an uproar. But the rumble of discontent did not wax any louder as the reporters talked it over. He heard one group deciding not to accuse Colby of buying time to hide the evidence, but to send one of their own in as a spy. But no one volunteered. In the end, a group of science writers made for the electric carts that would take them to the airlock for the probe tour. By ones and twos, the others followed.

The person Colby had sent through approached Titus with two computer media cases, the two copies of his catalogue. "If you'll just sign for these, Dr. Shiddehara, I'll leave them with you. Dr. Colby says you'll be through with them by the time of her conference in the morning. I'll pick them up then. And we'll be leaving guards here, if that's all right with you. This is legal evidence for the moment."

Shimon peered around Titus' elbow. "Which is which?"

One was the copy the reporter had brought, and the other bore the Project logo.

As he initialed the security man's electronic clipboard, Titus answered, "Good question."

As the lab emptied, Titus stared at the two boxes now sitting on top of one of the consoles. Where to start?

He saw two guards parting Inea from a pair of reporters. She glanced his way as the guards herded her toward the door with the others. Titus called, "Go on home and get some sleep. You'll have some real work tomorrow." Frowning, she took a step toward him. He shook his head. "I'll call you. Soon as I have anything. Promise." Slowly, she turned away.

He watched her leave, wishing mightily he could go with her. But she probably preferred solitude to his company. Again, he realized Abbot had never shown up to discover Titus hadn't Marked her. *At least she won't go looking for him!*

He hefted the two data cases. "Well, now what?"

Shimon called across to a group leaving. "Lorie!"

A chubby redhead wearing thick glasses limped toward them. Shimon introduced her, "Titus, Lorie here is a software wizard in her spare time." Quickly he briefed Lorie. "So how do we tell which one has been tampered with?"

"Good question," observed Lorie. "You mean Dr. Colby expects you to do this by morning, Doctor?"

"She's an administrator, not a programmer."

"With all due respects, Doctor, I don't think you're enough of a programmer to get it done in time."

"I agree. Can you help?"

She tapped one long fingernail on each of the boxes. "Whoever's playing tricks would've altered the data on the Taurus region stars— not anywhere else. Right?"

"Reasonable assumption."

"There's unpublished data in here on those stars?"

"Terabytes of it—some ten years' worth. I study dozens of parameters on each object. I use an ultra-customized Carrington-Worthy database that was made for me."

"I see. Do you have documentation on the customizing?"

"In my handheld."

Lorie sat down at a nearby console and called it to life muttering about needing the wireless network that just wasn't working. "Plug in and shoot me all of it, plus anything else on the catalogue's operation. I'll bet the saboteurs didn't know about the customizing. Next, I want an exhaustive list of everything in the Taurus region. And I need your index of attribute summaries. Then send out for enough sandwiches and coffee to last all night. Shimon, do you think you could stick around in case I need some help?" She raised her eyebrows at Titus as if to say, *Are you still here?*

"I'll see to it all, Lorie," answered Titus. And to Shimon, he added, "You're both on double-time overtime."

"I'll stay," replied Shimon, and began to connect the twin catalogue modules into the system while asking Lorie if she wanted tuna or chicken salad or maybe more pizza.

Titus retired to his office and transferred the data Lorie needed, then stuck with it as she demanded other data.

Nearly two hours later, he rocked back in his chair to watch her at her console, her intensity creating an aura of sexual beauty. She now had six monitors set up around her and was tapping away on three keyboards. Shimon was hovering in the background, loose cables festooned around his neck, ready to build her any configuration she wanted, his whole attitude betraying how attracted he was to her.

Idly, Titus pulled up Lorie's records, discovering her last name was unpronounceable, and her credits in her field were staggering. Small wonder she'd tackle the absurd at a moment's notice. She was simply having fun.

Finally, Titus relaxed enough to consider things in perspective. He made some notes in his Bell 990 handheld on Ebony, listing the flimsy evidence against her, her physique, her political background, her Brink's file entry showing lack of computer literacy, and that Gold was in one of her classes.

Gold. Gold! He sat bolt upright.

Assume Ebony was a terrorist and knew about the cloning project and about the sleeper. *Destroy the sleeper, and make it look like the Project was covering up after Gold's accusation.* That would be the end of Project Hail.

It might already be too late.

Titus tore out of the lab.

─── THIRTEEN ───

Titus rounded the corner into the Biomed corridor at a dead run. He pulled up short. All the guards were gone.

It was third shift, "night." But that was no reason for the corridor to be deserted. He crept along, holding his breath until he realized where the sense of wrongness came from. All the LED panels labeling the doors were dark.

He approached the short hall leading to the sleeper's chamber. The security equipment had vanished with the guards. The sleeper's door was dark. No security evident.

Disbelieving, he touched the hall floor with his toe, all senses alert for alarms. There were Brink's alarm systems he'd never heard of. Theft wasn't his field. *Nothing here!*

Fear put an edge on his senses. As he approached the door, he felt his way into the room beyond. *Abbot!* The feel of his father's Influence was unmistakable.

Half a dozen humans were in there, too, all intent on their work. Two bored guards flanked the door on the inside.

The sound of a power drill inside decided Titus. He opened the door and marched in, planting himself between the two guards and gazing through the double-walled bio-isolation airlock and shower into the chamber. Hands behind his back, he bounced on the balls of his feet and intoned, "I have to check progress here." He ignored the two heavy dart guns aimed at his back. "Well? How much longer will it be?"

"How should we know, Dr. Shiddehara?" asked one guard. The other added, "Sir, you're not on our clearance list."

"*I* know that," he snapped. "So does Dr. Colby." He didn't even have to Influence him to the desired conclusion.

Across the room, Abbot turned to look toward him with raised eyebrows.

"I'll be right there," called Titus, and stepped aside into the opaque shower alcove to strip and walk through the shower stall, then dress in the disposable suit and light bubble mask everyone else inside wore.

Abbot was waiting when Titus stepped out of the airlock and closed it behind him. Abbot greeted him with an ironic bow. "That was bold, but foolish. They'll report you."

"I expect. But this is an open secret now."

Cloaking his words, Abbot asked, "You expect me to handle Carol for you?"

"I can handle Carol. And I won't need Influence for it anymore than I did with those two back there."

Abbot studied him skeptically, then strolled over to two men who were wrestling an instrument up onto the workbench. The casing bore signs of having been cut open, then repaired. All the cloning equipment that had been in crates was now up on the counters, and showed similar signs of modification.

As Titus followed Abbot, he saw a crate that hadn't been opened— the variable womb. It was being used to support a piece of countertop which held a terminal and some locked file cabinets. When Abbot paused, Titus gestured to the scene about them. "Was this your idea?" He had to admit it was clever. The incriminating evidence had suddenly been modified into customized lab equipment unsuited for cloning.

Casting a pall of blurring Influence around them, Abbot demanded, "Titus, why didn't you come to me with the hunger? Why did you pretend you were all right?"

God. I did fool him! "I felt all right. And I am now." Around them, people wrapped up their work and one-by-one, began leaving.

154

"I shouldn't have believed you. I should have checked the data on how long you were dead. But I was worried about Sisi. I figured it was no accident you had her in there alone. When I found I was right, I admired your technique. I doubt if anyone else would have detected your work on her."

Titus glanced about and noticed that Sisi wasn't there. "I expected you to detect it," brazened Titus. "But I didn't plan on her getting hurt. I don't know how she could have escaped suffocation since I was driven dormant."

"She crawled down to a floor vent where there was a little more air. She was injured doing it, though."

"I see. I'm sorry."

Abbot frowned. "No, you don't see. You were dormant more than the three minutes the humans thought you'd been dead. After I checked on Sisi, I went into the wreckage of the centrifuge computers and found you'd suffocated at *least* eighteen minutes before they got that thing opened!"

Shit. No wonder I was so hungry.

"When I found that out," continued Abbot, "I looked for you, but couldn't find you. Then I ran across your unMarked, and discovered what you'd done to *her.*"

Titus bristled. "When I found out what *you'd* done to her, I wanted to kill you! Just be glad I didn't go even a bit feral, or I'd've ripped you apart when I got in here."

Abbot recoiled, and Titus wondered if he'd let a little too much ferocity show for a sane luren.

"Listen," said Titus. "The Law says you could have done worse and been within your rights. Blood Law means as much to me as to you, so you'll never catch me in a violation." *Inea's bare word is as good as any planted compulsion.*

"Let's hope I don't," Abbot intoned, gazing at Titus with wide-open eyes. "You know what my duty would be then."

Titus' confidence evaporated. *Maybe he knows she had been unsilenced!* Titus *had* checked Abbot's work on Inea, but he was no match for Abbot. He could have missed a clue. Then, sternly, he told himself to stop building his father up into a demigod. That tendency stemmed from the intrinsic physiology of being the man's son. He flogged his paralyzed brain back into combat. "I assume you've got the computer record to prove how long I was dormant in case you have to prove I'd gone feral."

155

"Of course, but have I ever used blackmail?"

"There's always a first time."

"You wrong me deeply."

"No. I know how much you want to go home."

"And I know how much you fear that my signal may get through. If you've gone the slightest bit feral, that fear could drive you to any unpredictable and dishonorable act."

Oh, it was a neat trap. Titus would have to toe the line as never before. Even his handling of Sisi Mintraub could be questioned. *Best defense is a strong offense.*

"I'll make a deal with you," offered Titus. "Promise to treat Inea as my Marked, whether or not she is Marked, and I'll tell you what the ninja's next move is going to be."

Abbot hardly blinked. "You think I don't already know?"

Oh, he's good! "You don't." Their eyes locked.

Abbot thought it over. "Why not just Mark the woman and have done with it?"

"It has to do with the nature of humans. Utterly beyond your comprehension." Despite what she'd said, Titus was certain Inea was loathe to wear a brand. *Abbot has no idea what it feels like to have a willing human ally.* "You wouldn't understand my motive if I could explain it."

"No doubt."

"You won't get a hint out of me unless you promise."

"Why would you give away an advantage? If knowledge of the ninja's next move is any sort of advantage."

"Not give. Sell. You'll get value for your sacrifice."

"If what I get is of as little value as what I give, I doubt it would be worth it. It shouldn't take me much effort to discover the ninja's plans."

"But do you have the time? I'll share what I know now if you promise to treat Inea as my Marked."

"For how long?"

"Forever."

"Suppose you Mark her and then release her?"

"Then, too."

"That's not reasonable!" objected Abbot.

"She's only one human. There are so many others."

He shrugged. "Never have understood Residents! So. Inea's off limits to me forever. Now what of the ninja?"

Titus recited his evidence. They were alone now except for the guards sealed on the other side of the isolation lock.

156

"Ebony statue you call her? Interesting. Ebony is her stage name. And Gold is in one of her classes? That's not a lot of information to get for selling a potential stringer."

"Think it through," urged Titus. "I'm surprised Ebony hasn't tried for the sleeper yet. She knew about the clone project from Gold hours ago. If she hasn't turned up—"

"When did you say you saw her with Gold?"

Titus told him.

Abbot went paler than normal. "A bomb."

In two bounds, he was beside the cryogenic equipment, yanking access hatches off the pedestal that held the sleeper's bubble. "Carol pulled the guards off and shut down this corridor to keep reporters from identifying this lab. But it was an hour later that I talked her into this plan for obscuring the cloning project. An hour unguarded!"

Abbot stuck his head inside the pedestal, examining the underside of the platform supporting the sleeper. His voice boomed, "Get the other side. Look for anything suspicious."

Titus ripped off panels. "What am I looking for?"

"A small, crude housing, probably not wired into the mechanisms. She had no time for finesse."

One of the guards called, "Is anything wrong?"

Abbot replied, "Could be a bomb or incendiary! Get—"

"Call that in," ordered one guard to the other. "I'll help them."

Abbot shouted, "No, don't come in! Get out of here, both of you! We can handle it." Despite the Influence Abbot threw into the command, they hesitated, then left.

As soon as the humans were gone, Abbot discarded his face mask, wriggling deep into one compartment.

Titus scanned the last of the compartments on his side. *Nothing! Must have missed it!*

Abbot ripped off the last panel, pushing himself inside. "I've got it!"

Titus scrambled around to where Abbot's feet jutted out onto the floor. Squatting on his heels, he surveyed the machinery that whirred and shushushed under the sleeper's platform. His eyes scanned the open pedestal restlessly as he tried not to think what would happen if the bomb went off.

What's that? Through the other open panel next to the one Abbot had crawled into, deep in the shadows to one side, Titus saw a glint of pewter, a lozenge shape that just didn't fit. He had studied so many of Abbot's fabrications implanted into his servers that he was sure this was another one. *Or a second bomb?*

But no, Abbot had checked that panel just after he got rid of his bubble face mask. Titus edged closer. The foreign shape was visible only from one very narrow angle. It was deep inside. To get at it, a technician would have to take his bubble mask off.

It's a transmitter component. Got to be.

Titus pulled his mask off and thrust himself into the pedestal. The pewter shape was held only by two wing nuts, not wired into anything. It had two expensive logic circuit connectors. *It's Abbot's.* Fumbling, heart pounding, Titus freed the thing. It was no bigger than the palm of his hand, and hardly as thick as his wrist.

He backed out, stuffed his find into a pocket of the disposable suit, and got his mask on before Abbot called, "This was set to blow half an hour ago! Get me a number eight hex key wrench—on the bench where I was working."

Titus dashed across the room. Abbot's tools were always laid out a certain way. He found the wrench and passed it in to Abbot, sweating despite the chill. What would taking the transmitter piece matter if the bomb went off?

Abbot backed carefully out of the hole. He held a flat brown box which he set on a corner of the pedestal. A numeric display on top had frozen. Abbot pried the top off. Inside, it was crude, but Titus knew it was potent from the way Abbot worked over the sloppily soldered connections. He looked up at Titus and grinned. "I'm glad I dined while you were showing off your computer! At least my hands are steady."

Titus didn't dare breathe, and he couldn't watch. He studied a wrinkle in the airlock wall and saw the emergency evacuation signs were lit, though the siren hadn't gone off.

Without warning, the door burst open.

Sirens were hooting out there in the corridor.

The insistent flashing of the corridor evacuation lights outlined a slim, black form that leaped into the room, an automatic dart gun in one hand, and a long knife in the other.

Ebony slashed through the plastic isolation curtain wall, leveled the dart gun and cut loose at the sleeper's bubble.

Titus dived across the room in a low tackle, under the line of darts, and hit her knees. She fell forward over his back, and the gun went flying in an arc, butt first, right at Abbot. Darts sprayed in a wild pattern before the firing stud popped up. Titus twisted and grappled for the knife.

Meanwhile, Abbot braced and let the dart gun slam into his shoulder, concentrating wholly on the bomb.

Titus got a purchase and used his strength to wrench the knife from Ebony's hands, only now thinking to Influence her.

But before he could exert control, she curled, planted a foot in Titus' crotch, and with a yell shoved him into the air, snatching her knife out of his stunned grip.

Abbot jerked, startled, then swore, surged to his feet, and hurled the bomb at the far wall. He hit the floor in a flat dive just as Titus landed jackknifed over the sleeper's bubble shield, the hard casing in his pocket ramming into his pelvis and abdomen with searing pain.

Then a hot wall of pure sound slammed into Titus.

When it was over, there was a hole in the wall behind the workbench, showing the plumbing of the adjacent women's rest room spewing fountains of water into the air. Under Lunar gravity, it was gorgeous. Shards of instrumentation caromed off the ceiling and rained slowly down.

The tone of the sirens outside changed, and those in the room cut loose with a barrage of sound more alarming than the explosion. But the decompression alarms remained silent. Abbot had put the bomb where it would do the least damage.

Titus dragged himself upright, to find Ebony charging at him—no, he realized, at the sleeper.

Still on the floor, Abbot focused Influence and spoke one word. "Halt!"

The command paralyzed Titus and froze Ebony in mid-stride. Her lips distorted into a snarl, and her muscles bulged as they fought one another. She even managed to inch forward despite Abbot's compulsion. Her hatred beat at Titus.

She's committed herself to a suicide mission. Titus knew now that he hadn't the power to stop her as Abbot had. Abbot rose with a leisurely grace and plucked the knife from Ebony's fingers. Then he dispelled his Influence. Movement returned to both Titus and Ebony, but Abbot pushed Ebony down and instructed, with less power, "Ebony, sit here until I tell you to move."

Abbot turned to Titus. "Sloppy of me. I apologize."

Titus swallowed hard. Abbot had not used anything like that kind of power in the Goddard Station men's room, but it was always his to command. *An object lesson.* "Think nothing of it," he croaked. "You saved my life."

"As I had expected you to save mine, child."

"Sloppy of me."

"You did your best. For that I thank you, though it was no more than your filial duty. But still, I claim her."

Titus slid off the bubble. "No! You can't kill her!"

Abbot's stare withered Titus' guts.

"I mean, we have to turn her over to the humans. If you claim her here, what will we do with the body? You know they'll find out she died of exsanguination."

"Cut with her own knife."

"And without bleeding all over the floor?"

He considered. "You have a point, but I'm not hungry. I could share her with you, and still leave enough mess."

"We don't have *time.* Damage Control will be in here soon, and then Brink's will get hold of Ebony. Ten minutes later the reporters will be onto it. Neither you nor I want this Project canceled. Therefore, *Carol* has to report this so it won't look like a terrorist scotched Carol's plan to cover up a cloning!"

"Perhaps I've underestimated you."

"Never mind," said Titus, fighting alarmingly mixed emotions at that praise. "Let's get to Carol. Now!"

Abbot insisted on replacing the access panels before they left to prevent water damage to the cryogenic mechanism.

The trip through the corridors was uneventful. Damage Control converged on the area, but civilians had already been evacuated. It was no problem to cloak themselves and Ebony, who hung limply between them, then just filter through the ranks of those intent on the disaster. Ten minutes later, they arrived at Carol Colby's apartment.

She opened the door at their first signal, and her jaw fell. She was wearing only the tee shirt she'd been given at Goddard. Barefoot, without makeup, hair in disarray, she did not look like a formidable administrator.

Behind her, Titus saw that her apartment, while larger and more luxuriously furnished, was about the same as his. Her carpet was red, the drapes a pattern with the same red in them. The furniture was softly upholstered in what seemed real leather, probably cloned at Luna Station. Planters divided the large room into areas.

Looking up and down the hall, Colby yanked them into the room, closed the door and leaned against it, lips pale. "You were there when the bomb went off!"

Titus hardly heard Abbot's reply. At the entry to an office alcove to the right of the central room stood Inea.

She had one hand on the controls of the vidcom, which displayed a news broadcast from Earth featuring the interview with Carol they'd all witnessed in Titus' lab earlier.

Titus locked eyes with Inea. Her face told him how ghastly he appeared. He still wore the isolation suit, *sans* mask. But it was soiled, torn, and disintegrating where water had splashed. His face felt flash-burned and sooty. His vision danced with spots from the explosion, and his ears roared.

"Inea, what are you doing here?"

"My civic duty. What are you doing here?"

Titus pointed at Ebony. "This is the ninja. She set the bomb. When it failed to go off, she tried a direct attack."

Colby stared at Ebony, astonished, then nodded. "She's the right size, and certainly has the strength." She urged them to put Ebony down on the bed, then filled Inea in on the crisis in the Biomed dome, finishing to Abbot, "Did we lose the specimen?"

"When we left, the cryogenic unit was intact." He gave her a version of how they'd located the bomb and how he'd tossed it at the wall away from the cryogenic unit.

"Then its biological isolation wasn't breached, and all we have to do is move it to a clean room and begin work. Good. Abbot, you've performed another heroic service and will be amply rewarded."

Before Abbot could make any modest disclaimer, Inea burst out, "Amply rewarded! Carol—after what I just told you? And you said you'd have to—"

"Yes," said Colby, suddenly doubtful and confused.

Titus moved to Inea's side, stopping when she retreated faintly. "Carol is very tired. And her *judgment* where Abbot is concerned. . . ." He shrugged, catching Inea's eye.

She absorbed that, watching Abbot. Titus felt her anger rise, knew Abbot would sense it if he weren't too occupied with controlling Ebony as well as Colby. Neither of the humans noticed how the ninja slumped docilely on the bed.

Colby's confusion cleared. "Don't worry, Inea. Abbot has just redeemed—"

"Carol!" Inea charged across the carpet to confront the director. "Call Mirelle in here. She'll tell you Abbot was with her—having sex—when he was supposed to be at the demonstration. That's insubordination. And if that's not enough, get Brink's to cross-check the signature on that order to Mihelich to start the cloning project. If the reporters get hold of that and don't find out Abbot forged your name, the whole project will be dead. You told me so yourself not half an hour ago. You said you'd fire him."

While Carol again paused doubtfully, Inea whirled and speared Titus with a triumphant glance. She had single-handedly vanquished the opposition Titus couldn't handle.

Oh, God! Titus felt weak all over, and he realized his own fatigue was catching up to him. He'd never lived like this before. His nerves weren't hardened to shock after shock after crisis after trauma without letup for whole days at a time.

While Titus leaned against the vidcom unit, Abbot chuckled. Adroitly, he manipulated Colby to take his laugh as a valid refutation of all the charges. "You signed the order, Carol. Surely you remember that."

But still Colby seemed confused. Her mind was strong and she had her ethics. Abbot would need more than gentle suggestion, or she'd begin to add up the inconsistencies in her behavior where Abbot was concerned, and that would be the beginning of the end of the luren on Earth.

The vidcom chimed.

Relieved, Colby hastened to answer. A small square cleared in the upper right-hand corner of the news broadcast. It showed a woman in a Damage Control uniform with Brink's officer's patches. "Dr. Colby, the Biomed dome is secure. No pressure leaks. However, four rooms will be out of service for a month and the engineers say this will cause another delay getting the wireless network up." She went on to describe the condition of the cryogenic chamber, finishing, "But there's no sign of either Dr. Shiddehara or Dr. Nandoha. I've begun—"

"They're both here with me. They've brought me the ninja, the terrorist who sabotaged the centrifuge. She also may be responsible for the bombing. Send four very strong armed men up here immediately. I want her questioned, under drugs if necessary, before my press conference tomorrow. We must establish who she works for and why she did this."

"Right away!" The vidcom window disappeared, restoring the news broadcast to a feature on the history of the Project.

"That takes care of that," said Colby in her usual command voice. "By the time Nagel sends me a policy decision on handling Gold's revelation, I'll know enough about Ebony to divert the reporters with facts. Now, as soon as they take her away, we should all get some sleep. Things will be more manageable in the morning. They always are." She ran a hand through her hair, increasing the mess.

Inea rounded on Colby. "I don't believe this. It's as if you didn't hear a word I said."

"Good description," put in Titus.

She shifted to him. "Whose side are you on, anyway?"

"You know that very well." He couldn't oppose Abbot in such a way as to reveal luren secrets. The guilt that knifed through him almost doubled him over. He dropped into a chair opposite the screen.

Colby said, "Think, Cellura. Abbot has cleared himself of any wrongdoing by his extreme heroism. He's an engineer, not a bomb expert. But he saved the specimen and caught the ninja." She looked at Ebony. "No mean feat, considering."

Ebony responded by straightening her back, but kept her head bowed, staring unfocused at the luxurious red carpet.

Abbot glanced at Titus. *Call off your woman.*

Wearily, Titus said, "You've got to concede Carol's point, Inea. The press will dance for joy at the chance to create a new folk hero. When Carol reveals how Abbot missed the demonstration to track down the assassin who tried to get me—and when she says that Abbot fielded that bomb with his bare hands to save my life—why, it'll make history."

Finally, Inea shrugged, defeated. "Is that the way you're going to handle it, Carol?"

"It sounds good," she responded vaguely.

"I don't think so," countered Abbot. "Why don't we just leave my name out of it. It's enough to say that members of the Project team subdued the terrorist. The image of a harmonious team is even better than a single hero. . . ."

"See? Now does that sound like a man who would defy his superiors and disrupt this project? No, it—" The door signal chimed and Colby broke off and started for the door.

As she passed Ebony, the black woman exploded into motion with a savage snarl of triumph.

── FOURTEEN ──

From Ebony's extended fingers flew a metallic gleam—a *shuriken*, a ninja's throwing star. The door opened.

Titus launched himself at Colby with a yell. As he slammed into her, Suzy Langton, seeing Titus attacking Colby, dove at Titus. The three of them collided and piled into Abbot, Langton on top.

Langton hissed and swore as the star grazed her face, leaving a line of blood as she dashed the sharp pointed weapon aside and brought the muzzle of her dart gun to bear on Titus' face—lethal if she shot him in the eye.

"Don't move or I'll—" was all she got out before another body hit her and knocked her aside. Out of the corner of his eye, Titus saw it was Inea. Her weight couldn't have added more than thirty pounds to the pileup, but Abbot, on the bottom, grunted and heaved to no effect. The bodies had the same mass as on Earth, and were just as hard to start moving—or to stop.

Ebony walked up and over the tangled bodies, planted a foot on Titus' neck and uttered a nerve shattering yell as she launched herself at the Brink's man—Langton's single partner—who stood framed in the doorway, dart gun drawn but pointed at the ceiling.

Titus heard a grunt and a sickening crack, and suddenly the air was full of anesthetic darts.

"What happened?" demanded Colby from under Titus.

Simultaneously, Langton jammed her foot into Titus' solar plexus and shoved off. Titus scrambled up and went after Langton shouting, "No! Suzy, she's insane!"

But Langton closed on Ebony with total confidence, as if she'd won matches against the weight lifter before.

The Brink's man lay against the doorjamb, head twisted unnaturally. His gun lay on the floor outside the door.

Ebony feinted with one foot, the beginnings of a kick which drew a reflex response from Langton. Then all at once, she was on the Brink's man's gun and spinning toward Langton. Titus redirected himself with one foot and flew at Ebony.

Three darts grazed his scalp and thumped into the door jamb. He slammed into Ebony, the two of them skidding out into the nearly deserted, night-darkened corridor. The anesthetic numbed his scalp.

Langton demanded, "Shiddehara, out of the way!"

One-handed, Ebony threw Titus at Langton, aiming the gun with her other hand. Langton side-stepped, whirled, and, with her leg at full extension, higher than her own chin, Langton swiped the gun from Ebony's grip with her foot.

Titus fetched up on the floor. "Suzy, she's suicidal!"

Ebony crouched and charged toward Titus, her hand dipping into her bodice again. The dark fingers emerged with a gleaming *shuriken* that spun at Titus.

Titus dodged the point-blank throw of the *shuriken*.

Simultaneously, Abbot roared, "Ebony, stop!"

But it was too late.

As Ebony obeyed Abbot's Influence, and failed to execute her dodging motion, Langton's heel smashed into the side of Ebony's head, snapping her neck. The black woman dropped like a stone, dead before she skidded to a halt at Titus' feet. He hardly heard Inea's scream.

In front of him, Suzy Langton had recovered from delivering the blow with her usual poise and stood swaying. Then she crumpled in a limp heap.

Titus scrambled to her side as her dying breath hissed out, forming the words, "Must have been poisoned. Damn her."

Titus gathered the woman up in his arms, hurting in a most peculiar way. *She died protecting me.*

Inea skidded to her knees beside Titus.

"She's dead," he announced, surprised how husky his voice was. "Just as dead as the other guard and Ebony. The *shuriken* that was aimed at Carol hit her. It was poisoned."

"You sure she's dead? Carol's calling the medics."

"Idiot-love, sometimes you ask stupid questions."

"I guess you can recognize death, huh?"

Abbot's shadow loomed over them. "You should have let me kill her in the cryo-lab. Next time you'll know better."

Inea rose to her feet and hissed, "You're no better than she was! It's you who ought to be dead."

"Call her off, Titus, or our agreement is void."

"Inea, don't. There's still a lot you don't know."

She looked down and her hand went to Titus' head and came away bloody. "You're hurt!"

He got to his feet. "Already healing up. If anyone asks, it's nothing. Okay?" His scalp wasn't even numb now.

"Titus, are you sure? If one of those poison things hit you, and Langton's dead—"

"Please don't argue. Not here. Trust me."

The way she looked at him made him hungry.

A Brink's squad jogged around the corner escorting a medical team which spread out to all three corpses. From her door, Colby called, "Titus, Abbot, Inea, come in here. It's safer." Then she asked the medics, "Are they all dead?"

"Yes, Ma'am," answered a woman who supervised them.

While Colby attended to the officials, Titus retreated to the chair opposite the vidcom and dropped into it, burying his face in his hands. He had known a sort of intimacy with Langton. It was amazing how much her death hurt.

Abruptly, the room filled with the crackling of flames. His head snapped up on a rush of adrenaline, then he realized it was only the news broadcast. As the camera closed in on a burning house, the neighborhood seemed strangely familiar.

". . . no one inside at the time of the blast. World Sovereignties Police will investigate, but firefighters on the scene say it's clear the house was bombed, and is a total loss. Dr. Shiddehara has not yet been reached for comment, though we have a reporter on Project Station and should have something for you by morning. This is Solomon Lawrence reporting for Independent News, North America."

"My house," muttered Titus.

"Oh, Titus," said Inea. Her sympathy almost undid him.

"No, you don't understand. The master copy of my catalogue's gone." *But now they've no reason to kill me.*

———

Hours later, Titus dragged himself to his own apartment. More than physical fatigue, he felt inwardly battered.

Colby had pulled herself together to deal with all the details of the official inquiries into three more deaths in addition to the guards in the cryo-lab. Ebony had sold her life for four others, but they had all been Brink's guards, not key scientists. The Project was not at all damaged—except possibly by the publicity.

And Colby was ably managing that. She hadn't allowed Titus and Abbot to be questioned, insisting that Titus' work was only just beginning, and Abbot's time was too valuable to divert just now that they must prepare a new cryogenic room.

She had them both record notarized depositions, and as soon as the reporters started calling in, she told them she would replay the depositions at the meeting in the morning, and would supply each of them with a copy.

Promising to send the reporters home tomorrow as scheduled, she cleared everyone out of her apartment. Seeing Titus to the door, she added, "How soon can you get us some reliable numbers? The situation on Earth is very bad. We'll have to move the probe launch up again."

Titus had grinned ferociously, and promised, "You'll have reliable figures when you're ready. Depend on it."

Now, trudging toward his door, he wondered if he could deliver. In the morning, he thought, he'd sift through every Taurus region entry in the two copies of the catalogue. Maybe he'd spot the tampered entries if the substitutions were clumsy. But now, he needed a meal and some sleep.

Fishing in the pocket of his disposable suit for his door key, he remembered it was with his clothes in the cryo-lab. The guard had been withdrawn from his door. He smacked his open hand angrily against the door. "Shit!"

He turned away, shoving his hands in his pockets. The transmitter component was tearing a hole in the flimsy suit.

"Titus?"

He spun in his tracks. "Inea!" She stood in the open door of his apartment. "What are you—how did you—"

"I still have your key, and you've got mine. Are you going to stand out there all night?"

He went in, shut the door and leaned against it. He couldn't take his eyes off her. "Your key is in my pants in Biomed. Want me to go get it?"

"Tomorrow." The microwave bleeped. "I figured you'd be hungry, so I heated some water. I hope I set it right."

"Inea, why are you doing this? You threw me out this morning. Or was that yesterday? And in Segal's Castle, you still wouldn't . . . ." He didn't want to think of the condition Abbot had left her in. "And then when you'd bested Abbot for me, and I had to help him win anyway, I thought—"

She turned away. "Maybe we'll never be lovers again, but we're partners. You owe me answers, but I'm not cruel enough to question you when you're hungry."

Titus went toward the microwave, tossing the metal box onto the table as he passed, noting that she'd straightened the room up a little. "You got the setting right." She had laid out the packet of blood and the scissors just as he always did. He put one hand on the packet. *She loves me.*

The truth of that poured into an aching hollow within him that he had not known was there. "You did this beautifully," he told her, meaning, *I love you.*

"Thank you," she answered abstractedly.

Titus turned to find her studying the pewter-colored object. "Titus, this is a smart power source for a miniature motor."

"It is?" He hadn't examined it closely.

"Where did you get it?"

"That's a long story. But I'll tell you all of it."

She sat down at the table to study the thing more closely. "Have your dinner first."

"Not now." The thready hope beating through him made him willing to wait.

She met his eyes and offered brusquely, "I'll hold the cup for you while you drink, but I won't sleep with you."

He felt her love tearing her apart. He went to his knees beside her. Folding her in his arms, he kissed her in the deep, open communion that stirred her to the core.

For her to feel it, he had to let himself soak ectoplasm from her which roused his own craving for blood to a sudden fever pitch. But before she had a chance to struggle, he forced himself away. "That's what we *could* have—tonight if you will it."

She bit her lip, breath suspended, then shook her head. "I'll hold the cup for you, Titus, but don't ask for more."

He knelt there, lips only centimeters from her bare arm, but blocking the deep contact. It was one of the hardest things he'd ever done. Feeding was reflexive, a function of the senses that supported Influence. "I thought you understood. It isn't for me; it's for you."

She took his face in her hands, her lips working. He felt her temptation, and her confusion. "I can't. Not yet."

He stood her touch as long as he could, blocking off his hunger, then flung himself away to fetch up against the sink.

Gasping for breath, he arranged his features into a calm mask, and turned to find her folded over, face in her hands.

She straightened.

168

"Inea, I dare not accept your energies if you won't allow me to restore them."

Mutely, she shook her head. "I can't. Just the blood."

"No. Eventually you'd become weak, listless, depressed. You'd sicken and die even with the best medical attention."

"Like Mirelle de Lisle?"

"What?"

"After I left the demonstration, I headed for the mall, but I saw Mirelle coming out of an apartment. I'd seen her with Abbot before, and it suddenly occurred to me he's been—*taking* her?" At Titus' nod, she repeated, "Taking. What a horrible term! Anyway, Mirelle looked absolutely ghastly—wan, dark circles—she staggered as if drunk. At first I thought only to help her, but then we got to talking and I realized what Abbot had been doing during the demonstration."

Titus nodded. "But one thing you didn't know—she wears his Mark. Though I'd expect him to treat her better than that." And he recounted the incident at Goddard Station when Abbot had stolen Mirelle from him in retaliation for Titus' destruction of one component. "He wanted her only for her position in the Project. She can't keep anything from him."

"I refuse to believe he can be all that invincible."

"Oh, he's not. That," he said gesturing to the box on the table, "is another component of his transmitter. I had it on me all that time and he never knew."

She gaped. "Holy shit. And I thought you needed help!"

"I do. Stealing *that* was sheer luck, and—I'm not sure the transmitter is still his highest priority." He took a deep breath, wondering if she'd run out in the corridor screaming at this next revelation. "Are you ready for another shock—one as bad as I laid on you this morning?"

She toyed with the component. "That I've been sleeping with something that's not even human? What could be worse?"

"God, you do know how to hurt a man, don't you."

She frowned. "I'm sorry. I didn't mean to hurt you. It's just that I still don't see how it could be true. After all, if you *can* interbreed with humans, then. . . ."

". . . we must be human? Well, maybe what we know of genetics is kind of like Newtonian mechanics—just a special case? Or maybe all life in the galaxy is descended from a common ancestor?"

169

"Occam's Razor. Who needs all life in the galaxy when Earth has enough spontaneous mutation? If such a spaceship had really crashed on Earth, somebody would have noticed!"

She was trying to convince herself that his stock was human so she could sleep with him freely. He wanted it almost enough to let her do it, too. Very quietly, he said, "Somebody did notice."

"What?" She frowned. "You mean those silly old cave paintings?"

"No. We think it was in the early seventeenth century—late in Russia's Muscovite period. Near Vanavara."

"Look, check your facts before you lie to me. The hit near Vanavara was in 1908, not the seventeenth century!"

"By the eighteen hundreds, we were in Transylvania," he continued. "In 1908, it was clear that scientists would *know* what that ship was when they found it. There wasn't much left after the crash, but the impact had not destroyed the interstellar drive. In 1908, with atomic power being discovered on Earth and satellites not far off, the remains had to go. Four luren returned to trigger that explosion, and minimize the damage without leaving telltale traces like radioactive dust." He resisted the impulse to recite their names, as Abbot had taught him. "They never returned."

She thought that over. "You mean that ship out there could—my God, it could blow half the moon away!"

"It's not likely to blow. What is surprising is that in 1908, we still retained enough knowledge to explode the drive. They're designed not to do that."

"What is amazing," she countered, "is that you'd do it at all. That was your last link with—home. Was it the Tourists or the Residents?"

"I doubt there were such factions then." He eyed the component. "They all knew what humans would do if they ever suspected us." Titus had not lived through such a purge. "Just think about how it makes you feel, to know what I am."

"But I'm not trying to kill you!"

"That's only because you love me. What about Abbot?"

"I'd want to get him, even if he was human. He's an overgrown bully with delusions of godhood."

"He just believes differently than we do. And he's terrified of humans." Abbot had known luren who'd fled Eastern Europe during an uprising against vampires.

"You're defending him again! Whose side are you on!"

He studied the power source housing. *I wish I knew.*

170

"Titus, we might have to kill him."

"I couldn't, not just because it's against luren law. There's a deeper—real physical inhibition." He'd never actually triggered it, but he knew it lurked within him.

"But you have defied him. You told me so."

"Only when he let me." He relived that paralyzing blast of raw power Abbot had leveled at Ebony, freezing Titus too. *Why didn't he use that power in the men's room on Goddard?* Because he was playing with his son, fostering his son's strength. He was overconfident.

"He'll let you once too often and we'll get rid of him."

"He'd be replaced. At least *Abbot* might be won over."

"Who are you kidding?"

"Myself, maybe. But I think it's our only real hope. Use his very strengths against him—his sense of honor. He isn't as bad as some of the Tourists."

"Then I'd hate to meet the real McCoy."

"Yes, you would. Look, that was sheer genius, getting Colby to fire Abbot. If she hadn't already been heavily under Abbot's Influence, you'd have gotten him sent home."

"I know. Before Abbot came in, she was ready to kick him off the Project. I don't understand why you let him change her mind like that. And then you defended him!"

"She was fighting the Influence!" he explained.

"Well, good!" she misunderstood. "She's no faint hearted, simpering clinger!"

"Which is not good! You want to know why that team blew up our ship? Because we fear *humans!* Think! How would humans tell Residents from Tourists? And who'd bother?"

"But—"

"Abbot has been playing fast and loose with human minds all over this station. What if people discover that someone is warping the minds of those making important decisions for all humanity—and is doing so for the advantage of his own species as separate from humanity?"

"But that's why Abbot has to be—"

"Yes, but how long until they discover me too, then trace us back to Earth? Our lifestyle is horrifying and we have power over humans. How long until panic triggers a global witch hunt? Look how you felt about sleeping with an alien from outer space, and you've known me all my life. You love me, for pity's sake—and look how you feel. Think, Inea. What is the only reason I'd ever side with Abbot?"

171

"To keep all your people safe."

"So, I had to prevent Carol from seeing the illogic of not firing Abbot despite what he'd done, then deducing that she'd been Influenced by him." He peered at his disposable shoes. "Betraying you was the hardest thing I've ever done. I hope I never have to do it again, but I will if I must. So, before you try again, you've got to tell me because, no matter how hard I try to tell you everything, there'll always be something you don't know."

"You haven't been doing a very good job of telling me everything so far. Like, for example, why did Abbot tell you to call me off, as if I were your dog—or as if you'd Marked me, and he couldn't deal with me himself?"

"I haven't Marked you! I've never lied to you. Not about where the ship crashed, or when, or anything, and especially not about Marking you!"

She arched her brows and waited.

He told her the deal he'd struck with Abbot in the cryo-lab. "So now you're safe from him. He'll keep his word."

"And if he doesn't?"

"He won't go for you. He'll come for me, directly—and he can do almost anything he wants with me." He told her of the data Abbot had kept to prove to a luren court that Titus had gone feral. "So if you break luren law, it's my neck."

"That's not fair. I don't even know luren law."

"So check with me before doing anything."

She shook her head and scrubbed at her face with one hand. "This's all too much for me. I guess I'm tired." She got up. "Well, if your deal with Abbot is your big shocker for the night, the one you asked if I was ready for—"

"It wasn't." He had to force the words out.

She sank back into the chair searching his face.

There was only one way to say it. "I've been trying to tell you—the luren in the cryogenic chamber—the reason we risked our lives with that bomb is that he's still alive."

For a moment, her expression didn't change. Then it went wooden. "Oh." After a long while, she added, "I should have guessed. You must think I'm awfully dumb."

"It's just too many shocks too fast. I haven't been too bright lately either."

"What are we going to do? I mean if they warm the corpse—I mean, dormant luren—to get a cloning specimen, it'll come alive—won't it—he? He'll be ravenous. He'll kill somebody. We've got to tell Carol. Somebody has to—"

"Carol is under Abbot's control, and Abbot signed Carol's name to the order to try the cloning, or got her to sign it and made her forget."

"Abbot. Abbot! He'll father it—him!"

"I expect so." He recounted his first sight of the sleeper, and his deductions about Abbot's language research. "He's going to send his message using what he's learned from the ship's computers."

"Oh, my God. And you've been living with this all the time we've been—you're right. I never did understand the situation." In a very small voice, she asked, "Is there any more? Because if there is, heap it on me now while I'm down. I don't think I can take too many more falls like this."

"I don't think there are any more really major facts you don't know, but the minor ones may defeat you."

"Plan," she said dazedly. "We need a plan to stop him."

He outlined his approaches, ending, "But if I knew how to stop him, I'd have done it already. Every time I tangle with him, he ends up saving me."

"Don't be a defeatist. You've proved you can beat him." She hefted the power supply. "By the time he finds this gone, so many people will have been through there, moving the alien—I mean luren—around that he won't know you stole it. We'll keep him guessing, underestimating us, and too overloaded to think straight, and maybe we'll win."

Titus hitched up onto the rim of the sink, mentally reviewing what things must look like from Abbot's point of view. "It may be he's keeping himself overloaded. Or undernourished. Tell me again about Mirelle?"

She described the French woman's condition again.

"It's not like Abbot to just fail to show up at that demonstration. He might have put in a brief appearance, then had himself called away before he could be interviewed. Or I could see him staging an emergency elsewhere as an excuse not to show. But careless, open defiance of orders? Conspicuous absence? No. It's not like him. Which means he didn't *expect* to spend that time with Mirelle. Which means he'd driven himself over the edge and knew he couldn't manage that demonstration in such a state of hunger. Why?"

173

Titus recounted Abbot's derision of Titus' dietary habits. "He's taking blood as well as ectoplasm from Mirelle and maybe four others. That's his usual custom. In such a small population, he has to be circumspect. He's keeping his string as small as possible, and he's rationing himself."

"What could make him hungrier than usual?"

"Using Influence. Healing wounds. Dormancy. Fathering the sleeper. But that hasn't happened yet. From what I learned from Mintraub, I'll bet he's not been sleeping at all while he's been using Influence too much." He described the way the medics had fought Abbot's Influence. "So he's got the beginnings of desperate trouble on his hands—trouble from trying to do too much, too fast, with too many people."

"If he's sweating, we've got to keep the pressure on."

"Think about Mirelle, and the others! He'll have to Mark another stringer or overburden the ones he has. And offhand, I'd say Mirelle needs vitamins and iron—lots of it. There was a limit to how much of that Abbot could have brought with him—" He had to pause to explain how responsible luren made sure those they bled took heavy supplements.

"But he's not doing that for Mirelle? How many others is he bleeding dry?"

"He won't kill. Not here. Not until he's desperate, with his goal in sight, and he's a long way from that. So he won't violate any of the safety rules he pounded into me."

"Pounded? Did it take a lot of pounding?"

"To be brutally honest, yes, it did. At first, I only knew how hungry I was—I didn't know what I was doing."

"You haven't lied to me, have you?"

"No. I try very hard not to."

"You have killed humans—for blood."

"Yes. But it was long ago."

Dully, she announced, "I should turn you in for murder."

"Do you see why, when it comes to exposure, I'm on Abbot's side? And he's on mine, however much it galls him?"

"I've slept with an alien, a murderer. How low can you get?"

He wanted to gather her up and comfort her, but she'd run from him if he moved. At the same time, part of him loved her *because* killing disturbed her so deeply. "Imagine all the women who've had to sleep with husbands returned victorious from war—with blood on their hands."

"Not the same."

"No, but there's murder—and murder. I've never killed deliberately. Abbot has, and doesn't see anything wrong with it." He told her how Abbot wanted to take Ebony.

Suddenly, she looked away, tugging at her hair. "When Langton went after Ebony, you moved like a blur. I mean no one could move that fast. And before, when Ebony moved on Carol, I swear you were in the air before Ebony's hand dipped into her bodice. If you're so set on concealing what you are, why did you do that?"

Titus had not been aware of it. He slumped. Abbot hadn't even called him down for it. It was inconceivable that he hadn't noticed.

"I know why you did it," asserted Inea. "Because you care, and Abbot doesn't. I saw your face when Langton died. You risked your life—and your luren secrets—to save two humans, and you lost one. And you grieved. I saw Abbot's face, too. Maybe you should have let him kill Ebony, then Langton and the other guard wouldn't be dead."

"He couldn't have gotten away with it."

"That's the point. He'd be sent to Earth for trial!"

"I keep telling you, that's no solution."

"Then what *is*?"

He sighed. "Convincing him we're right. Using his strengths against him. Working at his weaknesses. And thanks to your noticing Mirelle's condition, I think I understand now why Abbot wanted Ebony. He's not getting what he needs from his stringers. They're fighting him. They're hating him. He's not getting what you've given me—so while he's been getting weaker, I've been getting stronger."

"So I should go to bed with you as a duty?"

"No!" he snapped. *I'm too tired for this.* "If it's doled out through gritted teeth, or dragged out over suppressed defenses, it's no good. And it has to go both ways, Inea, it has to or you'll end up like Mirelle."

She was still toying with the box. "Both ways," she repeated. "Both ways! That's it!"

"What?"

She leaped to her feet, pacing in gigantic moon strides, and she gesticulated with the box. "Both ways—two-way communication. I'm such an idiot! Don't you see, Abbot's real advantage is in knowing what's happening before you do. He's got you always looking over your shoulder for one of his—stringers—right? He's got stoolies at every corner!"

"Not quite that bad, but—"

"Listen! No army is any better than its intelligence. You're beaten before you start because you don't have any stoolies. If you did, Abbot could pick them right out of any crowd, couldn't he? So, we're going to convince him he's being watched all the time, and keep him so busy wondering, he won't have time to act. And while he's all tangled up in confusion, we'll run around his end guard and capture his goal—the sleeper—and *you'll* father the alien!"

"What!" Shock echoed through Titus.

She waved the box under his nose. "Well, what else did you have in mind? Why would you have stolen this otherwise?"

"I don't follow. But never mind, I'm not going to go around picking the brains of humans—"

"Shut up! Do you think I'd want you to?"

"No." He felt ashamed. "But—"

She tapped him on the chest with the box. "It's a compact power supply! Rechargeable." When he still didn't see, she spelled it out. "I build this into a system of microscopic bugs, and you sneak around and plant them, and I monitor them and tell you what he's up to! And he thinks he's being watched by your stringers—which don't exist. He gets so spooked that we walk right by him. Just like when you stole this—you Idiot-love!" She flung her arms around him and kissed him resoundingly.

He sank into it almost afraid of it. But she drew back, cocking her head to one side. "I guess I shouldn't have done that. It's teasing. It's just—I forgot myself."

"I'll wait. As long as you need."

She looked at the box. "But this will take a while. How can you survive? I mean, you do need ectoplasm, too."

"I can get enough to survive just being around people. And—if I must—I'm sure I can find someone willing." She went pale. He hastened to add, "But I won't have to for a while. Take your time. Get used to knowing what I am and see if knowing makes so very much difference."

Very seriously, she said, "It does." Her eye fell on the clock. "Shit. We've been talking for hours! I've got to get some sleep. I can't think straight anymore." She pocketed the box and went toward the door. "I'll get Brink's to let me in my place, and I'll see you in the morning." Over her shoulder she added, "I never thought I'd be grateful for the shop training you forced on me, but now I am because I know exactly how to get Abbot Nandoha!"

Every step she took hurt. He had to clutch the sink rim to make himself stay there. She paused at the door, and he stopped breathing. "You'll be all right?"

He nodded and tried to focus on her plan, telling himself he was letting her take the component because, even though they probably wouldn't catch much of Abbot's activity with bugs, still it would keep her too busy to challenge Abbot. Besides, maybe it would help. "Go. I'll be fine."

As the door closed behind her, his hand strayed to the packet of blood crystals on the sink drainboard. He shied from the thought of that sterile fluid coursing down his throat. He had to force himself to reheat the water and make the solution. He had lived on it alone for months at a time with no problem. Now, it was all he could do to choke it down. But he had to, just to get through tomorrow.

Sitting at the table, he chuckled over what Abbot would say if he could see him now. That led him to ponder Abbot's condition, seeing Abbot's risky use of Influence and the merciless pace he set himself in a new light. Feeling Abbot's desperation in his own bones, Titus could suddenly believe Abbot's vision of the end of the luren on Earth.

Titus saw himself through Abbot's eyes as a wayward child who demanded the utmost patience. He felt his father's love then, as he'd shared it on the shuttle leaving Earth. *Maybe it's wrong to stop their SOS?*

The thought sent thrills of shock through him.

Had he let Inea take the component just so he wouldn't have to destroy it, to strike that symbolic blow against Abbot's mission? Could he have done it at all? *What if I've been wrong and Abbot's right?*

FIFTEEN

Inea was as good as her word. With a bit of help from Titus getting parts and security codes, she designed eight tiny bugs slaved to a central unit made from a gutted PDA and the miniaturized power source. She even put a memory into it, programmed to debrief the bugs at intervals and save the data. The central unit interfaced with Titus' console, and would also pirate images from security scanners.

Titus, however, had little time to plant the bugs.

When he got back to his office, he discovered his black box had captured a terse message from Connie informing him he'd have to contend with Abbot alone.

Though she had people in the Project's groundside Communications and Supplies, Connie couldn't get anyone up to the station through the security designed to stop assassins. But she'd arranged to have his security clearance increased.

"When you hear about the bombing of your house," the message continued, "don't worry. We got there first, but this channel is not secure enough to discuss further plans."

She ended, "We can now guarantee your blood supply." They'd perfected a way of turning the crystals into maroon packing chips to be used in boxes shipped to his lab. "Just microwave to restore solubility, and dissolve. Connie."

Titus reported Abbot's doings and the situation with the sleeper and the transmitter, but omitted mention of Inea.

Later that day, while Colby was struggling to convince the reporters that the bombing had been a terrorist act, not an attempt to cover up a cloning lab, Titus was informed that his security clearance had been bumped up to Abbot's level.

Within an hour, he was given a heavier meeting schedule than ever before. While it provided a better overview of the Project and of Abbot's activities, it cut into the time he needed to compare the two copies of his catalogue.

Lorie had called in five other programmers. The news, however, was bleak. They found files that had been erased from the directory on each catalogue, files that didn't have appropriate security or date stamps on them, files Titus didn't recognize. Two different methods had been used on the separate catalogues, so it was likely that Titus could sort out the mess of fragmented temporary and backup files to construct one correct set of numbers.

Titus had both versions of the data put on line, and carried his Bell 990 around, tapping into his console through the station's system so he could work during meetings. At the edge of despair, he cherished the idea that Connie had an un-tampered version of the data, and the Tourists might have kept one, too, when they took his flight bag. His life's work was not lost, just inaccessible.

In one grazing encounter, Abbot coolly informed him that a mature luren would not be having such trouble.

178

After that, Titus spent a night attempting to reach a depth of the luren's mnemonic trance he'd never reached before, but the numerical data eluded him. Relationships, equations, functions, and useful constants were clear, but it seemed the data one plugged into the equations or substituted for algebraic expressions had never been recorded in his memory.

He had always been able to determine if a result seemed plausible, but he had grown up relying on computers. To him, a number was just a number and he'd even been known to confuse a number with its own inverse.

So he worked painfully and carefully through the Taurus region star systems described in his catalogue, searching for any anomalies, such as a planet at an incorrect distance from its sun, or a planet that was too large for its position. Laboriously, he wrote a program to compare the two sets of data, and soon had derived a third data set which he considered better than 70 percent reliable.

As he worked, the stellar systems he was intimately familiar with revived in his memory. During meetings, when he would peck at his Bell, people thought he was checking every claim made by the speakers. In fact, as his mind leaped from one insight to another, he often missed whole hours of the ponderous speeches designed more to fend off blame than to inform.

However, he didn't miss the departure of the reporters. Colby had Titus speak at the send-off ceremony. But she scripted the whole thing, allowing the reporters to read prescreened questions, to which Titus read prepared answers.

He told them how the loss of his home was also the loss of his life's work, but that he intended to recoup his loss by reconstructing the original catalogue, and implied that success was a certainty, given just a short time. When the reporters departed, the whole station breathed a sigh of relief.

The situation on Earth, however, did not improve. Colby and Nagel had not convinced everyone that the Project was not planning an illegal cloning. Several countries mounted unilateral investigations into the Project, and though such wheels moved very slowly, they were a source of anxiety.

Carol Colby, seeming drawn and much thinner despite the low-gravity plumping of her face, ordered an increase in the working pace, convincing them all that the Project could well be scrapped unless it showed results very quickly.

The construction of the probe had been going smoothly, but was still the limiting factor in the race against time. The workers accepted the new schedule, but the feverish pace caused an increased number of accidents and lost man hours.

Meanwhile, Engineering finally kindled the ship's light fixture. Standing under it, Titus felt a pinched pain behind his eyes. He wished mightily he could take his contacts out and see what the light was really like.

The spectrum was only one datum among many. After all, most tungsten or fluorescent lamps didn't exactly mirror the sun's spectrum. They were just a handy way to make light, and people endured them as best they could.

On the other hand, Biomed held that light had various other health effects on the body, as it did on plants. They were delighted that both species of alien had eyes well suited to the spectrum produced by their lamps, and concluded that the ship was probably made by those crewing it. Others argued that a leased vehicle would have been altered to suit the clients, so the data proved nothing. The aliens may have bought their space technology from a more advanced species.

But that argument was nothing compared to the bombshell dropped into an otherwise dull meeting by one of the bright young men working under Dr. Andre Mihelich. "The alien's skin probably functions as a sort of third eye," he declared.

When the uproar subsided, he cited research that had allowed blind humans to learn to "see" with the skin of the face using instruments that fed the data to the optic centers of the brain. "It seems to me," he announced, "both these alien species would experience pain and possibly severe injury upon exposure to Earth's sun."

Titus kept his face expressionless. He was glad that crossbreeding with humanity had blunted his sensitivity to the sun, but how much of a disadvantage would that be if they went home, as Abbot wanted? Would Earth's luren be blind on their ancestors' planet?

On the other hand, Earth's furious rejection of the cloning of the alien made it obvious that his kind would never be welcome among humans. Abbot's determination to signal the home world seemed more and more reasonable.

Titus fought the louring depression his disloyal thoughts evoked by throwing himself into his calculations. It was more soothing than a night's sleep, more nourishing than the dead blood he choked down, and more intriguing than anything he'd ever done before.

He and Inea customized a program written by a student at U.C. Berkeley to predict surface conditions on hypothetical planets. They assumed the atmosphere of the luren homeworld filtered out most of the ultraviolet, which accounted for their optical and skin sensitivity, then used the customized program to concoct a model of the atmosphere for the luren homeworld, deduce the planet's gravity, and guess its size. This produced a model of the luren solar system and a very vague guesstimate about characteristics of the sun itself.

He had to guess the planet's magnetic characteristics which would, combined with the solar irradiation figures, predict the amounts of heavier atoms, such as oxygen, that the planet would lose from the ionosphere. But using Earth's known loss of oxygen from the polar regions due to solar wind funneled in by the converging magnetic lines, he worked up a range of plausible assumptions.

At every turn, he relied heavily on the legends and traits of the purest blooded luren known.

Many times during those long sessions, he was acutely conscious of Inea beside him, as caught up in the job as he was. Knowing where he was getting his assumptions, she didn't challenge him, but became as eager as he was to locate the home star of his species.

Contrasted with the tedium of his first three weeks on the station when he could not do astronomy or physics, this was a time of daily satisfaction. Sharing it with Inea, a willing partner, gave him a sense of boundless energy and limitless capacity. Yet, after the day's work, from the time he left her, and in his rare moments of solitude, Titus could not keep his thoughts out of a groove that wore ever deeper.

What if he did identify the home star? Should he give it to Earth? Would he? Could he? Should that probe be sent out at all? And should Abbot's SOS be on it?

The only way to answer such a question was to waken the luren, just as Abbot planned.

Preparing for that, he worked with the Linguists' files. Some of the material he had been stealing was now open to him, but he still needed the Brink's codes for the rest.

Even though he was attending the higher level meetings, and could follow Abbot's official work, he still couldn't divine how Abbot planned to get around security, wake the luren, and then keep him from killing. The few bugs Titus had planted, and the few glimpses of Abbot he caught via the security cameras gave him no clue, but they did provide

181

ammunition to keep Abbot guessing about how much Titus actually knew and where he was getting his information.

Two hours before anyone else knew about it, he told Abbot, "Nagel's sending up World Sovereignties inspectors to make sure nothing is done with the 'corpse.'"

Clearly surprised, Abbot replied, "Does that worry you?"

"Should it?"

"Depends on your priorities. If you'll excuse me?" And Abbot left the conference room with a jaunty stride.

Later, Titus told Inea, "I scored. He's stymied, but doesn't want me to know it."

"Good. That's progress. By keeping him distracted, we'll beat him yet. Here, I've got three more bugs ready."

"You must have been up all night."

"Not quite. Put them where they'll do the most good."

Where? Abbot was everywhere, helping so many diverse departments that nobody questioned his movements anymore. It was Abbot's way of reducing the amount of Influence he had to use. The best way to be inconspicuous is to be ubiquitous, but that also made him impossible to track.

Five days after the reporters left, Titus was at a conference of department heads, watching Abbot crowding Colby into okaying the warming of the alien "corpse." It wasn't working. Colby had her orders. Abbot dared not use Influence against that, and without Influence, Abbot could not handle humans. Titus tingled with anxiety, knowing he should help Abbot and yet reluctant to make the move which would be his first traitorous act. Or would it?

He was saved from decision by a messenger who tiptoed over to Colby and whispered in her ear. She paled, then said to the man, "Show her in. Everyone should hear this."

It was Sisi Mintraub, looking grim. Abbot rose to offer her his seat, but she said anxiously, "Dr. Nandoha, I couldn't find you, so I came for Dr. Colby, but—" She broke off, shook her head, then faced Colby. "I don't know how it happened. God, I'm sorry, Carol, but the alien specimen—the cryogenic chamber has been leaking for days. Maybe since the explosion. And nobody noticed." She looked up at Abbot. "Not even you, Doctor."

Dismayed, Abbot asked, "What do you mean, leaking? I checked it myself two days ago."

"Dozens of tiny leaks at some of the inner seals and gaskets, very slow leaks, but we've lost temperature control. Several gauges were off, and an intermittent short in one of the controlling boards masked the errors until just now."

Abbot faced Colby. "Then it's quite clear, Dr. Colby, we must warm the corpse, or risk losing it."

"Warm the corpse! Is that all you can think of?" asked Kaschmore, the head of Medical. "What of contamination?" She rose and turned to Colby. "I told you we never should have brought the thing in from the ship. I'm declaring the station under quarantine. At least we haven't received a supply caravan since the bombing, and those reporters never got into Biomed. Earth should be safe from us for the moment."

Before anyone could react, she was out the door. Mihelich started after her, but Colby said, "No, let her go. She's right."

Mihelich shook his head. "Contamination is not the issue. I doubt the aliens have any bizarre diseases our immune systems can't already handle. It is amazing—perhaps even horrifying—how similar their microlife is to our own."

One of the first jobs of those opening Project Station had been to collect specimens, then sterilize the craft. Mihelich had unraveled the genetics of all those specimens.

"Dr. Colby," said Mihelich, "Dr. Nandoha is correct. If that leak has altered the temperature, then it's imperative that we warm the corpse and complete the autopsy before deterioration sets in."

"No, you don't understand," interrupted Mintraub. "It's been room temperature in there for hours, and there's no deterioration at all! They said the wound had—"

Abbot seized her by the shoulders. "How long?" he demanded. "Exactly how long?"

"Uh, at least six hours."

"And it's night outside!" Abbot dropped her and ran out the door. It was the first public slip Titus had ever seen Abbot make. *He didn't know of the leak! I've rattled him.*

Pandemonium erupted. In a small voice, Mintraub finished, "—begun to heal." She was white and shaking, but Titus didn't stop to comfort her. He jostled his way through the press of bodies and took off after Abbot. Six hours at night, and the alien could be recovered already.

His palm print got him through the barricades and he caught up with Abbot as he sidled between the two Brink's guards inside the

183

cryo-lab door. In the sterilizing shower, Titus whispered, "You don't think the sleeper will—"

"Oh, yes I do," said Abbot. "This isn't how I planned it." The door opened and Titus crowded through behind Abbot, watching the scene beyond the plastic wall of the dressing room through a small window.

The cryogenic bubble had been opened, the body lying on the top of the pedestal as if it were an operating table. Dr. Kaschmore spat emphatic orders at the half dozen nurses and physicians who clustered about the body. Mirelle, on the far side of the pedestal, was leaning over the body, and the woman Titus thought of as Diving Belle was flexing the sleeper's fingers and dictating notes.

As Titus donned his mask, the shower behind him started up again. In front of him, Abbot charged out the door into the lab. "This is like a scene out of a bad science fiction movie!" he roared. They fell silent, turning toward him. "If that thing wakes up, it could kill you before it knows you're not enemies!"

His Influence carried a vibrant shame. Everyone backed away from the body as Abbot and Titus approached. A sterile sheet had been draped over the legs, but the chest wound was exposed. It had nearly healed.

"There are too many people in here," declared Kaschmore. She singled out the Diving Belle, Abbot, and Titus, "You have no reason to be here. Out. Now. How can we—"

Abbot cut her off. "I may be of assistance to Mintraub with the equipment." He went to the wall panel controlling the ambient environment. "If the explosion—"

At that point, Colby and Mintraub emerged from the shower room, Colby saying, "I gave explicit orders that the cryo-bubble was not to be opened for any reason. I—"

"He's breathing!" exclaimed the Diving Belle who was behind Mirelle, on the other side of the pedestal.

Abbot doused the lights, and the room filled with dismayed human voices. Dimly, Titus heard the outer door open and shut. Eyes still straining to adjust, Titus felt rather than saw Abbot streak by him, headed for the luren, moving by dead reckoning. Then he saw the dim blot of warmth that was Mirelle, Abbot's Mark glowing on her forehead, collide with someone and stumble toward the luren. Colby got in Abbot's way. Abbot tripped and Colby yelped.

Titus saw the luren hand go for Mirelle's throat. The luren body was room temperature, and the limb appeared only as a shadow against

Mirelle's warmth. Without thinking, Titus dove through the air, flung his body across the luren's and shoved Mirelle away.

The luren emitted a formless grunt as Titus' weight came down on him, then steel fingers closed over Titus' ears, and cold wet lips searched his throat. A strange paralyzing hum penetrated Titus' bones, turning his will to mist. He hardly felt the teeth cutting into his vein, but he knew it when the luren began to feed.

He felt it in the soles of his feet, in his groin, in his belly, and in his heart, a rhythmic pulling, that grew stronger, more intense, more insistent, until he was pushing with it, helping it devour him, wanting to pour himself into the other, needing to become one with it.

Around him, the paralyzing hum rose to fill the room, but he knew only the great demanding rhythm of his pumping heart, and the hot tendrils of thought piercing his brain, demanding more of him than he had to give, pulling him inside out. It was not unpleasant. It was like a good, long hard stretch, or a delicious yawn.

He melted into relaxation, nothing left in him that wanted to guard himself. Gradually, he became aware of the hunger he was feeding with his substance, and he could feel it abating with each pulse that rippled through his body. His pleasure was the luren's pleasure, the desire to live, the need to live, the demand to live.

And it was life that they shared, life and the glory of living. The pulsing rhythm of life and the love of life wove between them, and Titus wanted that life, to cherish it and let it kindle him forever. At some point, the luren's demand succumbed to Titus' overflowing insistence. The pleasure was now Titus', and the luren shared it with him.

Their heartbeats slowed, the distant pulsing hum weakened, and the urgency abated, leaving them floating in darkness. Distantly, Titus felt the luren's tongue stroking the skin of his throat. His whole body burned with the aftermath of pleasure too intense to recall.

A breath whispered in his ear, "Enough, my father. I would not take your life."

Warm hands pushed up on his chest. The words had been in the luren language, and the spell was broken. *I've fathered the sleeper!*

Stunned, he pushed his weight up, and then the emergency lights came on, Mintraub crying out triumphantly, "I got it!"

The alien gasped.

Abbot, with Kaschmore's help, was trying to untangle himself from Colby. Mirelle lay supine, the Diving Belle kneeling beside her.

Mintraub was at the power control panel, lifting off the coverplate. Mihelich stood in the door from the dressing room, mouth agape. The blackout couldn't have lasted more than a few seconds, but Titus would have sworn it was at least a year.

The alien screamed, an ululating shriek of pain and terror carried on a blast of paralyzing Influence such as Titus had never felt before.

Every human in the room froze, eyes blank.

Titus' hands went to the luren's face, needing to soothe the shuddering fear away. Their eyes locked.

"Wh-what are you?" choked the alien.

"Luren, of a sort," answered Titus.

"*What* sort?" His slitted eyes traversed the room. "Where am I?"

"On an airless satellite, in a building constructed around *Kylyd*. It crashed. You went dormant."

The alien focused on Mirelle and a cluster of medics. "What manner of people are they? They are people? Not orl?"

"Human," answered Titus in English. "Not orl."

The man's gaze locked again with Titus' eyes. "Your accent. I've never heard anything like it."

Titus himself was guessing at the luren's words. "I first spoke their language."

The alien's eyes went back to the cluster of humans around Mirelle. Then suddenly, Titus found his own eyes drawn to the alien man's and that profound Influence focused inside him. For a moment, the rapport of their sharing flashed into being, and the hot tendrils of a probing mind crawled through his brain. He flinched, and hard, bony fingers bit into his shoulders. He threw every bit of his training and skill into deflecting that raking, tearing probe, sure his sanity hung in the balance.

Without warning, everything went white, and the next thing he knew he was on the floor beside the pedestal, some bare feet dangling over his face and Abbot bending over him sealing his disposable suit's collar over a sore spot.

"Don't let anyone see that wound for an hour or so," he whispered and rose to meet the alien's eyes.

The man said, "Halfbreeds?" in English.

He snatched the language right out of my brain!

"You could have killed him," Abbot said to the alien in the luren tongue. "There are very few of us, and the humans don't know we're here or that we breed on them as well as feed on them because no orl

186

survived here. You must release them before it becomes impossible to explain, then leave them to me."

Straining over Abbot's accent, the alien asked in uncertain English, "I am your . . . prisoner?"

"No," countered Abbot, also in English. "*Their* prisoner. *We'll* get you out of this, but they mustn't learn what we are."

"Trapped in a herd of orl. A horror story."

"Don't stampede the herd," said Abbot, "and we'll all be safe."

The man fixed on Titus. "I did not mean to hurt."

Abbot asked, "He fought your orientation probe?" then repeated it using an unfamiliar luren term.

"He has not the capacity. I could not complete."

Titus said, "I didn't understand. You should have warned me; I wouldn't have fought you. I'm sorry."

"You must release the humans to me," repeated Abbot.

"I understand. Halfbreeds and intelligent orl."

Orl are considered animals.

"Release them to me and observe. One must be gentle with humans. Too much power can destroy their brains."

God! Titus had never heard that, but he was sure Abbot meant it. Abbot had that kind of power; Titus didn't.

Still holding Titus' gaze, the man asked, "Should I do as he says? He *is* your father, as he claims?"

Abbot glared at Titus. Mouth dry, Titus rose to his feet. He didn't dare oppose Abbot in front of a real luren. "He's my father, but don't do *everything* he says without thinking. This time, though—yes, do it."

He squinted at the humans. "Will they attack?"

"No," answered Abbot. "Let me show you how. Just wait until I put out the lights again."

He measured Abbot again, then studied Titus. The panic had been replaced by wariness. "Good, and leave them out."

"I can't. These are the dim emergency lights. If they seem bright, the real lights will nearly blind you. Cover your eyes. We're wearing protective lenses, and in a few minutes I'll provide you with some special goggles." With that, Abbot sidled around Mintraub who stood with one hand raised to the open panel, eyes unfocused. His fingers flew over the connections, and Titus realized Abbot had rigged the boards so he could have a power outage when he wanted one.

The lights went out, and Abbot said, "Now. Release them to me."

187

The alien emitted a low musical hum, and the pall of Influence gripping the room abated. At the same time, Abbot flicked the main lights on. Mintraub jumped back with a gasp. "Abbot! Where did you—"

Mirelle screamed. Sitting bolt upright, she crammed both fists in her mouth and whimpered. Then Titus saw that the alien had draped his sheet over his head and tied a fold of it over his eyes. He looked like a naked, albino Arab playing Blind Justice. *But he can rip the language right out of a person's brain!* He was that powerful, and Abbot was manipulating him as if he were a helpless child.

"Quiet!" ordered Colby in a low, penetrating voice. "Get back from him. We don't want to panic him."

Mihelich strode up to her. "That hardly seems likely after what he just did. I'd say he has the upper hand."

"You felt it too?" she looked around with a most peculiar expression. "It wasn't just me?"

Abbot went to her, saying with a touch of Influence, "Titus, what did he do to you? The last I saw before the lights went out, he had grabbed you."

"Yes," said Mirelle getting to her feet, "and the world froze solid."

There were murmurs of agreement as people checked chronometers. Titus interjected with a touch of Influence, trying to gloss over the lost interval, "He just grabbed me, but he didn't hurt me. Then the lights came back on."

Kaschmore said, "I lost at least six minutes." There were murmurs of agreement.

Diving Belle added, "My recorder shows seven and one half minutes elapsed. Let me see what recorded . . ."

"It sounds to me," said Abbot moving around to the woman, "as if our friend here has a formidable natural defense. But, even in panic, he didn't use it to hurt anyone." He lifted the recorder from the Belle's hands and ran it fast over the segment while exerting Influence over all of them, including the single Brink's guard by the outer door. *Where is the other guard? When did he leave?*

The humans heard dead silence on the recording while Titus listened to the chatter of speech at high speed. Then Abbot erased the segment from the recorder's memory and handed it back to the Belle. "Set it up. Dr. Colby will no doubt want the rest of this recorded."

All this while, the alien had been turning his head, watching them through the folds of cloth. Titus said, using his mildest Influence,

"Perhaps we should get the man some dark glasses and a suit of clothes?"

Colby nodded. "Kaschmore, see to it."

She waved a nurse toward the dressing room, while replying, "I wouldn't know where to get dark glasses that had been sterilized."

Abbot said, moving to a workbench, "I have some welding goggles here that might do for a while. Titus is right. It's the gesture that counts. We wouldn't want him to think he's a prisoner and panic again."

As the nurse brought the shapeless disposable suit to the alien, holding it out at arm's length, Titus lifted it from the man's grasp and shook out the two pieces to show what it was. Abbot came up with the goggles while Titus held the jacket for the alien's arm and, cloaking his words with heavy Influence, Abbot muttered, "Say thank you in English and explain that you learned the language from Titus. Say as little as you can after that—plead exhaustion—we've got to get Titus out of here before his hunger rebounds."

Twice, the alien started to say something else, stopped himself, then nodded. "This gesture means yes, correct?"

"That's right," said Abbot, cloaking the exchange.

"To show teeth is for friendship?"

"Yes," grunted Abbot, then added, "Titus shouldn't have fought you. You ought to be sure of these things."

"I will learn. Titus will help." But his hands shook.

Titus knelt to hold the pants under the alien's dangling feet while Abbot helped him shed the cloth and don the goggles. When they were done, the alien stood beside the pedestal, grinned, revealing sharp teeth, and said in Titus' intonation overlaid with another accent, "I thank you."

"Good grief!" said Colby.

"I don't believe this," muttered Mirelle, white-lipped.

"This one provided me your language, and him I thank most profoundly for the gift."

Abruptly, Titus' knees sagged. He put a hand on Abbot's elbow, and Abbot's hand clasped over his. Abbot muttered to Titus, "Just a moment more. You can make it." Aloud he said, "I suspected as much, from Titus' dazed state. Dr. Colby, I think we should offer our visitor a proper room in which to rest and whatever else may be required for his comfort." He turned to the alien. "Do you find it cold in here, uh, how would you like to be called, Sir?"

189

"H'lim is my name."

"H'lim," said Abbot with a creditable try at the luren accent. "We normally keep our rooms much warmer than this."

"That is good news. I hope."

Abbot named each of those in the chamber. Under his breath, Mihelich groaned, "Dear God, he's talking to him as if he were a person."

H'lim's eyes flicked to Mihelich, but the man didn't seem to notice. Colby, however, caught the comment and raised her arms for attention. "All right, folks, you've just witnessed the most important event in the recent history of mankind, but right now I think Abbot's right. We must show our guest a reasonable amount of ordinary hospitality. How would you feel if you were in his place?"

"I'd want to be left alone for a while," said Kaschmore.

Titus knew she meant to isolate H'lim among the medics. Cloaking his words, he told H'lim, "Later, ask for me. Don't let them keep you away from me."

H'lim nodded, then asked Abbot, imitating their light cloaking of speech, "Will Titus be all right? I didn't even realize you're not really luren."

"I'll see to my son. And I won't let them harm you." Aloud, Abbot said, "Dr. Colby has the right idea. We must show H'lim we are friends. Carol, if Titus and I may be excused, we will see that the lighting panel from the ship is installed in a room for our guest."

Kaschmore interjected, "Shiddehara will go to medical for a complete check—"

Titus threw off the daze that gripped him. "Oh no, really," he protested with Influence, Abbot's own power working with him. "H'lim didn't hurt me at all. I was only surprised. I want to help Abbot make him comfortable."

"Excellent idea. Kaschmore, install H'lim in the infirmary's executive suite temporarily. Mintraub, help Nandoha adjust the environment. And Mihelich, I want you to see about lifting quarantine. A man can't live in a sterile bubble, but we wouldn't want him to die of a cold either. De Lisle, you're to stay with H'lim and make sure there are no misunderstandings."

Abbot had Titus halfway to the changing room door by the end of this speech. He stopped, looking back. "He went for Mirelle first, didn't he?" he asked Titus privately.

"Yes—I—"

190

"H'lim," said Abbot, cloaking, "De Lisle wears my Mark. Do you honor such?"

"Mark?" H'lim looked at Mirelle. "I see no—oh. *That's* an orl-mark? It's so faint."

"It is my Mark. I expect it to be honored."

Mirelle approached H'lim, getting a better grip on herself. "We don't want you to be frightened."

"I accept the strange customs of this place, and I honor your hospitality," answered H'lim openly, then glanced at Abbot and Titus.

Cloaking, Abbot told him, "I'll see that your needs are met. Wait for me." He hustled Titus into the changing room. "What a mess! And I can't even blame it on you this time!"

"But I thought you wanted him revived."

"Only not yet. I wanted to drive Colby into ordering the corpse destroyed. Then I'd have shipped a sufficient part of the remains to Earth and we'd have revived him there. But I've been too busy to get in here, and didn't know about the malfunctions. Mintraub should have caught it sooner!"

Inea and I kept him busy!

As they were showering, Titus said, "Well, now that he's awake, it's my place to provide for H'lim."

Abbot sighed. "He can't survive on what you'd give him. Considering your diet, I'm amazed you're still on your feet, but don't stop to argue with me now. You can't surmount this hunger with that dead powder, so I'm giving you two of my—"

"No!" The disinfectant got into Titus' mouth as he said that and he spat, gagging.

"Titus, when the shock to your system wears off, you'll have no choice. He took more than blood . . ."

"There's Inea."

"What are you going to do, ask pretty please?"

They toweled off and dressed in smoldering silence. Titus was beginning to feel rocky, but he wondered if it was just Abbot's repeated suggestion. When he thought he had his temper leashed back, Titus said, "I can handle humans without Influence. I've been fending for myself since I left you."

"This is *different.*"

"I know. I can feel it. I'll take care of it." *God! What am I going to do?*

191

"Look, I know how you hate killing. You're going to be blacking out intermittently. I wouldn't want you to wake up and find you'd killed someone who matters to you. I've got two stringers who—"

"Residents have been parenting for generations!" snapped Titus. "I've broken the habit of direct feeding, and I won't go back, not under any circumstances. I don't want your help, and I don't want you teaching H'lim that humans are just orl."

He threw up his hands. "H'lim's my grandson! At least *he* has a proper respect, even if my own son hasn't the sense of an orl!" He started for the door, then paused. "But if you kill carelessly, I'll have to take you out. I'll have to, Titus, but I don't *want* to!" He stomped out past the Brink's guard who still stood at attention, but stared avidly through the plastic wall into the lab where the "corpse" was now chatting affably with the living.

——— SIXTEEN ———

At the end of Biomed's hall, a crowd of off-duty workers had gathered behind the security barricade. Their voices filled the area with an excited babble. Four Brink's guards held a fifth tightly between them, and the prisoner's hands were shackled behind his back. Titus recognized him as one of the guards who had been on the cryo-lab's door, the one who must have exited when the lights went out. On the security station console, a monitor showed a broadcast from Earth, with a bulletin header flashing over an announcer's image. *Alien Body Reanimated!*

"You shouldn't have done it, Chip," one of the guards said to the prisoner as Titus arrived. "That's a major breach of security."

"Security be dammed, what about infecting all Earth with some alien disease?"

Oh, shit! He's reported H'lim's revival! If there'd been the least hope that Connie could get someone through the anti-assassin security, there was no hope whatever that she could get anyone through a full-scale quarantine.

His eyes lit on Inea, almost invisible in the crush of humanity beyond the barricade. She spotted him at the same moment and began pushing toward him. He signaled her off to the left exit gate, a door made of spokes that rotated only in one direction. As soon as he got through it, the crowd surged toward him, inundating him with a barrage of questions.

He folded Inea into one arm and began shoving toward the edge of the crowd. "Dr. Colby will be out soon, and she'll have a statement for you," Titus repeated over and over.

They made it to clear air, and Titus staggered, gasping.

"You're shaking. What happened?"

"I fathered him."

"We won!" she yelped, kissing him. Then she bounced over to the lift call button and gave it a triumphal smack.

"Inea." To his chagrin, she had to catch him and prop him against the wall. "Abbot seems to have more control over H'lim—that's his name—than I do. If I'm going to keep Abbot from teaching him to despise humans, I've got to get back in there."

"But you're sick."

"Not sick. Starving. Ectoplasm exhaustion." The numbness was starting to wear off, and Abbot's predictions were proving right—again. "I can't—I've got to—"

"But the alien is all right? He didn't go feral?"

"He's fine—for the moment, but I've got to—"

An empty lift came, and she bundled him into it. "You're in no condition to be doing anything. But I guess this means that everyone knows about you and Abbot."

"No, no." He explained the way Abbot had handled it.

"Abbot again!" Draping his arm over her shoulders, she half carried him out of the lift. The corridor was deserted at mid-shift, with most of the off-duty people waiting in Biomed and the rest glued to their screens. Dimly he realized it was his own door he was staring at, and Inea was digging in his pants pocket for his key.

The next thing he knew, he was slumped in the chair by the kitchen table and the microwave was bleeping. And then the smell hit him. Staggering to the sink, he grabbed the pitcher, sloshing half-dissolved crystals over the rim, and gulped the gritty mixture. Then he gagged and vomited into the sink. Gasping, he cried, "Get out of here. If you know what's good for you, get out!" *I've got to call Abbot.*

Calmly, she refilled the pitcher and chucked it into the microwave. "Go rinse your mouth out, and stop telling me what to do."

When he didn't move, she grabbed him by the biceps and pushed him into the bathroom, shutting the door. Titus leaned over the sink, sick and ashamed, yet aching with a desperate hunger he'd never felt

193

before. He rinsed the dead stuff out of his mouth, then glimpsed his face in the mirror—eyes sunken and bruised, anguish graven in deep lines down his cheeks. He swayed, struggled for balance and fell against the door. It wouldn't open.

Panic struck, and he flung himself against the barrier, dimly aware of the life surging on the other side but wholly unable to think. The battering thud of his body hitting the hard barrier set up a rhythm in his mind, a pulse of hunger as strong as H'lim's had been.

The next thing he knew, the door slid aside and he fetched up hard against the opposite wall.

Inea held the pitcher filled with warm blood, surrounded by a haze of ectoplasm. He went for it, slobbering and gulping like an animal, the thick stuff spattering them both. He knew no shame until he'd finished the pitcher, flung it aside, and borne her to the floor, ripping at her clothing.

Then her arms went around him, and she put his face to her neck. His teeth caught the fold of skin, the great vein like rubber between them. And there he stopped.

Scalding remorse paralyzed him while her hands moved urgently on his bare back, and her lips plucked at his bearded cheek. And there was no reserve in her, no barrier between them. Her love and her substance penetrated his flesh, and her desire inflamed him.

He forced his jaws apart, muscles hardening as his will refused what his body demanded. The searing shame was worse than the relentless hunger.

"What's the matter? Am I doing it wrong?"

A raw sound tore from his throat, perhaps a sob. He rolled off her, pulling her on top of him and cradling her in his arms. "No. *I'm* doing it wrong. Can you ever forgive me? I never wanted you to see anything like that."

"It's okay, if you're all right now?"

"No. I need more." He struggled to his feet, pulling her with him and retrieving the pitcher. His hands were shaking even worse now.

"Here, let me." She rinsed the mess off and set another pitcher of water to warm. Then she ran cold water into the sink. "Get out of those clothes. They've got to soak right away." She stripped her clothes off into the sink, turned and found him standing still. "Come on," she said, unfastening his shirt. "*Oh, my God!*"

Her fingers danced over the wound in his neck. He captured her hand. "That'll be gone in a few hours."

"Titus, you've broken quarantine! You could be infect—"

"He's got nothing that hasn't been loose on Earth for centuries! If there was anything to bring, my ancestors brought it."

"You don't know that. There could be mutations—"

"Mihelich says there's nothing humans can't handle, and there's no reason to doubt that."

"I hope you're right." The bleep interrupted them, and Inea poured another packet of crystals into the pitcher, holding it close to her bare chest.

He smoothed her hair back from her face and kissed her forehead. "I don't know why, Inea, but the biochemistry out there is the same as that evolved on Earth."

She held the pitcher to his lips, but he wrapped her hands around it and stepped back to skin out of his stained pants, take his Bell and the bugs' control box out of the pockets, and drop the pants in the water. Then he got a glass and poured himself a drink. "To life— micro and otherwise!" When the elixir crossed his tongue, he knew he couldn't afford the bravado. He chugalugged it and refilled the glass, still unable to sip it.

By the third glass, his hands stopped shaking and he considered what all this must be like from her point of view. She had been unable to give her body to an alien, and now she'd been attacked by a slobbering animal who was about to ask her to go to bed with him. He dropped into the chair, burying his face in his hands. "I'm sorry!"

She slid into his lap and put her arms around him. "I know. But it's okay. You're the best man I know, and when you run up against something you can't handle, I know what kind of a thing it has to be. But the secret of love is that the two of us together can handle anything."

"Even the idea of sleeping with something that's not human?"

"Are you so very sure you're not human?"

"I used to think I was human, but now I'm not so sure." He told her how H'lim had extracted English from his mind. "He was in a panic and paralyzed everyone—even me—and then snatched the language from my mind. But no luren I ever heard of could do that. I fought him, and then I was ashamed I'd fought! Is that a human reaction to mind rape?"

"Was Abbot surprised?"

"I don't know. I was a bit out of it then."

"Out of it? I'll say. I had to haul you through the corridors like a zombie."

He kissed her. "The zombie's coming alive. Can you handle that yet?"

"Try me."

He emptied the pitcher into his glass and wrapped her hands around it. "First I have to confess something that may change your mind."

"Good. That's progress. You always used to hit me with those things *afterwards.*"

"I did a really stupid thing." He recited Abbot's warning that he might kill.

"And you think you should have taken his stringers and maybe killed one of them?"

"I vaguely recall thinking that in the bathroom. Inea, I lost control, I didn't really believe it could happen—"

"Now, you listen to me. You so much as lay a finger on one of them, and you'll never get me in bed again. Is that understood?"

"Inea!" he protested, the false strength of partial recovery deserting him. "We don't know what's going to happen. I may have to develop a string—"

"Well, we'll see about that, but you don't accept anything from Abbot, and you don't go to anyone else without telling me, first! *First*— do you understand? Not later!"

He nodded, but before he could say anything, her eyes went wide. "The alien! You said the hunger is harder after a dormancy . . . "

"He's fed for now, and Abbot'll bring him a stringer. I think H'lim will accept. He doesn't have much choice."

"We've got to get there first!" But a vague helplessness suffused her as the heavy drain of ectoplasm weakened her. Absently, she lifted the glass of blood to her lips, but when the smell reached her, her lip curled.

Titus lowered his head to sip from the glass. "We don't have much time. But first things first—if you're still willing?"

"We may still have to fight Abbot for H'lim, but we're in a better situation with you as his father than if Abbot had got him. So we've got to find out what kind of folk H'lim's people are, because maybe Earth shouldn't send that probe out at all." She shook her head. "Oh, I can't think."

He set the glass aside, and enfolded her in his arms. "It will all be clearer after this." He kissed her and discovered he was in an embarrassing hurry all of a sudden.

He didn't get it right for her the first time, but the second and third times made up for that. He woke to find her hanging up their laundry, and the fourth time was pure sharing. He let her sleep while he showered and worried.

Nothing was becoming clearer, and almost six hours had passed while events hurtled on without him. Dressed, he made up some blood, noting how low his supply was and hoping Connie's trick packing chips arrived soon. He infused the blood with his own ectoplasm, so replete he hardly felt the loss, then left a note for Inea flashing on the vidcom screen:

I don't know how you could face me when I behaved so shamefully. But you did. Now I've got to use the strength you gave me to tend to my obligations. You're right; together we can do anything.

I love you beyond all measure, T(DR)S

Tucking the Thermos under his arm, and cloaking it so it wouldn't be noticed, he headed for Biomed, a bounce in his step and a whistle on his lips. Those around him, however, trudged bleakly along, wearing grim frowns and muttering darkly about Nagel and W.S. having declared Project Station under strict quarantine. Colby had already invoked rationing anticipating curtailment of supply deliveries.

———

Sterilization showers were deployed at the entry to H'lim's suite, along with four Brink's guards, two outside and two inside. Colby had put Titus' name on the list of those to be admitted, and the guards signed him into the suite muttering how Kaschmore would have to take it out on Colby, not them, that H'lim had so many visitors.

Abbot had signed in several times during the last few hours, as had Mirelle and Colby.

Properly dressed, but still cloaking the septic Thermos, Titus entered the infirmary's executive suite. He found himself facing a long formal dining table behind which was a conversation pit done in gold and indigo. To his left a door opened into a private kitchen where someone was puttering about. The lights were dimmed, and the temperature was stifling. From the door in the far wall came the glow of *Kylyd's* one surviving light panel.

Through that door he found the bedroom. The hospital bed had the sheets turned down. To its left was a conversation group of three cloned-leather upholstered couches with computer consoles installed on the end tables between them, and a coffee table with two abandoned cups on it. Behind the couches was a closed door, and another faced it in the wall across the room.

To the right of the bed was a desk and executive vidcom installation. H'lim sat at the desk, chin resting on one hand, squinting at the bright screen. A top-security thumb reference file lay open beside his other hand.

When Titus stepped through the door, H'lim turned then grinned widely. "I am trying to learn this the hard way. I don't suppose you'd be willing to help?"

Give him my mind again? "Maybe later. How do you feel?"

"I've been distracting myself from that by learning this." H'lim gestured to the vidcom screen displaying an access menu. "I got your speech, but no graphics, and I'm very hazy on the inner harmonies of your language so I mischoose the applicable meaning too often. Your—people—are polite, and ask many questions, but they won't answer mine."

Titus gestured to the four surveillance cameras bracketing the room. "They're making recordings to study later, you know. They want to see what you're like before you learn too much of us and obscure the data."

"Recorders, yes. Abbot mentioned them. Lack of privacy does not seem to bother humans." His eyes went to the Thermos Titus carried cloaked. He had kept it out of the cameras' fields and now set it down on the floor by the door. Then he went to the desk and leaned over H'lim.

"They're actually for medical use, not spying, so they can be turned off easily. Watch." He poked in Colby's authorization code and the command to secure the room as he did at many meetings. The screen flashed, SECURED. "They might not be happy about that, but insist, then negotiate, and they'll yield a bit of private time to you."

H'lim looked up at him. "You seem to understand humans. Your Abbot does not."

"He thinks of humans as orl."

"A vast error." He squinted at the screen. "All my orl were killed, they tell me." He clenched his hands before him. Titus cupped one hand over the luren's fists, feeling his terror. He explained that Earth's luren had no orl, and that Abbot's people used humans instead. Then he offered the cloned human blood he'd brought, and held his breath.

H'lim clasped Titus' hand. "You are perhaps more human than you know, Titus. Andre Mihelich has begun to clone orl blood for me, but it will take time, and the hunger is now."

198

"You told them what you need?"

"I had to."

"I understand. Come, take this before they get Carol to turn the cameras on again."

They took the Thermos into the bathroom where there was no camera, and H'lim downed the contents, grimacing and shuddering with each swallow but not complaining. For a while, Titus was afraid it might all come back up, disagreeing violently with a full luren. But then H'lim bent over the sink and rinsed the taste away. He looked at himself in the mirror, and proclaimed his hunger appeased.

Titus was wrapping the Thermos in a sterile towel when he heard the bedroom door close and Abbot called from the bedroom, "H'lim? Titus?"

H'lim wiped his face. "Who is that with him?"

He's sensitive! "Probably a stringer to offer you." He raised his voice, "We're coming, Abbot."

He had brought Dr. Kuo, the short, middle-aged Oriental woman Titus had once followed into Biomed. Her eyes had the glazed look of heavy Influence. Abbot greeted Titus. "I see you've got the cameras off. That should stir everyone up. How long do you think we have?"

"Maybe another ten minutes."

Abbot introduced Kuo to H'lim. "Mark her for your own. My gift."

"You don't use them in pairs?"

"Pairs?" asked Abbot, frowning.

"As orl, so they replenish each other afterwards."

Abbot flushed. That was a rare sight. Titus said, "Humans are not orl. They don't replenish each other effectively. So—we lie with them ourselves."

H'lim compared the two crossbreeds before him, then said urbanely, "I see. I should have realized."

Abbot offered, "If the idea distresses you, I will take care of the matter. Do not hesitate. Mark her."

"May I ask you something first?"

"Certainly. My reticence was only because of the cameras. thought I explained that."

"How long have I been—dormant?"

"Luren time measures have not survived the generations," answered Abbot, and described the length of a year as one thousand four hundred sixty times the interval H'lim had been awake. "And you've been dormant about three years."

199

As H'lim gnawed on the mental arithmetic, Titus punched up a solar system graphic and gave the year's length in terms of earth's orbit.

H'lim nodded. "I don't know exactly how long that is, but it does explain why I feel like this. It will pass."

Titus wanted to ask all sorts of personal questions, but Abbot said, "Now you must take sustenance—"

"I have one more question," said H'lim, and Titus got the distinct impression that H'lim's mind was still open on the issue of using humans. "Is there any chance I'll ever be able to go home?"

"Yes, there is, if you can wait long enough," answered Abbot, and told of the message he was going to send. He spoke as if talking a distraught patient out of suicide, offering hope and so luring him into eating and surviving.

"I see," said H'lim at length, inspecting Kuo at closer range. "In that case, I must—regretfully—decline your generous offer."

"What?" exclaimed Abbot. "Why? Titus, what have you been telling him?"

"Titus has met his obligations to me as best he could, and I will be grateful."

"Met his—*Titus!*"

"I gave him blood, but didn't mention that my mission is to stop you sending that message."

H'lim's eyes darted from one to the other as Abbot glared at Titus, Kuo forgotten in her stupor.

At that moment, the door opened and Colby charged through, ". . . and I did not turn the cameras—oh! Dr. Kuo, I don't recall authorizing—"

Abbot turned Kuo toward himself briefly, as he said with pervasive Influence, "Dr. Kuo, do you think you'll be able to help Mirelle with the spoken language now?"

Her eyes focused, and she looked away from Abbot. "Oh, yes, there shouldn't be any problem now." She saw Colby. "Excuse me, Carol, I'll have that report by morning." She gave a polite little bow to H'lim. "Thank you so much." And she slid past Colby and out the door.

Colby blinked, frowned at H'lim, and rearranged her features. "I didn't think my security code was in those notes, H'lim."

His eyes darted to Titus, and Titus intervened. "I taught him the code. He felt the lack of privacy—"

"No harm done," suggested Abbot with Influence.

"No, I guess not," Colby said without enthusiasm.

Titus went to the console. "Watch this, H'lim. I'll turn them back on so the anthropologists will be happy."

As the cameras started to sweep the area again, Colby leaned against the back of a couch. "Titus, I thought you might have been hurt in the cryo-lab. Some of your blood was found on the sheet—"

Titus felt his face pale. Before he could speak, Abbot said, "He had a nosebleed, but it stopped right away."

Titus started to breathe again when Colby accepted that and went on talking. Silently, Titus blessed the programmer who had gimmicked the Biomed computers to identify his blood without revealing its peculiarities. Abbot was right that it wouldn't be long until Earth's luren could not survive unnoticed. When he came out of shock, Colby was saying " . . . have Titus checked for infection."

Abbot edged Titus away from the vidcom and typed rapidly, peered at the screen, and swore as if he'd made an error, then typed some more. "Here it is," Abbot said brightly. "Look, he's been checked and cleared."

Titus realized that Abbot had input that data right under Colby's gaze. She nodded at the screen. "Good that I have a competent staff. Now, H'lim, you know that your presence is causing quite a problem—"

Mihelich said from the door opposite the bathroom, "Not as much problem as you might think, Carol." As he advanced into the room, Titus saw through the opening behind him a small lab designed to serve the patient in the suite. "H'lim has been very helpful so far, and as soon as he learns to read, I'm sure he'll have a lot to teach us."

"I'll be very glad to do what I can to make things easier," H'lim put in with no Influence whatsoever. Then he invoked a touch of his power as he added, "It would surely help if I could go out to see *Kylyd.*" He glanced at Abbot who nodded.

Colby repeated the ship's name and H'lim explained it to her, adding, "I was escorting livestock I had designed for a new colony world. I know nothing about ships, but still I might be able to solve some puzzles for you."

Mihelich chimed in, "That seems reasonable to me. You won't believe what he knows! He *meant* 'designed' those creatures—the other species we found with him."

To H'lim, Colby said, "We have no spacesuit for you, and the ship's in vacuum. In a while, when they've built you a suit, I'm sure the engineers will be glad for any clues you can give them. Meanwhile, your first task is to regain your strength. The doctors are worried that you won't eat."

Mihelich explained, and Colby took the news about his diet woodenly. With no overt reaction, H'lim watched her swallow her disgust. Colby reminded Titus and Abbot of rescheduled meetings, made hasty excuses, and departed, a touch pale about the lips.

Mihelich ran fingers through his white hair and turned back to the lab. "H'lim, come look at this, and then I'll show you more things the vidcom can do. You can tap into cameras aimed at the ship. . . ."

H'lim followed him, glancing back once at Titus and Abbot with apology.

Titus gathered his Thermos disguised with the towel, and when he came out of the bathroom, Abbot said, "I'm glad to see you recovered."

Titus went past him without stopping. "There are some things, Abbot, that you'll never understand, but I hope you can finally grasp the fact that I do not want or need your help." *But I'd never have pulled off that trick with my medical records.*

"There may come a time when I'll believe that."

Titus went into the shower, then returned to his apartment. Inea had gone, leaving him a note saying she'd taken the "spare handheld." By that, he understood she had used the bugging system to tap the surveillance cameras in H'lim's room, so she knew some of what had happened. He took his Bell and went to his lab where Inea was working at the Eighth Antenna Array console in the observatory. He signed some forms, picked up status reports, and headed to the first round of meetings after H'lim's wakening.

As he started out the lab door, Inea came out of the observatory, yelling, "*Wild Goose* is alive! *Wild Goose* is reporting on relay through the Eighth!"

Wild Goose had, presumably, the best tracking data on *Kylyd's* approach vector.

Everyone rushed into the glass enclosure, crowding aside to let Titus through. The noise was deafening. When Titus worked his way up to the screens, he saw the data relayed from one of the outer orbital observatories. "Yeah, that's *Wild Goose* all right, but what is that stuff?" he asked.

"Mostly garbage," answered Inea and thrust a set of earphones at him. "Listen."

The technicians were arguing about what was coming in and what they could do to clean up the signal, about why the package had just started sending again, and about what to send back to get better data.

Titus handed the phones back. "I'm late, and Colby's going to be livid. Start this through our cruncher and let me know if anything useful comes of it." To the crowd, he announced, "This may be just what we need to nail that star! The alien, H'lim, says he knows nothing of ships, so I assume he doesn't know how to find his home star. Everything depends on us—on *Wild Goose*—now. Can you handle it?"

A cheer went up, and as Titus began working his way out of the observatory, they threw questions at him. "You've talked to it?" "Why is it alive?" "How could it have survived?" "Is it really a monster like they're saying on the news?" "Are we all going to die of plague up here?"

Climbing the steps to the hall door, he held up his hands. "There's no plague! H'lim is no monster, just a poor, lost castaway." Then, feeling like a hypocrite, he added, "Maybe we can get his people to come take him home, and if that happens, we want him to report highly of us. So let's see some level-headed competence around here, okay? I'm late for this meeting, so you get me those numbers, and I'll find out what's happening in Biomed and let you know. *Wild Goose* is alive!"

With that, he plunged out into the corridor.

———

It was a stormy meeting. The rumors Titus' crew had heard were nothing compared to what the press was disseminating. Panic was overtaking Earth's population, and already there were riots in some countries. Unsubstantiated reports indicated that some countries were funding the anti-Hail groups in open defiance of World Sovereignties law.

Colby's orders were to get hard data, taped interviews, and biological evidence on H'lim and beam it to Earth to counter the panic. Mihelich insisted on sending along his own report on the benign microlife the alien carried. "What little there is of it. His blood is practically sterile, and his immune system's biochemistry is virtually the same as ours." Privately, he told Titus, "He carries antibodies I've never seen before, but not the corresponding organisms. *Nothing* about him is human, yet there's no threat to us. Why are they so hysterical down there?"

Titus had no answer except that it was human nature to fear the unknown, which wasn't wholly irrational. In the days that followed Inea clung to the vidcom, devouring every tidbit on H'lim, and chafing at Titus' inability to get her in to meet him. But she still fed Titus willingly and abundantly of her ectoplasm even though he was rationing his remaining blood. She understood that Titus was supporting H'lim until Mihelich produced orl blood.

Under the imposed quarantine, deliveries to the station were now to be made by drop rather than by surface, so that crews would not stay overnight at the station. This cut the tonnage they could transport, so all requisitions were doubly scrutinized. Mihelich would not receive anything to support cloning, and Titus might not get Connie's new blood chips. Every report he filed with her mentioned the restrictions and his dwindling supply, but she only acknowledged, reminding him their channel was not secure from the Tourists.

Titus scoured his hardware for any bug Abbot might have planted and found none. Any leak was on the ground.

During the frantic days after H'lim's wakening, Titus hardly slept. In the lunar night, and with Inea supporting him, he had the stamina. He even squeezed in frequent visits to H'lim, both under the cameras and privately. He was present when the luren's eyes were examined, and learned that Earth's luren had lost sensitivity in the visible spectrum. Luren had not only the three sensitivity peaks that humans had, but also a number of infrared and ultraviolet peaks. Luren skin responded to the electromagnetic presence of human bodies. When one of the engineers presented H'lim with a pair of goggles to allow him to use station lighting, he told her, "All the colors seem odd, but I do thank you."

He was unfailingly polite and graciously cooperative, obscuring his reticence under an effusive generosity. "I know genetics and commerce, but not politics or cartography. Believe me, I'd like your message to reach my employers even more than you would. However, I don't know where I am, and I've even less idea of how to locate home from here."

Questioned on astrogation, he could only cite his ineptitude with that branch of mathematics. Of *Kylyd's* stellar drive he said, "I don't think anyone understands why it works, but it's revolutionized galactic commerce."

That was their first clue that there was a civilization out there. Closer questioning only revealed that there were many species allied into political units, which never seemed stable enough to traders. H'lim's people, however, dealt little with other species and even his ignorance was long out of date. How long? There was no telling, he claimed, since he did not understand astrogation, and never could anticipate the elapsed time of a trip. He sounded much like a time zone-hopping businessman who depended on his handheld to match local time zones, so no one considered he might be lying.

Knowing he was starving while waiting for Mihelich's cloning of orl blood to yield results, they offered him human blood from the infirmary's stores, cloned and guaranteed sterile blood. That's precisely what it was, cloned, dead and sterile. But he accepted it with good grace and did his best to choke it down. It took more fortitude than had the acceptance of Titus' supply, which he now welcomed whenever Titus could get some in to him. That, at least, was infused.

Meanwhile, H'lim redoubled his efforts to help Mihelich. He was under no constraints about working around the clock in plain sight— they *knew* he was alien. So late one night Titus found him poring over the vidcom. As Titus came in, he looked up. "You don't have much of a vocabulary, do you?"

"What?" That had never been one of Titus' problems.

"Chorion," challenged H'lim.

"Never heard the word."

"Choroid," he said.

Titus leaned over his shoulder to see what he was reading. "H'lim, that's a biology dictionary."

"I know. I'm a biologist—I think. The study of animals, yes?"

"Definitely not my field."

"True. Have you made any progress in your field?"

"We're getting some sense from *Wild Goose* now, and we've refined our guesses with all the new data. If you came along a direct line from your home planet, we'll find it."

"I couldn't begin to guess about that, but it doesn't really matter. The signal will be picked up by someone."

"Someone who'd care enough to respond?"

"Who knows? But I'm going to compose a message to go with Earth's, so that whoever hears it will route it to someone who would care."

"You want to go home."

"Yes." H'lim turned from the vidcom, waved cheerily at the surveillance cameras, then turned them off. "Do you really think that makes privacy?"

"I'm staking my life on it," said Titus, producing his Thermos from his briefcase. While H'lim drank, Titus mused, "I'd have found anything the humans left running, but Abbot might have a bug or two in here. I don't think so, though. He prefers to use Influence."

"What little you have of it, it seems to suffice."

"We wouldn't fare very well if we went back with you, would we?"

"Hard to say. From the two of you, I'd say your strain has become devious, perhaps sly. But then you admit you were sent as master spies to manipulate these humans and vie with each other covertly. I doubt such skills exist at home, however I've led a sheltered life—as you say Andre has."

Mihelich and Mirelle were the only two H'lim saw more of than he did of Titus and Abbot. "Andre's a specialist," Titus said.

"Yes." Even in private, H'lim refrained from criticizing Earth's lifestyle, though he often registered surprise at first encountering a peculiarity. Titus believed the man had traveled on diverse worlds and learned the trick of accepting the strange on its own terms.

Titus dug into the briefcase again. "Brought you some items from *Kylyd* that my analysts are through with. Can you tell me where these were manufactured?" He set some odd bits of metal on the desk.

H'lim scooped them up eagerly. "Where are the rest?" he demanded with an intensity that startled Titus.

"Rest? I think that's all there were. Were they manufactured from materials found on Lur?"

"I don't know." He began sorting them and counting.

"It might give me a clue to the spectrum to look for."

H'lim looked around. "Mirelle would demand to know what they're *for*, but you're not the least bit interested."

Titus really hadn't thought about it, but now he looked at the oddments. "Game pieces?"

"You've lost *Thizan?*"

"Abbot might know more than I." Titus pulled up a chair, suddenly intensely curious. "Tell me about it."

Several hours later, Titus left with sketches for the missing pieces of the board game which was not unlike chess but had more kinds of pieces and a more complex board. Technically, the time had been wasted, but he felt almost as relaxed and refreshed as if he'd slept a full night, and he wanted to forget all about everything else but building the set and mastering the game.

He was jarred back to reality when he found Inea in his office with a report on Abbot's doings gleaned from her little bugs. "He's discovered his power source is missing!"

He told her that H'lim would be adding a message to the probe's signal. "Abbot may not think his message is so important any more."

"He's been running around like crazy, gathering components to rebuild the thing."

"Are you sure that's what he's up to?" They spent the hours until Titus' first conference of the day analyzing Abbot's moves.

"Don't worry," said Inea as he left. "I'll stay late tonight and get those figures from *Wild Goose* cleaned up."

Titus went on about his business, sternly putting aside his infatuation with the board game. The news from Earth had worsened, the probe construction was going swiftly but not smoothly, and despite everything he'd learned from H'lim, he felt less confidence in his targeting efforts than ever before. *Maybe H'lim doesn't know much, but he's not telling everything he does know. Those starships don't travel in straight lines—I know it!*

But *Wild Goose's* preliminary figures had confirmed the straight-line trajectory constructed from all other detection devices operating during the approach. The very earliest figures though, had eluded them. *Wild Goose* had been the first to spot the approaching object, but that data had a lot of noise in it due to the onboard malfunction which still hadn't totally cleared up. The engineers hypothesized that some kind of wave from the ship's drive had disrupted onboard electronics, but there was no proof of that.

Late during the graveyard shift, the sun was coming up outside, making Titus suddenly tired as well as hungry. Inea wasn't in her apartment, so he returned to the observatory, worried that she'd fallen asleep over her desk.

The lab was deserted, the lights dim, and there were two figures behind the glass walls beyond the computers. A singularly strong Influence pervaded the atmosphere, throbbing with hunger.

H'lim!

Titus charged across the room.

——— SEVENTEEN ———

Before Titus reached the door to the observatory, H'lim cried out and backed away from Inea, the blanketing pall of his Influence fragmenting. Titus fetched up against the doorjamb and H'lim sank to the floor, doubled over.

Inea stood over him brandishing the silver cross, her lower lip caught between her teeth. Seeing Titus, she flung herself into his arms, sobbing. He whispered, "I have to Mark you. Inea, I have to!"

"Do it!" She huddled against his chest, trembling.

He raised his finger to her forehead and set his Mark, marveling at the tremendous wave of relief that washed through him with that act of possession. And in the next moment, he was ashamed of the feeling. To cover that, he demanded, "H'lim, *what* are you doing here?"

Gulping air, the luren rose and straightened his disposable suit. "You have taken the one I've chosen." There was no hint of defiance in him, just confusion.

"There's a complicated story behind that," answered Titus. "You shouldn't be here. If they catch you—"

"Could it possibly go worse for me?"

Inea stepped away to face H'lim. "You could have just asked me politely and I'd have shown you anything here."

"I did not wish her to report to you," he said locking gazes with Titus. "I Influenced only those you and Abbot used. Why is this one not held in abeyance, as Abbot does?"

"Abbot's a goddamned Tourist, that's why!"

Inea put a hand on Titus' wrist. "Don't swear. H'lim didn't mean any harm." She stood on tiptoe to reach his ear and, in a choked whisper, added, "Titus, he's *starving*."

Titus swallowed his incipient tirade and whispered back, "You may speak freely in front of H'lim, but only H'lim."

H'lim blinked at Inea, astonished. Titus said, "Tell me what you wanted from Inea. I'll dump the data into your personal files."

"I want to see the stellar map you've constructed."

"You know more of astrogation than you've let on."

"No." His gaze fastened on Inea, his hunger blunted but clear. "Why was she not Marked? Why isn't she controlled?"

"I'm not controlled," said Inea, "because Titus isn't afraid of me. Abbot's terrified of humans; Titus understands humans. Abbot knows only his own purposes; Titus knows others have the right to choose their own purposes too."

"Inea's not controlled," said Titus, "because Inea keeps her word. You declined Abbot's stringer, but now I find you at the woman who has, in fact, been supporting you *and* me. And you won't even explain what you're doing here."

H'lim sagged, leaning on a console. He scrubbed at his face, and Titus could see the ends of his fingers quivering. "I thought this place would be deserted. I only wanted to see if you were really doing what you claimed, if you really were what you said you were. A vidcom image is not data. I *had* to verify what you gave me. Can't you see that? Before I made them a message, I had to be sure!"

"Why would you doubt us?" asked Titus.

"They said they'd make me a spacesuit so I could go see the ship. They never did. It would be so easy to fake those pictures of *Kylyd*. The fragments didn't even have the name on them, after all. You might be holding all of us prisoner. You might *be* anyone, or allies to anyone, using me or my stock. Or the humans might. I don't *know* your species; I don't *know* who you are; I don't *know* where I am!"

"Titus, you've got to take him out to the wreck. You said yourself the cameras can't pick up the name." And she explained why the cameras couldn't see the luren paint job.

Titus asked, "If you saw the wreck, and the star maps, if you were convinced it's all true, what would you do?"

"Make the message they asked me to make."

"I'm not so sure that would be to our advantage."

"It would be to mine."

"Would the luren take this world from us?"

With genuine surprise, H'lim said, "No! It would—it would not be legal to do that."

"You're hungry. You'd have taken Inea. Who's to say some luren wouldn't come to prefer humans to orl?"

"It would not be legal. I'm glad you stopped me. I'm glad she stopped me. I'd face a dire penalty otherwise."

"Who out there cares about humans?"

"There are dire penalties for saying the wrong things to primitive peoples, too."

"Titus," said Inea, "not everybody as hungry as he is would worry about which food is legal."

"I know." To H'lim, he said, "If taking humans isn't legal for luren, then where does that leave Earth's luren?"

"I'm no lawyer." H'lim sketched a shrug. It looked awkward, like something Mirelle had taught him.

"Titus, we should take him to your apartment and feed him. It's hard to trust people who starve you."

Titus was wondering how a "sheltered" stockman could suspect humans and Earth-luren of creating the infirmary room to trick him. And what did he imagine they would want to trick him into? What was going on in the galaxy to raise such a suspicion? Industrial espionage? War?

"He's not so sure he wants my trust," said H'lim.

"No, it's not that," answered Inea. "There isn't much blood left, and there's no telling when there'll be more."

"Mihelich will have his first batch ready soon," said Titus.

"But H'lim needs ectoplasm, and for that humans are as good as orl." H'lim looked aside and remained silent. Titus added, "I did father you, H'lim, and I'll honor that commitment. But there's too much you don't know yet about life among humans. You've got to go back to your room and keep anyone from knowing you've been out."

"First I must go to *Kylyd*. There are things I need. If they've survived." Titus felt a wild surge of Influence that cut off abruptly. "I haven't been able to sleep since you woke me. Your people may have changed, but I can't—"

"Oh, shit!" Titus interrupted. "Listen, it's been night since you woke. Abbot and I have been wakeful, too, but now the sun's coming up, so we feel ghastly, too. It's the magnetic—" H'lim had Titus' vocabulary, but few concepts to go with the words. "We use a generator to relieve the discomfort and sleep. Abbot was making one for you. Didn't he mention it?"

H'lim shook his head. "On the ship, I have—"

"It's probably destroyed, or we'd have found it. Abbot's clever with machines. Work with him; he'll get the settings right for you. Now I've got to take you back—"

The outer door of the lab crashed open and armed Brink's guards in spacesuits poured through, dart-guns at the ready.

"Okay, H'lim, freeze!" shouted the leader, taking aim.

Moving very slowly, Titus raised his hands and stepped in front of H'lim, muttering, "God alone knows what those darts might do to you! They don't hurt me." Aloud, he called, "Hold it, gentlemen. He was only trying to verify what we've told him of ourselves. You won't need the guns."

Behind the guards came a cordon of Biomed technicians in isolation gear carrying an isolation bubble. "I'm sorry, Dr. Shiddehara, but we've got to detain you and the lady, too."

Titus' heart pounded into his throat. He wouldn't be able to eat, or to bring H'lim nourishment. But then Colby, in uniform only, pushed through, shouting for attention.

"Listen! H'lim has been through the outer observation dome, the spacesuit lockers, the arcade, the gym, and several refectories. No dome is untouched. Further quarantine is a farce. Worse yet, he can make people *see* things—or not see them. That's how he got out of Biomed. He could walk out that door and we wouldn't know it until tomorrow when we tried to figure out why we'd been here dressed like this!"

"Dr. Colby," said Titus, edging forward, "H'lim was scared we weren't leveling with him—especially when we didn't deliver the spacesuit we promised. He had to check in person on what we'd provided through the vidcom. Wouldn't you have done the same? Has he hurt anyone?"

H'lim stepped out from behind Titus. "Dr. Mihelich and I confirmed that there's no need for quarantine. And now I believe you've told me the truth, however unlikely it seems." He placed his hands on his knees, giving a sort of half-bow as he said, "Forgive me if I frightened you in return for the kindness you have shown me."

"You may," said Colby, "have condemned us all to live out our lives on this station. It could take decades for Earth to accept the absence of a health threat."

"You will have my cooperation in regaining trust." H'lim looked to Titus with the barest whisper of Influence.

Recalling the paralyzing blast H'lim had generated on wakening, and his puzzlement over the faintness of Abbot's Mark, Titus said, "As a physicist, I'm intrigued by H'lim's sensitivity across the electromagnetic spectrum. The human nervous system is electromagnetic, too, which could account for the odd effects he has on people's minds. Could those effects be a natural defense reflex of your species, H'lim?"

Titus underscored "natural defense" with Influence, and H'lim, after an awkward pause, took the cue. "I've never met a species on which my fright has such an exaggerated effect. I know you're not my enemies, so it won't happen again."

211

Titus said softly, to Colby alone, "Biomed and Cognitive Sciences will be fascinated to learn of a planet that evolved a dominant species with a reflex for becoming invisible when frightened. Dr. H'lim is a life sciences expert, and would help them." H'lim didn't blink at Titus' according him the ubiquitous title "Doctor." Titus asked, "Doctor, can you agree now to compose the message for the probe to send?"

"Yes. I can." H'lim glanced at Titus acknowledging how Titus had altered the mood of the crowd without Influence.

The hall door opened, and Abbot entered, halting on the top step to survey the tableau. He wore ordinary coveralls.

Colby didn't see Abbot. She knew that H'lim expected to survive the centuries it might take for his people to come, but that human knowledge of his language was too sketchy for them to verify what his message said. "We can accept such a message only on condition that from now on, you allow our cameras to record and monitor all your movements."

It's only sensible, thought Titus with despair. H'lim's terror surged into rising Influence, and Titus laid a hand on his elbow, feeling his tremor of hunger. How could he feed under surveillance? Titus was determined not to let Abbot take over this time. He said, "We're asking H'lim to vouch for us, but we're treating him like a dangerous animal. I wouldn't vouch for people who treated me that way."

"Titus," protested H'lim, "they are frightened." He addressed Colby, "You react to fright by using your power, and I react to your use of power by being frightened and using my power. In this small laboratory, can we not experiment with ways to prevent such a destructive cycle?"

"I don't think you understand how we feel about what you've done—or what we imagine you can do beyond that."

"Possibly not. But can you understand that I regret frightening you?" At Colby's cautious nod, he went on, "So let us break this cycle before it controls history."

"But I *must* have you under absolute surveillance. No other option is open to me." Her voice was hard.

"Allow me some freedom and some privacy with the chance to earn more by proving trustworthy, and I will aid you in every way I can. Deny me such necessities, and I will die."

Her expression altered. "Die?"

"My kind are not like yours. I have other needs. Are you so barbarous that you'd enjoy watching a death by deprivation? Is that why you revived me?"

Titus listened open-mouthed. H'lim had caught the knack of manipulating humans so fast, Titus wondered how much he and Abbot had been manipulated by him.

Abbot strode forward, threading between the Brink's and Biomed crews to stand beside Colby. "*Some* humans would enjoy watching such a death," he replied to H'lim, the whole room reverberating to his controlled whisper of Influence. "But I think everyone here is as offended by your remark as I am."

"Then I withdraw it." H'lim bowed again, this time with an Oriental flavor, yielding utterly to his grandfather.

Abbot said, not needing Influence with the deeply conditioned human, "Carol, I came as soon as I heard H'lim had left his quarters. I thought you might not realize he was so starved and so exhausted from being unable to sleep that his judgment has to be impaired."

Contrite, Colby said to H'lim, "Exhausted? And hungry, too. Together, they'd leave a human prey to fear and likely to overreact. Why didn't you say something—"

"I did ask to go to *Kylyd.*"

Abbot said, "We didn't understand, but now I think I've got a solution."

"We have other business to settle first," Colby said that hardness returning to her voice. Titus sensed a shield go up within her mind, shattering Abbot's hold on her. Abbot stepped away from her, puzzled, unsure of himself for the first time since Titus had known him.

Titus said, "Abbot's solution to H'lim's insomnia might explain why H'lim feels his life is threatened by confinement and surveillance. After all, Abbot is the Project's foremost electronic engineer and H'lim's most remarkable distinction from humans is his electromagnetic sensitivity. Am I right, Dr. Nandoha?"

Some of Abbot's apprehension vanished. "In a way. I found that the beds aboard *Kylyd* are rigged to produce a controlled magnetic environment. If they were functional, no recorder could operate within the electromagnetic noise they'd set up—at least, none of ours could." He turned to H'lim, highlighting his words with Influence, "You want the cameras off because they're noisy, right? You want to move about the station because you require sensory stimulus of shifting magnetic fields, not just muscular exercise."

213

H'lim assented, guardedly, and Abbot cast a reproachful glance at Colby.

"H'lim," she said, "can you ever forgive us? We never intended to torture you. Believe that, and tell us what you need, but please understand we can't tolerate being controlled as you have done. We'll defend ourselves against it, even if it hurts you. We won't enjoy your suffering, but we won't suffer in your stead."

"That seems reasonable," answered H'lim.

Titus said, "H'lim, do you understand the concept of giving your word of honor, the military usage of 'parole'?"

"In your mind, these concepts define your identity. It is even more central for us."

Colby gasped. "You can read our minds!"

H'lim flinched from her horror but denied, "I can't read minds. Titus gave me his spoken language and later provided graphics. I understand some things, but am missing others."

"Then how can you twist our minds as you have?"

"Titus is the physicist here, not I," H'lim answered.

"Physicist," said Titus, "not metaphysicist." That second session with H'lim had been a major trial, and he knew he had not done well. H'lim still stumbled over words with multiple meanings or with concepts he didn't have.

H'lim shrugged, and went on, "I will offer my word, my 'parole,' thusly. Let Titus and Abbot visit me, and me visit them. Let them, along with"—he scanned the crowd, appearing to select Inea at random— "this lady, determine the conditions in which I am to be kept. In return, I pledge that my power, such as it is, will never touch them. You'll be able to trust them, and if they judge I must be put to death, my defenses will not rise against them."

And he called us sly. He had given away absolutely nothing and claimed in return everything he wanted. Titus said, "I'd trust him to keep his word—more so, perhaps, than if he'd promised to include the whole station in the pledge."

"I believe him, too," said Abbot, without Influence.

"I'll take his word for it," added Inea.

H'lim glanced at her sharply, then inclined his head. "But the ultimate authority lies with Dr. Colby, no?"

"Your escape tonight," said Colby, "and the method you used to accomplish it, are already recorded on Earth. Ultimately, *they* will decide your fate, and by now they probably believe we're in your

214

thrall as well as disease-ridden. Nothing we say will sway their decisions."

An icy lump formed in Titus' guts. *They'll nuke the station!* But where on Earth could they find a hot bomb? He said, "Meanwhile, we have to live together. We can't stand here and work out the details. After a couple of good meals and a night's sleep, we can negotiate more sensibly. Carol?"

Cautiously, she said, "It may be necessary for me to replace Titus, Abbot, and Inea with others."

"I trust Titus and Abbot well enough to keep this promise," H'lim said. "It's an extreme one, you understand? Perhaps I could accept someone else, but please don't choose at random. I won't extend a promise I might not be able to keep."

Colby stepped closer and searched behind H'lim's dark glasses for some clue in his eyes. Then she nodded. "Titus is right. He's made his promise so small because he intends to keep it. But, H'lim, why do you trust these three?"

H'lim asked, "Is there anyone here who doesn't?"

The room stirred with nervous laughter, and from it came the distinct chorus of approval for the three. Titus felt Abbot tense, undoubtedly feeling naked when he didn't dare use Influence. Finally, Colby said, "Well, I agree. And Titus is right. It's been too long a day. We'll hammer out terms of parole at the department heads' meeting tomorrow, and I'll expect you to attend, Dr. H'lim."

"The family name is used with the title for those who do original work in science? I should be then Dr. Sa'ar."

It was a small thing for him to offer, but it somehow softened the hostility in the room. "Dr. Sa'ar," repeated Colby, then strode toward the door, firing orders right and left. When the door finally closed behind her, she had posted four guards outside, guards who would follow H'lim about, both to protect him and to protect people from him.

Inea, Titus, and Abbot were left with H'lim, who had stood ramrod straight through the whole confrontation. But now he sagged back against a desk, burying his face in his hands. "Titus," he warned, "I'm so hungry."

Abbot opened his mouth, but Titus cut him off. "I'll take him to my apartment and feed him. You and Inea go rig up his bed for him."

"You sure you can handle it?" asked Abbot of Titus.

"I'll go with you, Titus," said Inea.

215

"No!" protested H'lim. "Just—just get away from me, Inea. *Please.*"

She stepped back. "You sound like Titus!"

Abbot understood. He beckoned Inea. "Come on, let's not make it any harder for him. Life is going to be bad enough around here, after this." He led Inea to the door, trying to convince her to trust him.

As H'lim and Titus followed, H'lim said, "I've panicked the herd with my ineptitude?"

"Yeah. You saw Carol shake off Abbot's lightest touch. It'll be a long time until she'll be unsuspecting again, and Abbot doesn't know how to manage without Influence."

"He's going to have trouble—feeding?"

"Maybe."

"I'm sorry."

"I know. We all do what we must. Come on." He led H'lim and the four Brink's guards to his apartment, ignoring the wary looks and hard stares the party drew. Leaving the four men outside, he entered and held the door for H'lim who waited on the threshold, one hand raised as if resting on glass. "Come in, H'lim, and welcome." Cloaking his words, he added, "I didn't know if you'd feel the threshold."

H'lim nodded. "What I can't stand about that room they have me in—it's like trying to live in a hallway."

"Humans don't sense the threshold as we do. Even if you had a proper room, they'd come and go like that."

"I have to stop it, Titus, or I'll surely go mad."

"We'll arrange something tomorrow." As he prepared the blood, he asked, "Do you really sense magnetic noise, as Abbot said?" He gestured for H'lim to sit at the table.

"Yes," the luren answered.

Titus folded his arms and leaned back against the sink. "I don't. How bad is it for you?"

He looked away. "If Abbot's truly built a bed, I will discover that soon."

"You can trust Abbot's gadgets. What can I do to help?"

"Take my mind off it. Tell me why you took Inea from me." He looked young, lost and alone, bewildered and scared.

"I'll try." Titus started with how Abbot had taken Mirelle from him, and how he'd vowed never to do that, and then had no other choice. He struggled to explain what Inea meant to him, and was relieved when the microwave bleeped.

"I think I understand," said H'lim. "She is both mate and orl to you. It must be intolerable."

216

"No," said Titus, holding the pitcher and wishing Inea were there to infuse it instead of his having to do it himself. *She's safer with Abbot.* H'lim would gain ectoplasm, but Titus would only lose in this meal. "No, H'lim, it's the only tolerable situation for me."

"I—see."

As they shared the meal, Titus observed, "You've become pretty good manipulating humans without using Influence. I can't believe you learned it from me that quickly."

"I'm a stock breeder and a merchant. Though non-luren don't have much use for my stock, I deal with them for supplies. They frown on the use of Influence in business."

"I can imagine." Vivid pictures danced through Titus' mind of a galaxy where luren were ostracized and feared. "Shall I make up another pitcher?"

"No. Your supply is low and it won't be long until there is orl blood. I will share it with you, and Abbot."

"They'll keep a close accounting."

"I'll tell them I need more than I do. I must help you, as you must help Abbot if he has trouble. He has offered you his stringers more than once."

"I've explained why I can't accept."

"Yes." H'lim toyed with the last drop of blood in his glass. "If you know where Inea got that thing she used on me—"

"The cross?" Titus laughed. He told H'lim how she'd done the same to him and why. "It helps, but it is in even more limited supply than blood!"

"A religious object," he mused. Eyes veiled, he paused to think and Titus waited, avid for any clue to H'lim's religion. "Well," said H'lim, changing the subject, "there may be another way I can help. I note that you, more than Abbot even, tend to produce a bit of your own sustenance. Perhaps this is a trait from your human ancestry. You said once that you have more human ancestors than Abbot does."

Titus knew he produced his own blood faster than Abbot did, but ectoplasm too? "How could you see such a thing? I really have to study your eyes!"

"And I have to study your genes—your real ones, not the fabrication in the medical records. There's a stimulant we use on orl, you might call it a—booster for blood and ectoplasm both. I can adapt it to work on you through your human traits. Just get me tissue from you and from Abbot, and convince Dr. Colby to allow me access to a laboratory."

Titus was hungry enough that the idea didn't seem too exotic. "They'll balk at turning you loose in a laboratory."

"Tell them I'm improving my food supply. It'll be true, after all, for if you're supplied, you'll provide for me."

———

That simple trust moved Titus more deeply than he could believe possible. It sustained him throughout the tedious business of tuning Abbot's field generator, through H'lim's hysterical relief when he tried it, through Inea's impatience as he insisted on stopping at his office to record his report for Connie, and through the argument with Inea when she proposed asking another human to volunteer to support H'lim.

"What's the matter with you?" she demanded when Titus refused to consider it. "He's starving, and he won't even insist on taking the volunteer to bed!"

"*That's* the problem!" retorted Titus, hunger eroding his patience. "Any such volunteer would sicken and die! Humans aren't orl. Sex with another human isn't enough."

"How do you know!"

Titus sighed and quit keyboarding his report. "I've seen those of my blood cause a lot of death in a lot of different ways. If you doubt me, ask Abbot."

Inea recoiled, stung. Titus finished his report. She said, "Well, then maybe you could convince him to take the volunteer to bed? After all, *I* finally accepted you."

"He'd *never* do it. He thinks of orl as animals!"

"But humans are not orl!" she insisted.

"It doesn't matter. He'd never be potent with a human."

"Did you ask him?"

"I don't know him well enough yet."

"If you're supposed to be his father, you're supposed to tell him about the birds and bees."

Titus laughed. The release felt good, and when Inea joined in, he reveled in it. Then, out of the corner of his eye, he saw text from Connie scroll onto his screen.

Inea read over his shoulder. "*Barnaby Peter?* That's the ship you arrived in. It doesn't usually carry much cargo."

"It's bringing the W.S. investigators. And this"—he indicated one of Connie's code groups—"means it's also bringing enough blood for me, H'lim, and Abbot, too. So we won't have to recruit another human volunteer—yet."

"The blood isn't all you need."

"We can survive on what we gather from human proximity."

"But—"

"Inea! It's become too dangerous to use Influence, and stringers are much too dangerous without Influence. If we can't manage, we'll have to either go dormant or die."

"You really mean that?"

He nodded, acknowledged Connie's message, and shut down. "Will you come home with me now, or are you too mad at me?"

She put her hands on his shoulders. "I'm more scared than mad. I don't want you to die."

He relaxed into the warmth of her touch. "I won't—not as long as you're willing to be mine." He lifted her hands off his shoulders. "Let's not start that here, though."

———

The next day, after cautioning H'lim not to invoke the slightest whiff of Influence, Titus escorted him into the conference room flanked by a new set of four Brink's guards, two men and two women, who were punctilious but white-lipped.

Those at the long polished table were pinched and drawn. Conversation arrested, their eyes followed the alien around the table to his place at Colby's right. Titus admired H'lim's composure and wondered if the ordinary clothing he'd been issued helped him feel less like a prisoner.

The seat reserved for H'lim had extra space around it and was between Titus and Abbot. There was no water glass or electronic doodling pad in front of H'lim's place, and the computer terminal there was locked. Titus shoved his pad in front of H'lim, demonstrating its controls, then used his master key to unlock the terminal while he remarked to one of the Brink's guards, "We're short one pad here."

The woman looked to Colby who sketched a nod. Before long, the pad was produced. Enabling the large screen on the wall behind her to display their graphs, Colby called them to order, inviting each to report on the effect H'lim's escape had had on their work.

Titus marveled at the furor sparked by the escape. The station was being scoured for biological contamination; everyone was to be put through a psychological and medical sieve; Brink's was investigating for laxity; a copy of the computer records had been impounded; Food Services was shut down for sterilization and institution of stricter procedures; Environmental was double-screening every technician's move from a remote location; locks were being changed; the gym showers and swimming pool had been shut down; and progress on the probe had halted because all of these measures required staggering numbers of staff hours.

As each department head reported, Titus saw the others darting covert glances at H'lim who listened impassively, jotting notes in luren script. The proceeding took on the aspect of a trial, with H'lim the defendant. When at last Accounting gave an estimate of the cost of it all, it was as if H'lim had been indicted for grand larceny. The point was not lost on the luren merchant.

"It does not stop there," announced Colby. "Each of us will undergo psychological testing at short intervals. The tests will be administered and evaluated from Luna Station. Furthermore, every official decision, every act of every technician, will be evaluated at Luna Station. Personnel are en route aboard *Barnaby Peter* to Luna to set up a department there, and new landlines will be laid to carry the data without solar interference. Aberrant behavior or hypnotic influence will be detected immediately.

"Also aboard *Barnaby Peter* are the World Sovereignties investigators, a group now composed of volunteers who'll share our quarantine for the duration. Half of them will remain in Luna Station to review the decisions of those who come here. Are there any additions, suggestions, or questions?"

Absolute stillness wrapped those at the table. When Colby glanced down to consult her notes, H'lim said softly, "Dr. Colby, may I speak?"

Her head snapped up, then she scanned the tense faces about the table. Every eye was on H'lim. Titus suddenly wondered if anyone would note a resemblance between H'lim and the two Earth-luren flanking him. He had to restrain the surge of Influence that came unbidden. The meeting was being recorded and Influence wouldn't fool the recorders.

"As a matter of fact, the issues connected to your future situation are next on the agenda." Scanning the grim faces, she announced, "Dr. Sa'ar has the floor."

H'lim had heard the phrase more than a dozen times now, and copied the human mannerisms with haunting exactitude. "I understand I have put you to trouble and expense. The manner in which I did this is more disturbing to you than I had expected. I have made a grave error. I wish to explain and to offer to make amends. Would this be out of order?"

"Not at all," replied Colby.

H'lim painted a graphic picture of his awakening and confinement, emphasizing the control the humans had exerted on his information access. He cited the promised spacesuit that never arrived, and the "magnetic noise," the lack of privacy, and a pattern of deprivation that seemed to him to have been engineered by an expert in his people's physiology.

"When you asked me to construct a message to draw a ship here, I entertained two hypotheses. Either you were exactly what you said you were, or you were enemies bent on using me against my own kind. I had to ascertain the truth. I discovered, to my chagrin, that my suspicions were groundless."

Colby asked, "What precisely had you suspected us of? Who did you think we might be?"

H'lim gazed at the terminal set into the table. "You are like enough to one of the known species that you might have been recruited from them."

"But you admitted to me," said Colby, "that you had contact with Titus' mind. Surely, had this been an elaborate deception, you would have learned of it?"

"Not necessarily, though that would have been the most difficult and expensive part of the deception, and so the stakes would have had to have been very high. I'm a stock breeder, a merchant, an ordinary working man. These matters are wholly beyond me. But I'm now convinced that you are what you say you are, and that therefore I owe you a great debt.

"If you will launch your probe, then I will supply the message you requested. But I must know if you intend the probe to lure the respondent away from this solar system. If you were to signal from here, with the more powerful ground-based equipment, there would be a greater chance of attracting attention quickly, so later winning trust."

"Of those very people," said Colby, "whom you thought had kidnapped you? Whom you thought had tried to brainwash you with well designed torture? Who are those people who look so much like us?"

221

H'lim's eyes raked the tense humans. Titus could hear his shallow breathing, but he did not raise Influence as he answered, "Figments of my disturbed imagination, no doubt."

"*I* doubt it," said Colby.

Eyes fixed on his terminal, H'lim elaborated. "I have been told of well-funded espionage conducted between rival firms on your world. Your species is not so dissimilar from those of the galaxy. There are always wealthy individuals who would do drastic things to quadruple their wealth.

"I was escorting a herd of specially bred stock, my own product, and a closely guarded secret. Possession of that secret could have quadrupled the wealth of those who could afford to stage such a deception against me. Your work with the intact orl tissue supported that theory. The message you wanted me to write could have used my personal reputation to lure someone of even greater value than I into a trap."

He raised his eyes. "I understand that humility is valued among you. I apologize for not being humble about my value. I assure you, I do not exaggerate. Provide me freedom, privacy, and access to a well-equipped laboratory, and I'll help you with your next steps in conquering viral and genetic diseases. I won't 'give' you anything that would disrupt your civilization, but just the tools to meet galactic civilization with confidence."

H'lim focused on the recorder up in the corner of the room and spoke to those on Earth. "I'm only one person, isolated here, surrounded by vacuum, under heavy guard—and already my existence has disrupted the affairs of your world. But if you were confident, then there would be no disruption, not even at the arrival of a shipload of galactics. I offer you contact on an even footing with a huge commercial market. I ask only your help in surviving and returning home."

Titus could not have written a better presentation, but then H'lim's rhetorical style in English was no doubt derived from Titus' own. It was almost too good. It was eerie. An alien should seem more—alien.

Colby took charge, aborting a dozen private arguments. "Dr. Sa'ar has spoken very persuasively, but the matter will not be decided here. Dr. Mihelich has repeatedly confirmed that we are in no danger of biological contamination. Dr. Sa'ar has not, even under extreme provocation, injured anyone. We are fully isolated here, and our actions will have no consequences on Earth—unless we lose Dr. Sa'ar's good will by mistreating him. Therefore, I am ordering Lab 620, across from Dr. Mihelich's lab, turned over to Dr. Sa'ar. I am searching for suitable private quarters for our guest, and will provide guards and staff to aid him."

The main screen flashed white, then resolved into an exterior of Goddard Station, with an announcer's voice-over ". . . enormous destruction! It's getting hard to breathe in here!" He was screaming over a background roar. Titus made out chunks of debris spreading from a gaping hole in the station's wheel. "—take you now to Quito Orbital Control, Max Simon reporting. Max?"

The image shifted to a shirt-sleeved reporter muttering aside to someone, "Oxygen masks up there?" Then he touched the button in his ear and glanced at the camera. "Oh. Good morning from Quito Control. Here we've been getting conflicting reports of the explosion." Behind him, a large screen held another view of Goddard. "Only one thing is absolutely certain. Nothing is left of *Barnaby Peter.* According to scanners here at Quito, none of the pieces is larger than a man. I have—" His hand went to his ear again, and his manner changed.

"We have a bulletin just in, and for that we return to Terry Rogers at Houston."

The scene shifted to the fountain plaza of the familiar Orbital Control Center building in Houston. A brunette in a yellow silk suit held a microphone between herself and a young man with thick glasses and a fringe of beard. "Dr. Raymond Sills here will comment on . . . oh?" She glanced off camera, to someone who handed her a flimsy, then started again. "I'm sorry. This just in. A group calling itself the Coalition of Earth Advocates has claimed responsibility for the destruction of *Barnaby Peter* and the World Sovereignties Investigative Board. Their spokesperson—"

She cut off as another flimsy was shoved into her hand and someone whispered off camera, "No, no, read this!"

She began again, "The Coalition of Earth Advocates is supported by—oh my Cod!" She went white.

Yet another paper appeared before her, and the top of a head bobbed into the shot. Titus could see the young bearded man's arm supporting the reporter for an instant, and then she stood on her own feet again, took a deep breath and declaimed in the calm but grave voice of a reporter covering a funeral, "I have here official confirmation that the Coalition of Earth Advocates is supported by sixteen countries *formerly* signatories to the World Sovereignties compact. They have, as of this date, seceded from our union. We take you now to World Sovereignties headquarters."

The screen showed the cavernous General Assembly room, a scattering of delegations present and more arriving by the minute. At the lectern stood a swarthy, turbaned man with a full black beard reading a statement in the ponderous style necessitated by simultaneous translation.

". . . do not declare war upon those still signatory to the World Sovereignties compact. We have banded together to protect all of Earth, and to do so, we will use our military might to block any action of World Sovereignties that endangers our species. To this end, we the undersigned nations of Earth, declare Project Station under full blockade. Project Hail's probe will never lift, their signal never go out. Project Station is now isolated and those within left to die in the arms of their gods. Never again will any human being set foot on or near Project Station. We hereby declare it forbidden!"

——— EIGHTEEN ———

The department heads watched the coverage for two hours until it began to repeat. Twenty key W.S. figures asserted that the probe would go on schedule and that the station would be resupplied even if the blockading nations had to be defeated militarily. No one on the station believed this would remain a unanimous opinion, or that supplies would arrive soon.

The next three hours were spent creating a new, tighter rationing schedule, and when they finally broke up, Colby had the unenviable job of presenting their immediate, urgent needs list to Irene Nagel.

The moment Titus was free to leave his seat, he charged out the door, heading for his lab and his only link to Connie. Fractionally ahead of the others, he reached the lifts while they were still clear. In his lab, he found his people glued to the screens watching the coverage of the blockade or the station's official announcement of rationing.

They turned to him the moment he appeared. Dismay, indignation, even rage colored their fear. They had all accepted the hazards of lunar duty, but none had signed on to fight a war, harbor a living alien, or die on the moon.

"I say we should execute that unnatural beast!" shouted someone. "Finish what the crash started. Then—"

"Didn't you hear?" interrupted a woman. "They consider the station contaminated. Killing H'lim won't change that."

"They can still send us supplies—even under quarantine," argued Shimon. "We won't die."

"They want us dead. They don't want H'lim's knowledge to reach Earth. They're scared enough to nuke the station."

Titus held up his hands for silence and declared, "A few people, a few nations, on Earth have panicked, but that's no reason for us to panic. The majority of humans are level-headed, sane, practical people who value life—even ours, even H'lim's. We will survive until sense prevails, and we will do the job we were hired to do."

With that, he ducked into his office and shut the door, wishing he could believe his own words. They'd sounded awfully weak, but the noise level subsided.

Fingers trembling, he sat down and tapped his message buffer. Sure enough, there was word from Connie, but it cut off in mid-sentence as communications were disrupted. With only minutes' warning of the attack on *Barnaby Peter,* she had managed to send a brief admonition to stop Abbot at all costs and sit tight until she could resupply him.

He wrapped his arms around himself and let the shock course through him. *Going to starve on the moon after all. I should listen to my intuition!* After a while, he began to think and plan again.

If the blockade worked despite W.S. determination, it would change everything. They wouldn't be able to finish building the probe, they couldn't launch it, and so they wouldn't need any messages *or* targeting data. There was no way to defend the station, the probe hangar, or the launch pad from direct attack. The residences might be safe from low-yield explosives, but the surface installations would go—even the solar collectors and antennae. Despite everything W.S. could do, the blockade might work, and then what would the Tourists—more specifically, *Abbot*—do?

Titus had given up trying to tap Abbot's communications with the ground-based Tourists. He could only guess what Abbot's orders were. He pulled up his note file and listed his questions. What had Abbot been building after he discovered his transmitter's power source was missing? How much damage had he done to H'lim's attitude toward humans? Titus thought he'd scored more points with H'lim than Abbot had, but he couldn't be sure. How did Abbot intend to survive now that the use of Influence on his stringers was so dangerous?

Clearly, whatever Abbot intended, he would be working against a nearer deadline than he'd ever expected. Would haste drive Abbot to make errors, take chances? Titus put himself into Abbot's shoes, looked at the entire situation again, and suddenly *knew.*

The secessionists would seize all the lunar facilities Project Hail was using, including the antenna Arrays. W.S. had rejected the idea of sending the message from here in order to prevent possibly hostile galactics from getting a directional fix on the beam and following it right to Earth.

But their decision didn't bind the Tourists, and if the probe didn't go—or perhaps even if it did—they would not hesitate to use the Arrays. They *wanted* the luren to know Earth's location and come here as quickly as possible.

Thinking about it, Titus wondered if the Tourists had known of the blockade in advance and had sent Abbot orders to shift to the use of the Arrays on the assumption that the probe would never go. Abbot could have been building a second transmitter designed to use the Arrays. And Connie knew, which explained her admonition to stop Abbot. Her other operatives would be trying to stop the Tourists, who were no doubt infiltrating the secessionist forces on the moon to use them to get at a broadcast antenna Array.

Titus' fingers flew over the keyboard, bringing up a list of the seceding nations as he strove to recall everything Connie had told him of the Tourists' deployment around the globe. *They can do it! By damn, they can! But can Connie stop them?* How ironic! The secessionists, the very humans most opposed to summoning aliens, would actually facilitate that call. Abbot would find that delicious.

Meanwhile, as long as there was hope, the Tourists' main objective would still be focused on the launch of the probe. Either way, probe or ground-based, they needed H'lim's text, and that would be Abbot's job. After H'lim's mere presence had triggered armed rebellion, Abbot wouldn't expect W.S. to include H'lim's text in the probe's official message.

Titus bounded out of his chair and was halfway across the lab when Shimon and a group of others accosted him. "Dr. Shiddehara, what are your orders?"

The question was more a challenge of authority than a simple request for directions. These people were scared. He adopted a calm, positive tone and supported his words with a faint Influence. "Dr. Colby expects to receive supplies to finish and launch the probe immediately, even without the full load of instruments and experiments.

"Given this whole new situation, this department will be called upon to deliver a final decision about the target within a matter of days. Therefore, I'm going to hold a department meeting tomorrow morning, and I'll want written reports from each of you on the status of your work. I want summaries of the data from *Wild Goose* and of the new physiological data on the alien. I'll want verbal summations from each of you. Consider yourselves on overtime." He went to the door, then turned back with a calculated, "Oh, and there will be bonuses if we pull this one off."

He left while their stunned silence held.

He found H'lim in Biomed, off an underground corridor, surveying the empty room that was to become his own lab. The four guards were posted outside the door. Inside, Inea was scuffing about in a far corner where equipment had been ripped out. Near her, a door stood open revealing a small lavatory. Abbot stood next to H'lim, taking notes on a requisition pad. "I think we have some variable temperature incubators still in stock—new and perfectly sterile. About this high and this wide." Abbot gestured against a wall. "You've seen them— with movable shelves?"

"Yes. I know the kind you mean. But I will also need running water, and—"

"No problem—comes with the wet benches." Abbot pointed out several clumps of plumbing connections sticking up from the floor. "Now the centrifuges—we had three in for repair last week, and I think we can—oh, Titus, we wondered where you'd gone."

"I'm glad you're getting H'lim's lab organized," Titus commented obliquely as he surveyed the room for cameras.

Following his gaze, H'lim said, "Dr. Colby has graciously allowed the removal of the cameras, and Abbot has offered to build magnetic shielding around everything else. It should be possible to work here."

Inea came toward them, greeting Titus, and saying to H'lim, "I think the computers can fit in that corner. Do you want to face the wall or the room?"

"I don't care as long as I can use the data files I've already built, and I don't have to contend with these lights." He adjusted his goggles and eyed the closed door behind Titus. Lowering his voice, he said,

"Give me ten, maybe fifteen days after I have your tissue samples analyzed, and I'll have a batch of my booster ready to test."

Abbot cautioned, "You may be overestimating what our equipment can do."

"Maybe. But if Andre comes through with the orl blood as promised—"

"His first batch was a failure," observed Abbot.

"I found what he'd done wrong," argued H'lim. "It is my field, you know." His tone was flat, but there was no mistaking the challenge. "I believe there'll be just enough for all three of us. When my booster is ready—"

"You mustn't forget," said Titus, "that you'll have to spend most of your time on producing something for Colby to pass on to Earth, something innocuous but commercially viable. If we show you're a valuable resource, not just a liability, the blockade won't last long."

Apologetically, Abbot said, "My son is an idealist, and somewhat naïve about human politics, but he's right. Your highest priority must be to produce for Colby, and you have a lot to learn before you can be effective."

"My background is sufficient. No, the time problem lies mostly in concealing my real work from those familiar with the field who will want to learn what I'm doing. That's why I need access to the notes I've been making. I have to devise something I can say I'm doing when I'm really tailoring the booster. When will all this be ready?" He gestured at the empty room.

Abbot glanced at the requisition pad. "Tonight."

"I can have your computer installed in about three hours," offered Inea. "And I've requisitioned a direct tap for your room, when you get one, so you can work from there, too. I'll get started now." She turned to the door.

"I'll go with you," said H'lim and she paused. "Maybe I can find someplace to sit down and work on that message you wanted, Abbot. It's a challenge to make it that short and still convincing. What's the matter, Titus?"

Abbot's serene expression had frozen. Titus asked, not taking his eyes off Abbot, "What message, H'lim?"

H'lim's gaze shifted to Abbot who said, "Basically, the same message Carol wanted drafted. Nothing remarkable."

A great silence blanketed the room. H'lim asked, "It is a point of disagreement between you? I thought—"

"Nothing's changed," said Titus. "Earth belongs to the humans, and it's up to them what message to send."

"They won't send any, not now, not under threat of war," said Abbot. "And we will die. All of us. You know it, Titus. They've learned too much about luren from H'lim. Someone will spot us soon and we'll all be hunted down and killed. Don't interfere, son." The air congealed with Abbot's Influence. It was an order.

Inea moved to Titus' side. H'lim's gaze flicked from Titus to Abbot. Inea, oblivious to the tension, said, "Abbot doesn't understand people. If I were you, H'lim, I wouldn't take Abbot's word for anything."

Abbot's lips twitched, as if he were suppressing a snarl. "Titus, keep a rein on your stringer."

Teeth clenched and throat tight with the effort of defying Abbot, Titus whispered, "She's right. H'lim, Abbot's got to translate your message into burst-code and provide a decode template for whoever receives it. He knows enough of the language to make your message say anything he wants. You'll never be able to check if—"

"I've figured out *Kylyd's* communications protocols," said Abbot. "You can see for yourself if I change anything."

"Can you read burst-code, even your own people's code?"

"No," H'lim answered Titus, "but Abbot's repaired the machines that can. Carol Colby knows this. Using proper galactic protocols instead of one of Earth's digital codes, the message will be readable by anyone."

Titus had heard they were working on *Kylyd's* electronics but he hadn't heard of their success. Perhaps it had been bumped from the meetings agendas in order to focus on the problem of H'lim's escapade. "But Colby doesn't know that *Abbot* understands the protocols and the language, does she?"

"No, Titus, she doesn't," answered Abbot.

Titus skewered H'lim with a finger, "And you won't know exactly what message Abbot actually sends! You said yourself the legal position of Earth's luren was questionable. Abbot wouldn't stop at tying you into our fate in the galactic community, if he knew a way to do it."

H'lim paled, if that were possible for one so chalk white to begin with. Titus watched his stiff shock and suddenly doubted everything H'lim had implied about how luren would treat humans and Earth luren. H'lim did, after all, want their help in sending a message home. He wouldn't have mentioned anything that might deter them from helping him.

Titus added, "And if I know Abbot, I'll bet he does know a way to do it. Does that bother you, H'lim?"

"Not really. I just wouldn't want to be tied up in law courts for years. I have a business to run. I could go bankrupt waiting to testify for you."

It sounded almost plausible, but Titus felt there was more to it than that. Abbot said, "I wouldn't trap you into an untenable situation, not after all the help you've given us. I only want to program your message into my transmitter and make sure it's in the probe when it's launched. That way, even if the humans make the probe nothing but a receiver, your message will go out and you can go home."

Titus' neck hairs stirred. Abbot's Influence was still a palpable force in the room, but Titus suspected he was lying and H'lim believed every word of it. "H'lim, as a father to you, I want you to understand that the only message you are to compose is the one for Carol Colby."

"I don't really need him to write it, you know," said Abbot, his Influence growing heavy and invasive, "but it would be safer if he did. I might make some error that would bring battleships instead of merchants here. Would you want to risk that?" Abbot's Influence clutched at Titus. "You wouldn't oppose your First Father, would you? You wouldn't order your son to oppose your father, would you?"

Despite himself, Titus shook his head. "No, I wouldn't want to risk any of that."

"Titus!" protested Inea, but he hardly heard her.

"Stop!" snapped H'lim. "Abbot, he's your son!"

The pall of Influence lifted, but Titus was still held rigidly silent, emotions distanced, knowing intellectually that he'd gone too far this time.

Abbot said, "He has defied me."

H'lim asked, "Is everything a matter of hierarchy for you? Well then consider this. Titus is not my first father, but my fourth. I owe prior loyalties, stronger ones, and to fulfill those I must do my best to call for help no matter how Titus feels about it, or for that matter how you feel about it, Abbot." He faced Abbot again and H'lim's power throbbed through the room, clashing with Abbot's.

They stood silently, locked in a battle of wills until H'lim's Influence blotted out Abbot's, who staggered back, gasping. Suddenly Titus gulped air again, free.

H'lim said, "If strength is your only criterion, then only my will prevails, for I'm strongest here. If *Law* is your only criterion, then you can't displace my First Father or his needs. But I prefer to conduct business as business. Trade translates across all boundaries of custom and law, and in trade value replaces strength. You have given me value— my life, sustenance, a chance to go home. In return, I offer you value— some bits of science, sustenance, and a chance to contact your ancestral roots. Surely it makes better sense to bargain than to fight."

"It sounds very civilized," said Titus, his throat dry and aching from Abbot's clutch of Influence. "But around here, the only ones authorized to trade with you regarding that message are the owners of the hardware that'll carry it, Earth's humans."

"If the probe doesn't go at all," said Abbot, "you'll be stuck here with us until you die. Do you want that, H'lim? Isn't this place— alien?" He gestured at the walls, but encompassed the whole installation.

H'lim followed the gesture thoughtfully, then turned somber eyes back on them. "Not as much as you might expect," he murmured cryptically.

Before Titus could ask what he meant, Carol Colby entered trailed by Mirelle de Lisle carrying a stack of media cases with colorful book covers showing. Mirelle had circles under her eyes, and her fingers danced as if with caffeine jitters. She'd lost weight, and the angular planes of her body showed through the loose uniform. Her hair seemed to have lost luster, too, or perhaps it simply wasn't as well cared for. But Titus knew the signs of depletion and silently cursed Abbot for it.

As Colby greeted everyone, Inea inspected Mirelle with a grim twist to her mouth.

Colby turned to H'lim. "I've cleared an apartment for you, as agreed. You can move in anytime. Inea requisitioned you an Exec terminal so you can tap into your lab's files from the apartment, so I had to put you next to Abbot." She handed him a key, white and glossy with its code strip showing.

He ran a finger along the strip, musing, "On the other hand, the philosophy behind the technology *is* very odd."

"Have I missed something?" asked Colby.

"Not at all," said Abbot, proffering the notepad in his hand. "I've got the complete equipment list now, so I'll go get Mintraub on it right away." He filled Colby in on their proposed schedule and she signed the requisition.

As Abbot departed, he caught Titus' eye then glanced at Inea, lips compressed in disapproval. H'lim followed the exchange silently. Titus said, "Inea, I'll show H'lim to his room while you get his computers installed, all right?"

She nodded and started for the door, but Colby said, "Abbot, wait! I'm calling a special department heads' meeting for tomorrow at noon. I'll want reports on the new rationing schedule and I may have news from Earth, so be prompt."

"I'll be there," replied Abbot, and ducked out between the guards, followed by Inea. Beyond the door, Titus glimpsed a small knot of people craning their necks for a glimpse of the alien.

"And leave the door open," called Colby to Inea as she moved so that they were visible. Lowering her voice, she said, "Dr. Sa'ar, there are some grim realities that you must face. As soon as I leave this room, I'll be tested for lingering traces of hypnotism. You might slip something past us, but if we find *anything* you've done to someone, your life may well be forfeit. And don't give your guards the slip. There are a lot of people on this station right now who would like to see you dead, and though we don't have any homicidal types here, mob violence is always a possibility among humans. Some may sympathize with the blockaders. Do you understand this?" She glanced at Mirelle whose job it had been to teach H'lim the rudiments of human behavior.

"I comprehend my danger, Dr. Colby, perhaps even more keenly than you do."

Mirelle said, "I believe he does."

"And I am eager to work to prove you all wrong about me. I'm a simple merchant who would like to go home, and I'm willing to pay my way."

Colby folded her arms and paced a small circle. "So you keep claiming. We shall see. We're very cut off here, very vulnerable, with suddenly limited resources. Do something to alleviate our situation, and you'll be a hero. Do you understand what a hero is?"

"Yes," he answered simply and Mirelle corroborated him.

"Show us any threatening behavior and you shall be dead. Do you understand that?"

"Yes."

"Dr. de Lisle says you exhibit the classic human reward-response behavior. I'm going to trust her judgment. I've entered a security clearance for you commensurate with that of my department heads, and I've put you on the payroll so you can make purchases—though I suggest you don't go strolling through the shopping mall. It could upset people."

"I understand."

"I'll expect you at the meeting tomorrow with a report on your progress here. Let me know who you want assigned as your staff or get Abbot to select them for you. You'll need a good secretary. It takes a lifetime to learn how to handle W.S. paperwork, and God alone knows what to do about income tax. I'll expect you to report on the schedule you've set up with Biomed to teach them what you know, and Cognitive Sciences has requisitioned a portion of your time to study you."

"That's understood."

She rounded on him. "I hope so," she said in a hard, tense voice. "I'm putting my career on the line for you, Dr. Sa'ar. You'll be treated as one of us only so long as you behave as one of us."

"Have I broken my word yet?"

"Not that we've found—yet. But in the meantime, don't let anyone catch you out of your apartment without either Titus, Abbot, or Inea. Is that clear?"

"Perfectly."

Colby turned to Titus. "The work of your department is no less important for all this added duty," she began.

"I figured that," answered Titus and reported the overtime he'd authorized so his people could prepare a summary by morning. "My staff is handling things, but Cellura is badly overworked. I've put her on overtime, too."

Colby nodded and made a note on the board she carried. "Just see she gets enough rest and exercise. I don't want anyone cracking up. Not now." With that, she departed, leaving Titus alone with Mirelle and H'lim.

Looking after Colby, Mirelle said, "She's not herself lately. Too much pressure and not enough rest."

"She's frightened," said H'lim.

Mirelle blinked at him, then cracked a dazzling smile that wiped away the fatigue. "You learn fast!" Proffering the stack of books she'd brought, she recited dully, "Here, these are the books I promised. I annotated them for you, so you don't have to read it all." She selected two saying, "This is Burke on Rhetoric, and this is the *Kine Variant Tabulation,* unabridged. Chapter Twenty lists the fifteen degrees of eyelid closure, but most human cultures only recognize five at the most. The chapters beyond Twenty have to do with complex kinemorphs, so don't bother with those. They'd just confuse you."

H'lim caressed the plastic media cases. "Oh, I think this will be most valuable. Thank you, Mirelle."

She looked at Titus without any of the flirtation she had always shown him.

"Would you like me to go with you to H'lim's apartment?" She seemed wholly disinterested.

Overwhelmed with pity, Titus said, "No, no. I know where it is."

"All right." It took a moment for her to gather strength, then she bid them au revoir and slipped out the door just as a man and a woman were preparing to jockey a long workbench into the room. Seeing Titus and H'lim, the man knocked and called out, "Ready for this yet?"

"All yours," said Titus. "We were just leaving."

They squeezed past the obstruction and the guards fell in around them leaving them no privacy to talk until they reached the apartment. Titus didn't want to risk cloaking their words for fear someone might discover how the guards, walking close, couldn't remember anything that had been said.

When they opened the door, they found an apartment much like Titus', but done in stark black and white, with a gray carpet. The kitchenette had black marble and gold fixtures, and there were some African paintings on the walls. H'lim winced at his first sight of the place.

"Is black and white offensive to you?" asked Titus.

"No. Oh no, it's fine." He moved his hand across the threshold barrier as if pushing through molasses. "I will work to make a home of it. Meanwhile, won't you please come in?" He uttered the polite phrase with stiff but proper intonation, so proper that Titus almost laughed when H'lim peeked at him to see if he'd done it right.

"Thank you very much," intoned Titus with a bow and crossed the threshold, closing the door on the guards.

The few personal possessions H'lim had acquired were piled on the bed beside folded sheets and blankets. The wires from the field generator Abbot had built were tangled but unbroken.

As they untangled the mess, made the bed, and Titus showed H'lim how everything worked, Titus asked, "Do you think your people would give me as much as Colby has given you? I mean, positions reversed."

"Possibly. Colby is an unusually courageous individual. I'm awed by her boldness."

"I think she's hoping that if you do get home, you'll remember how you were accepted here and say a few good words for Earth's humans."

"Of course. Positions reversed, there would be no compelling reason for those in authority to seek your good opinion. So the situation wouldn't be the same."

Titus seized on that new datum. "Why wouldn't luren out there value our good opinion of them?"

"I thought that was obvious. You have only one little planet, and so far I've seen nothing much worth trading for except art curios. Should Earth decide not to trade, it would be little loss. However, we have many planets full of things you could use and a wealth of technology you don't have yet. In that situation, how would humans behave? Wouldn't one group be more eager than the other?"

"Well, if we have nothing the galaxy would want, why should we bother trying to communicate?"

"I'm only one person and I've seen little of this world. Perhaps your world has commercial potential it would take experts to discover. Where there's a chance of profit, such experts will come and search hard to open a new market. But there are strict laws to protect newly contacted cultures. Mirelle has told me your world has already documented the vulnerability of cultures in a mismatched relationship. Surely you can understand—"

Titus interrupted, suddenly realizing how smoothly he'd been led away from his question. "Of course I do, but you're not being totally honest, H'lim. You're intent on going home, but you don't want to be associated with us—with Earth's luren—after that. And I want to know why."

"Don't be too hasty," cautioned H'lim as he surveyed the bathroom. "Earth's luren could be a market for my orl."

"Not big enough to matter."

"Maybe. Maybe not. But I tell you one thing that makes me uncomfortable. Mirelle. She wears an orl-mark and acts like a teacher. She's Dr. de Lisle sent to teach me of human communication and she wears an orl-mark which isn't mine."

"Does that make you hungry?"

"Hungry? I'm always hungry. But not for humans. I've traveled widely, Titus, but I've never run into anything that discomforted me so. I think I would sell you orl at a loss, just so I could feel good about myself again."

He did it again, thought Titus as he wanted to ask what H'lim would accept in payment—art curios? "Selling us orl wouldn't compromise your position in the galaxy?"

"What?" H'lim seemed genuinely confused, and not just because he'd turned his attention to his new console.

"You are reluctant to be associated with us, yet you'd sell us orl?"

"Hypothetically, Titus, hypothetically. In reality, Earth's trade status will be decided by law as will the status of Earth's luren. It's a complex matter, and I'm not qualified to try to explain it. Those whose profession it is to integrate new worlds into galactic trade have equations to calculate how much contact a culture can stand, how quickly, what products, what sequences. As a merchant, I look up what I may sell and what I may buy with it on any given world. I don't always try to understand why this and not that. But I do understand my own field and how to introduce it to new cultures. I make good money as a consultant in such matters, and we're usually first on the scene."

And again! marveled Titus and retreated, knowing when he'd been bested. "We should go back and see how the lab's coming."

"Wait," said H'lim. "What's this?" He bent over his vidcom. The screen showed a tricolor graphic of a stomping bull against the stars.

Titus leaned over his shoulder. "Inea's playing games." He told of her demonstration program, then made some suggestions. Inea got the signal and responded. They spent a few hours troubleshooting network connections and security protocols while teaching H'lim the remote commands he had available. In the course of this, they discovered the accounting files Colby had assigned for H'lim's use, and Titus began showing him what records a department head was responsible for keeping.

"I think Dr. Colby was right. I need a secretary."

Using the link, Titus found out that Abbot was almost through supervising the setup of the lab, and told Inea to go get some dinner and meet him at his apartment to discuss the reports Colby wanted tomorrow. Then he escorted H'lim back to his lab and left him with Abbot, not without some trepidation. But Mihelich was also there, along with an ever-changing mob of technicians. *Can't be with him every minute,* he told himself and bid them good evening.

He stopped by the refectory nearest home and picked up a dinner tray, one much lighter than usual. Already the rationing program was cutting allotments.

When he arrived at his own apartment, he found Inea swabbing out the microwave, her own refectory tray on the table. "Ought to do this more often," she said, pushing a wisp of hair back with her wrist.

236

He took the towel and pushed a chair behind her knees. "You're exhausted. I'll do that. It's my stinking mess after all. You're right. Shouldn't let it get this bad."

She dropped into the chair, yielding the chore to him but saying, "I'm not as tired as Mirelle. That woman's out on her feet. And it's not just from following H'lim around."

Titus whipped his head around. Her eyes were closed. She didn't see his reaction. He stuck his head into the microwave looking for a way to pull the roof of the cavity out for cleaning. "I didn't know you realized H'lim is drawing ectoplasm from everyone around him."

"You as much as told me so. Besides, he's draining to be with. Not like you. You're stimulating."

"I keep telling you. You can't just feed me. You must accept my gift in return. H'lim can't offer, but he's starving."

"But Abbot's not starving, and he has sex with Mirelle. Why's she looking like a corpse?"

He got the top loose and stuck it in the sink with the other parts that needed soaking, resolving never to try reheating blood again. Concentrating, Titus rinsed and replaced the parts. At least rationing hadn't tightened the water allowance. The recyclers were efficient enough.

"Titus, you're not answering me."

"He's taking too much of her blood. He doesn't have enough stringers, and apparently he *likes* Mirelle."

"That's how he treats people he *likes?*"

"Yes. It is."

After a long silence during which Titus heated himself some water, she said, "That's why you left him."

"Yes."

He heard the tone of his voice and wasn't surprised when she asked, "What's wrong?"

"I don't know, Inea. But nothing's—simple—anymore."

"I know what you mean."

"No you don't. Inea, you came to me because I convinced you of my loyalties. I'm not so sure they're so solid as I thought. Maybe—maybe I'm not human. Maybe you *have* been sleeping with an alien from outer space after all and not the boy next door you were about to marry. I just don't know!"

Her mouth fell open.

237

The microwave bleeped. The painful silence held Titus rigid until the echo died away. Feeling as if his body would shatter, he forced himself to extract the pitcher of water, dump in half a packet of crystals and stack both plates of food in the microwave. Punching up a reheat, he said, "From now on, you'll eat my rations so I don't have to discard scarce food." *What does a microwave sound like to H'lim?*

She still hadn't breathed a word, and he felt as if her eyes were boring holes in his back. He fled into the bathroom to hunt for the supply of supplements he'd brought in case he needed stringers for blood. Connie had insisted. He had to ransack the medicine chest because he'd forgotten what they were disguised as. *Some secret agent!*

When he returned, Inea was clutching the pitcher to her breast, bent over it protectively. It took a moment for him to realize that she was crying. Eyes closed, wooden-faced, almost not breathing, she sat with tears dripping from her chin into the pitcher.

He felt more helpless than he ever had before in his life. *Me and my big mouth.*

He brought his glass over to the table and took the pitcher from her hands, pressing the bottle of pills into her palm as she raised streaming eyes to him. "These are for Mirelle, if you can get her to take them without anyone else knowing—not even Abbot. Especially not Abbot."

She swallowed hard, blinking at the bottle dazedly.

"Ignore the label. It's a supplement specially designed to replenish blood. Just vitamins, nothing like what H'lim's been talking about."

Unaccountably embarrassed by her silence, he poured blood into his glass and drank it down, praying for the microwave to bleep. He could taste her tears in the diluted blood and the acrid tang of her pain. Almost gagging, he poured another glass before it got cold.

Tear-choked, she rasped, "Why?" and shook the bottle.

Why? Because he couldn't stand to see Inea suffer? Because he'd wanted Mirelle himself? Because he hated Abbot? Or because of the inexorable physical bond to his father that made him unable to stand to see Abbot starving?

He turned to inspect the microwave timer. "Because I trust you with my life, with the lives of all Earth's luren. Because I'm confused. I don't know whether H'lim is lying about everything or only some things. Because I don't know whether I really ought to stop Abbot's message. Will Earth's luren be more likely to survive if Abbot's message is sent, or not sent? *Should* we survive at all? It used to be such a

238

simple issue! Now, I just don't know. Only one thing is certain. Whether Earth's luren live or die should be decided by Earth's humans—victims and volunteers alike. Have we taken more than we've given Earth? Or have we given more than we've taken? Considering what we take and how we take it, does it even matter whether we pay our way or not?"

He faced her. "Inea, if anyone discovers what's in that bottle and that you're feeding it to Mirelle, they'll find out why she needs it, which will expose Abbot's use of her. Abbot's right. Now that humans know about H'lim's physiology, the smallest clue will reveal our existence."

"Then why's he still using her like that?"

"He has no other choice. He's probably able to fake her tests so they can't trace his Influence, but he couldn't fake them for his whole string, so he's leaning on her too hard. He probably thinks he can complete his mission before he's discovered and before Mirelle collapses."

She shook the bottle. "This would give him more time. It would help him. Titus, I don't want to help him."

The accusation that *he* did was etched in the air between them. The microwave finally bleeped. Titus ignored it. "I don't know whether I do or not."

"You're copping out. You're leaving it up to me."

That stung. But it was true.

"Your mind isn't working because you've been starving yourself, living on half rations to feed H'lim." She shook the bottle. "If this would work for Mirelle, it would work for me, too. With some *real* blood in you, you could figure out which way was up. After all, you're a brilliant astrophysicist. This isn't such a difficult problem."

"I'd rather write a whole new cosmogony. It'd be simpler to decide that stars are born under cabbage plants."

She burst out laughing, a free, musical sound that delighted the ears. Titus hadn't meant it as a joke, but all at once it seemed very funny.

Their voices harmonized, and he reveled in the purely physical sensation until silence wrapped them together. After a moment, Inea took the pitcher from the table and came to refill his glass. "I meant it. You'll never beat Abbot when he's fed and you're half starved. Until Andre comes across with that orl blood, take some of mine. I haven't given to the blood bank in weeks. I can afford it."

"I can't. It's addictive."

"You broke it when you left Abbot. You can do it again. Right now, you and I have to best Abbot or die trying. That's what I know and that's all I know."

"It's not enough. You heard H'lim. He intends to go home, no matter what. And I think he knows what damage he'll be doing to us. He doesn't *care*, though. That makes him not a whole lot better than Abbot. Which means that besting Abbot won't help unless we also best World Sovereignties. Should we join the secessionists?"

"Titus! That's treason! And we're at war."

He held the glass up between them. "Treason? What's drinking human blood, then? Loyalty? Respect?"

"Do you hate yourself?"

"Sometimes. When I'm tempted." He drained the glass.

Very quietly, she said, "You know, it really isn't up to us alone to make a judgment like this. Who are we to decide the fates of species and worlds?"

"Who is anybody to make decisions that affect others?"

She frowned. "Are you drunk? Maudlin drunk?"

"Maybe a little." He stared at the glass. A victim's blood alcohol had never made him drunk. Now, the bitter dregs of Inea's tears were affecting him. *Like alcohol on an empty stomach.* He set the glass aside. "The moment I suspected what Abbot would try next, I ran to stop him. And I don't know why. If I was merely following orders, then I'm no better than the worst humanity has ever produced. I don't feel good about myself for following orders blindly. I don't feel good about myself for opposing my father and my son. What luren could? Inea, let me feel good at least for helping Mirelle in what way I can, and for trusting at least one person, loving one person. I think I need that more than blood. It may be a pathetic gesture in the face of the real problems, but it's all I've got in me at the moment."

She studied his face. "It's physical, isn't it?"

"What?"

"This business of opposing your father. There's some kind of a real physical link between you that makes it impossible for you to fight him. It's not just law or custom or emotion—it's a profound physiological response."

"I think I explained that long ago."

"I didn't understand you meant it literally. You're like this now because a couple hours ago you threw yourself against him, and now you're somehow depleted inside. Your central nervous system's in shock and you can't think. Your self-esteem and sense of identity have been almost extinguished. Abbot did that to you, didn't he?"

"Don't judge him too harshly. He could have killed me. Quite legally, too. Maybe exposure to H'lim is showing him that the Tourists' attitudes aren't so honorable after all. Inea, just a few weeks ago, Abbot *would* have killed me instantly for such defiance. All through this, he's helped me out of tight spots. Maybe he's changing."

"Maybe it just wasn't politically expedient to kill you in front of H'lim—who, after all, ended up defending you as well as defying you. If it comes to a choice between Abbot or H'lim, I'll pick H'lim. He's a better man than Abbot, even though he may not have a human cell in his body. So just because you have luren in you, that doesn't mean you're worthless as a person."

"And what if everything H'lim has told us is a lie?"

"In his place, would you tell the truth and die for it?"

"More likely I'd edit heavily and grit my teeth."

"H'lim, unlike Abbot, has a conscience, and his teeth are gritted to nubbins. If I have to choose, I pick H'lim."

"So you'll let Colby send H'lim's message."

"Yes, but not Abbot. You were right. He'd cheat."

"And what of Mirelle?"

"I'll slip her as many of these as I can—tell her they're for headaches. She's always cadging headache pills."

"One at a time. Don't let her take any home."

"Why would it bother Abbot? We're helping him!"

"Technically, it's an infraction. She wears his Mark. I should give *him* the pills."

"Then why don't you?"

"He'd never remember to give them to her, even if he thought it was a good idea. It's not a Tourist habit to care for stringers any more than you'd try to refill a pen. They're disposable."

"Ugh!"

"Besides, though he might not object to the pills making Mirelle last longer, he'd be furious at the risk of leaving them around where the human medics might find them. He'd class that as endangering Earth's luren—which would be true. So be careful with them."

She shook the vial. "I'm holding your life in my hand."

"You have for weeks and weeks now. Nothing's changed."

"I love you, Darrell. I always have and always will."

He bent to kiss her, but she recoiled. "Brush your teeth first."

He laid his cheek against hers and drank the sweetness into his soul. "And I want you to eat first."

———

The next morning, Titus collected all the reports from his department, hastily assimilated the mountain of material and rearranged his list of possible target stars, stared at the data, then called H'lim. "Is your home star a *binary?*"

"Of course not! Binaries don't have inhabited planets!"

"I thought you didn't know anything about astronomy."

"I don't. *Everyone* knows that, though."

Titus would have given his right arm and two gallons of blood for what "everyone knew" out there. "Are there two gas giants in the home system?"

"No, only one. I've told you what I know."

"Yeah." He'd told them of the space stations and domed colonies, of tourist attractions and discount fare structures, but little that was of real use from here. "See you at the meeting."

He rearranged his list again, combed his hair, polished his shoes and went to the conference room.

Colby was late. They had the war news up on the big screen, bits and pieces compiled at Luna Station. As developments in different regions were covered, people in the room took sides, defending their homelands or attacking the enemies of their regions.

The moment Colby entered, though, silence fell. She looked as if she hadn't slept, but she was impeccably groomed. In dark tones, she announced that World Sovereignties official policy was now to run supplies through the blockade, with the first shipment due in a few days. It would be mostly parts for the probe, which was to be finished and launched in stripped form. Earth's and H'lim's message were to go as planned.

"If the probe penetrates the blockade, the secessionists will have lost their main point and their movement will die. The need then will be to unite Earth and prepare for contact. We will be Earth's first priority and no longer in danger."

Colby called for reports from all departments, finishing with Titus, who could only offer them a 60 percent chance of success. "From *Wild Goose* we got not only a better fix on the craft's approach trajectory, but also half a dozen new possible stars that can't be seen from here. We're building a house of cards out of untested theories."

"If it's your best," replied Colby, "we go with it."

"Accuracy isn't important," supplied H'lim. "*Anyone* who hears it will relay the signal."

"So you've said before, and we're counting on it." Colby turned to Abbot. "We have to tap the blockaders' communications. Can you build a device to do that?"

"If I can have access to the Eighth Array to capture their bursts, I can build a decoder—maybe even a transmitter—so we can jam or decoy them. I heard the com-techs talking this morning. I think we already know what frequencies they're on, and I can probably find a way to track them when they change frequencies and encoding."

"How soon?"

"I'll give you an estimate tomorrow."

The Eighth Array! But he can't send H'lim's message openly! He wished he'd tapped Abbot's ground link. What was he up to? He hadn't Influenced Colby, that was clear.

Then H'lim gave his first department report, revealing how very alien his thought processes were. All the required data was there, displaying a spectacular virtuosity and competence, but the organization was so bizarre not a single person at the table—except perhaps Abbot—followed a word of it. Colby assigned him a ghostwriter as well as a secretary, both men drawn from the Cognitive Sciences staff and eager to study the alien.

The meeting broke up and they returned to work with a sense of tackling a gigantic but possible task. A few days later, the first W.S. blockade runners were destroyed by secessionist ships directly over the station. Debris rained down, holing one of the domes, but no one was hurt.

The tight surveillance continued on H'lim despite Biomed's excitement about what they were learning from him. It seemed he had considerable experience translating his science from one system to another. Nothing fazed him. That, perhaps more than anything, contributed to the distrust but he never Influenced the humans where they'd notice.

Watching Mirelle, Titus saw her condition improve and not just from the occasional supplement Inea got into her. Abbot became haggard, gaunt-faced, and snappish. He was rationing himself hard. Inea's spy devices revealed how much time he spent at the Biomed computers. It was a struggle now to falsify Mirelle's tests, not to mention his own and Titus'.

Titus ached inside for his father, counting the hours until Mihelich's cloned orl blood became available. He was in his office watching Inea and Abbot out in the observatory, bent over the console that controlled the Eighth Array, when the call came from H'lim.

"Stop by my apartment as soon as you can, and bring Abbot. I have something to show you both."

The blood!

——— NINETEEN ———

The black and white austerity of H'lim's apartment had been broken up by the makeshift mesh cages Abbot had installed around all the electrical devices and draped over partitions that contained power cables. H'lim had pronounced the measures acceptable in the wan tones of a teacher giving an E for Effort and then proclaimed the place his home.

Now, when Abbot strolled in unperturbed, Titus had to pause at the threshold for invitation. Never had he felt such a strong barrier. Its surface stung his whole body.

H'lim reached out to him, pulling Titus and Inea through while saying in the luren tongue, "Thank you for honoring my threshold." He added, "Your manners do you credit, since the threshold is merely symbolic."

"Symbolic?" repeated Titus dazedly.

"Perhaps," added H'lim wistfully, "when I've regained my strength, I will again have a real home."

Titus looked back at the now closed door, understanding anew the gulf between Earth's luren and genuine luren. He switched to English for Inea's sake. "I hope you don't mind that Inea came along? I can. . . ."

"It is to be expected," answered H'lim looking at Abbot, who had come alone. "You did understand my message? I have the first sample of genuine orl blood for you."

Abbot turned away and Titus knew he was only pretending to examine his mesh installations. "Have you tried it yet?"

"Yes." H'lim's tone was curiously flat. "Andre insisted. It was a great trial to conceal . . ."

H'lim's goggles angled toward Inea and Titus said, "She's seen the worst. She won't be offended."

H'lim turned to study Abbot's back. "You know, don't you, Titus?"

Overwhelmed with sympathy, Titus asked, "You've never had to use cloned blood before, have you?"

"I thought I was prepared—after what you and the humans have been supplying me." He met Titus' gaze steadily. "I wasn't."

"Mihelich—"

"I managed to choke it down without letting him see how—inadequate—it was. At least it was *orl,* and that helps. I feel better than I have since I woke."

Neutrally, Abbot asked, "It's that much different, orl?"

"*Yes!*" With an eloquent shrug, H'lim apologized to Inea for his vehemence. "I hope it will help you as much as it does me. Here." He went to the kitchen counter where a large barrel Thermos sat, the spigot thrust out over the sink. Titus caught the hard glitter of barely suppressed esurience in Abbot's eye as they both converged on H'lim.

He took down two glasses, gorgeous examples of the unique lunar product. They were beautiful enough to have been exported to Earth rather than consigned to lunar use. It was cheaper to manufacture glass here out of rock and solar power than to lift it from Earth. And it was cheaper to recycle wash water than to use disposables. Titus realized he was dwelling on the economics of lunar life to avoid admitting his own eagerness for the orl blood. "H'lim, have you any idea if this might be harmful to us?"

Filling a glass with the thick, purple-red fluid, he answered, "I cross-matched as best I could. There doesn't *seem* to be any gross incompatibility. But I've hardly started my analysis." He handed a glassful to Abbot and turned to fill one for Titus. "It might, however, prove unpalatable."

As H'lim handed Titus his glass, Abbot sniffed and then tasted his, expression unreadable. The fumes invaded Titus' head, seeping through his brain and triggering responses he'd never felt before. His hand did not want to bring that glass up to his lips, but his hunger demanded it.

Out of the corner of his eye, he saw Abbot's hand trembling, his face chiseled from granite as he tilted the glass. A distanced part of himself admired his father's self-control, knowing full well what this experiment was costing Abbot and knowing also that the Tourist could not have resisted the chance to taste orl, however artificial.

Titus closed his eyes and tilted the warm fluid to his lips, touching it with his upper lip before sipping. The texture was wrong, the smell was wrong, but it wakened a searing hunger. His lip arched to let a drop past. It was dead, flat, like all reconstituted blood. But that was familiar, and his throat closed willing around the first runnel of the strange stuff.

He swallowed again, the odor filling his nose. On the fourth swallow, his gorge rose. Simultaneously, he heard Abbot stagger to the sink, and bend over retching, coughing, fighting for breath. Seconds later, Titus shoved H'lim out of the way and joined his father, tied in knots. His brain seemed on fire and he needed to scream but couldn't.

Abbot's knees buckled, and from somewhere Titus found the strength to grab him around the waist as together, almost in rhythm, they emptied themselves convulsively of every last drop of the foreign substance. As H'lim stood helplessly aside, Inea turned on the water to wash the stench away.

She made them rinse their mouths out with water, which almost triggered more retching, and said to H'lim, "I guess that experiment was a failure."

This jarred H'lim into action. From somewhere, he produced a blood pressure monitor and a body fluid specimen collector. Pushing the two down into chairs, he administered a very thorough, very competent medical once-over sampling tears, saliva, blood, sweat, and vomitus while demanding an exact description of what had happened.

In the end, it appeared that Titus had swallowed more than Abbot before experiencing the rejection, and the two rejections had been different.

"My eyes are still burning," said Titus, "and my head feels full of hot coals."

"My stomach," said Abbot. "I've never had such cramps."

H'lim pondered for a moment, then speculated. "Abbot, perhaps it's just as well that you tried it unenergized at first and that caused you to reject it. It could be wholly incompatible with your metabolism. But Titus—you seem to have had a central nervous system reaction. Nutrient had begun to pass into your blood before you rejected it."

"Those are the worst poisons," agreed Titus. "I probably swallowed more than Abbot because I'm used to the flatness of uninfused chemical." He glanced at Inea. "It's a hellishly difficult thing to learn to tolerate."

Abbot climbed to his feet. "Some difficult things are worth doing," he observed, "and some aren't. Thank you for the instructive experience, H'lim, but I won't try it again."

"Wait until I've done some more tests," protested H'lim. "I can tolerate human blood. Certainly you can—"

"If you clone an orl, I may consider trying it again." With that Abbot was gone.

Titus glanced at Inea. "Maybe we should have tried to infuse his first?" *Could I order her even to feed Abbot?*

H'lim said, "No, I don't think so. He might have drunk more, and it might have poisoned him."

"You think I'm poisoned?" The way his head felt, Titus could easily believe he was about to die the final death.

"Your genetic makeup is very different from his. I think there's something in orl blood that your body is equipped to use, but that you've never encountered before."

"You mean that I'm more luren than he is? I don't think so. He's much older, has fewer human ancestors."

"Yes, that much is immediately evident. But the interbreeding has selected for different factors. It will take some time, but I can determine if orl blood is really a poison for him—or for you for that matter."

"Interbreeding," said Titus heavily. "Just why is that even possible?"

Ignoring Titus' direct question, as always, H'lim mused, "Perhaps I can filter out the incompatible factors for Abbot."

"It wouldn't be worth the time," said Inea unexpectedly.

"Why?" asked H'lim blankly.

"Haven't you figured Abbot out yet?" she asked. "It's not the blood that nourishes him, it's the subjugation. He *is* a vampire, not a luren."

H'lim frowned. Titus, unsure if it was in disapproval or disagreement, changed the subject. "Inea's got a good point. We don't have time for pure research. You not only have to do this in odd moments stolen from Colby's work, but you have to hide it from everyone looking over your shoulder. Between the limited time and the risk, I think your better investment would be your booster. If that works on Abbot *or* on humans to stimulate blood and ectoplasm replacement, it would be acceptable to Abbot and would let us survive."

"Time," said H'lim heavily. He toyed with the specimen kit. "Do you know if you'll be getting a shipment soon?"

"No. If any convoy does get through, though, I'd expect some of my supplies to be on it." *Connie is that good.*

H'lim seemed skeptical, but he said, "Since the booster was designed for orl, the two projects are related. I'll pursue both goals simultaneously. It's not as difficult as it sounds, you know. I've made orl for use in medical testing. The genetics is flexible and the blood composition can be altered to mimic that of diverse peoples." Staring at the Thermos, he lapsed into the luren tongue.

Titus puzzled over the words "teelee-odd" and "metajee." Those were the only terms he could separate from the mass of the unfamiliar ones, and he realized that his own lack of a biological and biochemical vocabulary had left H'lim unable to think professionally in English. What other flaws had he left him with? What other communications problems lurked beneath the façade of normality?

Inea followed H'lim's gaze and rose to fill a glass with the orl blood, returning with it cradled between her hands. H'lim tracked her movements with a quiet reverence then dragged his attention from the glass she held and asked Titus, "Did you tell her to do this?"

"No. It's her own idea." He wasn't sure it was even a good idea, but he followed her reasoning and her heart, so he said nothing as H'lim savored the act of a sentient orl—a willing human. Ectoplasm carried a different texture when it was a deliberate, wholehearted gift.

He was curious to see how this would strike H'lim. But the luren didn't reach for the proffered glass. He clasped trembling hands in his lap. "Titus, she wears your Mark."

"Only to keep you or Abbot from taking what you will of her. She's a human being, free to give what she chooses to whom she chooses. You've partaken of her gift before."

"I don't like being discussed in the third person."

H'lim seemed perplexed, so Titus explained, "It's impolite most places to ignore a person's presence."

"Oh, I'm sorry. I didn't intend—Inea, there's no way I could ignore your pervasive presence. I would like very much to accept your gift." He held his hands out just short of the glass waiting for her to place it in his grasp.

She breathed on it one last time, then put it in his hands, cupping hers about them. "This is so you'll have the strength to find a way to feed Titus—and Abbot too. I just wish I could do more to help."

Titus thought H'lim didn't even hear her last words. His attention was riveted on the glass and he was shaking. When at last he drank the energized orl blood, the beatific expression on his face made Titus' hunger surge like a trapped tiger. *She is free to give as she chooses. Besides, damn it, she's right!*

———

Two weeks later, Titus was in the centrifuge with Abbot and H'lim. Colby had noted the drawn, haggard appearance both of them presented and had ordered them off duty to sleep, eat, and exercise. "I don't care what the medical records show about you two, you're both about to fall on your faces. You've each been doing the work of three men for months now. Nobody can sustain that kind of pace."

She had gone on to warn them that a parts shipment for the probe vehicle would arrive soon, and *then* the pace would increase tenfold. "So I'm doubling your rations for a week, and taking you off the duty roster—except for escorting H'lim. If I catch either of you at work, I'll commit you to the psych ward!"

Looking in the mirror, Titus couldn't argue with her appraisal, only with her therapy regimen.

But he did need the time in the centrifuge, as did H'lim, who was willing to wear a special suit Abbot had made for him to attenuate the noise the centrifuge motors made. As uneasy as the centrifuge made Titus, especially the first time he'd gone in there after nearly being killed, it was worse for H'lim.

For the alien, they dimmed the lights, increased the gravity and adjusted the air mixture. Biomed invented half a dozen new telemetry sensors, and the physical therapists who ran the gym devised a new exercise machine to accommodate H'lim's physique. When H'lim used the centrifuge, only Titus and Abbot stayed with him—and that was only after Abbot had reprogrammed the computers to show proper human stress patterns under the new conditions.

Actually, Titus enjoyed the changes. His body had to work harder, but afterwards he always felt better, especially when he spent some time sweating and straining on H'lim's bicycle while H'lim jogged around the track.

The one great advantage about time spent in the centrifuge was that it was utterly private, so they could talk as they wished. The noise was great enough so that H'lim, working out on the opposite side of the drum, couldn't hear Abbot and Titus, who were riding side by side on the ordinary bicycles, unless they shouted.

249

"Abbot, I'm sure of it," Titus insisted in low, urgent tones. "He's not telling all he knows. When you ask him anything truly important, he pours out data on other intriguing but irrelevant topics. He's a master of the snow job."

"Would have to be," grunted Abbot, peddling hard, "to be a successful merchant in intragalactic trade."

"Maybe," conceded Titus. "Have you ever dealt with an Arab? They don't cheat—not by their code—so they always come across as honest because they are satisfied that their honor is spotless. But there are certain things they don't feel obligated to disclose, even if you ask. It's your fault if you believe what you want to believe."

"H'lim is just protecting himself," countered Abbot. "He explained that when he gets home, they'll have ways of checking to see if he's broken any laws. He's not *allowed* to tell us everything. That's for others, later."

"Maybe, but I'm sure he's withholding something crucial. If we knew it, we might not be so eager to send his message."

"Oh, so that's it. You're still trying to convert me. Well, I might be willing to listen if you can show me another way for our people to survive. I don't know why you keep losing sight of that single fact. We're battling for our lives, and it's now or never. Doesn't the secession tell you anything about human attitudes?"

"What that message brings down on us may be worse than all the panicked humans on Earth. And I think H'lim knows it will be worse. Abbot, I like him, but I don't trust him."

Suddenly, his father turned to him with a most peculiar expression. After a bit, he observed, "That's exactly how I felt about you a week after I revived you."

Their eyes met. A momentary rapport flowed along Titus' nerves like honey. He suddenly realized that part of his chronic hunger, the part Inea could never fulfill, was the deep need for his father's approval. H'lim had said something about that, once. *"I've read that humans have no instincts. If this is true, it's a point on which human and luren differ, for luren do have some important vestigial instincts. The parental power is one such. The gratification can sometimes be worth dying a final death."*

In that moment, Titus could believe it. When Abbot murmured, "I still like you, Titus," he could see in his mind the contrast between this lined, haggard, and worn Abbot and the young, zestful, and immortal Abbot. It took all he had to dismount his bicycle and begin

250

his job. He was able to regain his perspective only when he recalled, in gory detail, just how that young Abbot had taught him to feed. But the perspective tended to slip whenever his concentration did.

Five days later, Colby came to H'lim's lab for the broadcast to Earth of a demonstration of his progress against Alzheimer's Disease. The preventive regimen introduced decades ago on Earth had recently proven only partially effective, and now H'lim was close to being able to reverse the progress of the disease without wiping the patient's brain clean of memory.

"Life in the galaxy," lectured Dr. Sa'ar in a perfect Harvard accent, which he had not acquired from Titus, "has followed certain broad patterns. Earth belongs to one of those patterns, and so solving its problems does not require so very much original work as one might expect. This is one reason that Earth has nothing to fear from the infectious diseases of the galaxy. Most are analogous enough that your existing defenses are sufficient. The rest, you would encounter only if you travel widely, and in that case you will be properly immunized first."

He was about to key up a computer model of the relevant molecules when the monitor screen that was showing what Project Station was sending to Earth went blank, flickered, sizzled, and then cleared to a stock view of the lunar landscape. A news announcer was saying, "We regret that we have lost Project Station's signal. Please stand by."

"We're getting them, how come they're not getting us?" asked a tech by the pile of broadcast equipment.

Colby answered, "That's what you're paid to know."

Blushing, the tech fiddled with connections as Abbot knelt over a digital circuit probe. H'lim drifted toward them. He was wearing the contact lenses Biomed had made for the broadcast, so people could see his whole face. Circling Abbot, he announced, "The fault is not in your equipment."

"I wouldn't expect so," muttered Abbot. "Blockaders are jamming us, of course."

Unless there's a traitor on the staff here, thought Titus. He knew that no new assassins had been brought onto the station, because nobody had been allowed onto the station—nobody at all. However, that didn't prevent factions from developing among the station personnel. It was mostly among the workers, but Titus had seen it at the highest levels. Still, people on the station tended to see themselves as a third faction in the war, a faction dedicated to galactic exploration yet unwilling to sacrifice their lives just yet.

251

As he listened to the bursts of static produced by the technician, Titus wondered how much longer they all could endure. He glanced at Abbot. *When will desperation create heroes and martyrs?*

Abbot raised his brows in silent query.

Then the screen flicked to stars, the Earth cutting across one corner of the shot. ". . . view from Central Pacific Stationary, the only satellite that can see the battle." The news announcer's voice wavered under bursts of static. "*High Changjin,* the orbital station that was relaying Project Station's signal, has been destroyed with all aboard, some five hundred souls. Secessionist forces continue to fire on the unarmed supply ship. We have no confirmation yet that this ship was indeed heading for Project Station with parts for the probe vehicle, as the rebels claim. There are three men and two women aboard that unarmed ship."

As everywhere on the station and on Earth, the group in the lab remained glued to the screen for the next several hours. As they analyzed the flash of destruction and the burst of particles that had arrived at the lunar detectors, the tension broke into despair.

Grimly determined to keep up morale, Colby had them record H'lim's presentation, and a few days later got it through to Earth piecemeal despite the jamming added to the loss of the vital relay station. Computer reconstructed, the presentation went over very well in W.S. territory and shored up W.S. determination to launch the probe, which meant W.S. had to get a supply ship through the blockade with parts for the probe and supplies for the Project.

Titus, still unable to communicate directly with Connie, focused his efforts on keeping track of Abbot. He was still not certain Abbot's message had to be stopped, but he was even more skeptical of H'lim's honesty. He could only pray he'd know what to do when the time came, and that he'd be ready to do it.

To that end, he was at his desk at home, using Inea's bugs to watch Abbot puttering about H'lim's lab, when Inea arrived with Mirelle in tow. As the door closed behind them, Mirelle wavered, and then collapsed. Inea draped the limp form over her shoulders in a fireman's carry and deposited her on the bed. She turned, hands on hips, eyes blazing, and spat, "Well? Now, what are you going to do? This is all your fault, you know!"

Stunned, Titus bent over Mirelle. He could sense the wispy character of her aura before he found the weak, thready pulse under the sheen of cold sweat. The crook of her elbow showed recent needle marks, and from the look of it he knew it was Abbot's doing. Over his shoulder

252

he said, "There are extra blankets in the closet. I think there's a heating pad in there, too. Get it."

He began loosening Mirelle's clothing, then he noticed Inea was not moving. "Move! She's lost a lot of blood."

Silently, Inea helped him to wrap Mirelle and, as she regained consciousness, to get some fluids into her. But Inea was still angry when they'd done all they could. "Titus, I want to know what you intend to *do!* You can't let him get away with this!"

"Why didn't you take her to the infirmary?"

"And let them find out? They would, you know, and then the witch hunt would be on."

Titus nodded. "Exactly. We've held off that witch hunt by adhering to a very strict set of rules. One of those rules is the respect for the Mark, and another is the filial duty. I can't do *anything* about what Abbot chooses to do to Mirelle."

"Not even if it threatens to expose you all?"

"I don't know why she's walking around in this condition. He's usually more careful."

"Walking around in this—" she repeated, aghast. "All you're worried about is that she's '*walking around,*' not that she's in this condition to begin with? Titus, he's *killing* her!"

Her outrage beat against him. He wanted to make excuses for Abbot, and he wanted to placate her all at the same time. And he ached horridly for Mirelle. She was so pale and thin, the glowing beauty of her faded to gray.

He turned away from them both and spoke to the computer console which still showed H'lim's lab, Abbot's back to the pickup. "Inea, there is something about luren law that you have to know — about luren politics on Earth."

"Politics? Politics! How can you—"

He lowered his voice and cut across her hysteria. "I know how you feel, Inea. It's the reason I left Abbot to begin with. I've had moments when I wanted to do more than leave him. I've actually wanted to kill him. I got over that only when I discovered he's not one of a kind, but a representative of a group, the Tourists. And Abbot's one of the least worst of them. He's kind, considerate, and sane by comparison."

She approached as if creeping up to a cesspool. "Titus, the way he's treating Mirelle isn't kind, considerate, or sane. If anyone finds out—"

"Listen to me! The Tourists constitute fully half of the luren on Earth. My presence here constitutes an act of civil war, but it is war under more strictures and conventions than humans have ever heard of. If we had known *who* the Tourist would be here, I would never have been sent here. *Never!* They've tried to send someone who could deal with Abbot, but he couldn't get through. Even if he had, he couldn't do anything about Mirelle. Abbot is within his legal rights with her, and no Resident will challenge that. We don't kill humans, but *they* do, and the Law of Blood says Marked stringers can be killed. Abbot can kill Mirelle, and it's perfectly legal, under some circumstances."

She recoiled, white-lipped.

"Yes, it's disgusting, and yes I hate it, and yes I'd like to wring his neck. But I won't. I wouldn't if I could. Not for this." *Don't remind her she's Marked!*

"Titus—" It was a tiny, strangled plea that stopped his heart. He watched her lip quiver, somewhere between disgust and tears of bereavement, and he realized that he had to do something or lose her forever. He couldn't argue that Mirelle would probably survive the few days until H'lim's booster was ready. That must be what Abbot was thinking. Or maybe he wasn't thinking too clearly. Hunger could impair the ability to assess risks. And the vision of how much hunger it would take to do that to Abbot horrified Titus.

Damn the blockade! Damn this goddamned war!

"There is one thing I can do. I don't know if it will work. I can only try." He went to the cupboard and stuffed the few remaining packets of blood into a net bag lined with a lab coat. At the outer door, he said, "Maybe this will keep him from leaning too hard on her. Take care of her while I'm gone." Then he turned to meet her eyes. "I'll be back soon, Inea."

In H'lim's lab, he found H'lim and Abbot tinkering with the temperature controls of an empty incubator on a workbench screened from the rest of the lab and from the one bug he'd planted, by a noise partition. H'lim was shoving a notepad under Abbot's nose, the screen lit. "In the Teleod, both luren and human-stock people are legally enfranchised, and this is the genetic tag they look for to determine stock. You have it, so you should have no trouble with the courts."

He's lying. Why is he lying? Why do I think he's lying? Titus had never been one to suspect others of prevarication, but he could not shake this conviction. Simultaneously, he filed away the datum that Teleod was a political alliance, not a chemical term, and in the Teleod legal enfranchisement was a matter of genetics, not loyalties. The lessons of Nazi Germany sprang to mind, but he put aside his suddenly dark suspicions and strode forward.

Without looking up, Abbot said, "You're early, Titus."

H'lim thrust his handheld at Titus. "Look!"

H'lim's screen was divided into five areas. In the center, four colorful molecular models were superimposed over each other in three dimensions. Around it, each of the four curled helices was displayed alone.

H'lim pointed as he explained with real enthusiasm, "This is you; here's Abbot; here's a textbook example of human, and here's me. I have orls, too, but this pad is too small. I haven't translated any galactic races into your coordinates yet, but just by inspection I can tell you that you and your humans have some peculiar anomalies. Other than being oddly suggestible, your humans might be the find of a lifetime for me." He pointed at various parts of the screen. "I've never seen or read about anything like this—or this—or even this! Once I discover what traits are linked here, and there—and this one, too—I may actually have found the single most marketable commodity on Earth. And Titus, I assure you, *I* am the one who can best market it."

Abbot turned, gesturing with the probe he'd been wielding. *"Now* do you see that I've been right all along?"

Triumph, and Mirelle's blood, had glossed over Abbot's hunger, but Titus saw an ashen tinge of exhaustion in him even before he noticed the way the probe vibrated with his hand's uncontrollable shaking. *He's on the edge, and it's partly my doing.* His efforts to stop Abbot had only amounted to harassment and inconvenience, with his mistakes adding a modicum of busywork, but all together it had taken a toll on his father and Titus felt a luren's guilt for that.

Absorbed in his models, H'lim mused aloud, *"This* may account for the suggestibility of humans, though why it should vary so much, I don't know. Can you get me a specimen from Inea? And one from Mirelle? Comparing the strongest with the weakest, perhaps—"

"It's Mirelle's weakness I've come to discuss," Titus interrupted. "Her exceptional weakness today."

"She'll recover," declared Abbot.

"What?" asked H'lim, yanked out of his reasoning.

"I *intend* it should be so," said Titus.

H'lim backed off a way, suddenly sensing the cold tension. Titus advanced to set the net bag on the counter beside Abbot's tools. It sagged open, partially revealing the contents, which Abbot recognized.

"Inea half carried Mirelle to my room. She fainted on the floor. What if someone *else* had found her and taken her to the infirmary? In the name of the Law of Blood, take what your son offers. Use it. Let her recover."

Abbot's fingers rested thoughtfully on the packets. "My son. Truly my son again, at last?"

He met Abbot's eyes and yearned with all his soul to say yes. The moment stretched unendurably as his lips almost formed the word. He felt the first tentative stirring of Abbot's power, offering the enfolding warmth of a parental welcome, stirring the depths of his being. The tentative joy dancing in his father's eyes, the scream of hope poised at the edge of his Influence, and the ache in Abbot's soul at the loss of his son—an ache Titus, only recently a parent himself, could now understand—all combined to show Titus that Abbot had two distinct objectives in coming to the Project: to save Earth's luren by getting their message out, and to win Titus back from the darkness, to do his parental duty by his son whom he loved as any luren would.

Yes! The word pushed up from his heart, threatening to explode from his throat. But there was the vision of Mirelle sagging helplessly in Inea's grip.

With a wordless cry of anguish, Titus broke away from Abbot's seductive gaze and fled, running into the corridor and not stopping until he got to the lift where he fetched up against the closed doors and pounded his fists against them. It was only sheer dumb luck that nobody saw, and that he recovered before the security camera swept across him.

Facing his own apartment door, he straightened his clothes and smoothed his expression, suddenly realizing that for all the pain still surging through him, he felt uncommonly good about himself for the first time in a very long time. He had done his filial duty. *I feel good about starving so Abbot can feed? God, I must be insane.* But there it was, a tremendous release of tension he hadn't felt until it was gone. *I can't fight him. I can't win against this because it's inside me.*

But he also knew that he couldn't win as long as his own son opposed him—and had won Abbot over with lies. Yet if he had been in H'lim's place, he would have done the same. He couldn't blame the luren.

Squaring his shoulders, he went in to confront Inea. She was spooning soup into Mirelle, who was propped up in bed, eyes drooping half shut. She was wearing one of Titus' pullovers now, cuffs rolled into massive donuts around her wrists. Inea looked up. "I went and got my ration. And I've given her two of the pills. I'll take her home in a while—if you think I should."

The implication was, *If it's safe.* Titus answered her unvoiced question. "I don't know, Inea. But there's no choice. She doesn't belong here."

He didn't feel awkward discussing Mirelle like this because there seemed to be a dull film over her awareness, the cumulative effect of heavy Influence. How Abbot had avoided detection so long, Titus didn't know. But both he and Abbot knew it was too dangerous a game to play now. Or if Abbot didn't know it, H'lim would convince him of it.

In a heavy silence, he helped Inea prepare Mirelle and then take her to her own room, which was a tumbled mess, tangible evidence of depression and enervation. There wasn't even a threshold barrier, so diffuse was her presence. But Titus could sense the dregs of Abbot's presence—bitter, savage dregs summoning images of what had occurred here. That almost turned his self-satisfaction to self-hatred. While Mirelle fell into a heavy sleep, they straightened up the place as best they could, then left her alone.

Back in Titus' apartment, Inea stripped the bed and remade it while Titus went to the refectory to get his own rations. They worked together with only casual comments on what they were doing, as if the deeper subject was a glowing coal, too hot to touch. But while Inea was nibbling on the last crusts of the inadequate meal, she asked point blank, "How long until you'll have to take my blood?"

Startled, Titus recoiled, "What?"

"You heard me." Her expression shifted. "You weren't thinking—of taking from someone else without telling me? Titus, I won't permit it."

He laughed out loud. He couldn't help it. After all the grave, grim tension of the last few hours, the image of a human woman sitting over his kitchen table, eating his rations, wearing his Mark, and dictating terms to him in a "be reasonable" tone was just too much.

Catching the edge of hysteria in his laughter, she frowned. "What's the matter with you?"

"I wouldn't think of disobeying you," he said through a veil of chuckles, and suddenly, she understood the irony and together they laughed uproariously.

In the end, she said, "Well, Delilah could wrap Samson around her little finger, why shouldn't I boss a vampire around?"

That almost set them off again, but Titus sobered. "Inea, I had no intention of taking your blood—or anyone else's. I've been well-fed, compared to Abbot. I'll be all right until my supplies arrive."

"There's no way to know how long that'll be. You'll have to take some blood. What had you planned to do?"

He thrust himself out of the chair and caught himself against the edge of the sink, wanting to run, wanting to accept, and wanting to appear in perfect command. The truth was like bile in his mouth. "I didn't think about how I'd survive."

He turned to watch the bewildered shock flicker across her features. "Inea, you're going to have to grasp something else that may be even harder than the idea that Abbot has the right, under luren Law, to kill Mirelle. I will not take the living blood of a human. I don't *want* it."

"That's not true. I've seen the look in your eyes, over a bleeding wound."

"So? I'm mortal. I'm subject to temptation. I thought I'd explained this before. Haven't you grasped yet what it is that deters me when I am tempted?"

"How could I? I'm not even sure what's so tempting. Cloned blood is genetically identical to real blood. If it's infused with ectoplasm, it ought to be really identical. All this fuss makes me wonder if maybe there isn't something—unique—in giving blood directly to a vampire. Maybe I'd enjoy it!"

He surged across the floor and plucked her out of the chair by the shoulders, shaking her. "Don't you dare—!"

The hurt shock that flashed through her knifed across his anger and he froze, horrified at himself. He enfolded her in his arms, burying his face in her hair and rocking her back and forth as he moaned, "I'm sorry! I'm sorry!"

How could he explain to her the ghastly trap he had dug himself out of when he'd left Abbot? He pushed her away, caught her eyes, and repeated what he'd told her so many times. "Inea, it's addictive. I don't know if I'd have the strength to break away again. I *could* do worse to you than Abbot has done to Mirelle and feel just as little remorse over it. I've done that, under Abbot's direction. I lived that way, Inea, and I won't go back to it. I won't. Can you understand that?"

"You're scared," she said. "That I can understand. Maybe I'll come to—"

The door signal interrupted her, and only then did Titus feel H'lim's familiar presence. But not Abbot's. Not the four guards. "Oh, my God!"

He dashed to the door, flung it open, grabbed H'lim by the elbow and yanked him inside, shutting the door and leaning against it. It was the middle of the night for the station. Hall traffic was light, but not wholly absent.

"H'lim, you fool!" hissed Titus.

"I won't stay long," he answered with equanimity. From under his capacious lab coat he produced a fat Thermos. "I was trying to explain before you left, that I think I've got orl blood you can manage to take. Abbot can't use it, but I talked him into accepting your gift."

Titus let him shove the Thermos into his numb hands. "What about your guards—the recorders? Carol will—"

"They'll never know I was gone!"

"H'*lim!*"

"I'm going. Don't worry." With one hand on the door, he paused to say over his shoulder, "I just wanted you to know, I'm proud to count you Fourth Father. And I'll be proud to introduce you to my First Father."

Then he was gone.

Titus sank into a kitchen chair, his knees too weak to support him even in the lunar gravity. The Thermos clutched to his chest, he bowed his head over it and blinked away unaccountable tears. *I must be as close to the edge as Abbot is.*

Inea lifted the Thermos from his grasp. With her help, he choked down the alien substance and kept it down, and by morning, he had regained his equilibrium and soaked up some of Inea's optimism and determination with her ectoplasm and her love.

—— TWENTY ——

Over the next few days, Titus survived on what H'lim provided, though he sometimes vomited up most of what he swallowed. Mirelle's improvement was evidence that Abbot wasn't at her again, not yet.

Abbot was as horrified as Titus that H'lim had eluded them and the guards to bring Titus blood. H'lim argued, "I made sure it was safe enough. Filial duty takes precedence."

"You could have *called* me," Titus repeated doggedly, and H'lim insisted Titus had even less business stalking the halls in such condition than H'lim had, and besides they couldn't trust the monitored vidcom channels. For Titus it was a new experience, having someone worry about him. In the end, Titus understood that the restrictions were chafing on H'lim, and this had been his way of asserting himself as well as seeking that peculiar gratification Titus had discovered while providing for Abbot. And H'lim *hadn't* been caught. He hadn't made any of the mistakes he'd made the first time. He'd learned a lot about humans.

But after that, Titus, Abbot, and Inea clung closer to H'lim. Inea, having fewer obligations than the department heads, had the longest duty hours alone with the alien. But he never gave her any trouble. They seemed to be developing a kind of friendship as Inea became ever more fascinated with the evolution of the orl and luren.

During this time, two ships penetrated the blockade, dropping bundles of supplies near the station. Soon the probe construction was resumed, and rations were increased, though there was no blood aboard for Titus. He understood security must be ferocious, and though his spirits sank, he didn't blame Connie for the failure.

After that single W.S. triumph, the frenzy of the orbital clashes increased. Colby instituted a more vigorous regimen of decompression drills. At rumors that a blockader ship blown up in Earth atmosphere had been slated to bomb Project Station, she ordered more lower levels under the residence domes equipped as survival bunkers.

With the new hardware in place in the probe, programmers began installing the software, both guidance and message. They installed extra shielding on the assumption that the probe would launch through a dense veil of heavy particles. During this phase, Abbot spent much of his time at the probe hangar. When Titus planted one of Inea's bugs on the vehicle, guards caught him loitering and Colby ordered him not to go out there after his targeting program was in place. "You're too valuable to lose, and that hangar is *the* primary target on this station."

With the installation of Titus' program, his crew's job was over. They were exhausted but still tense because they knew they could have done better, given time. Titus sent them to rest "You've got to be back here on Launch Day, fresh and ready to work. We have to track the probe, probably without backup from Earth." Every day, news came of another attack on W.S. orbital control installations and even University observatories.

Now it often fell to Titus to escort H'lim at meetings of the joint Cognitive Sciences and Telecom committee that was designing Earth's message. And one thing stood out, even above the achievement of a broadcast signal intelligible across such a gulf of space and culture: H'lim was gradually winning the humans over. They had begun to trust him. And as that trust grew, the factionalism on the station precipitated by the war began to melt away. There was a feeling that only those on the station had any grasp of what was out there in the galaxy, and of how Earth could benefit from it all.

Titus' distrust of H'lim, however, was not assuaged by seeing how he manipulated humans without even using Influence—or how he'd learned to do that in such a short time. One other thing bothered Titus: H'lim had no difficulty understanding the war. His strange, backhanded grasp of English never got in the way on that topic. He had the concepts down pat.

After one meeting, H'lim confided, "Now I'm glad Abbot's sending a real message, or I'd have been tempted to deceive the humans. They're clever, Titus. Especially Mirelle. They'd have caught me." Seeing Titus' expression, he'd added, "I'm sorry you and Abbot are at odds over this."

It was one of the few times Titus believed the luren. He pressed him. "What exactly did you put in Abbot's message that's not in this one?" It wasn't the first time he'd asked, but it was the first time he got a straight answer.

"A code that'll tell my company that I'm sitting on a genetic gold mine. If they can only get here first and dig me out, we'll all be rich— Earth's luren as well as the humans. I told them to file a claim that will protect your legal rights, and to make all the appropriate appeals to create a special category for you. We're one of the few firms in all the galaxy, Teleod and Metaji combined, who can do this for Earth. Trust me, Titus. I wouldn't do anything to harm a parent of mine!"

Abbot came to take over escort duty, and Titus watched the two walk away. *Maybe not to harm, but to risk, yes.* Then he wondered where the thought had come from. H'lim had *sounded* so sure. But on the other hand, under Mirelle H'lim had mastered the body language and kinesics of the Near East, China, and Australia as well as North America. It had made him so effective in his dealings with the committees studying him, even the ones who understood the power of the unverbalized languages, that he didn't need Influence.

Throughout this period, Inea and Titus still watched Abbot's movements closely. One evening, about two weeks prior to the rescheduled launch of the probe, Inea was at Titus' vidcom screen drinking coffee and sifting the newest data on Abbot. Titus was sprawled on the bed doodling equations on a handheld, his old mathematical proof that Influence, and so H'lim's ability to grab language right out of Titus' skull, couldn't exist. Meanwhile, most of his mind was inventing methods of prying truth out of H'lim. Inea's voice penetrated his reverie. "Either he's installed his transmitter in the probe or he's not going to at all."

"What? Who?" Titus sat up. "Abbot? He's supposed to be with H'lim."

"He *is* right now, but I mean all this last week."

He went to look over her shoulder at the graphs she'd made. "You're right. He hasn't been out to the probe hangar in days." Heading for the door, he shrugged into his jacket.

"Where are you going?" She followed him.

"I'll be right back."

She slipped out the door behind him. *"Titus!"*

He put his hands on her shoulders. "I know Colby ordered me not to go out there. I'll just check out what Abbot's done, and be right back. Don't worry, it's night outside. I'll be fine."

"Titus, what will he do to you if he catches you destroying his work? You can't just go rushing—"

He kissed her. "You're supposed to relieve him in half an hour. Go early, see if you can keep them both occupied. I'll come to the lab when I'm done." He turned and strode away before she could object again.

Suited up, he rode with a shift change out to the probe. Colby had not lifted his clearance, so he was quite open about his presence. His mind, however, was on how he could possibly identify Abbot's transmitter and what he'd do if he found it. From studying the plans of the hastily redesigned probe, he had a fair notion of where it must be. He had entertained ideas of editing Abbot's message, or substituting one of his own, but had been unable to break into Abbot's files to steal either his message or the program that cast it into galactic communications protocols H'lim had given them. Titus hadn't spent enough time on the luren language to draft his own message. Besides, what could, or should, a Resident say?

I'll have to remove the transmitter. I can put it back again before launch if it seems H'lim's honest. How he'd explain such an act to Residents who had sacrificed to put him here, he didn't know.

The illumination outside the hangar cut the area into a crazy quilt of stark, flat pictures embedded in black, like a limbo set on a stage, because there was no air to diffuse the light. But the floods were cleverly aimed to prevent disorientation or dazzling on approach to the open hangar doors. Despite his contacts, Titus could make out traces of what existed in shadow, infrared images that would have been clear had there been no light, because the workers produced a considerable amount of heat that could escape only by radiation and conduction.

He climbed the scaffold into the probe and took a few moments to sort out who the electricians were. He hung over their shoulders asking questions as he examined each of them for trace of Abbot's Influence. It would not be perceptible unless triggered by work involving Abbot's modifications, so he checked only those at work. At last, he came to one woman squatting before an open panel consulting a circuit diagram.

She kept tapping a single component with a probe, and then following the circuit diagram *away* from that spot, clearly frustrated that she couldn't find it. *That's it!*

He hunkered down next to her and introduced himself. "Why are you checking this out? It's been approved." He pointed to the band of tape that had sealed the access port.

"Oh, this is just another surprise double-check, along with all that anti-hypnotic conditioning they're putting everyone through."

"*All* that conditioning?" As far as Titus knew, they'd only done one round of hypnotic conditioning, unsure that H'lim's power was related to hypnosis.

"Yeah, an experiment. They make you do a job, then they flash lights in your eyes for a while, make you do the job over again, flash lights at you again, and so on. Who knows when it'll stop! If you ask me, the higher-ups were raised on too many old movies. *This* blood-sucking monster from outer space turned out to be a nice guy!"

"Sure seems like it." *I better not miss any more meetings!* Titus couldn't be hypnotized, but he had no idea if he could fake it without using Influence. Finger quivering inside his glove, he pointed at a familiar area of her diagram. "That's my stuff. Here, let me. No use both of us rechecking what's been rechecked before. You must be tired." He didn't even have to use Influence. Tedium had taken its toll. She shoved the display handheld into his mitts.

"All yours, Doctor. I'll be up top when you're done."

"Right."

Aware that Abbot's shift with H'lim was officially over, Titus kept looking over his shoulder expecting his father to appear. *It can't be*

263

this easy, not after all these months. But connection by connection, memorizing what he was doing, Titus excised Abbot's assembly, checked everything by the diagram, ran a systems check, and buttoned it up again, satisfied it would now work the way the humans had intended.

Even with the lumpy appurtenances where Abbot had improvised parts, the whole transmitter fit neatly into his outside leg pocket. He was still sweating after returning the diagrams to the electrician.

Titus found himself climbing down between a welder and a shift supervisor who were arguing with each other, when their voices in his phones were cut off by a piercing whistle. "Clear the probe hangar! Clear the hangar! Incoming bogey at ten o'clock. Clear the hangar! Two minutes to contact."

Swearing, the men above and below Titus pushed off from the ladder to land yards apart and running for the nearest dome. Titus copied them, and then lost ground when the lights went out as the station secured for attack. Titus followed the sparks of suitlights around him, and once outside the hangar, dug his toes into the compacted soil of the path. His mass was too great, his feet clumsy, his vision obscured by the helmet but he had to keep up with the swarm of men and machines behind him, driving toward the safety of the dome's underground bunker, or be run over.

The Disaster Controller's voice chanted the countdown in his ears. He didn't dare look up when the voice announced defenders on the attacker's tail. He'd gained such momentum that he had to concentrate on keeping his center of gravity over his feet.

An oddly detached corner of his mind worked Newton's Laws, calculating his stopping distance, and impact force if he didn't stop in time, a freshman final exam problem. *This isn't going to work!* But the crowd seemed to be bounding along in nightmarish slow motion, and no one dared slow down even when the narrow opening in the dome gaped before them. It led into a small garage, still floodlit inside. The first arrivals skidded onto the smooth paving, yelling frantically when they realized they would hit the far wall hard. Way short of the door, Titus slowed, yelling for others to do the same despite the instinct that screamed, *run!*

Then the ground jerked from under him as something hit his back. He sprawled, chin first, momentum driving him on. In front of him, others fell, knocked over the staggering who piled into the fallen, who slid with relentless momentum into a tangled jam in the doorway.

Then molten fragments of metal rained down. Screams filled his earphones.

Swimming in squirming, suited bodies, Titus struggled forward to throw himself across one man's slashed leg, trying to keep air and blood in. It was a mindless act, but it saved his life. Where he had been, a large wedge of hot metal sliced into the man who had been under Titus. It stood quivering, its pointed end skewering the writhing body, its upper end glowing red hot in shadow. Panic drove others forward despite the pile of suits jamming the doorway, burying Titus in squirming humanity. Many of those on top died, suits holed by hot missiles floating down under lunar gravity, or plunging down with the energy of explosion behind them.

The eerie thing, the most frightening thing, was that it all happened in such utter silence. Spacewar movies always had sound effects. All Titus heard was the screaming. He had not even heard the ground rumbling because his boots were too well insulated.

For a long time, he lay buried under a mass of dead, injured and dying, pinning other dead, injured and dying to the ground with his own mass, and all afraid to move for fear of holing their suits on sharp fragments. *At least I don't have to smell the panic and the blood.* After a while, his suit radio ceased working, so he was even spared the patient Disaster Controller's voice instructing them not to move and not to panic to conserve air.

Eventually, people came and pulled the pile of bodies apart, heaping the stiffened corpses for identification and burial, setting the survivors onto their feet in the awkward suits. Those too injured to walk were carried off, and the others were told to report to the infirmary only if there were signs of concussion or serious injury.

When Titus was at last extricated and set up on his feet, one leg numb from lack of circulation, a small suited figure that had been attaching oxygen hoses for those still trapped, turned toward him, froze, then flew at him, almost knocking him over again.

Across the helmet was written, I. CELLURA. Through the faceplate he saw sweat on her forehead and her lip quivered. He let her support him all the way back to the airlock, because he didn't trust his leg, and because it felt so good to hold her, but he made it clear that he was fine.

When it was his turn to be cycled through the lock, Inea reluctantly returned to her work, and he entered the corridor leading from the suit dressing rooms to the airlock.

Abbot and H'lim both were inside, helping survivors off with gear while others supplied drinks and first aid. All at once, Titus remembered the transmitter in his leg pocket, the lump that had cut off his circulation.

They pushed Titus down on a crate and H'lim pulled the exterior, insulating boots off him. Abbot hovered over him, cutting out other helpful corpsmen, and ostentatiously used a penlight to check if his pupils dilated properly, making notes on a medical pad as he worked. Along the line of dazed survivors, the four Brink's guards who usually shadowed H'lim were wrapping sprained ankles and bandaging facial cuts.

"Thanks, Abbot, I can manage now," said Titus, heart pounding as Abbot worked over him. He struggled to his feet to shed his suit. "Go help someone who needs it."

"What were you *doing* out there," hissed Abbot.

"My job, what else!" snapped Titus. In a very non-regulation move, he pushed the suit's torso down to dangle over the legs, as if it were a pair of wholly flexible overalls. Abbot began to object, but H'lim tugged at his sleeve, moving off to help clean up someone who had vomited.

With a scowl directed back over his shoulder at Titus, Abbot went, but cloaking his words, he added, "It doesn't matter what you were doing. The probe's gone now."

Watching them, Titus was struck by the way H'lim's ministrations were accepted. He sat back down, pulling his feet out of the suit's attached boots. He'd worked his right foot up to the knee when the lock opened and a woman was brought in on a stretcher, stifling screams. It was the electrician Titus had relieved in the probe.

Her leg was broken. Two corpsmen converged on her to cut the suit away and start an IV. All the suitcutters were in use, so they employed powered metal snips, awkward and dangerous if she moved. She bit the rim of her suit collar and tried her best to remain still, but it wasn't good enough, and nobody had come yet with medication.

After their third failure, H'lim plunged across the room and lifted the snips from the corpsman's grasp. "Let me," he said, without Influence.

The electrician readily accepted his help, but she was unable to remain still. H'lim reached for her face, Influence gathering about him like a rising sun. Titus almost came off his crate, one leg in his suit, the other bare, but swallowed his protest when the room fell silent. H'lim murmured, "Let me take the pain away. Please, we've got to stop the bleeding or you'll die."

266

She glanced at her audience, and Titus followed her gaze to see Colby coming through the hatch. Defiantly, the electrician told H'lim, "All right, but just for a moment."

Titus was certain that, concentrating as he was, H'lim was unaware of Colby. Though the power H'lim raised was stunning, his touch was delicate enough not to derange the suggestible human nor to disturb Abbot's work on her.

Her eyes closed and tranquility altered her face to that of a young girl. H'lim wielded the clumsy tool with fine precision, excising her arm for the IV, then exposing the tattered mess that had been her leg. Everyone there knew what H'lim considered nourishment, and not a one saw a hint of anything on his face but clinical detachment as he wrapped a tourniquet and announced, "It's not as bad as it looks. Only two breaks. They should be able to save the leg." To the corpsman who had finally seated the IV, he added, "If the surgeons doubt it, have them call me."

Before he could answer, a nurse arrived with a shot for the patient and H'lim released his hold on her mind. As he turned away, Colby moved up to challenge H'lim. "You are under injunction not to use your power." The Brink's guards, who had watched from a distance, snapped to.

H'lim met her gaze unwaveringly. "If my life is forfeit, then so be it. I acted as required by an oath and ethic older and more honored than your Hippocratic Oath. And I *did,* Dr. Colby, gain her express permission first."

"As I recall, permission wasn't a factor in our agreement, nor have you ever represented yourself as a medical practitioner." Her awareness of the onlookers was clear in her stance and tone.

"The divisions of labor you practice are not universal, Dr. Colby. My field is the integrity of the physical body, in health, in illness, in reproduction, and in trauma, regardless of species or planet of origin. Were it not so, I could not have learned your biological notation system so quickly, could I? But this is the seventieth, or maybe eightieth such system I've encountered, and *at least* the hundredth physiological variant. I could repair that woman's leg as easily as I could grow her a new one." His expression hardened. *"Therefore, I am not free to ignore her plight."*

Colby's eyes flicked about the room, and what she saw there gave her pause. H'lim had won. "There is still the matter of manipulating her mind with your power. You gave your word you would not do such things."

H'lim also directed his attention to the audience, aware that Colby had politics and morale to consider. "At the time of that discussion, neither of us was considering such an emergency. You're not a sadist, Dr. Colby. Had I asked your permission, you would have granted it." He raked the humans' faces with a measuring glance. "Would you *prefer* to find that you were harboring an alien life form so devoid of compassion that he would withhold succor because his first thought was for his selfish fears?"

Masterful, thought Titus, *but he talks like a textbook when he gets nervous.* And H'lim was scared, there was no doubt of that.

Surreptitiously studying her audience, Colby announced, "Your— *patient* will be thoroughly tested. If we find you've done anything *but* relieve pain, your life *will* be forfeit."

"Then I have nothing to worry about." Which was true, Titus reflected as Colby strode out the door.

Everyone started to breathe again. A corpsman clapped H'lim on the back and set him to wrapping a sprained ankle. From the tone as the buzz of conversation rose again, Titus knew that H'lim had just passed the final test. The station no longer considered him inhuman or a menace. *If they can accept him, maybe they can accept us eventually.* Abbot caught Titus' gaze, and Titus knew his father was thinking the same thing—only to him, it was an alarming thought.

As more casualties came through, Titus pitched in to help Abbot and H'lim. Inea joined them, and for a while, Titus savored what it could be like to have a family again.

Later, he found out that not only had the secessionists hit the probe hangar with several bombs—others having gone wild and dug new craters in the landscape—but two of the W.S. ships defending Project Station had crashed into each other, raining deadly fragments. One dome had been breached, and was currently airless, the survivors trapped in the lower levels behind pressure seals, rescue workers trying to get to them and their casualties.

This was why there was so little help for the probe workers. Meanwhile, one of the blockaders' ships had crashed nearby, and a party had been dispatched to search for survivors. However they might regard the secessionists' politics, they wouldn't let anyone suffocate. Not that they'd be thanked, considering the quarantine.

"Besides," observed a woman carrying a welder's helmet, "they might know something worth learning. H'lim could get it out of them."

Titus didn't like the enthusiastic response to that, but H'lim's attitude reassured him. The human mind was off limits to him, he told them, and that meant all humans. "Besides," he pointed out, "you don't need me. You have Dr. de Lisle and her colleagues. They are difficult to lie to."

Four days later, rescues completed, they paused before launching the repair effort to hold the mass funeral. Colby's oration concluded with a promise to revise evacuation plans and to increase disaster drills. She bolstered their courage by pointing out that when Earth finally realized what H'lim had yet to offer, the war would end. After the day of intense grieving, life returned to something resembling normality. But now there was no further need for Titus' department. There would be no probe to target or track.

Late that night, while Abbot and H'lim were working in H'lim's lab, ostensibly on a project for Colby, Titus let himself into H'lim's apartment using a borrowed maintenance key. He hid Abbot's transmitter where neither H'lim nor Abbot would ever look, inside a casserole dish heaped in the back of a kitchen cabinet with pots and pans. He didn't even tell Inea for fear she'd telegraph the guilty knowledge to H'lim, who was becoming all too wise in human ways.

Titus retained only a copy of the message he coaxed the transmitter to spit out. Its targeting data were, of course, his own, and of no particular interest, but the message was long, detailed, and obscurely coded. Titus was certain it would have brought the whole galaxy to their doorstep. With little to occupy him now, he spent time attempting to read the message, but without luck—except for the section that identified Earth's sun in both digital code and in something that must have been *Kylyd's* coding system. His real purpose, however, was to access H'lim's part of the message and read it back to him to see if Abbot had altered it. It was a longshot, he admitted, but he had to do something to jar the whole truth out of the luren.

The work served another purpose, too. It kept his mind off his hunger and his growing inability to keep the orl blood down. H'lim, aware that his try with the orl blood had not been a success, wanted to risk cloning human blood in his lab, but Titus wouldn't hear of it. If the luren was caught, the whole attitude of the station humans would change. "You might be torn limb from limb, and I mean that literally. Humans can be savage."

When Abbot, looking worse than Titus did, supported Titus' position, H'lim capitulated, and redoubled his efforts to refine his

269

booster. With the mystery of why Titus was rejecting the orl blood nagging at him, H'lim wasn't nearly as confident of the booster now.

The work went slowly, and Titus often saw the alien's frustration with the best of Earth's equipment. But he never compared the hardware to what he was used to. He only worked harder to master the primitive tools and to understand the hazy images the microscopes produced in color schemes all wrong for his eyes. Titus believed the luren's boast that he knew seventy or eighty different scientific systems and was undaunted by learning one more, even one based on an "oddly disjointed model of reality."

Titus could never get H'lim to elaborate on that observation, and in fact the luren apologized profusely, trying to convince Titus that he hadn't meant to disparage Earth's achievements. "Perhaps it's just that I haven't had time to investigate all your uniquely divided specialties. And you are a devoted specialist, Titus. There are so many of your world's disciplines that you know nothing of—not even the basic vocabularies. When this war is over, I expect I'll have plenty of time to learn all of Earth's other ways of studying the relationship of space, time, will, vision, and the life force."

Titus allowed that mysticism was indeed not his field, but that Earth had a plethora of such disciplines. Not wanting to start an argument by revealing his aversion to the sloppy thinking of mystics, Titus dropped the subject. In retrospect, he later realized that he'd missed his chance to convert H'lim into an ally of Resident policy at a point where it would have saved a lot of lives.

One afternoon soon after that, in H'lim's lab when the Cognitive people had finally left and H'lim had secured their privacy, the luren commented, "It's only a question of time, now, Titus. Abbot's had to start using Mirelle again, but I've asked him to go easy on her. A few hundred hours, and I should have a test quantity of this formula to try."

"The war could be resolved before then." *When Inea sees Mirelle fading, what will she do?*

As H'lim worked, they discussed the war. The luren understood that W.S. might not win, but in that event, he intimated, the Tourists had a plan for smuggling his dormant body to Earth. H'lim did not believe he was revealing any secrets when he told Titus that the Tourists had infiltrated the blockaders, and could just about guarantee his safety regardless of who won, provided he could manage to die with his spine and brain intact.

Either Abbot's lying through his teeth, or he's got his communications working again. Outwardly, Titus just nodded as if it were old news. "The secessionists want this station dead and kept quarantined. If they win, it'll be a long dormancy for you."

"I doubt that. You mustn't underestimate your father."

Really? Watching H'lim putter about, he was certain the luren had no idea of what he'd just revealed.

Noticing how Inea's log showed Abbot's attention focused around the observatory and the Eighth Antenna Array's console, Titus had searched the console and all connecting installations clear to the edge of the station looking for any way Abbot had of getting the Eighth to transmit his message. It had never before been a top priority because the Eighth hadn't had a window into the volume of space H'lim had come from. But now, with his old theory returning to haunt him, and with just such a window coming up, Titus went through the hardware again, found nothing, and rechecked all the software.

They had used the Eighth to communicate, via relays, with *Wild Goose* as well as several other experimental stations. It had been built to serve the manned exploration program, which had been abandoned for lack of funds again. But the Eighth was still equipped to be linked to its seven other counterparts around the moon, providing global coverage of the entire firmament.

A good deal of Titus' department's computing power had been designed to link the Eight Arrays with the satellites and mobile observatories, forming what might have to become the solar system's first global defense network communications system.

It had never been used, or even tested. The nearest they'd come was Abbot's being ordered to use the Eighth to break into the blockaders' communications. To date, he had reported only sporadic successes, with recordings that had revealed little. He hadn't even been able to give warning of the attack on the probe. *Did Abbot know and just not say anything? Is that why he wasn't concerned about the humans finding his transmitter? Would he have knowingly sacrificed the device?* Or maybe, since Titus hadn't heard of the increased use of anti-hypnotic conditioning and rechecking of work, perhaps Abbot hadn't heard either? Perhaps he hadn't known how close his transmitter had been to being discovered. Or if he had known, perhaps he wanted the probe destroyed in the attack.

Fruitless speculation, Titus told himself. But one thing seemed obvious. Abbot must have been using the Eighth to communicate

271

with Tourists among the blockaders to set up H'lim's escape. He might even be able to communicate with his control back on Earth, Connie's opposite number. In any case, when the window opened, Abbot would be ready to send the Tourists' message to the stars.

If he was planning to have such a stunt go unnoticed, then he must have a way to prevent Maintenance from noticing the power drain. *Ah, but that's Abbot's department. He could gimmick all the monitors and nobody would ever know.*

Renewing his study of the Eighth's console, Titus figured a way to configure his black box to use the Eighth's transmission capability to contact Earth. It was an absurd use of an Array, like swatting flies with a baseball bat, but it could be done. Since it was possible, if not feasible, Abbot had probably done it. But Titus couldn't see how to hide his transmission without an official transmission from Colby to hide it under.

What little official traffic went in and out of the station now went via moving ships in space. Their news came audio only, or with black and white video at the most. Personal mail was totally cut off. And in the attack on the probe, they'd lost one of their last transmission masts. Though a crew was working on reconstructing it from the debris, there was little hope it would last long. The landline to Luna Station had been cut and repaired, debugged and retapped so many times nobody trusted it.

During one of the interminable committee meetings on the subject, Titus brought up one of his earliest suggestions. "We could use the Eighth to guide an unmanned supply ship in to a hard landing out on the mare, then go out and truck the supplies back. It's dangerous, but it could be done."

They kicked the idea around, and in the end decided that though it was technically feasible, the military types wouldn't go for it because of the danger of interception. "The blockaders need supplies, too. They've been getting most of theirs by stealing ours. If they heard us pulling a supply vessel in, they'd just outshout us and bring the supplies to *their* doorstep. Or if we kept control and landed it, they'd be there first. It'd be hand-to-hand combat for possession. Are we ready for that?"

Colby decided they weren't and tabled the idea. But it was only two days later when she called Titus into her office, wrapped the place in security shielding, and told him, "This is for your ears only, a job for your hands only. You were chosen out of your whole department because you're the only one whose background check shows no ties with secessionist countries. Do I have your word you won't confide in a soul?"

Mystified, he nodded. *Background check!? Oh, Connie, sometimes you're too thorough.* "Darrell Raaj" had relatives in every one of the seceding nations. Titus kept his lips from twisting at the irony. "I take security seriously."

"The secessionists have Goddard. They destroyed, captured, or crippled the other installations that can do these computations. Your server is the last fully operational, wholly trustworthy, completely secure facility we have capable of this kind of precision."

"What do you want me to calculate? Shimon—"

"No! You must do this with your own hands and wipe out all trace of its having been done. You must say not one word to anyone. All our lives may depend on it." Titus saw the circles under her eyes, the aching fatigue dragging her down. "Besides, the whole thing was your idea to begin with."

"My idea? I don't understand."

"When our first supply ships were hit by the blockade, you suggested unmanned ships, and you've been pushing for it ever since. I passed your idea on, but I thought it had been discarded. Only it hasn't." She wiped her forehead with the back of her wrist and ironed the frown off her face. "World Sovereignties is losing this war, Titus. We've lost so many computers we can't fly orbital missions properly, which is why the blockade is nearly impenetrable. We can't threaten them with the probe anymore. H'lim is doing all he can to supply us with proof of his value, but it will all be for nothing if the station dies.

"We need supplies, Titus. I haven't let people know just how desperate we are, but I'm telling you. This is our last chance. This consignment must arrive or we'll all die out here. And everything depends on you."

"I don't understand."

"Cargotainers, not ships—unmanned missiles, launched from Earth's surface and aimed at us. If they hit us, they'll act like bombs and will destroy the station. If they land close, but not on us, the W.S. will win the war because the secessionists are at the end of their resources, despite their victories. You can do it, Titus. It's an elementary ballistics problem. The 'tainers will have simple correction jets for use in space, to compensate for unpredictable atmospheric effects on launch. They'll be controlled from here by the Eighth Array."

273

It was a simple problem. He had the programs. "I'll need data—mass. . . ."

She clapped a data case onto the desk before her. "It's all here. The timing—everything."

He took it, hand trembling as he realized Connie would probably have blood aboard for him. By now, she had to be inside their security. He had been vomiting up the orl blood so violently, he'd begun to think seriously of accepting Inea's offer of blood, which she repeated every time he had trouble. He gripped the data case in both hands and told Colby, "I'll let you know when it's done."

"There's one other thing." She checked the bank of meters and alarms in front of her, then raised her eyes somberly. "They're protecting the supply missiles with a decoy. The missiles will be sitting ducks if spotted, so the plan is to keep the secessionists busy—" She broke off and leaned forward urgently, sweat showing at her hairline. "Titus, three men died bringing this information across the surface from Luna Station, on foot, because they didn't dare broadcast it or attract attention with vehicles. We've got a leak on this station. If you breathe a word. . . ."

A traitor. He wasn't surprised. Between the rescues of crashed secessionists and now some W.S. messengers, there could even be another assassin on the station. "I won't say anything. Do I have to know about the decoy?"

"Yes. For the timing. It's all there for you, but not the reasons why it has to be so precise. A surface convoy just like what they've been trying to get through to us will be timed to draw enemy fire just before the 'tainers are to arrive. The decoy will be loaded with explosives. The 'tainers must arrive on time and on target. If they hit the station, we're dead. If they hit too near the decoy which will be set to blow, we lose the supplies, the war, and our lives. The blockaders need supplies, too. They'll attack that decoy to capture, not just destroy. This is a gigantic, tightly planned, high-precision operation. You can't improvise. You can't create or embroider. You must do precisely what you are instructed, exactly as demanded.

"Do you understand this, Titus? It all depends on you."

"I can see that."

"Good. Let me know when you're ready to transmit the data. And don't forget the time lag."

He just looked at her.

Embarrassed, she grimaced. "Yes, well, everybody else forgets the time lag."

He went to work on it immediately, and it wasn't nearly as difficult as it sounded. The W.S. planners had in fact thought of everything, even the problems caused by computing on the moon and launching from Earth. *They must have been planning this since I first suggested it.* But he was also sure that the suggestion had been so obvious that others must have thought of it before he did.

Inea was curious about his activities, but he told her truthfully he was reopening communications with the Resident operatives who could ship him blood. Shimon hung over his shoulder until he convinced the Israeli that he was going over *Wild Goose's* data again, just for the hell of it.

Then Abbot caught Titus dismantling the Eighth's console in the observatory, getting ready to connect his black box. "Titus, *what* are you doing?" he demanded.

"Spying on you, what else?"

Abbot hunkered down to peer into the mechanism, hands dangling over his knees. "You don't seem to have done any damage. Listen, whatever you do, don't use the Eighth to send any sort of signal. I'm only getting fragments of messages because I haven't been aiming the antennas, but I'm convinced that the blockaders believe the Eighth is dead. If anything moves out there, they'll bomb it. If they pick up any kind of signal from it, they'll bomb it. It's too valuable to lose, Titus. Don't risk it."

"Do you really think they'd destroy something so valuable? I don't believe they think it's dead. They've decided to spare it because it's the last operational one."

Abbot studied Titus for a moment, then edged closer. "All right, listen. My—friends—among the blockaders have reported that the Eighth is dead, and so it's being overlooked. After their triumphant destruction of the probe, the secessionists feel they are winning, Titus, and they are! If they take over, there will be no money for rebuilding your orbital observatories or Arrays or anything. We've got to save what we can, so don't energize or aim the Array."

"I understand the situation," said Titus.

Two hours later, he had connected the Eighth console to his black box, slaved to the special channel they'd use to communicate with Earth.

At the first opportunity, Titus reported to Colby that Abbot believed the blockaders considered the Eighth dead. "I'm not so sure we should go ahead with this. We'll have to aim and energize the Array twice, once to send the launch data, and once to correct the orbit. If Abbot's right, it could cost us the Array and our only way of intercepting blockaders' communications."

"Abbot's project didn't save the probe, and the Array isn't really the right tool for signaling Earth. If we lose it, science loses a lot but our strategic position won't be that much worse. The other antenna mast is almost finished and might be powerful enough to reach Earth without a relay." Colby couldn't ask Earth for a decision, so she paced around her desk like a caged animal several times before she finally told Titus, "We've got to risk the Array. With the diversions planned, it's possible they'll never notice."

As the sun rose over the station, Titus' vitality sank, and he forced himself to check and recheck everything for fatigue errors. But a few days later, he had the tabulations ready for transmission with every eventuality covered. He also had a test message ready for Connie, with a full report set to dump if she returned the code signal. It was a risk. If ground control at the ballistic launch site caught the interference their computers were filtering out of Titus' signal and realized that it, itself, was a signal, it could blow the entire operation because they'd think it was the secessionists breaching security. The resulting tightening of security could ruin all of Connie's plans.

Just before the transmission time, Colby cordoned off Titus' lab, filling it with Brink's auditors, claiming that they had to keep up with their paperwork. This attracted no attention because the auditors had been working constantly, all over the station, and since the blockade, Colby had been using them to keep people too busy to brood.

With that security in place, Titus wanted to make sure his black box was functioning properly, so he pulled the console apart to go over all the connections. It was only then that he found one board he couldn't account for. At first he thought fatigue was dulling his mind, but when he couldn't find that board on any circuit diagram, he realized he'd found Abbot's alternative transmitter—or, at the very least, his means of communicating with the Tourists.

"Something wrong, Dr. Shiddehara?" asked a guard.

"Uh, no, just have to replace this. Intermittent short." He wasn't challenged as he deposited the board in his office and brought forth another, wholly meaningless, one which he inserted without connecting it to anything.

On Colby's command, Titus sent his calculations, tying in local weather predictions at the launch site and known orbital movements of the blockade ships. The media had surmised that the blockaders were preparing to take Luna Station, the last bastion of World Sovereignties on the moon's surface.

As planned, Titus got no acknowledgment that his data had been received, only the computer's tedious, digit by digit handshake with groundside. The data went somewhere, but he had no way of knowing who got it.

As they waited for the launch hour, and the moment when Titus would have the chance to correct errors in the orbit, Titus went into his office to pocket Abbot's device. He didn't expect to be searched on the way out, but if so, he'd just say he was taking it to the shop to get the short fixed. Checking the console, he found that Connie had solicited his report with her proper code, and in return his black box had captured a brief note from her. "Next caravan from Luna Station has supply for you. Stay on top of A. We're doing our best."

Heart pounding, he began to enter a warning to divert her efforts to the 'tainers, and then realized that the 'tainers were already buttoned up, and no doubt the decoy caravan was now loading at Luna Station. *It's too late.* Whatever miracles had been pulled off, whatever sacrifices had bought those miracles, the blood would be destroyed when the convoy blew up in the blockaders' faces.

It was with heavy but shaking hands that he brought up the Eighth Array, grabbed the orbital data, recomputed the orbit, and nudged the 'tainers back on target, a circle a hundred fifty yards wide not half a mile from the station. It would be a "hard" landing, and there would be some loss, especially since the target area could not be cleared of all rocks. But it had been leveled and smoothed at one time, for use as a staging area when the station had been built. Most of the supplies would survive impact.

When Titus emerged, he found Abbot talking to a guard. He cut his conversation off and followed Titus. "You had the Array up, didn't you? Colby wouldn't let me in. Titus—"

He didn't break stride, the stolen board stiff and heavy in his lab coat pocket. "If you want to know what the auditors found, talk to Colby."

"Titus, you don't know what you're doing—"

"—and right now, I'm too tired to learn." Titus hit the lift call button and was shocked when a door opened before his nose. He slipped in and hit the door close before Abbot could follow. He left his father sputtering. *I can't believe I've got his transmitter and he never knew!* But Titus didn't even feel a sense of triumph. Abbot had seemed so haggard.

By the time the doors opened again, Titus felt the letdown of tension. Nothing would happen now for days with the 'tainers in freefall orbit.

He returned to his room, weary from the weight of the daylight outside and the cold knowledge that there would be no blood for him after all. Even Inea's squeal of delight as he showed her his plunder didn't raise his spirits.

Together, with a kind of solemn ceremony, they broke the board in a dozen pieces and stuffed some of them down the disposal. Titus felt like a traitor not telling her that he had the other transmitter intact, hidden in H'lim's room.

That night, despite everything Inea could do, not one drop of orl blood would stay down. Covered with cold sweat, Titus curled around his aching middle and huddled in one corner of the bed, struggling to breathe gently enough not to set off the perpetual dry heaves.

I could live. If I develop a string. He'd accepted this job with the knowledge it might become necessary, but the idea had never been real to him before. *I'm taking ectoplasm from Inea, and in this condition, I can't help her replace it. I can't go on like this.*

He hugged himself tighter and tried not to think. In a few moments, he'd get up and rig his wires around the bed so he could sleep. Presently, trickles of a seductive aroma invaded his sinuses. His throat melted open and surrounded the sweetness as if to swallow the nourishment.

No. Inea! Before he could move, she thrust a hard rim against his mouth and tilted it so the blood ran down his throat and he was forced to swallow. Fresh human blood. Her blood, still warm from her body, replete with her life, aching with her love. Shaking with the need for it, he tried to thrust it away, knowing there was no end to what he would do for more.

She pushed the glass back at his mouth, and he saw the tourniquet still around her arm, the clumsy mark where the needle had gone into the vein. "Drink, Titus, or it will go to waste."

He did. He couldn't help it. After a bit, he found himself sitting crosslegged, cradling the glass he'd licked clean and inhaling the aroma. It hadn't been enough. Would any amount be enough? "Abbot put you up to this."

"No. It was my own idea. H'lim told me it probably wouldn't be as addictive if I gave it to you in a glass."

"H'lim said that?" His eyes fixed on the tourniquet and he reached to release it.

"You can have more," she said, proffering the arm. She registered surprise, and maybe disappointment, when he only removed the tourniquet. "H'lim said maybe human blood would settle your digestion so you could accept some orl blood."

He coiled the tourniquet expertly around his hand and tied it. "Inea, you shouldn't have done it. One human can't support one of us, and I don't dare start with anyone else."

"Very soon, H'lim will have his booster ready."

"If that's no more successful than the orl blood, it will be worse than useless."

"The blockade can't last much longer, then your own supplies will be coming through."

"You don't understand. If you think my reaction to the orl blood is bad, wait until you see what the reconstituted blood will do to me after *this*." He gestured with the glass. On the other hand, he felt much better.

"H'lim said it wouldn't be as bad as if taken directly."

"He doesn't understand. It'll be bad enough."

Finally hurt by his rejection, she pulled away. "If I wanted gloom and doom I'd turn on a newscast."

"Then why don't you!" he snapped and instantly regretted it.

She whirled away and poked at the vidcom controls.

He set the glass aside, went up behind her and put his arms around her, pulling her suddenly pliant body against him. "I'm sorry. It helped. Obviously, it helped. H'lim's right, it does make a difference. The heart's electrical, you know. The impulses are perceptible in arterial blood. There's nothing quite like it, and nothing at all like the strength it gives—or the mad desire for more. I love you more than life itself, and I'd have drunk from you until you'd died if you'd forced that on me just then. You hit a reflex, Inea. Now that you know what power you have over me, I hope you'll exercise it with restraint."

She kept her eyes on the screen where the reporter was reading lists of battle casualties. "H'lim says the orl have a kind of power over the luren, too, but they're just animals and don't know how to use it. Titus, I'm not an animal. I won't hurt you. And I *know* despite what you think, that you won't hurt me. You're afraid you would, but I can't let that fear kill you—for nothing."

"I'm a long way from dying of hunger." *The feeding frenzy would come first. No, I can't chance that. I'll have to take drastic action long before that.* Since bodies would not be shipped back to Earth due to the quarantine, what he was contemplating meant a final death.

She twisted in his arms, locking her fingers behind his neck. "Titus, you didn't see yourself on that bed a few minutes ago. When I came over there, I thought you *had* died, that I'd lost you even though we finally defeated Abbot!"

He couldn't disillusion her about Abbot's defeat. "I understand why you did what you did, but I don't want you to do anything like that again. Inea, it could be dangerous for you. And—mutilated corpses are difficult to explain."

His brutal phrasing finally got through to her, but before she could answer, the ground shook with an ominous rumble that rolled through the complex. The screen sizzled and went dark. The lights flickered, then steadied, and in the distance there was a brief shrieking of a decompression alarm.

She clamped herself to him with a whimper as he reached to shift the screen's controls. Colby was on an internal channel, and the news was not good. ". . . landlines that control the Eighth Array have been cut, though the Array itself has not been damaged."

Colby betrayed none of the hope that the supplies would come in on target, that the decoy would deplete the blockaders' equipment when it blew up, and that W.S. would come out on top. She'd rather face despair on the station than risk a premature leak to the blockaders.

Courage. Human courage. Watching her, Titus felt his own courage revive and felt the line of kinship with humans that was so meaningful to Resident philosophy. "I think maybe you might be right, Inea, maybe—just maybe—I wouldn't hurt you. I don't want to try it, you understand, because it's too risky, but—"

"Just don't you dare try it with anyone else without telling me."

"I don't intend to try it at all. I just want you to know how much I love you, before I ask for more orl blood."

——— TWENTY-ONE ———

At least the Array is safe. Titus struggled awake against the syrupy drag of nightmare. *The Array is safe, but the probe is gone.* Already the memory of horror was fading, as it always did, though the dream itself lingered in images of being buried alive under scentless bodies that screamed and writhed in slow motion. The nightmare was shorter now, and he was waking up sooner, healing inside.

And, he realized, for the first time since the sun had come up, he'd wakened refreshed, without the urge to vomit vying with ravening hunger. Still, what Inea had done to him the previous night rankled.

Sitting up, he discovered she had gone, turning off his magnetic field generator so he'd be sure to wake up eventually. A note was flashing on his screen. Scratching absently, he bent to read it.

"Couldn't bear to wake you. I'm covering your shift with H'lim, and I've switched our gym appointments, too, so you take over from Abbot this evening. Don't forget your Medical at noon. Word has it there's some new treatment that takes an extra hour, so be early because you have the Department meeting right after that. Colby wants those reports this afternoon, too. I'm on K.P. this evening. See you around midnight."

"Whoever said life here would be dull and boring was flat out wrong," muttered Titus, knowing full well what the new medical treatment would involve. He wasn't worried about Inea. She wasn't under any Influence. The Mark she wore wouldn't show up, and the silencing would be evident only if they knew what questions to ask. But for him, it would be a challenge.

As he might have expected, Abbot was on top of things, though he looked ten years older than he had a month ago. Just outside Biomed, he took Titus into a lavatory. "I've programmed the instruments to read normally, but there's the problem of pupil dilation. Titus, we're going to have to help each other on this one."

"I can't control my pupil contractions! And what about the contact lenses?"

"They'll let you keep the lenses in. They don't *appear* tinted. They want you to see normally, but think their way. I've read their recording and I know the cues. If you'll let me, I can Influence your subconscious to provide the correct autonomic responses."

Titus recoiled. Abbot pressed, "I'll let you do it to me first. Titus, we don't have much time!"

He still doesn't know I got his transmitter out of the Array! Maybe Abbot hadn't been able to get back into the observatory yet. He might be assuming the loss of control of the Eighth had come *after* his message was sent, under cover of Titus' use of the Array. The Taurus window had been opening at the time, though Titus' message had gone outside that window, to Earth, not deep space. The instruments had not registered any antennas pointed wrong, nor had there been any abnormal power drain. Still . . . .

Titus assumed Abbot knew of the cargotainer project because he knew everything that went on. If Abbot thought that his message had gone out as planned, that he had summoned the aid he believed Earth's luren needed, despite human opposition to revealing Earth's location, and that his action remained undetected, then his offer of help in passing the medical could be genuine.

Even if Abbot thought he'd been defeated again, his offer of help ought to be genuine because he felt that the secret of Earth-luren's existence had to be kept at all costs, at least until the galactic luren arrived.

On the third hand, Abbot might know what Titus had taken from the console and be totally unfazed by the theft. He might already have another plan brewing, despite loss of the Eighth. In that case, Abbot's offer might be very dangerous.

What could he do to me besides plant physical reflex controls? The exploitation of Influence had never been an interest of Titus', but Abbot was an expert.

"Come on, Titus. This will take at least five minutes."

"All right. Show me what to do."

Abbot had a handheld that displayed the list of verbal cues the hypnotist would use juxtaposed against a list of the proper responses. It took Abbot several minutes to teach Titus how to direct the pencil of Influence to induce the effects. Then Titus had to treat and test Abbot, to be sure he'd gotten it right.

By then, Titus trusted Abbot's motives and submitted to him with some confidence. But he was late for his appointment, and subsequently late the rest of the day. Inea did come in just after midnight, but fell asleep over the orl blood she brought for him. He choked it down, and it stayed down producing only a slight queasiness that passed quickly.

The next few days, running late all the time, he had no chance to dwell on the impending arrival of the 'tainers, or even to speak to H'lim about his advising Inea. H'lim was constantly surrounded by the Cognitive or Biomed people, and Titus wondered how he could find a moment to work on the booster. The day before the scheduled arrival, Titus again overslept, tremendously relieved by the few ounces of her own blood Inea had surreptitiously mixed with his ration of orl blood. Even the resulting quarrel, and lack of sexual release, had not impaired his sleep. The sun was still up.

Waking to the groggy miasma of lunar daylight, Titus realized he felt better than he had in months, and the mirror confirmed the impression. Despite the effectiveness of Inea's treatment of him, his opinionated and willful woman had been given the worst advice in the galaxy, and, he decided, today was the day of reckoning. Tomorrow they might all be dead, or in the hands of the secessionists. But if they survived it all, he didn't want to go through the whole ordeal he'd faced after leaving Abbot. *If it's not too late already. Dear God, don't let it be too late already.*

When he arrived at H'lim's lab to relieve Inea, the guards let him through with a perfunctory warning that the security cameras were off.

Since Cognitive had tried to spy on H'lim's private hours, and he had caught them every time, Titus knew he could speak freely and somehow tell the luren to butt out.

Inside, Inea was seated on a tall stool leaning over the *Thizan* game board, looking tired but wholly absorbed. H'lim, welding mask over his dark glasses, was in the safety cage using an acetylene torch to mend a piece of glassware. His movements were deft, his concentration total, and a fog of absentminded Influence filled the room brighter than the torch fire.

Titus watched until H'lim had finished the delicate job and the subliminal throb of Influence had abated.

Inea looked up. "Titus. I thought you'd be late."

"I am."

She checked her watch. "Ha! I must have lost track of time! Well, it's only fifteen minutes. I forgive you."

Titus looked at H'lim, knowing the luren had, perhaps unconsciously, Influenced her attention to the gameboard. His objection died on his lips, however, because he was more astonished at the deep tremor of *violation* he felt, and the pure animal rage lurking below it. *Maybe it is too late.*

Inea came to his side, gripping his elbow. "Are you all right? You seemed better. . . . Look, I'm sorry I said all those really rotten things last night. Forgive me?"

Titus shrugged that off, eyes on H'lim. "It wasn't your fault." *Did he Influence her to do that to me?* He wouldn't be surprised if H'lim's touch slipped right through Biomed's anti-hypnotic conditioning and past him. But the thought of H'lim's Influence focused on Inea made his lips peel back from his clenched teeth. *He wouldn't violate my Mark!*

H'lim tilted back the welder's mask and scrutinized Titus. "Earth's luren are very different from the parent stock. Only in the last few days have I come to see just how different—and how uniquely valuable—Earth's mixed genetic stock is." His tone carried a note of apology that checked Titus' outrage, capturing his curiosity instead. "Last night, Titus, I discovered, *after* I spoke to Inea about what she had to do for you, that I'd overlooked something vital."

Titus' arm went around Inea's shoulders. "You only *spoke* to her?"

"I only *spoke* to her. You see, I thought the key fact was that a particular living orl provides its luren with a vital central nervous system stimulation, a personalized bioelectrical signature, that the luren may come to crave.

"From what Abbot said about you, I thought that's what you hadn't understood and so you were resisting a tie to Inea and sickening for lack of her blood. But I was wrong about your motives. I can see that now, in what's happening between you—and in your outrage about it. You knew very well what would happen, and had set yourself to avoid it. What I still don't understand is why."

"Orl are animals. You don't have to wait for their consent to have your way with them. And you don't have to deal with having consent withheld or delayed. You don't have to worry about overtaxing them because they're replaceable. And you don't have to contend with your own guilt if they break your patience and your hunger rules you."

"Ah. Well, consider this. A luren's own signature changes, attunes to his herd—uh, string, as you say. It's like Mirelle's kinesics, only more so. That mutual attunement is what makes our Marks so much stronger than yours, and so inviolable, not sheer power of Influence, as Abbot assumed, and not the power of Blood Law. The mutuality of the orl tie between human and Earth-luren, *should* solve the consent problem."

Suddenly, a covetous note beneath H'lim's scientific tone jarred Titus into associating a dozen things H'lim had said and done. *There's some kind of stiff penalty for a luren who takes blood from a human, and that taboo makes luren crave humans even if the blood isn't compatible.* It fit. H'lim had refused Abbot's stringer in favor of cloned human blood because he wanted to go home, and they had some way to tell if he'd used a human as an orl. *Must have been a letdown to find human blood so vile, but he's still wondering what it could be like.*

Inea tugged at his sleeve. "He explained it all to me, Titus. With Earth's luren, the ability to make the orl-tie is vestigial. But you and I, Titus, we have it. I *know* we do." Her eyes shone. "I'm going to make it as beautiful for you as you've made sex for me."

He hugged her closer. "I don't care what you call it, Inea it's not a healthy thing. I'm going to break it. I'm not going to take your blood again. Not ever."

"Titus," said H'lim, "your fears are groundless. One never harms an orl one is tied to."

"A *luren* doesn't harm such an *orl,* perhaps, but you've a lot to learn about humans and Earth's luren." Titus remembered all too well how he'd felt about the humans he'd fed on and then killed. They'd even enjoyed it.

"Why are you holding her like that?"

Titus jerked away. Inea nestled closer and he froze, aware of his need to *possess* having gone far beyond the normal sexual need of a male. Just holding her, he was soaking ectoplasm from her.

"You see, that's what I missed! I never saw you two, only Abbot and Mirelle, and there's no tie there, despite his practices. But when Inea told me how ill you'd get on orl blood, even after I'd filtered out the irritating component, I realized what brain site that component stimulated—the vestigial orl-tie site! You were sick because you resisted the natural completion of that tie. But what I didn't grasp is that this isn't exactly the same as an orl-tie. You see, Abbot was instantly and repeatedly sick because his brain receptors differ from yours, so his nutritional absorption is different, and so he reacted to other trace chemicals as well as the absence of various human blood components."

H'lim interpolated, "I don't think Abbot can survive on cloned blood. The differences between the Residents and the Tourists may be physiological, not philosophical."

I hope not! thought Titus, clutching Inea. If so, it would come to a war of extermination when it was discovered there was no way to persuade the Tourists to stop killing humans. "Abbot's been controlling his appetite."

"At a terrible cost," agreed H'lim, pacing back and forth, warming to his topic. "I wish I knew enough math!"

"Surely, *I* know enough math! You got it all from my mind."

"Just words I don't have the concepts for!" Waving his hand in a gesture Titus recognized from a favorite physics professor he'd had for three courses, H'lim continued, "The difference between what you and Inea have and an orl-tie must be at the ectoplasmic/ Influential interface." He wagged a slender white finger at Inea. "If you knew *how*, you could augment Titus' power to Influence! No orl could ever do *that!* But I'd wager it can't be done to a genetically purebred luren.

"Even without access to my library, I swear there's nothing else like it anywhere. But there really isn't so much on the genetics of consciousness or the conservation of volition—"

Genetics of consciousness? Sometimes H'lim put words together grammatically and still uttered nonsense. As usual when that happened, he lapsed into luren terms. This time, as he paced back and forth, his lecture sounded like a physics lesson on the relationship between space and time, conscious will, metaphorical vision, and the life force. At the same time he seemed to be talking about the evolution of human brain chemistry as the result of the "genetics of volition." He mixed up orl-tying with ectoplasm absorption and cross-linked them to Influence, but Titus only understood every third word, and missed half the tenses. *He can't be saying that all of Earth's biology is the product of genetic engineering, that the nature of human brain chemistry was* done *to* us!

"Which is of course," concluded H'lim, "why human stringers having sex with each other is insufficient to replenish the human, and the luren must service his string."

"Of course," said Titus dazedly in the luren language, glad Inea didn't know a word of it. How could he ask all the questions surging into his mind?

H'lim came out of his creative reverie, and reverted to English. "So now you understand, Titus, why you don't have to be afraid. She can defend herself handily."

"Against what?" asked Inea blankly.

"Against Titus."

"Why would I want to do that?"

"Or against Abbot, or any Earth luren." He shrugged.

Titus interrupted, "H'lim, you're a galactic-class geneticist, not an Aikido instructor. She may have the genetic potential, but she doesn't know how to use it and there's no teacher. Besides, I don't attack people I love, and that's that. I won't take any more of her blood."

"That's beside the point. Don't you see, this means Earth might become the richest planet in the galaxy! What we have here is genetic coding for enhancing—oh, I don't know your terms! Just take my word for it, this could be the key to a giant leap forward in space-faring technology. It's so basic, it could solve the biggest riddle in the galaxy. But even if we can't work out the applications immediately, it's sure to win the w—" He broke off to stare into infinity.

"Sure to what?" prompted Titus. His mind was spinning. He'd just gotten more information out of H'lim in the last ten minutes than he had in the previous ten days, but he felt less informed than at the moment he'd fathered the alien.

H'lim is an ambitious adventurer who is working everything out as he goes along. But that assessment told him nothing except what he'd already known. He didn't dare trust H'lim's word that it was safe to send his message. It was a good thing that he'd pulled out Abbot's Array transmitter.

"Never mind," shrugged H'lim. "There's something so hauntingly familiar about this genetic algorithm, or maybe it's just some random association it keeps triggering off when I try to translate human/Earth luren gene structure into other notation systems. I *know* I've never seen anything like this before, and yet . . . Well, perhaps it's a word you gave me that I don't have a concept for, or some Earth-evolved redefinition of one of your luren words." He paced away.

"None of that matters, Titus. One thing is straightforward." From the refrigerator he extracted a flask of clear purple fluid labeled only with a strange luren symbol. "Finally, it's ready for testing! Considering what I've just learned about your biochemistry, it ought to work on the humans and you, maybe on Abbot, too, if he'll try it."

Inea cried, "We've *made* it! We've won!"

In her jubilation she spun Titus around in a low-grav dance.

Titus stopped her. "H'lim, your message didn't go out as Abbot planned. I've destroyed the transmitter he embedded in the Eighth."

"Because of what I told Inea to do for you?"

"No. Before that." He eyed the purple fluid. "You don't owe me any more help."

H'lim leaned against the refrigerator as if he needed the support. He swirled the flask thoughtfully. "I didn't make this to bribe you into betraying your oath and your conscience. I *knew* you opposed Abbot, and I didn't expect you to change your mind. I just hoped he might win—not an absurd hope since he's your First Father, but by no means a certainty. My filial duty does not derive from my chance of getting home, but only from the renewal of my life."

The ache of dashed hopes was plain enough as H'lim added, "I'm ready to test this whenever you are. I need a volunteer, but we must go carefully. I don't want a repeat of the orl blood disaster if I've missed something else."

"I volunteer," said Inea. When Titus strangled on his objection, she added, "Titus, he's already tested it on human bone marrow the surgeons supplied and it increased blood production. It'd be a big to-do to get bone marrow from you or Abbot without anyone knowing, so test it on me first!"

"It doesn't make sense to risk the life of someone whose life isn't at risk to begin with," argued Titus. "If you had a bad reaction, how could we explain it to Biomed? Abbot's a genius at covering for us, but they're getting awfully close." Abbot's method of coping with the new anti-hypnotic conditioning had been pure desperation and Titus knew it.

Abruptly, H'lim shoved the flask into the refrigerator. Titus didn't like the thoughtful frown that flickered across Inea's features. He'd seen that look before and it made him very nervous. But before he could say anything, H'lim announced, "Someone's coming." He turned on the recorders just as Colby arrived at the head of an entourage.

As she introduced the engineers and physicists who hadn't met H'lim before, Inea left the luren in Titus' care saying, "I have to log some gym time or Biomed will be all over me. I skipped yesterday, and skimped the day before."

Titus had no chance to reply because everyone was talking to him, as if he had to translate to make H'lim understand what they wanted of him. He held up his hands for silence, then said, "Ladies and Gentlemen, may I present Dr. Sa'ar, H'lim." Feeling a bit foolish, he turned to H'lim. "I never have discovered which name actually comes first, family or given."

H'lim laughed, breaking the ice easily. "Actually, neither, but the rest of my designation is irrelevant. My family name is Sa'ar, my given name H'lim, and you may use them as you see fit."

With that said, they began "Dr. Sa'ar-ing" him from every direction on topics ranging from computer conventions to *Kylyd's* drive assembly and power plant.

Colby shouted the babble down. "We came here, H'lim, to take you on your oft requested and oft promised tour of your ship." With that, someone walked a spacesuit forward that had H. SA'AR stenciled on the helmet.

"Now?!" exclaimed H'lim glancing at Titus in a panic.

Shit! It's daylight out there!

"I doubt there's any danger of us being bombed today," said Colby. "I regret we've put it off this long, but your suit has just been finished. The outcome of the war may end our investigations, and though your lab work promises to change minds back on Earth, still we mustn't overlook the chance that you may know something about the ship that will trigger even more impressive advances."

"Impressive advances," repeated H'lim, circling a workbench and nervously repositioning glassware. "Here in this lab, I know what I'm doing. I won't accidentally provide you with some bit of technology you can't yet control. But the ship—Dr. Colby, that's not my field. Some offhand remark could do your civilization a great deal of damage."

"You won't come?" asked someone in the back.

"I will go," answered H'lim gravely. "For my own reasons, I must. I'd prefer to explore *Kylyd* in solitude, but I understand that is not to be. Therefore, I'll go." He tapped a used Petri dish on the bench, frowning at it. Someone had cleaned pizza crumbs off the bench into it.

Titus could almost see the thoughts churning in H'lim's mind. For the first time, he no longer cherished hope of escape and riches. Titus had won. Abbot's message had not gone and, with the probe destroyed, neither had the humans'. "I'll answer your questions, but only to satisfy your curiosity, without providing any 'impressive advances.' At least I hope I shall not destroy my generous hosts."

He snapped the dish down onto the hard surface and strode out the door. As they all crowded out of the lab, Colby edged over to Titus who was wrestling with his own whirling emotions. "Have you any idea where Abbot's gone? He was supposed to meet us here. I've left messages for him everywhere, but nobody's seen him in hours."

Oh, no, now what? "You tried my lab?"

"Several times.

"Maybe he's in *Kylyd* and plans to meet us there?"

"Maybe, but it's not like him to just disappear."

Titus grunted noncommittally. He didn't even have time to drop Inea a message warning her that Abbot was up to something new. As H'lim's trusted escort, he had to hurry to catch up. *Maybe it's a false alarm. Maybe Abbot's sleeping.*

On the way to the locker room, Colby walked beside H'lim, assuring him of the various protective features Biomed had designed for his suit. When they'd all dressed, she led the way back to Biomed, saying, "Protection or no, we won't make you face the direct sunlight."

As soon as they emerged from the airlock into the connection tube to *Kylyd,* H'lim's knees sagged, and he eyed the flimsy material around them with distrust. Titus, too, felt the drag of the sun like the impact of the noise of an unshielded jet engine. When they reached *Kylyd's* hull, the luren leaned against the bulkhead and closed his eyes, taking attention away from Titus as they both recovered.

Seeing the alien wilt, everyone spoke at once. "Are you all right?" "My God, if we've hurt him. . . ." "It can't be ultraviolet this time." "He's sensitive to magnetics, remember?" "Hardly any flux out there." "Less in here, by Dearman's measurements." "What about particles? This hull stops everything—maybe even neutrinos. Has anybody measured . . . ?" "Quiet!"

That last was Colby's voice. Titus stiffened his knees and moved up beside H'lim. "Better now?" he asked the luren, only then noticing the single Cognitive representative, who had a camera trained steadily on H'lim.

"I wish I could stay in here." H'lim's voice gained strength and he finally stood away from the wall and looked around as if to get his bearings.

This corridor was distorted and crumpled in spots, but had been cleared, leaving gaping holes in the walls. H'lim scanned a wall, muttered something about human lights in the luren tongue, then led off with purposeful strides. Titus, squinting at the spot where the luren had stared, imagined he saw some dim variations in the paint that might have been symbols. There might be spectral studies of the interior on file by now, but Titus hadn't had time to look them up.

And suddenly, he was more excited than he'd been since he was a boy. H'lim was finally in a mood to reveal the very things Titus had always wanted to know. But more, he might well give away the secrets Titus had been digging for—how both Earth's peoples would be regarded in the galaxy.

As escort, Titus had the privilege of clinging to H'lim's elbow, catching every gesture, every prolonged look, and he intended to make the most of it.

Trooping after H'lim, the humans jockeyed for position, vying for attention. Finally one physicist won out, a gruff-voiced barrel of a man with a slight limp even under lunar gravity. "You handle that suit as if you know what you're doing," the physicist observed, "but this ship didn't carry a full complement of vacuum suits. Nor does it have escape pods. Is that the height of arrogance, the depths of depravity, or simply bad design?"

Amused, H'lim answered, "Try flawless workmanship."

"Ah, but you crashed. Not so flawless."

"It's an old ship," answered H'lim.

"Ah, broken down, then."

"Oh, no. It was flawlessly designed for conditions other than encountered."

"And what conditions were encountered?"

"You've got me there." H'lim's command of idioms Titus seldom used had grown rapidly. He seemed to have mastered English, but that, Titus reminded himself, was an illusion.

H'lim led them to what had been identified as a crew dormitory—until they'd discovered that orl were animals. "You've cleaned up in here."

"I've told you," said Colby, "that we've saved every shred of orl tissue we found. Most of it was in here and the adjacent room. You've seen what explosive decompression did to the tissues."

The room had been twisted off-true only a little. H'lim toured the place, touching wall fixtures and the fittings where bed frames had been stapled to the floor, lingering wistfully at the broken lighting panels.

Someone noticed, and prompted, "Perhaps with a little more data, we could duplicate those lighting panels."

H'lim shook his head. "If I knew how to make them, I'd have made some by now." Then he led the way on a whirlwind tour through the rest of the ship, identifying for them the captain's office, the crew's quarters, the orl feed lockers, the water recycling plant, the air scrubbers, and the room where he'd been found, which had retained some pressure.

"I was preparing to—dine," he explained delicately. Titus hung on H'lim's every word, but his eyes roved down each cross corridor seeking Abbot, worrying about what his father was up to now. Had he discovered his transmitter missing? If so, how long ago? Was there any way to get word to Inea? He saw the opening where Brink's had their security checkpost. It had a line into the station. He toyed with the idea of cutting away just for a moment to leave Inea a message that it wasn't all over yet.

Remembering the look on her face when H'lim had put the purple fluid, the precious booster, away, he took a few steps, but Colby called him back. "This way, Titus!"

291

Nearby was H'lim's living quarters. Inside, he opened wall panels nobody had suspected existed, found a dead computer terminal, shook out some liquid containers long since boiled empty, collected a set of grooming tools, a couple of suits of clothes, and the rest of the pieces to his *Thizan* set, stuffed it all into a small bag and presented it to Colby. "Do I have to beg or fight to keep these?"

"Neither, but I suspect someone will ask to examine them." She gestured to the open compartments. "Is the whole ship equipped with these?"

"I suppose, though I doubt they'll open the way the ship's frame is twisted. And don't ask me where they are, what they have in them, or how they ought to open. I was just a passenger. I actually didn't expect these to open."

She hefted the bag. "You do travel light."

"One learns."

"Mass limits?" asked someone eagerly.

"No. Regardless of what has been dragged along, it's never what's needed. Much simpler to acquire items appropriate to the local conditions."

A woman at the rear laughed ruefully.

When asked about the still minimally operational work stations along the central corridor, H'lim said, "They have to do with running the ship, but I don't know how to operate them." Having seen how quickly H'lim picked up the station's programs, Titus thought the luren might figure these out, if he wanted to. Abbot had broken into some of the ship's systems that Cognitive and Technical didn't know about.

They came to an intersection where H'lim swung right, and Titus stopped him. "There's a gap in the hull and the sun's coming from that direction."

"Let's go down this way," suggested someone, "and we can circle back to Biomed without going outside." She led the way confidently down into the nearly flattened underside of the ship. Titus recognized her as an engineer who'd been studying the propulsion system, and his interest quickened. Though he hadn't revealed anything important so far, H'lim was more helpful now than he'd ever been. *Or*—Titus stopped dead in his tracks, then shuffled forward as people pressed up behind him. *No, he couldn't be creating a diversion for Abbot.* On the other hand, Abbot might have arranged the timing of this tour to get Titus out of his way.

Titus squeezed back beside Colby and made small talk while he inspected her for any trace of Abbot's renewed Influence. "Do you really think," he asked her, "that our study of this ship will be stopped when the war is over?"

Since the suitphones were all on the same channel, everyone listened to Colby. "Even if the W.S. wins, public support for our work may have dwindled by appropriations time. It's important that we come up with results very soon."

"I heard," said someone else, "that W.S. might just fold up, in order to stop the war. It could easily just scratch the whole program, and then the secessionists' organization would fall apart leaving W.S. in power as always. After all, with the probe gone, what's to fight about really?"

"Us," said a woman with Brink's markings on her suit and an Australian accent. "The secessionists think we're a plague station even though there hasn't been so much as a cold here in months. Even if we could build duplicates of this ship and fly them, we wouldn't be accepted again on Earth."

"We don't need your gloom-and-doom, Irena. We may never drum up enough support for the probe again, but this station will be operating long after we die of old age."

"Yeah. *Here*"

"Game's not over 'til it's over," said a Thai accent.

Colby cut in, "That's the spirit. Watch your heads, everyone!" They had to duck low and scramble down a newly cut makeshift ramp.

The lower area was a maze of squashed and buckled corridors propped up by stanchions where the lower hull had been torn away and they'd had to excavate into the lunar rock to create a walkway. As he went, Titus became convinced that Colby had not been Influenced by Abbot recently, except to smooth over some of the memories Abbot wanted to stay buried. Dangerous but not reckless.

Still, Abbot could have controlled the timing of this jaunt simply by delaying completion of H'lim's suit.

H'lim stopped to examine an area where the broken hull was curled and buckled. The woman who led them had to stop him from touching the torn metal. "It could cut suit fabric."

H'lim looked at his gloved hand with trepidation and Titus could see his opinion of humans' vacuum suits plummet. Oblivious of this, the engineer commented, "You know, the pilot of this ship should be decorated, even if posthumously. He almost made a soft landing, dead stick and all. And there was no subsequent explosion."

Titus had asked H'lim about the absence of explosion before, recounting the story of his ancestors' arrival, and H'lim had told him there were older ships than *Kylyd* still in service, not very well-built ones that did carry escape pods and vacuum suits because they had a lamentable tendency to explode. As far as Titus had been able to gather, newer ships, ships built within the last century or so, also carried more safety equipment, for some obscure reason.

H'lim ignored the engineer's bait and corrected, "She."

"What?"

"The pilot. She."

"Did you know her?"

"No."

"Did you know you were about to crash?"

"No. Else why would I have been—dining."

"But the ship's approach was long and slow enough."

H'lim repeated the answer he'd always given Cognitive. "I understood they intended to orbit—a star or a planet, I'm not sure—recalculate our position, and proceed to our scheduled destination. We were *lost,* not broken down. Nobody aboard expected the disaster."

"That seems clear from the evidence," said someone.

A little farther on, the engineer squatted before a wide but low opening that had been cut, Titus was sure, by Gold's magnetic shears. The room beyond was several feet lower than the corridor floor but there were no steps. There were some lumpy casings strewn about inside.

"This is one of the things that's puzzled us," said the engineer. "Have you any idea what this room was for?"

He peered inside. "I think you know very well, young lady, what a power plant looks like."

She flashed a grin from ear to ear. "Well, that's what we *thought,* but we weren't sure." She stood up, aborting a dust-off gesture, as she added pleasantly, "It wasn't the only power plant, though. It's barely adequate to handle the environment and internal power requirements. And we've never found any fuel. What *does* fuel this ship, anyway?"

As always with that question, H'lim answered, "I don't know. It's not my field."

"But everybody knows what fuels airplanes!"

"Of course. They call it jet fuel." H'lim could be maddening when he wanted to be. But this time, he relented. "Actually, I don't know what this particular ship used for fuel. Almost anything you can name is used by someone. If we were carrying anything dangerous, it was likely discarded in a stellar dump when the crash became inevitable. They don't tell passengers about fuel dumps. Tends to upset us."

Mollified, the engineer grunted, "I see," then led them off down a slope toward the rear section of the ship.

"Oddly enough," she lectured, "this is where we found the only intact lighting panel." Titus remembered the room, but much more radical dissection had been done on everything in it, walls and floors included. "Possibly another power plant was in here, but the two plants couldn't have driven this ship—certainly not anywhere near lightspeed."

"I've never been in this area before," said H'lim.

"Step carefully," she warned, leading them through the grid pattern of the debris, "and I'll show you something we found back here that's got us really stumped."

In a far wall, a hatch stood open. It was thick, like a bank vault's door. They had cut the cowling out of the wall and jacked the whole thing aside. "We thought the ship might blow up when we did this. That door—and this wall—seem to be the most heavily insulated. But even here, the seams were sprung and there was no radiation leakage."

She paused, faceplate swinging toward H'lim, who made no comment. Titus thought he was reading the labels on or around the door. Politely, the luren looked over the engineer's shoulder and Titus edged around to see too.

It was a large, totally empty room, with a fantastical floor that might have come from a sultan's palace. Precious metals and colored stones which had to be gems were patterned around a large, dark area in the middle of the floor. The dark area was gold-rimmed, and the rim was marked like the points of a compass.

"Now *logic*," said the engineer, "dictates that this must be the interstellar drive. The walls and floor are thick, the floor is overlaid with heavy metals and stone like marble and granite and nobody knows what all else in tiny chips. Mass wise, this room accounts for almost a third of the mass of the entire ship. You don't carry something like that around unless it's useful, and the only use that could justify it would be power-generation. But the room's hardly damaged, and I don't see any drive, just a ruddy dance floor! Or is it just a dance floor?"

"No," answered H'lim.

"A temple?" asked Cognitive's photographer.

"No. Were there any bodies found in here?"

"What would it mean if there were?"

"Not a whole lot. But I knew the people who worked in here. I'd like to know what happened to them."

With shame in her voice, the engineer told him, "No, there weren't any bodies. Would they normally work with the door locked?"

"Of course."

"Then you know what they did in here?"

"Of course not. Astrogation is a very tight union, and besides the math is way too difficult for me. Only those who enter the pool ever learn it, and *that* naturally is a very private business." He said this as if it made perfect sense.

"Astrogation?" The engineer latched onto the word. "This is a guidance center? Then where are the computers?"

"Oh, that kind of math is too hard for computers."

Titus was holding his breath, afraid his respirator would drown out H'lim's soft voice, reminding himself that H'lim, for the first time, felt stuck here and obliged to make long-term accommodations. He wouldn't by lying, or even kidding. But he couldn't be serious. Unaware of the effect his words had on the scientific minds around him, H'lim added in genuine relief, "But at least there were no bodies. They must have gotten out." There was an odd tone in his voice.

"And left the door locked? From the inside?"

He examined the door mechanism, everyone crowding back out of his way. "Yes, it does appear to have been locked from the inside. Good." He *sounded* serious.

Suddenly the engineer threw her head back and laughed. "Oh, you almost had me!" she gasped. "That's *good*, Dr. Sa'ar, that's *very* good!"

Others joined in as they realized that H'lim had to be joking. There was no way out of the bare room with the bank vault walls. And what sort of math could a living person do that would be too much for a computer?

At length, the chuckles died down, and the engineer said, "Well, you did warn us that you wouldn't answer all our questions. But now this room is going to get more attention than you'd ever believe. Dr. Shiddehara, if this is astrogation, not the interstellar drive room, it's in your department. Would you care to ask some questions? Perhaps walk inside? The designs could be a map of some sort. We've made records of them, of course, for study after we tear up the floor. But it's not the same as the real thing." Over her shoulder, she said to a colleague, "Martha, the computers have to be under that floor, and the central area must be the display tank. It just can't *be* any other way."

"Lack of imagination will prevent you from solving the puzzle," warned H'lim. "It *is* another way. You won't find any computers or other equipment inside that room. That's the reason the walls are insulated—for *silence.*"

As H'lim gestured for the engineer to precede him into the room, Titus thought the luren was finally giving them something new, but the other engineer, Martha, said, "So! I win! It is insulation for the luren senses. But why, if it's not a temple?"

"Not luren senses," corrected H'lim. Then in an odd tone, he added, "There are no luren astrogators, at least not yet." He paused at the door and looked back at Titus with that same distant gaze he'd had in the lab a while ago, speculating, weighing, looking into a distant future while simultaneously groping for something only dimly remembered.

And he did say that a genetic code could be the key to a giant leap forward in space-faring technology. For the first time, Titus recalled how H'lim had lumped the study of the relationship of space to time in with human will, vision, and the life force. By "life force" he might have meant genetic code. Genetic codes and space technology.

And he remembered the time when H'lim had dealt with the pain of a woman's broken bones and explained that Earth's customary divisions of disciplines were not his own. *In that kind of a science, could astrogation and interstellar drive be one and the same thing?*

Unbearably excited, Titus stepped up to the threshold to stand at H'lim's side. He felt the subtle resistance of a mild threshold effect, something like a hotel room, and recalled all his attempts to prove mathematically that Influence could not exist. Yet it did.

"H'lim," he asked, "why would the room be insulated like this, if luren don't use it?" He was almost afraid of the answer.

"I really don't know. I told you, Astrogation is a very tight union."

"Well, come on in," said the engineer, "and tell us what you can of all this. Please."

H'lim gracefully stepped across the threshold. "Come, Titus, you may want to look this over." To the engineer and everyone else, he said, "I don't know how astrogation is done, but I can guess that from the time the collision course with your moon was known, they must have been in here trying to alter our course to prevent the crash. They must have been the first to know that our situation was hopeless."

"And they would have bailed out?"

From the tilt of H'lim's body, Titus thought the luren was struggling with the idiom. Since H'lim hadn't had time to look at any fiction, it was small wonder he'd never heard the term. "To abandon ship," supplied Titus.

"Ah! Yes, I suppose they would have tried. I can only hope they succeeded. Just hope. Please believe me, I know nothing about the exercise of their skills, or the way they use this room. Such matters are a specialty for the talented and trained. I couldn't begin to assess their chances of getting out alive. I can only hope they did."

Talented. Genes reveal talent?

"And if they did survive," prompted Titus, "they'll send help for you."

"No. *If* they survived, they'd assume total destruction." He gestured at the ship. "Hardly an unwarranted assumption."

"I hate to be a killjoy," said the engineer, "but except for the door which was locked from the inside, there's no way out of this room."

"Not at the moment, no."

Ah! "So the motion of the ship through the galactic fields creates something in this room—a vortex, an anomaly, a singularity which interfaces with—what?" For that moment, Titus forgot about Abbot, messages, threat of exposure to humans, and Inea's diabolical self-determination. He felt tremendously *alive* for the first time since the takeoff from Quito.

Disjointed. Our science is disjointed! Little bits and pieces of comments and allusions H'lim had made coalesced. "A pool," said Titus aloud. "You said a pool must be entered to learn this variety of math. A singularity might look like a pool." He was standing on the black glass at the center of the design. He tapped one foot. "This looks like a pool! It makes some kind of a spacewarp, doesn't it?"

H'lim was utterly still, his boots no longer scuffing at the mosaic. Even the susurration of everyone else breathing vanished as they waited.

"Spacewarp?" asked H'lim.

The word was part of Titus' vocabulary, but mentally filed under "fantasy" along with everything else he knew about philosophy, psychology, Tarot, palmistry, and dream interpretation—unreal and therefore unimportant. *Mysticism.* He had dismissed the most important clue H'lim had given him as mysticism, not physics.

It's real. It's not mysticism, it's real. They can really make spacewarps — maybe wormholes? It was the simplest explanation for everything they had found—and not found—on this ship.

"Explain it to him, Titus," said one of the engineers, and Titus could hear the suppressed chuckle.

"I'm sorry, H'lim." Titus sketched a definition, stumbling embarrassedly as he gave his sources.

"*Science* fiction? And I thought science training knocked all the imagination out of humans."

They were all breathing again, but softly, tentatively. Titus replied, "Oh, we still dream, even as adults."

With intense, searching curiosity, H'lim asked, "What do you dream of achieving, Titus? Travel among the stars you study?" His tone made it a personal, private moment, almost as if he were seriously offering Titus the stars.

Titus answered with bald honesty, "Yes. Every night."

H'lim took a step closer, and Titus could make out his pale features behind the helmet. "Every night?" he demanded with a peculiar intensity.

"Every night when I can sleep, anyway. *Tell* me, H'lim, how does this thing work?"

H'lim retreated two steps, and Titus thought he could make out the negative movement of his head as he brushed the plea aside, his concentration focused elsewhere. "I don't know, Titus. That's the truth. I don't know."

In jerky stages, H'lim's left hand went to the top of his helmet, as if absently trying to touch his forehead. The glove remained suspended there. Titus sensed aborted surges of Influence, as if the luren were choking down a fear/fight/flight response as he muttered, "Dreams," as if tasting the word's nuances for the first time. "Not aspirations or ideals. Something else entirely, some other biochemical function of consciousness."

Titus offered, "Dreaming is the healthy way the human mind has of editing and organizing memories of the day's events, and is psychologically vital to human health."

Titus expected that was enough to dredge up all of the untapped associations lurking at the back of H'lim's mind where Titus' vocabulary was stored. It usually didn't take very much to bring a word up into active use for the luren, but now Titus understood better what blocked the luren's comprehension. Earth's languages carved the universe up into chunks of very different sizes and shapes than the galactic languages. *The genetics of consciousness.* Earth's physics talked of conserving momentum, mass and energy, not volition.

Before Titus could pursue that thought, H'lim dropped his hand, muttering in the luren language, "So *that's* what Abbot meant." The room filled with a beat of Influence that built from shock, to dismay, and edged into panic. Titus gathered his own power. Knowing he couldn't protect the humans if H'lim were to seize them as he had when he first woke, Titus focused narrowly on H'lim and spoke with all his own power, "H'lim!"

Somewhat to Titus' surprise, it worked. The bright throb of Influence vanished and the luren turned to look at the cluster of humans by the door. "I'm sorry," he began, then turned back to Titus, who was still standing on the black area of the floor. He seemed to realize the humans had never been aware that he'd violated his word and invoked Influence. "Uh. I've just had a sudden insight. I've got to get back to the lab." He started for the door. "Titus? Can you hurry?" He chattered to the scientists as he sidled through the crush. "You know how it is when you're stumped and you take your mind off the problem. Besides, we were finished out here anyway."

The crowd parted, and Titus caught up with H'lim, casting his own apologies about him as he went.

—— TWENTY-TWO ——

"*What* did Abbot mean?" demanded Titus when the two of them were momentarily alone in the airlock.

"Later, Titus." There was still panic in H'lim's voice, and the aura of Influence he held tightly about himself was like a clenched fist, white-knuckled and trembling. Titus had never felt anything like it. Two feet away, it wasn't perceptible, not even after they'd shed their suits.

Emerging from the Biomed section, through security and into the main corridors, H'lim turned the wrong way. Titus caught up with him. "Lab's that way," he offered.

"I *know* that!"

Stung, Titus fell silent. He'd never heard annoyance in H'lim's tone before, nor had he ever imagined a tone that conveyed both annoyance and fear. The two of them almost outdistanced the four Brink's guards.

At his apartment, H'lim opened the door and paused while the guards glanced inside, hands on their weapons. H'lim never allowed the Brink's people in, and had proved many times that he could detect unauthorized intrusion, so it was just a ritual. While waiting, H'lim said, "Titus, I didn't mean to snap at you. I've got something on my mind I have to think about, and then I'll want to talk to you. I'll call you."

One of the hardest things Titus had ever done was to reply casually, "All right. Abbot comes on duty in a couple of hours. Meanwhile, I'll be in the gym if you want me." In his mind, he was already preparing a list of questions he was going to demand answers to. And he meant demand. This time he wasn't going to be put off, no matter what. H'lim owed him.

H'lim went inside, pausing on the threshold for a moment as if puzzled, but closing the door gently behind himself and not looking back. Titus stood between the guards, rubbing the back of his neck and shaking his head.

One of the guards offered, "You didn't do anything. He probably just realized he'd been wrong about an equation or such and he's feeling like an asshole."

"That's the impression you got?" asked Titus.

"Scientists are always confident, then crushed. Then they get mad at having been wrong and snarl at everyone."

"Really?"

"Shut up, Sid. *Dr. Shiddehara* isn't like that."

Titus grinned. "Thank you."

"I was going to say," said Sid, "you're not like that."

Titus waved a hand. "I haven't been wrong about this job yet. Between the breakdowns, the theft, the war, and the haste, I haven't had a chance to do the job right!"

H'lim's door opened partway and the luren stuck his head out. "Titus. Come in. I need to talk to you."

Inside, Titus sensed what had disturbed H'lim at his threshold, the odor of human blood—and something else.

"Brace yourself." He led Titus to the bathroom.

Blood.

The walls, the floor, but mostly the shower stall were covered in blood, puddled, smeared, congealed, blackened, and reeking. Holding his breath, H'lim opened the shower door and Titus staggered back.

An arm clad in a black peignoir sleeve oozed fresh gore from the detached surface of its shoulder. Some legs and a head were stacked on a female torso.

Mirelle!

Titus felt his lips curling and trembling as they shaped her name and the word, "dead." His gorge rose, and all at once he recognized the other odor. H'lim's vomit.

Helplessly, he gestured for the luren to close the door, and backed out of the cubicle. H'lim shut the bathroom door. They stood, breathing hard, looking at each other. Titus barely recognized his own face reflected in H'lim's goggles.

"It was Abbot," said the luren. "She was dead when he brought her here." He indicated the clean floor. "But not bleeding. He wants people to believe I did that. I don't know what to do. Titus, you've got to help me."

Dead humans don't bleed like that. "Why would he want you accused of—*this?*"

"He's deduced that once I discover that humans—and worse yet, Earth's luren—*dream,* I will do everything in my power to prevent him from sending any message—especially not with your targeting data, and emphatically not with *my* too explicit message coupled to *this* planet's position!"

Titus' mind gibbered, *Do something. Anything. Fast!* He groped for the logic that had to be here, somewhere. "But you were on *Kylyd* when this was done. You can't be blamed."

"Do you think facts will override panic? You know humans, Titus." He paced a small circle. "They'll say I fed from her directly. Abbot knows Andre Mihelich discovered the similarity between natural luren enzymes and those of some leeches—hirudin, hementin, orgalase. . . ." As H'lim's fear grew, he lost the human body language and became truly alien. "Andre dubbed mine orgalentin and wrecked three Sepracor membrane reactors to grow a batch to keep the orl blood fresh. If Abbot stole it and injected it into Mirelle, it could have killed her and made her body a storage sack! That would account for the excessive bleeding after death—no clotting for hours, maybe days, without exposure to air."

Abbot's frames stick. He probably framed H'lim for the enzyme theft, too. "We've got to think. What would he expect you to do when you found the body? That's what we must not do. This is not at all like

Abbot—not in a closed community where he can't change identities and disappear. What's driven him to this? What's his objective?"

"That's easy," said H'lim and went to the disused kitchen cabinet where Titus had hidden the transmitter. He brought out the casserole and removed the lid, displaying its emptiness. "Yes, I thought so. Somehow, he's planning to send that damn message anyway!"

Titus blinked. He'd never heard H'lim swear before. "How did you know about Abbot's probe transmitter being in there?"

"You left your spoor all through this room when you hid it. All I had to do was follow it to discover what you'd planted."

I thought I was so clever. He lets me in all the time. How could he tell that one time from all the others? But he asked, "So how did Abbot know the transmitter was here?"

As soon as he asked the question, Titus *knew*. He buried his face in his hands. "It's all my fault. He tricked me!" The memory, transparent as a ghost, floated through the periphery of his mind: Abbot asking with incisive Influence and Titus babbling out the whole story of his trip to the probe, and his hiding the transmitter. *I never should have let him use Influence on me! Not even to fake autonomic responses for the new medical anti-hypnotic conditioning.*

"No, it's not all your fault. He tricked me, too. Not a flicker, not a twinge, but he knew all the time!"

Titus raised his head. "Knew what?"

"That humans *dream*."

The whole long list of questions Titus had been concocting moments before came surging back to the forefront of his mind, but what he said made no sense even to him. "Dreaming isn't volitional. So it must be genetic?"

"Titus," said H'lim as if the question were not nonsense, "there's no time to explain it all right now. Later, I promise. But right now everything's changed." He glanced at the closed bathroom door. "That message must not go out, not where Abbot's going to send it with your targeting data!"

"Because humans dream? My targeting is wrong because humans dream, and that's why all of a sudden you're willing to be marooned here instead of getting rich, and of course, logically, Abbot had to kill Mirelle in your bathroom." *My God. My God in Heaven!* Titus' eyes were fixed on the bathroom door, a nightmarish feeling swelling up inside him as the image of body fragments clad in black lace and oozing blood floated before his eyes.

Some oddly detached corner of his mind told him glibly that now he knew how Inea felt all the time she was fighting off understanding of what he had become—had always been.

I must do something fast . . . hurry . . . something . . . anything! Mirelle's in there, dead because I couldn't keep her out of Abbot's clutches because humans dream. You see, I'm a scientist and all of this makes perfect sense! He was aware that his eyelids were peeled back too far and his mouth was open.

With forced human mannerisms, H'lim brought a flask out of the refrigerator and poured two glasses of a thin, orange liquid reeking of orl blood. "Drink this."

"What is it? I can't—"

"Stripped orl blood with a dozen enzymes, nutrients, and a stimulant. Taste it. It won't hurt you. You need it. You're hysterical."

Hysterical? Hardly. But his hands curled around the glass. It was not as repellent as plain orl blood. It seemed to evaporate into his sinuses, exploding into his brain. He'd had nothing like it since he'd died. He drank down half of it and was surprised to find his mind clearing.

"Drink it slowly," advised H'lim, "so it won't make you hungry. I've no blood here." He sat down opposite Titus, cradling his glass. "These are the immediate questions. What is Abbot planning to do with the transmitter? What did he expect me to do when I found the body? What can we do to stop Abbot?"

"He's going to transmit the message, and he wants you tied up here so you can't stop him, which means you *could* stop him. How? And why?"

"Now I know where I am, I know Earth is interdicted—"

"You know where you are?"

"On the other side of the galaxy from where we were supposed to go!" he snapped. "If Abbot sends that message I wrote, the luren species may well be exterminated. And if the Teleod and the Metaji fight for possession of Earth's dreamers, Earth itself may have to be destroyed. Earth's humans are as dangerous to galactic order as luren. Maybe worse. I think—from what Abbot said—he plans to buy the Tourists a place in galactic affairs by selling Influenced humans as spies."

"You've told Abbot more than you've told me."

"No, just a chance remark about a planet way across the galaxy— I thought! I don't know how I could be *here*, but I should have known just from the genetics. I should have guessed! But your genes are classified top secret, so of course I've never seen anything like them. No, I can't go home. I wouldn't dare communicate with *anyone!* With what I know now, they'd. . . ."

As H'lim trailed off, Titus' eyes swept back to the closed bathroom door. He'd been right all along to distrust H'lim, but H'lim had in fact been innocent of duplicity. "What chance remark? It's important, H'lim. I have to know what Abbot knows—and doesn't know—if you want me to figure his moves." He glanced at the hall door. "We'll have only one chance to get out of here. If we walk into one of Abbot's booby traps—"

The luren twisted to gaze at the bathroom. "Discussing an old Genentech article on genetic engineering, I told him planetary scale bioengineering had been outlawed millennia ago, and only two such planets survive, both failures: our own and one on the edge of the galaxy that harbors a race of powerful telepaths who can't tap their power alone. Asleep, they involuntarily recapitulate the day's events, though in fragmented and broken symbols when not linked to the right receiver.

"Their planet is under interdict because, linked to the right receiver, the people they were engineered to link with, they make great spies. Everything experienced by the sleeper that day is uploaded into the receiver's mind. And with a telepathic link on that level of consciousness, there's no distance limit. We had been discussing the current galactic war and Earth's achieving peace with its consequent loss of practical standing armies, and I mentioned that such a spy could be placed within the tactical planning councils of one side and be untraceably passing information to the tacticians of the opposing side.

"Abbot replied, 'That's interesting. On Earth, reliable spies are valuable.' On *Kylyd* I finally understood what he'd meant; that Earth's luren could sell humans as reliable spies. In retrospect, it seems obvious that he would think that way, knowing that humans 'dream,' and knowing that there is only one planet where this occurs."

Current galactic war! Telepaths! What else had H'lim discussed with Abbot that he'd never mentioned to Titus? The thousand questions clamored in the back of his mind, but there really was no time for that now. "Is there anything Abbot doesn't know?"

"That it won't work. This interdict is the strictest law on record, the only one obeyed everywhere," said H'lim, then lost the façade of Earth culture as he added, "except for the laws controlling us."

305

Titus pounced on that. *"What* controlling law!"

He refused to squirm under Titus' challenge, but his Influence betrayed him. Yet he needed Titus' help now, and when he spoke, it was pure truth. "That we may not, as you know, take sustenance from any but the orl, nor use Influence on any but orl, nor interbreed with any race on penalty of death for breeder and offspring alike." He lunged across the table to grab Titus' hand as if to stay a blow. *"Listen!* I know we could have gotten around the law, considering the immense value of this unique genepool! I had *no idea* where I was! Titus, Abbot's message must not go out."

I was right and Abbot was flat wrong. They'll come to Earth and exterminate us like vermin, and never tell us why.

Titus doubted Earth really was this mysterious planet of telepathic spies. Dreaming couldn't be that exotic a talent. But as long as H'lim believed it was, he wouldn't risk the anti-luren laws of the galaxy. He put his other hand over H'lim's. "Abbot doesn't care about the Taurus window or my targeting program now. He knows that to cross the galaxy, your ship had to use a spacewarp, not a straight line, which means he doesn't need the Taurus window, so never mind the window closing for the Eighth—he's gone to the Eighth!"

"Across the surface? In sunlight?"

"Abbot can do anything he sets his mind to." The more he thought about it, the more likely it seemed. "He's been planning this for days. He Influenced the hiding place of the transmitter out of me the morning after we lost the landline to the Eighth. He must have found out I got his observatory transmitter, though how he'd know his message never went out. . . ." He shrugged.

"He's your First Father. You understand him. Go on."

"If we're across the galaxy, it'll take a long time for an answer, so he's decided the secessionists have to win the war, which is the reason he framed you. He killed Mirelle so he'd have the strength to cross the surface, but he framed you for it, so the W.S. would lose the war."

H'lim nodded. "If I'm really a monster, then my backers are discredited and the W.S. falls. But why? Why would he want that?"

"If the W.S. wins, order will be restored because it can run the world. But if the handful of small countries that have seceded win, they'll lose control. Economic and political chaos will break up the giant databases that interfere with Tourist activities."

"I see. He's playing for very high stakes. He must feel he's sacrificing minor game pieces—Mirelle—and me."

"And me!" He'd have planned another trap to keep Titus busy, which meant using Inea as bait somehow.

Titus remembered the look on her face that morning when H'lim had shown them the booster. "Mirelle! *That's* what Inea had in mind!" Titus slewed his chair about to face H'lim's vidcom. "Did you show her how to use the booster?"

"A few days ago. How did you know?"

"Oh, I know that woman's face! I should have realized. Not that it would have done any good. She never does what I tell her to! Why's this taking so long!"

"Calm down. The tonic has speeded up your synapses. We've only been speaking for a few minutes."

Checking the time, he saw it was so. The gym records came onscreen, showing Inea and Mirelle had been in the centrifuge, but had quit early. Mirelle had been in bad shape. He hit EXIT. "She was in Mirelle's room when Abbot arrived. She'd given Mirelle the booster. Abbot would have been livid at her transgressing his Mark." He turned haunted eyes on his luren son. "H'lim, would he have killed her, too?"

H'lim's lips compressed. "Titus, maybe Abbot didn't kill Mirelle. Maybe Inea did."

With numb fingers, Titus keyed for Mirelle's room, trying to recall how Abbot's override worked. If he could get a picture—suddenly, the vidcom lit up with an incoming call. Titus hit ACCEPT, and the screen cleared to show Inea leaning into the pickup, a gag across her mouth, her hands bound behind her. She was seated, and from the way she was trying to poke at the keys with her nose, Titus thought she must be bound to the chair. The color scheme behind her indicated it was Mirelle's room.

Her eyes rose to the screen as Titus made inarticulate sounds. H'lim bent over his shoulder. "Abbot did this?"

Vocalizing strenuously, she nodded. Titus felt H'lim's bony fingers dig into his shoulder and knew what the decision had to be. "Close down," he ordered her, "and get out of range of the pickup. We'll be there soon."

At her relieved nod, he cut off. "Is there an enzyme that will eat bone? And not ruin the water recycling plant?"

H'lim thought a moment, then he, too, fixed on the bathroom door. "Yes," he choked, "and Abbot knew about it."

"Where is it?"

307

"A storage room Andre and I both use, near our labs. Yesterday, there was enough to decompose her body."

"*That* is where the other booby trap set for you would be. Mirelle's room—or maybe Inea herself—will be trapped for me. Let's go. I'm going to need your help."

H'lim paused, looking at the bathroom door. "It would be convenient if the body just disappeared without a trace."

"That is the way Abbot expects you to react, and that's the last worry we can afford to have. Let the W.S. lose the war and the secessionists execute all of us, but that message must not go out."

Momentarily, H'lim assumed a preternatural stillness, then replied, "Yes. You're right, of course." When he moved again, it was with all the bustle of an animated human.

It was the work of a moment for H'lim to cast his Influence around the guards. Titus marveled at the powerful but subtle touch the luren now used to mask their passing from all human eyes, but when he commented, H'lim said, "I can't keep this up too long. Earth humans are just too sensitive. But of course, now I understand why that is."

Titus didn't have a chance to inquire. Mirelle's door was before them. He and H'lim both went over it, looking for Abbot's traps. Mirelle had given them the threshold before, so when H'lim picked the lock they had no trouble slipping inside. Inea, still bound to the chair, hopped it across the room, calling mutedly through the strip of sheet gagging her.

The chair itself trailed a twist of sheet that had tethered it to the kitchen sink fixture. Another piece of sheet lay across the sink, frayed end draped nearly to the floor. Titus inserted his fingers and tore the gag across, then pried the wrist and leg bonds away.

Instead of the torrent of gratitude and narrative Titus expected, Inea grew very still as she gazed up at H'lim. As Titus knelt, rubbing circulation back into her feet, Inea said, in a voice and cadence eerily like Abbot's, "I submit, Senior, that Titus Shiddehara has violated law and custom in permitting me to act uncontrolled and thus to endanger all his kind on Earth."

Titus hurled the bonds down. "*That's* his trap! He's Influenced her! Lord knows what else she'll say and to whom!"

There was a glassy, unfocused look in her eyes as H'lim knelt to examine her. "That may be all he left for us."

"Not if I know Abbot. He no longer expects you to enforce the letter of *our* laws."

"Doesn't his using Influence over your Mark constitute a capital offense as well?"

"No. He's my father, and he's only scripted her to expose me—probably to any other luren as well as to Colby, though what she'd tell Colby I don't know."

H'lim cradled Inea's jaw in his hands and inspected her eyes. "I can counter it. It's very superficial."

Titus reached forth with his own senses to confirm that, swallowing against the ache in his gut. "Yes. Abbot's always scrupulously legal." He removed H'lim's fingers. Titus could see that ferreting out all the triggers Abbot had left would be a delicate job if he wanted to have all of Inea there when he finished. "Stand clear."

When H'lim had moved back, Titus administered the Influential equivalent of a sobering slap, and Inea blinked hard, twice, shook her head, and gazed at Titus as if he had no right to appear out of thin air. Quickly, he explained what Abbot had done to her. "I can undo it when you're ready to let me, or H'lim can, but it will take hours. Inea, we don't have hours—"

She suddenly turned white, rose, and lurched to the bathroom where she shut herself in. The sound of water running almost covered the sound of retching. Titus picked up the bonds and shoved the chair out of the middle of the floor, starting after her. "Did I hurt her bringing her out of it so fast?"

"No," said H'lim, restraining him and examining the room. "It was Abbot who hurt her. Give her a minute."

The bed was tumbled, the mattress half off its foundation. A blood kit lay on the floor, parts scattered. He pushed the mattress back in place and found Mirelle's customized PDA had been shoved between mattress and foundation. *Odd.* He turned it over. It was activated, showing the Rosetta stone. His hands shook. *It's a message. She left me a message.*

He wondered obliquely how she could have done it under Abbot's Influence, but then remembered Biomed's anti-hypnotic conditioning and wondered if the humans had wrought better than they knew. He sat down on the bed, and H'lim knelt beside him to see the tiny screen. "What is that?"

"Archeological treasure. It's too complicated to explain." He suddenly recalled an utterly cryptic list he'd found in one of Abbot's station files that he had penetrated. Of their own accord, his fingers moved over the keys, trying the few codes he had labored over so long he'd memorized them.

The screen danced, flickered, then settled in to display luren script. H'lim exclaimed, "I wrote that!"

Twisting his head to look at the pale, goggled face, Titus said, "*That's* why I've never been able to get anything useful out of Abbot's files! He's been using Mirelle's handheld to dump data!" He shook the thing. "If I only knew how to make it scroll."

H'lim reached a slender finger over Titus' shoulder and poked a key. The image shifted to the next line of text, and the next. "She showed me, once. Titus, this is only the message I wrote for him. We can't stay here and—"

"No, wait." Titus used one of the other commands on the list, found some machine code, then tried another and yet another. He was coming to the end of what he remembered when they hit on a second file of luren script. "And *this,*" said Titus, laboring over the foreign language, "has to be the message he's sending now!"

It was built out of the components of H'lim's message, but omitted all mention of the luren stock breeding company and of the luren home world. Instead it invited responsible governments to bid for the services of those galactic citizens who now controlled Earth. *Or who will control Earth by the time they get here if the secessionists win and the Tourists use the inevitable chaos to take over.*

Titus looked up when H'lim moved back. Inea was standing braced in the bathroom door, her hair slicked back, a little color around her lips now. But her face was chiseled from stone, and her eyes sparked. When she spoke, it was not in metaphor. "I'm going to kill him."

Titus rushed across the room to gather her up. "No!"

"He's gone crazy. He'll kill us all if we don't get him first. And after what he did to me in the restaurant—and now—it would be worth my life to take him down with me. You can't, and H'lim shouldn't because we don't want an interstellar incident. Which leaves me. I've got to do it."

"He's not crazy, and he's not out to kill anyone else."

"Titus, you don't know what he did to Mirelle. He made me watch. He made me watch him drink until she convulsed and died and he told me that's what you'd do to me for what I'd done to Mirelle. But I didn't do anything to Mirelle, nothing wrong. I only gave her a shot of the booster."

Convulsed?! Titus couldn't bring himself to probe for details. H'lim asked, "You gave Mirelle the amounts I'd told you? But you used the batch I showed you this morning?"

"Yes."

"What happened after that?"

"Mirelle fell asleep, just as you said she would."

"How much later did Abbot arrive?"

"Oh, maybe an hour. He couldn't rouse her and I told him I'd given her the booster. He threw things around and raged at me. I couldn't understand what he said, but he wouldn't let me out the door. Every time I went for it—" She buried her face in her hands. "Snakes and scorpions. It was awful. He's mad, totally mad."

Titus didn't need any more words for what she'd endured to come vividly alive for him. *I'd have broken!*

H'lim, however, seemed unmoved. "What happened when Abbot went to take her blood?"

"She bled—too easily, he said. It tasted peculiar. He raged about that, not always in English. But then he said he had no choice, and he—he—he drank until she died."

In the luren language, H'lim said, "She'd have died anyway. Inea gave her twenty-two times the dose she should have used, a hundred times what I'd have started with in Mirelle's weakened condition. Don't tell her now."

Titus turned to H'lim and Inea asked, "What'd he say?"

"Will Abbot get sick from the booster?" asked Titus.

"Probably not. In fact, it could act to increase his own renewing ability, to give him endurance he hadn't expected. Titus, he just might make it, even under the sun."

"Inea, will you go with us? Outside? To stop Abbot from using the Eighth to call in the galaxy."

"Shouldn't someone stay to cover for you?"

"It's too late for that. Besides, no matter your intentions, you'll do whatever Abbot commanded because we don't have time to untangle the mess he made of your mind."

"Then I'm going." She headed for the door.

"Wait!" said H'lim cutting her off. While he extended Influence beyond the panel to mask their escape, he asked, "Titus, do you realize what this means?"

"That Abbot has several hours head start on us, and we'll be pursued, too?"

311

"No. That Abbot didn't plan everything he did."

Inea's eyes went to the tousled bed. As he opened the door and gestured them out, H'lim told her, "He cut her body into six pieces and smeared her blood around my bathroom."

The words were out before Titus could stop him. Inea choked and almost gagged. Titus gathered her tight against him, guiding her steps as her eyes closed. "She was dead before that."

"This is important," H'lim said. "Titus, he's not a demon with godlike powers. He's a fallible mortal, and thanks to you, nothing's gone right for him in months. Inea has ruined his last, desperate plan. He surely didn't intend to kill Mirelle."

"He did. Tourists kill stringers." Inea shuddered under his arm. He imagined Abbot had explained how he'd taught his son to do it thusly, so she'd never willingly touch Titus again. "Abbot enjoys killing humans."

"Hacking them apart? Framing blood relatives for it?"

It *didn't* sound like a typical Nandoha scheme.

"You've got the upper hand," insisted H'lim. "Not only can you win, but he knows it, and when he learns I've joined you at last, he'll be twice as deadly."

"You trying to scare me off?" asked Inea.

"No, Dr. Cellura. This isn't a hopeless, suicidal mission. We can stop Abbot, possibly without killing him. I don't kill those of my blood."

They suited up in the deserted locker room, guarded by H'lim's powers. Titus, who had labored his way, heart in mouth, through the station before the ban on Influence, marveled at how easily the luren moved through the multiple layers of the surveillance net. "I've had a while to study it. Besides, it's not hard. The instruments are very noisy and their operators are always easy to spot."

"Their *operators?*" squeaked Inea.

"H'lim, the control center is across the station!"

The luren looked at them both blankly, holding his vacuum suit's helmet above his head. "It's not very far."

"My God," whispered Inea, sealing her own helmet.

As he led them to the dock where long-range, enclosed Toyotas were stored, Titus grinned. "Colby would crumble! She's so sure you can reach only a room or two."

In the earphones, H'lim sounded uncertain. "Should I have told her?"

"No," answered Inea gravely. "But if they find out now, you'll be considered to have kept it a secret, and that will be seen as a threat."

"I sometimes think I understand Earth's humans."

They had no trouble commandeering a well-fueled vehicle. Since the quarantine, none were used beyond the station perimeter, and Colby, true to her absolute security on the operation, had not yet sent crews to stand by to collect the 'tainers cargo. The vehicles, however, had been serviced and were ready to roll. The Brink's guards, having nothing to do, were playing a modified version of *Thizan* on a crude board.

The three of them simply walked past the guards, cycled themselves through the lock, picked out a pressurized Toyota with a silver streak and a half-finished rendering of a cartoon Roadrunner hand painted on the side, climbed in, and drove off, just as easily as Abbot had. It wouldn't be long though until the checks and surveillance methods discovered what had happened.

Titus guided the windowless bus across station territory at a tentative creep, bemused by the idea of a Roadrunner as mascot of something that lumbered like a juggernaut over broken country, its tracks making its own road. H'lim Influenced those on duty at the scanners to "accidentally" turn the recorders off and to ignore the moving blip on their screens. "They'll never notice," he told Titus. "I've introduced a number of spurious failures into their efforts so that, should I need to move about, another little problem wouldn't stand out."

"And you called *us* devious!" said Titus, jouncing over a boulder. His steering needed improvement. *Maybe we'll have enough time.*

"It's a good thing you know how to drive these things," gasped Inea, grabbing her helmet before it rolled away.

"I don't . . . yet," answered Titus. "I'll get the hang of it in a bit. See if you can find a map stowed somewhere."

"You mean," she howled, "you don't know where we're going?"

He answered with a straight face. "I just don't want to go the wrong way on a one-way street. Could cause gridlock."

She sputtered. H'lim, barricading himself into an equipment locker he'd emptied, paused. He was the only one who hadn't removed his helmet because the radiation level was already too painful. Noticing his agitation, Inea laughed so hard she doubled over. "Titus, he thinks you're serious!"

Over his shoulder, Titus said, "H'lim, I know it's that way." He pointed then singled out the stellar markers. In the process, he began to realize the time. "How much of a head start do you think he has on us?"

313

"Maybe three hours, could be four," said Inea, "depending on how long he spent . . . in H'lim's room."

"I'd guess it would take him at least a couple of hours to rig that transmitter," said Titus. "He'll have modified it into a mismatched nightmare. If just one fitting is the wrong size, we may get to him before he's ready to send. But that's the least of our problem." Titus had studied the strategic maps carefully. "Blockaders will be crossing between us and the Eighth right about the time we get there, unless I've misread the stars *and* the clock."

Inea drew back warily. "How do you know?"

Promise or no promise, he had to tell them about the 'tainers and the decoy loaded with explosive—and the blood Connie was sending him amidst the explosives she hadn't known about. "I don't think Abbot knows, unless the Tourists among the blockaders found out the supply caravan from Luna Station's a decoy and the real supplies are coming direct from Earth's surface to our backyard. And somehow, I doubt Colby's security has been broken this time."

—— TWENTY-THREE ——

The little eight-passenger Toyota filled with the intense weight of H'lim's Influence, potential energy that gathered like an approaching hurricane. They rode in silence while Inea puzzled out the Cobra control board, producing an occasional squawk of voices as she flicked across World Sovereignties channels.

Then, nosing past the station outbuildings, they heard the flurry of traffic as the station prepared to receive the 'tainers, which, Titus was gratified to discover, were on course and on schedule. Listeners, not knowing of the plan and its code words, wouldn't have made any sense out of the brief messages audible before scrambling was invoked and the Toyota's radio lost the signal.

Titus found a double ribbon of tracks going off Project Station toward the Eighth, no doubt made by the maintenance crews based at the station, the closest habitat to the Eighth. With a sigh of relief, he ran the shield over the direct vision port, cutting out the painful sunlight and Earthlight, then stepped down the screen images so the sun was bearable, Earth only hinted at, and the stars invisible.

Just past the station perimeter, he spotted a crude sign made from a dented oxygen bottle with an 8 painted on it and the glyph of a frowning face. As they passed it, he saw the reverse side showed a smile and a "P.S." When they had lost sight of the station and had not yet seen the Array, he was very glad of the track, and the occasional frowning face painted or carved on rocks.

H'lim's power pounded through him, reaching for Abbot, casting a shimmer of unreality over everything. Even the dim images of the sky, human symbols electronically cast, seemed unreal to his luren vision.

He tried to shake free, building in his mind an image of how Earth would look to H'lim's naked eye, five times brighter than the moon, faint swirls of infrared, throbbing with colors only luren could see. He knew all the graphs, but until this moment, they had remained just mathematics. Now, fighting the pall of Influence, he synthesized breathtaking spectacle, the Cosmic Artist at His best.

Then he thought of H'lim, suffering from the negligible particle flux within the Toyota, and knew what the luren had meant when he labeled his species a bioengineered failure. *To see the spectral beauty they were designed to see, they must endure being scorched by their own sun!* All his deductions from the output spectrum of the lighting panel had been hogwash. Luren built their lighting systems to suit their artificially designed senses, not to replicate a sun that had not guided the evolution of their genes.

He tried to explain this to Inea, but she shook her head, crouching over the scanner board, hunching inside her suit.

Titus became aware of Abbot's presence, hurling a spear of outrage through the haze of H'lim's power. It took no telepathy to know why. His son and his grandson were defying him, H'lim trying to paralyze Abbot even from this distance.

As the battle raged invisibly around her, Inea stifled a whimper. Titus hitched over as far as he could and gathered her up. Through the odd tactile effect of suit against suit, he created for her a bubble in the flow between H'lim and Abbot, explaining the battle. "So the overwash is getting to you, like a fourteen-cycle note. Understand? You're afraid because it stimulates your nerves, not because you're afraid."

"Oh, that surely helps a lot." Her voice quavered, but there was a thin smile on her lips now.

H'lim's tinny voice issued from the helmets. "He's slowing, but I can't hold him."

315

Titus read the suppressed agony in H'lim's tone. The solar flux was depleting the luren's strength. "I'm not expecting miracles," Titus replied, "just do your best."

They passed the left-hand cutoff up to Collector Six, the station's furthest and largest outlying power source. It was plastered up an inside curve of a crater opposite a bulldozed rim so the panels got the most direct sun. Hundreds of panels sent energy to superconductor storage tanks for the long night ahead, keeping the station independent. The Sixth was the newest on the moon, so efficient the station sold power to refineries, factories, and supplied the Eighth Array.

The Collector fell behind them, the path becoming fainter and narrower. Gradually, Titus noticed he was struggling with the steering. Something was wrong with the left tread, but he refrained from mentioning it. H'lim's power filled the cabin with such pressure, Titus thought it would surely burst. He wasn't about to disrupt that kind of locked concentration. He'd heard tell of Influence duels to the death, but never witnessed one before. *I don't understand how H'lim can do it!*

Then he remembered that H'lim had claimed the higher loyalty to his First Father. If Abbot's message went out, his First Father would be in danger. *He'll kill Abbot before we even get there!*

Without conscious decision, he found himself adding his weight to the luren's, supplying energy for that stupendous field. His lips peeled away from his clenched teeth as if he were making a physical effort.

From the helmets stowed on the instrument hump between him and Inea, H'lim's voice erupted in a karate yell. All the gathered energy exploded outward. Titus felt it connect, felt Abbot recoil, and then abruptly, everything cut off. For a moment, he thought he'd gone blind and deaf, too, but then realized that only the luren senses had been paralyzed.

"I got him!" shouted H'lim. "Did you hear me? Titus? Inea? Are you all right?"

"Is he dead?" asked Titus, oddly bereft and frightened.

"No. I am merely a co-mortal, not a god to work miracles. I distracted him, and something happened to his vehicle. I believe the terrain was the real victor."

Ashamed yet relieved, Titus answered, "It may be enough." His whole body was ringing and aching, and all he could do was put a gloved hand over Inea's clad knee and try to convey confidence. She didn't look well.

A nerve-wracking and tedious time later, H'lim announced that a large number of humans were converging on a point off to their right. "Shall I divert them?"

"No! Must be blockaders after the decoy caravan," said Titus. "Inea, get a fix on them. This thing must have radar. Read the labels. That's how I found the ignition."

"This is all Cobra stuff, just like the observatory." A screen lit with an overhead radar scan. "I make it seven ships at two o'clock—those converted two-seaters the blockaders use as bombers." She checked the readout. "I'm guessing, but I think they're over the decoy caravan. Whatever it is, it's heading toward the quarantine dock they built outside the station perimeter, but going cross country, not on a path. It'll pass within two klicks of us."

"Got to be the caravan, then." Titus fought with the controls.

"Titus, it's changing course! It'll intercept us—somewhere over that big sharp hill ahead, the one with the spike sticking out the top."

"What?" He checked his odometer and her readouts. "That spike is the radio mast of the Eighth. The decoy caravan is heading into the Array basin!" Clumsy in his vacuum suit, he hitched himself out of his seat pulling Inea around him. "Quick, you drive." He squirmed over the instrument hump and reached for the scanner controls.

"Titus! I can't drive this thing!"

"Nothing to it. Just follow the frowns to the spike," he said while he fumbled at the scanner controls. They hit something and bounced, causing H'lim to cry out as the loose equipment shifted. "You okay?" he asked H'lim.

"Yes. The suit's not punctured."

The speaker rattled to life. "Got it!" As Titus had feared, it was the screech of computers handshaking on the decoy's remote command frequency, where there should have been silence. Frantically keying instructions and swearing over error messages, Titus coaxed the little Cobra to identify the sources, one of which was high above the other. The higher one had been stripped of its legally required I.D. response and the other transmitted only a request for a security code.

"Blockaders! They've seized control of the convoy—must have discovered it's unmanned." It was nothing more than had been planned, yet nobody had anticipated they'd take it into the Eighth. *But of course they would. It's got the nearest landing field! And when it blows. . . ."*

317

Titus gnawed his lips, unable to remember seeing any of the communications protocols for the convoy. He couldn't redirect it. He didn't dare warn the blockaders, assuming he could get through to them on any frequency his equipment could transmit. Inea had just gained control of the Toyota when the screech of computer chatter resumed, one signal overriding the other. The blip on the ground ponderously changed course again, and Titus fought the computer until it yielded a map of the ground. *Should have thought of this before. Of course there are maps aboard!*

Picking out the decoy's new cross country course, Titus found where it intersected their path and went on toward the Sixth Collector. Then he knew. "It's Abbot. He's at the Array and using its mast and the Array's power to command the decoy's guidance computer! He's going to blow up the Collector! If he's solved the code."

"He's solved the code," predicted H'lim. "But he won't blow up his power source until after he's sent his message. What would he do to buy time? What could he do while working to attach his transmitter to the Array?"

"Talk," said Inea. "He always talks when he's breadboarding. Titus, scan the other frequencies."

As they rumbled up the last steep grade toward the mast, he got voices—one of them Abbot's.

". . . *friend,* repeat, *friend.* Do not approach the Convoy. It's packed with explosives. Repeat, packed with explosives. Do you copy?" Abbot paused for the reply.

"Who are you that we should believe that?" a voice asked, directed at Abbot, but louder. Echoing as if far from the mike, a female voice commented, "Wonderful way to make us keep our hands off the supplies we need." A third voice yelled, "Holy shit! The Array's moving—all of it!"

Abbot's signal came back, broke up into hash, then steadied, louder than the blockaders'. " . . . told you I have rerouted the convoy. If you stay clear, it will blow up Project Station's Collector Six, the large one that makes them independent of their landlines. You'll have total control of the station's power supply. Do you copy?"

"We copy. Who are you? Where are you? Why should we believe you? You got a code name? A password?"

"Never mind, just check this out. In a descending orbit heading down on the far side of Project Station is a string of cargotainers. They contain the supplies you think are in the convoy. The landing

318

field is beyond the quarantine limits, the stationers aren't armed to speak of, and the W.S. defense forces are busy elsewhere—as you well know. You want supplies—go get them, but leave that convoy alone."

Inea spat, eyes sparking at Titus, "He's a traitor!"

She had the knack of steering the Toyota now, easily keeping them on the track, pushing into the hard climb. The entire forward view consisted of crushed rock passing into the black shade of their shadow. Black and white. Was anything ever so simple?

"No, Inea," Titus said. "Abbot's completely loyal. To the Tourists. Not to the secessionists, Inea, to the *Tourists.*"

"I don't know how you dare defend him! He's framed his grandson for a murder he himself committed, he's sending death to the station and all the humans on it, he's ruthlessly used and slaughtered Mirelle, and he doesn't give a damn if he kills all the humans on Earth if his vicious Tourists survive! The only reason he's ever helped you is to further his own plans! Titus, don't let him get away with it!"

"Watch out!" yelled Titus, lunging for the controls.

But Inea jerked around, saw they were cresting the rise heading directly into a boulder that jutted skyward, blocking the straight path. She yanked the sticks over left, steering servos whining as the treads bit into the sharp turn then ran off the path that curved around the obstruction. The right side scraped rock.

Titus' hands closed over hers. It took all their combined strength to veer back onto the path. Then the ground disappeared from under their treads.

The front end of the Toyota fell abruptly while the rear end rose, sending H'lim's barricade tumbling toward them. Titus fended off a First Aid kit, stopped an air cylinder with his foot, and suddenly found H'lim in his lap, arms and legs flailing, spitting luren epithets. Then they were grinding down the inside lip of the crater into dark shade, the Eighth Array spread before them in dazzling sunlight.

Titus gaped at the view, time standing still. The Array filled the bottom of the giant bowl, like a bouquet of alien silicon-life flowers, fragile and glittering. The identical antenna modules were set at precise intervals, all in the same attitudes. None of the structures—made of slender poles and thread-thin guy wires—could have withstood Earth gravity or weather.

Cables tunneled through the lip of the crater from the Sixth Collector and fed the mammoth superconductor tanks clustered between the Array's landing field and the sparkling white control hut. On top of the hut was a security camera turret that could view the whole basin, and attached at one side of the hut was a supply shed for recharged vehicle power cells, oxygen, replacement parts, lubricants, and survival kits for stranded travelers. Loose rubble dislodged from the slope had gathered near the walls of the hut and someone had sculpted and painted the rocks into a mock flower bed.

Neither hut nor shed was ever pressurized, and now the hut's door stood open. Directly ahead of them, on the steep path down to the hut, lay another Toyota, canted onto its side, treads still moving, half in, half out of bright sun. Held by a paralyzing sense of *déjà vu*, Titus thought, *We're going to die.* The boulder that had caused the wreck lay on the tread marks, a smile painted on it.

"Inea!" But she had already hit the brakes. The faulty left tread snapped loose, ends smacking the cabin with sharp reports. They lost power, and even Titus' strength couldn't budge the sticks. The cabin tilted to the left, the vehicle pivoted, but momentum carried them on in horrifying, nightmarish slow motion, on into the wreck before them.

"Helmets!" yelled Titus, shoving H'lim away and grabbing for his, which was on the driver's side. H'lim canted awkwardly across the console, kicked Inea's helmet toward her groping fingers. In the back of Titus' mind, the drill took hold. *Secure your air first, then help others.*

Training held, and Titus pulled his helmet on while everything in him wanted to reach out and affix Inea's for her. Then they hit.

The toppled vehicle skidded ahead of them down the slope, soaking up the momentum just enough to prevent the collision restraints from being triggered. The high-pitched whistle of escaping air penetrated Titus' helmet, and he squinted hard against the shaft of raw sunlight that came through the front window, where the covering plate had been torn away. H'lim came to rest curled up on the instrument console, head tucked to his knees, back to the cabin, facing the dark screens, a streak of light bisecting him.

The last thing Titus heard before the sound from the speakers was lost in vacuum was the muffled timbre of Abbot's voice saying, ". . . three of them in the second crawler, and one's the alien. The alien's in the second crawler!"

Inea pulled herself back up onto the canted driver's seat, helmet in place. Titus breathed a sigh that was almost a sob. *She's all right!* He pushed himself up. "There's a jack here somewhere, to connect a suitphone. . . ."

While Titus searched, Inea crawled onto the console where H'lim lay curled. "Maybe he's already dead." She tried to straighten the huddled form. He jerked away.

Titus got the phone jack into place just in time to hear the commander's voice say, ". . . no wild stories! Now I don't believe—" He broke off, and his voice was muffled as he asked, "What? They did? There are? You mean he's legit?" Then more clearly, he ordered, "Ben, Roger, peel off and take a look at those crawlers. If that monster's there, get him. Rendezvous over the station. Go!"

Power was flickering on and off. Titus couldn't tell what the seven bombers were doing. He helped Inea straighten H'lim out, muttering encouraging words in the luren language. Then as Titus watched H'lim's skin turned pink. He rolled the stiff body up in his arms and climbed back into darkness, scrambling awkwardly over the loose junk that had gathered at the lower end of the cabin.

He wedged the luren back into the cubby he'd chosen for a refuge, then built up the pile of junk again as best he could at the high end of the slope. "Better?" he asked as H'lim began to stir.

"Yes. I'm sorry."

"Nonsense," cut in Inea. "You saved my life. I could never have reached my helmet."

Titus patted a last cylinder into the pile, to make a natural looking mess that searchers could pick at without exposing H'lim. *Clumsy amateurs. Amazing we survived this long.* He turned to find Inea stuffing small oxygen cylinders into the arms and legs of a spare vacuum suit. It was the untailored sort with adjustable everything. God forbid you should have to do anything in it.

"Don't just gawk! Help me."

He held it while she strapped. "What's this for?"

"They don't know H'lim can't get out even in a suit. They'll count three of us going for the hut, and they'll follow. When they find an empty suit, they'll never believe Abbot again! Come on. We've got to hurry! Abbot's already got the Array in motion, and it doesn't have far to go!"

"Titus," whispered H'lim through dry lips, not a scrap of Influence around him. "Listen to me. There are higher instinctive loyalties than to a First Father. To save us all, our planet, Earth, all of us—you can win if you know you must."

"Don't worry, I'll get him, or die trying."

"'Bout time you realized that," grunted Inea.

"Yes." They tore a cushion from one of the seats for the torso and left the helmet empty. Draped over Titus' shoulders in a fireman's carry, the suit did look occupied.

By the time Inea and Titus emerged, two bombers were circling the Array's landing field dropping small bombs, testing for booby traps. Laden with the extra mass of the stuffed suit, Titus veritably flew down the rest of the hill. He caught stride and let momentum carry him, knowing exactly how hard he'd impact the hut and refusing to think about it.

At the last minute, when he was out of sight of the bombers, he hurled the suit against the hut wall as a kind of "breaking jet" and turned so his shoulder hit first. Even so, he almost blacked out. Inea smacked into the hut right beside him, gasping, and slid to the ground.

Titus rolled sideways and rounded the doorjamb in a crouch, looking for Abbot.

The interior was a study in black and white, laced across with dazzling cones of light. The panel readouts had been carefully designed for use in vacuum, through suit helmets, but by human eyes. There was the oppressive inaudible thrum of high gauss fields which Titus had never identified before meeting H'lim. And parts of the machinery casings glowed with infrared colors that filtered through his faceplate, his glasses, and his contacts. *Or is it my skin that's "seeing"?*

Bent low, he circled left, keeping behind consoles and housings, focused on locating the distinctive tang of Abbot's Influence. He was half hoping his father had been permanently crippled by H'lim's efforts.

There!

Abbot, his back to Titus, bent over a console nested in a nearly complete sphere of display screens. The console desk was made of two semicircles with an operator's chair in the center that could pivot to bring each segment into reach. Abbot, outside the circle, leaned awkwardly to consult the screens. There was a chair behind him, and others around the desk facing inward, a sloping control board in front of each. A team of five could operate the entire Array manually, debug and test, evaluate and correct anything that could go wrong.

Parts of the console were lit, and some screens showed data shifting as the antennas rotated to point clear of Earth. One set of screens showed exteriors of the two crashed Toyotas and of the landing field, the two bombers still making cautious passes testing for mines or traps. A black cable tethered Abbot's suit to the console.

322

Titus dug his boot toes into the floor and charged, leaping onto a console and pushing off in a flying tackle, ignoring the anticipatory twinge in his bruised shoulder.

He hit, and the two of them tumbled, bounced, and rolled in the narrow space between screens and desk. Titus tried one of Suzy Langton's low-grav moves, and marveled when he ended up on top. Abbot grunted, heaved, and sent Titus flying over the round desk. Arms flailing, he crashed into a display panel, which cracked behind him.

He got to his knees, searching for the black casing of the transmitter amid the glittering electronics. That was his target, not Abbot. He spotted it, nested inside a cavity in the desk where the panel had been removed to expose the works behind the keyboards. Titus figured that had to be the board connected to the console back in the observatory, which meant it was the masterboard that could control everything here.

Then Abbot's Influence engulfed him like a clenched fist. His muscles locked, leaving him half crouched.

Getting to his feet with an air of utter finality, Abbot plugged in his black cable again, and resumed settling the transmitter into place, suitgloves making him fumble. At the edge of Titus' field of view, the screens showed the landing field, where the bombers were now settling down amid clouds of dust and small rocks.

Titus gathered his power tightly about himself. *I've got to move. I've got to break this.* He recalled the moment in the lavatory on Goddard when he'd turned his hand over despite Abbot's will. Fixing on the black lump of the transmitter now just barely visible, he strained forward against the force that held him. *The barrier's in my own mind. It's human to suffer divided will.*

He summoned the image of Earth overrun, humans taken away to slavery under Tourist Influence, used the way Mirelle had been used. A blast furnace deep within his soul opened and his will fed on outrage.

"They'll never buy it," he said, his voice rusty.

Abbot jerked around then fiddled with his suit frequency. He hadn't heard the comment, but only felt the crack in his control of Titus. Now that Abbot was on Titus' frequency, Titus could hear the distant chatter of the blockaders Abbot was monitoring through the suitjack.

". . . convoy! It'll get too damn close. Let's go!"

Titus' arms knotted with strain, and he thought he felt movement. To distract Abbot further, he grated out words. "You can't sell humans as slaves to the galaxy."

Again, Abbot seemed startled. "So you got into Mirelle's handheld. *Such* a son to be proud of if only . . . Well, no matter. It's too late, Titus. I've won."

"They don't want us—or our dreams—loose in their galactic war." Titus moved a step forward.

Abbot turned from his work, and Titus felt the whole of his father's strength come to focus on him. He strained against it. His front foot shuffled forward. A trick of the lighting gave him a glimpse of Abbot's face through his helmet, mouth twisted with strain.

Distantly, Titus sensed the flavor of H'lim's power wafting through the hut. Abbot's attention flickered to counter the luren, but H'lim was too weak to affect the struggle, except that now Titus was able to pull his trailing foot up. He had taken a step. Filled with the triumph of that, he jerked his right arm forward, reaching toward the transmitter, like a badly articulated robot.

"Don't make me kill you," said Abbot, voice betraying nothing of the expression on his face. His hand reached out for a tool lying on the console—a laser cutter. He started toward Titus. "What sort of nonsense has H'lim been selling you that you'd turn against your own blood?" He stopped with the laser cutter inches from Titus' chest.

"Humans are of my blood, too. And so is H'lim." Titus managed another step, angling toward the console, not Abbot, daring him to use the cutter.

As he shifted angle, a movement on a screen caught his eye. Titus turned to see H'lim scrambling up the trail to the top of the rim. The four blockaders abandoned the approach to the hut and went after him. Abbot's suitphones relayed the tiny voices cursing and guessing who they were chasing. But even when he reached the deep shadow, H'lim was hurting. *He'll never make it without Influence!*

Abbot followed Titus' gaze. "The fool! Doesn't he know he can go to a final death in that solar flux?"

"H'lim's more of a tourist here than you, and he doesn't want to see war roll over Earth and leave it a cinder."

"What does that stock breeder, who has never been honest with us, and has often been wrong, and whose knowledge is way out of date, know of current galactic politics? Or of the desperate situation we face on Earth?"

Titus asked, "We? And what of Earth's humans? What will happen to them if we summon the galaxy's—"

"You believe that dreaming crap?" Abbot interrupted. "This *isn't* that planet, if it exists at all."

You didn't see Kylyd's *astrogation room!* thought Titus. A technology that uses imagination to steer a starship could easily send information via dreams and telepathy, or concoct a law for the conservation of volition. "Listen, Abbot, it doesn't matter whether this is the only planet where people dream. My mission is to prevent you from violating a World Sovereignties decision to prevent the galaxy from discovering Earth's position. So I took the transmitter from the probe, and the other from the observatory."

"I never thought you'd find it before transmitting the ballistics data. If I had, I'd never have involved you in the scheme." There was genuine admiration in Abbot's voice.

"Involved me?" Titus pushed forward. The screen showed the four blockaders approaching the hut, deployed for a fight. *H'lim got away!* From a distance, the luren's Influence flickered around the men and one fell, the others stopping to help him up. Weakened now, H'lim couldn't hold them, and when they arrived, Abbot wouldn't be able to control everyone and still finish his work. *Gotta delay.*

Abbot ignited the laser. "When I decided to use the Array, I needed a legitimate signal to cover mine, and I chose your scheme of bringing up cargotainers. It wasn't hard. We have most of the key decision makers controlled. It won't be much more difficult to take over after World Sovereignties is overthrown."

Titus' will flagged. It had all been Abbot's doing! Abbot's grip on him tightened, triumph blossoming.

Off to the side, Inea popped up and hurled something small, bright, and glinting, at Titus. "Catch!"

Abbot swiveled to face her, the glowing laser still pointed at Titus but his Influence freezing her into a statue that tumbled over grotesquely.

Reflexively, Titus' gloved hand intercepted the object. A great, sweet light burst through his nerves. Inaudible sound penetrated his spirit. The silver glint of the crucifix reflected all the colored displays, sparking and whirling deep into Titus' being. It was weaker than before and had a different texture, but there was a sublime energy, collimated and coherent enough to break him free of Abbot's grip.

Inea gasped, "I don't believe it. You can't make me see Titus as a monster! You can't!"

Abbot staggered back from Titus. Never before had he been effectively defied by a human. Titus wanted to grapple for the laser cutter, to jump in and save Inea. Instead, he lunged for the transmitter. His right hand closed on it as Abbot whirled and brandished the cutter at Inea's throat. Influence pounded into her. He spat, "Don't!"

Titus froze, gripping the casing. "Abbot! She's mine!"

"Touch that rig, and you forfeit life and stringer."

It was legal, from Abbot's point of view. He had documented proof that Titus might be feral. Only a feral would turn against the Blood and rip out the transmitter.

Inea struggled, exerting an amazing force against Abbot's will, and he had to grab her physically to control her. "What have you taught this one?"

H'lim was right! She can defend herself!

"Inea, remember when I was mad at H'lim for what he told you to do to me, and he told us what you could do because of it?" *If only Abbot doesn't catch on!*

"Yeah," she gasped, against Abbot's control.

"Now!" shouted Titus. Simultaneously, he yanked the transmitter away from the connections and threw all his might into raising Influence. Then he hurled the transmitter directly at Abbot.

Deep within himself, a blast furnace of power reopened. But this time, it was white hot and focused to a narrow pencil of intent. He used what Abbot had taught him when they had to Influence each other against Biomed's hypnosis check, and cut through Abbot's defenses, inducing Abbot's reflex move to bring the weapon around to ward off the flying object. Now!

The laser came up and flared. Two pieces of transmitter flew onwards, struck Abbot, and bounced to the floor.

With an inarticulate howl he discarded the laser, not caring that its activated tip ate a hole in the stone floor. He sank to his knees over the twin pieces of his last hope.

Inea, released from thrall, picked up the laser, moving at Abbot's exposed back with deadly intent. Titus flung himself across the space and pinned her arm up. "No!" he said aloud with no Influence behind it. "He's neutralized. Kill him in cold blood, and you're no better than he is."

He couldn't see her face, but he felt the muscles in her arm tremble with the smoldering need to slice into Abbot. Urgently, Titus demanded, "Would the priest who charged the crucifix approve of killing for revenge?"

She made a sound that was part sob, part laugh, and part shiver of terror. "*I* charged the crucifix, praying while he had you." She let him pluck the cutter out of her grip.

Awe struck, he flung it haphazardly aside, not noting where it landed. *It* had been *different. Very different.* "Come on, we have to help H'lim. He can't handle those four without Influence, and he's going to—"

Deep inside him there was a tearing, rending pain as if someone had ripped his heart out by the roots. *H'lim!*

The ground danced.

Titus staggered, hanging onto Inea, who didn't have the mass to hold him upright. They parted. Abbot struggled to his feet. Then a fluid wave of loose rock pushed into the hut, shoving everything before it. The roof majestically folded downwards. The floor jerked sideways.

One of the screens, detached and seemingly floating on nothing, showed the two crawlers sliding down toward the shed amidst a rock avalanche. Then it went dark.

Everything went dark.

The bright tip and the short cutting rod of the laser was clear even through Titus' suitvisor, and so was the dim form of Inea staggering off balance right across its beam.

Titus grabbed her arm, dancing onto the leading edge of flowing rock, and yanked her out of danger. But that sent him stumbling forward, pivoting in freefall. Suddenly, he realized that Newton's laws, the coldest of equations, had now condemned him to death. The laser, its butt caught in the moving rocks, would pierce his left eye.

A large, heavy vacuum suit slammed into him. *Abbot.* Spinning sideways, he landed on his back and bounced. In midflight, pain such as he'd never imagined could be endured lanced through him. Paralyzed, he couldn't even scream when a light that had been inside him, disregarded since he'd first crawled from his grave, winked out.

He rolled and turned to find Abbot sprawled, half buried in debris, the back of his helmet severed from the back of his suit, leaking infrared colors like drops of blood. Two polished ends of vertebrae were exposed, the froth of boiling blood hardly obscuring the fact that Abbot had gone to his final death, a fact that lived in ashen darkness within Titus where no other could see. Mixed with that gasping agony was the throb of another mortal wound. *And H'lim, too.*

327

Movement of the rocks had almost stopped.

Inea pulled herself out from under a ceiling panel, and shoved aside a piece of the roof camera turret. Bits of shattered sunlight pierced the gaps in the rubble over them, though without atmospheric scattering, they didn't illuminate much. One of them outlined Abbot's hand, clutching half a transmitter. Inea waded over to Abbot, knelt, and eased his body into her lap. Short little coughs that might have been astonished sobs came over the suitphones to Titus as he got his knees under him and began to crawl toward them.

"Ti-Titus, did you hear what he said? Did you hear?"

"No." He pulled up and examined the wound. The spinal cord was severed. Fatally.

"He said—he said, 'You're still of my blood.' I was wrong. He loved you. He was crazy, warped, *horrible,* but he had enough good in him to love you. I'm glad you didn't let me kill him." And then she cried.

"You can't cry in a spacesuit. It's too hard to wipe your nose."

"Titus! How—"

"When we have time, we'll both cry. But for the moment, we've got to—"

"H'lim! My God! We've got to go get him—" She tried to struggle free of the corpse.

"Inea."

She stopped.

Titus swallowed hard. "He's dead. Not dormant. Dead."

"But how could you—"

"I *know.* A father knows. When there can be a revival there's still a—connection. It's gone."

He put a hand on her elbow, remembering all the times he'd helped other fathers rush to the aid of suddenly dormant children. There was no trace of that feeling in him. *My first son is dead.* "H'lim blew up the convoy when it came close—"

"But why?"

"To keep those four men from getting to us, to keep the convoy from blowing up the Collector and putting the station at the mercy of the blockaders, and probably to distract Abbot as best he could without Influence to help me."

"What do you mean without Influence?"

"He was so hurt from the sun, so exhausted from battling Abbot, he couldn't even divert the blockaders."

"He's dead," she whispered.

He stared at her, savoring the feel of her with all his senses. Her acceptance of the loss somehow let him accept it, too. *And I'll never know what kind of science uses a math too difficult for computers.*

"Yes, Inea, he's dead. Permanently, this time. Now come on. We've got to see if any of those men survived. There must be first aid supplies in this mess somewhere. And then we have to dispose of Abbot's body, make ourselves a sledge of some kind to carry extra air, and trek back to the station—unless we can fix the radio and signal for help. But meanwhile we have to concoct a plausible story we can both stick to, and see about disarming any compulsions Abbot left you. And we have to do all of those things before we both break down and cry, or run out of oxygen."

Titus laid Abbot's head down on the rocks and shards of console and promised he'd make his father proud, always, even when he disagreed with him.

—— TWENTY-FOUR ——

Two days later, exhausted and depleted, Titus and Inea trudged past the last of the painted smiles, the one at the Project Station border, and saluted it as they had all the others that marked the road home.

They were hauling the sledge they had fashioned from wall panels and wiring in order to carry the two injured blockaders they'd found among the wreckage H'lim had made of the caravan. One of them, they were pretty sure, was dead, but the other might still have a chance.

Leaning into the harness they used to pull the thing, they trudged back onto station territory, heads bowed, eyes to the ground. There were still three spare oxygen bottles next to the two lashed-down spacesuits.

Inea staggered with exhaustion, and Titus said, "Don't stop. We may never get started again, and we might not be noticed for days." Their suitphones wouldn't necessarily be heard this far away.

"Don't worry about me," rasped Inea. "I could go another day or two. But you must be starving."

"Not—"

"Titus!" The bull roar had an Israeli accent and a joy Titus had heard only when a program ran on the first try.

"Inea!" came another voice. "Shimon, call the ambulance!"

Two suits were sprinting toward them out of the setting sun. Titus could barely force his eyes toward the glare, but made out one form with a portable flood, and another with the whip antenna of a powerful transmitter waving over his helmet. Inea called, "Shimon! Ernie! Ernie Natches!" Her pull on the sledge increased and Titus staggered, trying to keep up with her. But when they were closer, he was certain their rescuers were indeed his own lab's Israeli genius and Inea's electronics mentor.

Twice during their trek, they had seen flyers overhead, but had not known if they were friend or enemy, and so they'd hidden instead of signaling. Now, in a confused babble of questions, answers, and intensive debriefing that lasted through the four hours it took Biomed to clear them through into Carol Colby's office, they found out why they had seen no identifying markings.

Security had found Mirelle's body a few hours after H'lim and Titus had left, and Colby got that news through to Earth. Public opinion of the alien in W.S. controlled territory had instantly turned about. A monster that could masquerade as a friend was worse than an overtly monstrous monster.

World Sovereignties had immediately capitulated with regard to the alien. Earth would no longer seek contact with anything from "out there."

All the secessionist support had faded immediately when that proclamation was made. Rhetoric shifted to being ready in case the galaxy ever discovered Earth, and that meant a united Earth.

With the war over and World Sovereignties once again in control, secessionist insignia had already been eradicated, the bombers reconverted to freighters.

As Colby ushered Titus and Inea into her office and installed them in two comfortable chairs before her desk, she said, "I'm sorry to tell you the man you brought in, the one who they thought would survive, died a few minutes ago. He never regained consciousness."

Titus swallowed hard. *At least there's no chance now that our story will be contradicted.* Then he was instantly ashamed of the thought, and aching with new grieving. *All that dying, and only we survived.*

Inea buried her face in her hands. No amount of cold water had been able to subdue the puffiness from her long delayed cry.

"It's no reflection on you," Colby hastened to add as she seated herself and tilted her screen so she could read it and see them at the same time. "You're still counted heroes. Ah! Here it comes! Biomed has issued you a clean bill of health. No trace left of the hypnotic coercion that monster inflicted on you."

Inea gasped, choked back a sob, then flung her head back, sniffed, and faced Colby. "Even though I don't think he's a monster?"

"You haven't seen what he did to Dr. de Lisle."

"He gave his life to save the Collector and the station's independence from the blockaders."

"The war is *over,*" insisted Colby. "It has been since the W.S. ships came to meet the blockaders attacking the 'tainers and announced the cease-fire."

"I understand," said Titus, "that the 'tainers arrived safely, and on target."

"Yes." Colby seized the chance to change the subject as she tapped her keyboard. "Your work was perfect, even if my ground crews didn't measure up. *Here* it is—some spectral grade solvent was sent to your lab. Shimon found it there yesterday, but could find no requisition filed for it. Nobody can figure out what you'd need solvent for—not in this quantity, anyway."

Abruptly, he could taste the cloned blood, a vile deadness after Inea's living gift. But perhaps coming off this long a fast, it wouldn't be so bad. "Oh, that solvent wasn't for me," lied Titus, meeting Inea's gaze. "If it's what I think it is, it had to do with a project H'lim had in mind—or maybe Dr. Mihelich—or something H'lim wanted Mihelich to do. I don't recall. I'll look it up—"

"Never mind. I'll just have it trucked down to storage."

"Oh, no! Don't worry about it. I'll take care of it. You have so much to do, and my department is going to be dead weight around here with the Project scrapped. In fact, if space exploration is to be abandoned, I may never get another job." That hadn't occurred to him before.

"Don't worry. You're both accounted heroes and will be substantially rewarded for everything you've done. I've put you in for hazard pay for the time you spent in the alien's company, and there will be a decorating ceremony when we all return to Earth. Oh, and Titus, a few days ago, the insurance payment on your house came through, full replacement value. You can have it rebuilt before you go home, or wait and supervise it all yourself."

"Someone said the station would remain under quarantine indefinitely," commented Inea, "so we're stuck here."

"Only five years," answered Colby. "It's to be announced in a few hours. A compromise was reached and some biotech people will be coming up to verify Dr. Mihelich's findings. Meanwhile, the nearspace program is not being totally abandoned. After the furor dies down, there will be a drive to strengthen Earth's defenses and early-warning network, which is what Titus' department was originally intended to do. You won't be out of work. That is, if you're still interested. Considering what that monster did to you two and Abbot, as well, no one would blame you if you—"

"Oh, no!" objected Titus and Inea in unison.

Their carefully constructed story was turning into a spider web. They had declared that H'lim had used his power to take them to the Eighth, which was true. People assumed they had been held in thrall, as had Abbot. Titus and Inea insisted that all H'lim had wanted was to go home, and the threat of not being able to call for rescue had driven him to desperation. That was true, too, and also true of Abbot for a different reason. The minor aberrations in Inea's and Titus' physiological responses under questioning were attributed to the horror of their ordeal, so nothing more than a routine investigation was planned. Abbot's clandestine software had protected Titus during the hypnotic deconditioning session, and now security was satisfied.

Titus told Colby, "Nonhuman people are out there. Pretending they're not there won't protect Earth. Now more than ever, we have to *learn* about the galaxy, and about the principles that drove *Kylyd*. We just have to do it without attracting attention. Maybe, by our grandchildren's day, the galactic situation will have changed. Maybe there can be peaceful contact eventually. We have to hope and pray and prepare for any eventuality."

Colby cocked her head to one side, smiling. "That's exactly what I told them, almost word for word. You know, you may end up with my job." *If I had Colby's job the first thing I'd do is get the wireless network running.*

Titus weighed Inea's expression. The idea of staying on the moon, or returning often, didn't seem to upset her. He took his courage in his hands. "Inea, shall we ask her to marry us? Now?"

Her eyes widened in astonishment. She darted a glance at Colby, then said in apology. "He wouldn't let me move in with him . . . ."

The corners of Colby's mouth turned up and her eyes twinkled. "Well, if that's the way it is—when would you like to do it? In a week or two, we could manage some decorations and a dress . . . There hasn't been a wedding on the station yet, and everyone would—"

"No!" said Titus. "Now." They were both wearing disposable suits with Project Hail logos, and he had no ring except his class ring, part of the Shiddehara persona. He pulled it off. "Call your secretary in for a witness. We're ready." He caught Inea's eye. "We've put this off too long. I'm not going to let another accident get in the way. That is, if you're still willing, all things considered."

"All things considered, there's nothing under this sun or any other that I'd be more willing to do."

Now Available
from BenBella Books